PENGUIN BOOKS

Maybe Next Christmas

Emma Heatherington is the *Irish Times* and international bestselling author of sixteen novels, including UK number one ebook *This Christmas*, as well as Amazon Top 10 and USA Kindle hits *The Legacy of Lucy Harte*, *One More Day*, *The Promise* and *Secrets in the Snow*.

Her novels are set in Ireland, each exploring life-affirming issues combined with heart-warming love stories. Emma's distinctive style, full of poignancy and warmth, has developed a loyal and ever-growing fanbase.

Maybe Next Christmas

Emma Heatherington

PENGUIN BOOKS

PENGUIN BOOKS

UK | USA | Canada | Ireland | Australia
India | New Zealand | South Africa

Penguin Books is part of the Penguin Random House group of companies
whose addresses can be found at global.penguinrandomhouse.com

Published in Penguin Books 2024
001

Typeset in 10.4/15 pt Palatino LT Pro by Jouve (UK), Milton Keynes
Printed and bound in Great Britain by Clays Ltd, Elcograf S.p.A.

The authorised representative in the EEA is Penguin Random House Ireland,
Morrison Chambers, 32 Nassau Street, Dublin D02 YH68

A CIP catalogue record for this book is available from the British Library

ISBN: 978–1–804–94187–4

www.greenpenguin.co.uk

For Daddy, with love, always.

Just always be waiting for me

– J. M. Barrie – *Peter Pan*

Maybe
Next
Christmas

Chapter One

Bea

The Carnation Hotel, London
Christmas Eve

'You're running incredibly late, Miss Beatrice. I recommend you stop fussing over trivial details and get a move on to the airport before the snowstorm gets closer.'

My favourite colleague and confidant Leroy taps his smart gold wristwatch, shaking it out from beneath a crisp white cuff as a cutting December breeze whips in through the open hotel door.

A light dusting of powdery snow covers the steps outside. Leroy nods in my direction, tugging his dark green and gold uniform jacket to keep out the cold. I'll never take for granted how my place of work is found in one of London's most serene locations. Just across the street, Kensington Palace sits in frosty sparkling light while the royal park's ancient trees are wrapped in an enchanting morning mist.

In welcome contrast, the small hotel foyer where I work is toasty and bursting with festivity.

Jingling tunes fill the air as our resident black and white Collie mix Nana snoozes by the open hearth. The centrepiece is a towering tree with expensive blue, silver and red baubles that I bought from Harrods when November said goodbye and it was officially time to celebrate Christmas.

But just as was predicted, a winter storm is brewing, and as London prepares to lock down for a bitter, frosty Christmas Eve, I'm delaying the need to leave here for more reasons than the weather.

'You're panicking as usual, Leroy. There's no need to panic, my love,' I call, flying round the reception area's deep red and gold interior, fixing everything from the positioning of the thick cream church candles to the vibrant poinsettia and carnation displays to the *Welcome to London* brochures along the way. 'I have everything under control, so please don't worry. I still have time.'

I do have time. And I do have everything under control. I always do.

As front-of-house manager at Kensington's most opulent and intensely charming five-star boutique hotel, The Carnation, I take the utmost pride in never, ever taking my eye off the ball.

The elegance and history of the hotel is a far cry from my upbringing in rural Ireland, where I worked my way up in hospitality, dipping my toe in every sphere, from washing dishes to serving in the bar in my local pub to weaving magic at weddings in a romantic Irish castle resort.

The Carnation in London is rich in style, yet it oozes

warmth and old-world charm with original oil paintings hanging on wine-coloured walls. No two bedrooms are decorated the same – each one has been curated with love and attention by the hotel owner who is now in her nineties, but who still pops by to say hello now and then.

I knew from the very first day I stepped into these warm, traditional surroundings on what was meant to be a temporary transfer from a hotel back home that I'd found my true vocation, not to mention a home from home with the most dedicated team who offer much more than five-star service to our guests.

Leroy, a gentle giant and second generation of the Windrush movement from Jamaica, is as rich in character as the paintings and furniture. He is as sharp as the wind that whistles into every corner outside, and his smile is as warm as the fire that dances in the majestic hearth.

Leroy was the first person to greet me on that first day three years ago at the top of the steps that lead to the polished front door of The Carnation. And despite a thirty-plus-year age gap, he and I have formed a friendship since that makes my heart overflow every time I see him.

'You remind me of my Coral,' he tells me at least once a week, referring to the love of his life who once did the same job I'm doing now. 'She always stayed calm, no matter how busy we were in the run-up to Christmas.'

'And you remind me of all the goodness in the world, wrapped up in a Leroy-shaped bow,' I reply.

Now, where was I?

'Oh, yes. So, dinner reservations tomorrow,' I tell Sita at the front desk as Leroy rolls his eyes to the ceiling, tapping his watch again for effect. 'I know it's your first one with us, Sita, but Christmas Day here at The Carnation is, what can I say? It's *legendary*. So we can't afford the slightest mistake while I'm away.'

Sita rolls her dark eyes which makes me giggle.

They are right, of course. I do fuss, but I adore this place and everything to do with it. I always make sure I leave no stone unturned.

Or maybe I'm delaying the inevitable. Maybe I'm putting off the reality of going home to Ireland for Christmas – a prospect that has given me sleepless nights for at least the past seven in a row with a mixture of true excitement, anticipation and overwhelming nerves.

'OK . . . I don't think I've missed anything. Or have I?'

I notice Leroy and Sita exchanging wry glances as I run my eyes over the computerised booking system. I take my pen which is, as always, tucked behind my ear and scribble instructions on to a thick writing pad on the reception desk.

'I should have emailed you this, but a handwritten note sometimes goes a long way,' I say as I write down a few pointers for Sita.

First impressions count.

Eye contact is essential.

Always go the extra mile.

People remember how you make them feel more than what you do or say.

I underline the word 'feel', much to her amusement.

Cheesy, yes, but it works a treat on a family or an excited couple who have saved up their hard-earned pennies to stay here in luxury.

'Your attention to *detail*, Miss Beatrice, is *legendary*,' says Leroy, doing his best to imitate my singsong Irish accent. 'But you need to stop fussing and you need to stop talking. Just go. Now. *Adiós. Au revoir. Slán.* Please?'

I wring my hands.

'And don't forget there's one pre-arranged late check-out this afternoon,' I remind them both as I pull on my padded yellow coat, flicking my springy dark curls so that they bounce just above my shoulders. 'The American couple with the cute little three-year-old? It's on the house. It's Christmas Eve after all.'

Sita nods.

'You're very kind, Bea. But you *have* told me this at least five times,' she smiles. With her doll-like face and huge brown eyes, Sita, who is an auditioning West End actress, is picture perfect and has the charm inside to match her outer beauty.

'I can't help it, I'm a fusspot. OK, OK, so you've everything under control, my love,' I tell her, much to her delight. 'I know you're still new here, but don't ever be afraid to tell me to shut up and trust your judgement. I talk far too much for my own good, don't I Leroy?'

Leroy makes a signal to zip his lips and we all burst out laughing.

'And I know you won't forget, but on Monday the Kensington Suite is booked for a five-star VIP guest who goes by the incognito name of Johnny—'

5

'Madrid,' Sita interrupts. 'And I'll know him when I see him, for sure.'

'Excellent.'

'And I'm to stay totally calm, even if it really *is* Tom Hanks.'

'Exactly.'

'Miss Beatrice!'

'I'm going, I'm going,' I mutter, resisting the urge to check the bookings one last time. 'Oh, I'm so going to miss you, Nana!'

The hotel's resident furry friend puts her paws beneath her chin where she lies in front of the roaring fire, making my happy heart soar. Leroy and I named her after finding her as a young puppy on the streets begging for food not long after I started here. She has become part of the family, and we wouldn't have it any other way.

'Nana and I have a very deep understanding of life,' I remind my colleagues, ruffling the dog's downy black and white fur and staring into her big, dopey eyes. 'I tell her *all* my secrets on our walks every day, and she doesn't judge, nor does she tell a soul, do you Nana?'

I lean down further and kiss the top of Nana's head, feeling the pain of goodbye for Christmas etch my insides. I've always hated goodbyes, even if it's only for seven days and even if I've longed for this opportunity to spend time with my parents for ages now.

'We'll look after your best buddy, we promise,' says Leroy. 'Except on days like this when it means walking her on freezing dark mornings and evenings with bitter cold snow which will soon be thick on the ground.'

'Leroy!'

'I'm kidding. I will walk the dog this afternoon at four, just like you always do,' our concierge laughs. 'Now, London will wait for you forever if it must, my friend. Get home to your precious family. It's Christmas Eve and you deserve this break. You *need* this break, Miss Beatrice.'

'It's Christmas Eve and I do need this break,' I echo with a sigh. '*And* I'll be with Sean for seven whole days if I chicken out of my plan and he can tear himself away from his precious farm. You will pray for me, won't you?'

Leroy rolls his tired, sunken eyes.

'Oh look, the baubles on the tree have been tampered with, don't you think?' I enquire, fixing my fluffy red scarf around my neck before I finally leave. 'Not much point investing in overpriced, fancy decorations if . . .'

Leroy places a gentle but firm hand on each of my shoulders, turns me around to face the heavy golden double doors of the hotel and marches me towards them.

Across the street, snow-covered Kensington Gardens twinkles under the morning light in the distance. It's a place where I've solved many of my problems, work-led or personal, and although I'm only a 'blow-in', Kensington Gardens has taken up residence in my soul.

'Now, deep breaths,' whispers Leroy when we pause in the doorway.

'I can do this,' I whisper.

'You can do this,' he echoes. 'We love you and we'll miss you, but we really want you to go and take a well-earned holiday. And don't worry about Sean. He's a big boy.'

I'm not so sure.

'Let him down easily,' says Leroy. 'He's a good guy, just not the guy for you and that's all right.'

Leroy opens one door by its heavy round handle with a nod and a smile, then tips his top hat as Sita flashes me a warm smile to bid me on my way.

'Merry Christmas, Bea,' she calls, peeping out from behind a bunch of signature red carnations to match our hotel brand. 'Did you pack some red velvet cake for your mum?'

'She did,' says Leroy. 'Please don't encourage her to turn back.'

'And don't forget: *you* are important too, OK?' calls Sita. 'Text me if you need me! You are important too!'

I will remember those words. I need those words. Hot tears sting my eyes when I think of what lies ahead of me and Sean at this most wonderful time of the year.

'Reason and emotion will guide you,' Leroy tells me, holding my gaze as a blast of ice-cold air hits my face. 'You're our girl.'

I'm not sure I can hold back the wave of emotion that clutches me inside.

'You take good care, you hear? I'll be thinking of you,' I say to Leroy. He shoots me a smile in return that plucks on my heartstrings, his happy grin a stark contrast to his sad eyes which reflect a depth of hardship. I know he's hiding something from me.

But before I can wallow with him, my now awaiting taxi beeps its horn.

'I will take the most excellent care, my dear,' he calls after me. He carries my brown suitcase as we carefully walk down the steps and on to the wide pavement on Kensington Court. 'Don't you worry about a thing. Love to Mum and Dad, you hear? And Patsi too, of course.'

'I will,' I mumble, feeling the weight of guilt sink my insides already when I think of Sean. 'See you all in seven days. Love you.'

'We love you too,' sings Leroy. 'Have a wonderful holiday!'

The frosty wind catches my breath as I cautiously tiptoe towards the cab and away from The Carnation Hotel, my home from home, away from Sita and Leroy and the warm familiarity of a place I love so much it never feels like work to me.

I'm going home for Christmas, to my own precious family at last.

I'm also going home to face the music with Sean, to set him straight after pretending and brushing my real feelings under the carpet for far too long. My stomach goes to my throat at the very thought, but no, I can do this. I have to do this.

I'd better not miss my flight.

Chapter Two

Ollie

London
Christmas Eve

I'm going to miss my flight.

'Stay cool, Ollie. I've got this, mate. I've totally got this.'

Scott, my wingman, room buddy and best friend since I first came to London from the wilds of Donegal as a young student ten years ago, does his very best to weave through crazy Christmas Eve traffic to get me to the airport on time.

His infectious enthusiasm, his endearing Liverpudlian accent and our shared love of gym workouts and Liverpool FC, the best football team in England – as well as the fact we were the only two male students on our nursing course at university – drew me to him and made sure I've always had someone to lean on.

And boy, he's taken my weight so often lately. He's the one true friend I know will always have my back.

Christmas Eve traffic in London in a snowstorm is not to

be underestimated though, and my nerves aren't coping well after a ten-hour marathon on the cardiac ward at the Royal Elizabeth Hospital.

It was an eventful one where we had three emergency admissions, one ending in surgery, and a false alarm when an engaging old guy presented with chest pains which turned out to be the result of some early festive overindulgence.

As horns blare and the city's famous red buses weave in and out of traffic lanes to take shoppers into the city, we do our best to get out of it and reach Heathrow Airport on time.

I know I should have taken the train or Underground to the airport, but Scott insisted on driving me instead. The storm moving in is totally against us, I'm beyond exhausted and Scott is talking ten to the dozen which isn't doing much for my frazzled nerves.

'Do you know how much it meant to Jane that you covered for her last night?' he asks as he whizzes out on to the M4, the car's wipers swishing the slush off the wind-screen at what feels like lightning speed. 'I mean, seriously Ollie. That was a champion move. That's the one thing I can say about your team on Cardiac Ward Three. You work together. You *are* a team. My crowd in the Emergency department wouldn't swap a shift for you if you were on the floor taking your last breath. Ironic, yes, but *not* an exaggeration.'

Scott's eyes are everywhere except on the busy road that leads to Heathrow, which isn't helping the fear I have. Nor is the blinking clock on the dashboard that seems to be on fast forward, or the updates from the airline apps on my phone that keep reminding me time is ticking on. Why does time go so much more quickly when you're in a mad hurry? We are now twenty-five minutes by car from Terminal 2 according to the Google Maps I'm following on my phone.

'Jane wanted to take her daughter to see Santa at their village Christmas Fayre yesterday evening,' Scott continues, his voice cracking with emotion, which is very 'Scott' – but he's also incredibly hungover, which only heightens his moment of reflection and praise. 'I mean, sometimes I do believe my heart is as hard as the ice on the road out there. We've seen it all at work, haven't we? Life hanging by a thread, death on an almost daily basis. It does harden you, Ollie. But by doing that, champ – by doing that one unselfish act all in the name of Christmas spirit, you melted it.'

He punches his chest for effect, then we sit in silence with only BBC Radio 2 for company for miles on the motorway, both of us knowing that we're cutting it very fine to make my flight.

The familiar voices of the presenters do nothing to ease my anxiety, nor do the jolly tones of Elton and Ed Sheeran who are wishing us all a merry Christmas in song.

We approach the turn-off for the airport at last. Thank God for small mercies is all I can say, but then cars line up in front of us at a set of lights which I just know will stay on red for far longer than I need them to. The tailback ahead of us grows longer and slower, until traffic comes to a standstill.

Then we come to a standstill too.

'Seriously.'

Scott stares at the lights as if that's going to make a difference.

'This isn't moving, Scott. It really isn't moving,' I say, gripping the door handle of the Volkswagen Golf. The lights finally change from red to green, but we've only moved what feels like a few feet ahead. 'I can jump out here, honestly. I'll walk the rest. Snow or no snow. What do you think? Should I walk the rest? Scott?'

Despite my festive deed the night before and how warm and fuzzy it felt to cover for our good friend Jane, I'm feeling more like Scrooge than a Good Samaritan right now.

In fact, I'm kicking myself for not thinking ahead.

It's Christmas Eve and I need to get back to Ireland to my dad. If I hadn't agreed last minute to work a night shift into the wee hours, I'd have been well slept and at the airport long ago.

And although I know missing a flight isn't a life-or-death situation (I deal with those in my workplace every day), I really want to get home to my family this Christmas.

I've been counting the days. I've been watching the clock for weeks. I've made so many promises to my dad that I simply can't let him down by missing my flight on Christmas Eve just because I've been foolish enough to sleep in.

'I said I'd drive you to the door of Terminal Two, so I'll drive you to the door of Terminal Two,' Scott replies, leaning forward in the driver's seat as if that is going to speed things up. 'Look, we're moving now! OK, we're moving! See? We'll be at the entrance in minutes. No, in seconds. Once I stop, you jump out. No big goodbyes, mate.'

I'm not one for big mushy goodbyes anyhow, especially when I'll see Scott again in a few days back in London where we spend our time talking movies over takeaways, cheering on Liverpool on TV on Saturdays, and packing in gym sessions around serving our inpatients and outpatients who keep us both busy throughout manic ten-hour shifts at the hospital.

'Is it too early to say it's going to be a white Christmas?' I ask, leaning my head back on the headrest. I'm clutching at straws to look on the bright side here, I know.

BBC reports the worst of the storm coming in closer, but from what I can see through the windscreen, it's already well under way.

I'm exhausted in a way that makes me feel sick, but adrenaline thankfully is taking over. All I want to do is run, not drive at this snail's pace as the minutes tick by. Every festive song on the radio, from new releases to old classics like Bing Crosby, adds to the tension, and even a blast of 'Fairytale of New York' can't settle the nerves that tickle my bones as we sit here in gridlock traffic.

'You'll make it. I'm going to make sure you make it,' Scott mutters, but all I can feel is the world closing in as the likelihood of me being on that flight to City of Derry is growing slimmer and slimmer. If I miss it I could hopefully jump on the next flight into Belfast, but there's no way my elderly aunt Nora could drive so far to pick me up.

I can't miss it. I just can't.

'I really do think I could run the rest. I'll break and bolt,' I suggest again, with my hand already on the handle of the door. 'It might be quicker than sitting in this bottleneck?'

'You could end up breaking your *neck* if you run in that weather.'

He has a point, to be fair.

'Seriously, buddy, I need to make this flight,' I plead. 'I need to see my dad. It could be his last Christmas. I'm going to run the rest.'

'Hang on! We'll make it,' says Scott in a confident tone, but he looks like he might cry. He's never one to do anything by halves so I'm hoping he'll give in to defeat on this rare, very important occasion.

In return, I bite my nails. A habit formed in childhood but one I haven't visited in a very long time, which tells me I really am on the edge right now.

We sit in silence. I almost open the door in frustration. I want to scarper.

'Actually, no, look at the time,' says Scott, putting his head in his hands against the steering wheel. 'I think you're going to have to walk or run the rest after all. I did my best. I'm sorry, mate.'

'Hero. Thank you for getting me this far,' I reply, throwing him a twenty for petrol which will more than cover the relatively short but slow journey.

'Have fun at home and give your old man a hug from all of us. You're one of the good guys, Ol!'

I grab my rucksack from the back seat, then I wave back

at him under the weight of my bag, jogging along the slushy ground with trepidation while praying I make it on time. The last thing I need is to fall and end up back in my workplace A&E on Christmas Eve.

Everyone and everything seems to get in my way as I scramble through the front doors of Heathrow, physically bumping into every single obstacle, from people to trolleys to a bin I didn't even take the time to see.

'Excuse me. I'm so sorry. Excuse me!'

Slipping and sliding with only forty minutes to get through airport security was not how I'd envisaged kicking off my first Christmas holiday at home for three years.

I've been dreaming about this trip forever. Meeting Buster and Simon for a pint down at The Rusty Mackerel in my home village of Teelin in Donegal, watching the boats bob on the water at the pier with a coffee in my hand on frosty mornings, walking along the spectacular cliffs of Slieve League with their breathtaking views and the wind cutting through my hair, taking Murphy, our old Irish Red Setter, for long walks on the horseshoe-shaped Silver Strand Beach at Malin Beg.

Most of all, I've been dreaming of spending quality time with my dad.

I slow down my pace at the very thought of my father. The great Jack Brennan, former Gaelic football goalkeeper with hands like shovels, farmer of the land and mender of everything in the village from bicycles to car engines to old rickety chairs. Big Jack Brennan could breathe life into anything that needed repairing.

They call him the Fixer Man at home. Yet the one thing no one can seem to fix is his ailing health.

A lump forms in my throat. My eyes sting. No, no, I can't think about it too much. Not yet.

I start running again.

I do my best to distract any darkness in my mind by thinking of how my tastebuds are longing for a soothing pint of Guinness and a tasty bowl of Irish stew by a turf fire.

A real Irish Guinness in a real Irish pub, none of that inferior stuff I've appeased myself with in London for far too long.

I've also been dreaming lately of my Aunt Nora's famous turkey and ham dinner at home in Oyster Cottage, which will be a far cry from the hospital dinners I've dined on for the last three years at Christmas. She does a mean stuffing too, not to mention the gravy.

It's all so close I can almost taste it.

I'm on my way home for Christmas to Ireland. I'm on my way to spend what is likely to be my very last Christmas with my dad.

I never thought it possible to be so excited to see someone yet so absolutely terrified at the very same time.

Chapter Three

Bea

Terminal 2, Heathrow Airport, London
Christmas Eve

Those who believe that every airport across the world on Christmas Eve is a romantic sea of smiling faces, warm hugs and other cheerful displays of affection has watched far too many Richard Curtis movies.

Arrivals is a pleasure for the most part, of course, but the Departures lounge in Terminal 2 at London's Heathrow on Christmas Eve morning is a manic nest of city-based single-tons like me, or frantic young families embarking on a last-minute rush out of the big smoke at the same time to a place they really call home.

For me, home is the rural village of Benburb in County Tyrone, a stone-walled haven with an ancient castle and priory on the banks of a wide, foaming river. The familiarity of everyone knowing your name feels like a cosy blanket on a cold day compared to the anonymity of London, and my parents' house that sits in view of the swirling rush of the

River Blackwater is the closest thing to heaven I've ever experienced.

Every year in London I'd long to be home where I can walk on a crisp December day in the grounds of the priory on Christmas morning, enjoy a catch-up with old friends in the one and only pub, and then tuck into my mother's famous 'all the trimmings' dinner before settling down by a blazing fire with a hot chocolate and reminiscing about happier days gone by.

But the hotel in London has needed me for the past three years, and now that the opportunity to spend Christmas at home comes upon me at last, I'm not so sure it will be as picture perfect as I've always imagined it to be, due to the decision I've made.

I adore going home, but for many different reasons I always am ready to go back to London after just a few days have passed.

I loosen my red woolly scarf as a lump in my throat thickens.

'Worry gives small things a bigger shadow,' I mumble on repeat, remembering Leroy's words of wisdom from a few days before.

I need to stick to my guns. I need to go with my gut instinct. My mother has always told me to trust my gut. It's rarely wrong.

The smell of cigarette smoke on damp clothes of strangers lingers in the air in the Departures lounge as I scan the information board for details of my flight. I've cut it pretty fine time-wise but now I'm on my way, all I need to find within me is the strength to go ahead with my plan. Much easier said than done.

I check my boarding pass on my phone, smiling when I see my seat number is 13B. Thirteen for my lucky number, and B for the initial that stands for my very own name.

'Miss Beatrice, just like the princess,' Leroy often teases, nodding to the royal gardens that sprawl across from The Carnation Hotel, and although I always shoo off any comparisons, inside I kind of like it.

Life in London is kind to me, and although it was only ever meant to be a short-term transfer from my time at the prestigious Ashford Castle Hotel in Ireland where I learned my trade, I've settled in more than nicely to the company's flagship Carnation Hotel just off Kensington High Street.

It fits me like the proverbial glove.

A three-month-long stint has turned into a three-year-long stay in what felt like the blink of an eye, allowing me to live in the very best of both worlds. I've a quiet, cosy, rural home life in Ireland where I'm nestled by family who I love and adore, and a bustling city lifestyle where I can be anyone I want to be.

I let out a lengthy yawn.

Did I remember to tell Sita not to show obvious disappointment if our VIP guest Johnny Madrid isn't Tom Hanks after all? I'll text her just to be sure.

She's already six months into the job, but I've seen her go all giddy back in late summer when a Mr I.P. Freely turned out to be Slash from the rock band Guns N' Roses, despite my advice to keep her cool.

I close my eyes and breathe. Everything at the hotel is under control. I will repeat this to myself until it sinks in completely. I'm looking forward to giving my mother some of our signature red velvet cake which is always a welcome surprise for guests when they check into their rooms.

We take immense pride in the finer detail to make sure everyone who stays at The Carnation Hotel wants to tell their friends all about it. To me, that's the secret of good hospitality. Instagram and TripAdvisor are essential, but word of mouth after a wonderful experience from a friend to a friend is the best advertisement of all.

The airport is bleak compared to the festive warmth of my workplace, which reminds me what I love most about working in hospitality. The smile on the faces of our guests when after a long journey they finally get to relax with a hot or cold drink depending on the season, the look of delight when a staff member goes that extra mile to make their stay comfortable like the turn-down service after a busy day, or a complimentary newspaper at breakfast.

'When you give, you receive with compound interest,' Leroy often says when a happy customer leaves with a full belly and a fuller heart. I enjoy every one of Leroy's pearls of wisdom. My mother told me to write them down as they might come in handy one day, so I've started to do just that. In fact, I've started to write most things down I want to remember.

An extra special connection with a customer, or a tricky one indeed, or even my walks in Kensington Gardens with

Nana and the thoughts that go through my head when I'm alone. I write it all down.

With fellow weary travellers to my left, right and everywhere in between, the best place I can find to rest is against a wall, so I shuffle in next to a family of four who are doing the same while glued to their phones.

'Home for Christmas?' the friendly dad says to me when he catches my eye. They're Irish too. I nod and smile in return once I hear his accent.

I often wonder if people from the same country have a secret radar that lets them recognise each other before they even open their mouths to say a word.

'Can't wait,' I reply.

I slide my back down the wall and sit on my hand luggage, wishing that was totally true while I wait for my gate number to be called.

'I bet there's a delay,' I hear the man's wife say beside me. 'Why haven't they announced the gate yet?'

'Oh, don't even say that, love,' he replies, but to be honest I wouldn't mind an extra bit of time to put off the inevitable, even if it is Christmas Eve.

It's all beginning to feel very real. I've a big task ahead, but I don't want to let it take away from the joy I should be feeling about spending Christmas with my family.

I wonder what they're all doing back home right now. I check my phone to read through our family group chat but all is quiet, except for a selfie from Patsi and her French boyfriend Jacques with the famous Benburb Castle in the background.

At only eight months into their relationship after meeting in Paris where Patsi is working as an English teacher, she and Jacques are so overflowing with the first flushes of romance it's either sickening or joyous depending on your mood. Patsi was singing in a jazz club as a side hustle. Jacques was working behind the bar around his law studies. He heard her voice, they locked eyes across a Parisian dance floor, and the rest is history.

A pang of homesickness claws at my gut when I see my sister standing by the castle. As much as I'm dreading facing the music with Sean, I can't wait to get home to Benburb, my parents and the people I love most in the world. And as much as I love London, I know there's no place like home at Christmas.

In just a few hours our Patsi will be in the Bottle of Benburb pub by the open fire, singing and sipping a pint of Guinness with Jacques, while a singer in the corner strums his guitar to get everyone in the festive spirit.

Patsi's hot pink hair and nose piercings will stand out like a sore thumb amongst the locals, but she'll have them eating out of her hands once she hums a lilting tune, especially her unique, husky rendition of 'Last Christmas', which is famous at home by now.

I giggle to myself as I imagine her ramping up the Irish Christmas vibes for Jacques, who is bound to get a bit of a culture shock coming from his sophisticated Parisian lifestyle.

Patsi is a natural singer, while I've always been the one who has a way with words, both in the written form and verbally. My mother jokes how I've enough chat for another row of teeth, but my ability to talk to strangers is what makes me so good at my job, or so I'm told.

Mum and Dad will have the stockings hanging up by the mantelpiece at home, just like when we were youngsters, and there'll be three on display – one each for me, Patsi and Peter – for the family we once were before our world fell apart.

And as for Sean . . .

A cool shiver runs through my bones.

I hug my knees, surprised when tears spring in my eyes for what could and should have been by now. When I was young, I'd always imagined I'd be married with children by the age of thirty. And here I am at thirty-two, about to end my long-term relationship with a man who was once my everything.

I do wish I was still head over heels in love with Sean, but while he is established for good on his family farm, I've settled too well with my life in London, and I don't foresee making any changes to that in the near future.

I've never said it out loud, but I can't see myself ever living back home again. It's too painful for me to think about. It's all too painful in so many ways.

I often wonder why I can't be like our Patsi and Jacques, so madly in love and so certain about how they're going to spend the rest of their lives together.

Why can't I be so confident when it comes to my own love life? Is it because I've got the best of both worlds right now? Or is it because I simply haven't found the right person?

Sean is a good man. I know that deep in my heart. It's what attracted me to him in the first place all those years ago when we were in our twenties and we clicked one night after I came home from a long summer in Australia. He is kind, he is gentle, he is a hard worker and he's funny – sometimes. He tried living in London with me in the beginning and lasted four months, a proverbial fish out of water, and we've been ever so slowly growing more and more distant since. I know he'll make someone an amazing husband one day. I just don't think I want him to be mine.

Is this why I'm holding on to life in London? Am I simply avoiding the truth? I've been with Sean, albeit with the Irish Sea between us, for seven long years now, yet even my colleagues at the hotel know there's something just not right about our romance.

Maybe I'll always have this wanderlust within me. Maybe I'll always be running away from reality, never allowing myself to settle. But then who wants to just *settle*? I want magic. I want to feel my heart rise when I think of my lover coming to town to see me. I want to feel at home in his arms, like I've found my one and only. Yes, I know that true love isn't all hearts and flowers, and yes, I know it's hard work sometimes and ever changing. But I also know that what I have with Sean, as lovely as it is, is just that . . . lovely.

And I don't want just 'lovely'.

I picture him waiting for me later in City of Derry airport with a wide grin, teary eyes and welcoming open arms. I usually fly into Belfast, but the cost of Christmas Eve flights isn't for the faint-hearted, so I chose the extra miles on the other side to save a few pounds. Sean's cheeks will be ruddy from the winter cold, he'll smell of home baking and cinnamon from his mother's kitchen and he'll be full of plans for heading to the local pub where he'll show me off to his friends like I'm a prize turkey. But this time I'm determined not to go along with it like before. This time I plan to tell the man the truth he deserves once and for all.

He deserves better. So much better. And so do I.

Yes, in just over two hours I'm going to say what I have to say. In just over two hours I will have it over and done with. To be more precise, in just two hours and twenty-seven minutes from now I'll talk to him on the ninety-minute journey home from City of Derry to Benburb from the airport. I'll finally have the conversation I've played over and over in my mind a million times but still haven't worked out exactly what I'm going to say.

'It's not you, it's me.'

Christ, that's a cop-out.

'Do you think we've drifted apart, Sean?'

Or:

'Look, Sean, I've been thinking . . . are you happy?'

No, that won't work either. That's only a recipe for disaster because the answer will probably be 'Yes, of course I'm happy, sure don't I have you in my life.'

Even if we do see each other only once a month at the most. Even though our conversations on the phone every evening mainly skirt around people we know rather than how we're really feeling inside. Even though the last time we were together we had turned into that couple who scroll through their phones over dinner instead of engaging in real life conversation.

Even though every time I see him, I feel like I don't really know him at all any more.

Oh, can I really tell him today? On Christmas Eve? This should be our seventh Christmas as a couple. This should be a time of celebration, not a break-up. But those seven years were patchy at best, with most of our relationship being long distance.

It used to be enough.

But it isn't enough any more.

'I just need a little bit more time to think,' I whisper, hugging my knees from my place on this cold airport floor as if they have the answer. I'm so close to figuring out what I'm going to say without destroying the man, but two hours isn't enough.

'I told you there'd be a delay! Oh, for crying out loud!'

The voice of the man beside me diverts my attention to the information board where a delay has indeed been announced, and a notification on my phone follows to confirm their worst fears and my saving grace.

My eyes widen. It's only a one-hour delay but to me it's like a lifetime. It's exactly what I need – a little more time.

'Thank you,' I whisper to the heavens, but as relieved as I feel inside, those around me don't seem to share my delight at the announcement.

Another man to my right coughs, groans and curses at the delay. The pleasant father from earlier lets out a deep sigh, as does his exhausted wife. The smallest child cries in case she is too late for Santa coming. I understand their frustration, even if I don't share it.

The airport is stuffy, cramped and smelly, but I can't help but feel a tiny bit of pressure easing away. I know exactly what I'll use this time for. I'll write it all out. Yes, that always helps me sort out my mental dilemmas. I'll write down my feelings in my notebook. I'll spill it all out on paper and prepare my script properly now that I've time away from the hubbub of my day job and all the demands that come with it.

I'll do that.

I glance across to a pub called the George, which like all the others is packed at the seams. Maybe there'll be a spare seat by the time I get that far?

Yes, I'll go and have a nice cup of tea. And then I'll have a gin and tonic. And maybe once I've written down my thoughts, I'll even treat myself to a glossy magazine to catch up on all the celebrity gossip.

A drink of any sort and a bit of scribbling can work wonders for the soul, that's my motto.

In the next sixty minutes or so, I will plan my break-up speech to Sean Sullivan once and for all.

It might ruin his Christmas, which I feel incredibly sad about, but as Sita reminded me, I'm important too.

I'm trying my best to remember that.

I need to believe that it's true.

Chapter Four

Ollie

Terminal 2, Heathrow Airport, London
Christmas Eve

I make it through security with my heart still racing.

I can slow down a little now. I'm through the worst part. I can walk to the gate. I search for the screen to tell me where to go next when I hear a familiar accent next to me. A young lady wearing an oversized Santa dress and reindeer antlers stomps her Dr. Martens boot on the floor. To say she doesn't sound impressed is an understatement.

'You have got to be kidding me!' she squeals while tapping into her phone. 'I've a party to go to! How on earth can we be delayed on Christmas Eve?'

'City of Derry?' I ask her.

She has tears in her eyes. Oh dear.

'Yes, it's delayed by an hour,' she wails. 'Browse, shop and enjoy, they say? Anyone who still has shopping to do at this time on Christmas Eve deserves to be stuck in never-ending queues. I need a drink!'

She storms past me and I stare up at the board to see that, sure enough, the flight into City of Derry is delayed by an hour, but I can live with that.

In fact, it's music to my ears because after a very stressful start to the day including a lack of sleep, no breakfast and a white-knuckle ride against the clock to get here after sleeping in, I can now browse, relax and shop for an hour.

And I know what I'll be shopping for, too. A long, cold, creamy pint of Guinness.

It might not be lunchtime yet but as the saying goes, it's five o'clock somewhere. Looks like Christmas has come early for me.

'Excuse me, is this seat taken?'

After a lengthy wait at the bar of the George, I hold my pint glass like a precious prize trophy near where a very busy dark-haired woman sits at a tiny round table in the bar, her head buried in a notebook, a pen in one hand and a teacup in the other. She holds the cup poised in mid-air, deep in thought.

'Is this seat taken?' I ask again.

She waves her pen towards the empty chair, her eyes still attached to the paper in front of her.

I feel the weight off my feet when I sit down.

'Aah, that's a relief.'

I didn't mean to say that quite so loud, but my company doesn't seem too bothered. It's hard to hear anything over the din that surrounds me as frantic travellers either race to their gate or scramble to the bar to make the most of this short delay.

I'm surrounded by Irish accents of all sorts, which is both exciting and comforting at the same time. Looks like I'm not the only one to wait until Christmas Eve to leave the city.

As I sip my pint, the clock on the wall seems to slow down too, which is just what I needed.

I'm going home at last.

I almost choke as the reality of my dad's illness clutches my throat, but I can't think about all of that too much yet. It's too raw. It's too real. I gulp my pint then slam the glass down a little too enthusiastically on to the table which makes my company glance upwards.

'Whoops. I'm so sorry about that. Sorry.'

The woman catches my eye and squints a little, but instead of going back to her work she studies me, tilting her head to the side.

'Do I know you from somewhere?' she asks. 'You look familiar.'

She is beautiful in her vibrant red scarf and bucket hat to match, which is incredibly festive compared to my dull black winter coat that has seen better days.

I've never seen her before in my life. If I had, I wouldn't have forgotten her, that's for sure.

'Ah, you probably have seen me before on the cover of *Vogue* magazine?' I jest. 'And I was Person of the Year for *Time*. Ring a bell?'

To my relief she gets my attempt at humour. I wipe a creamy spill of Guinness from the table with a napkin.

'What year was that?' she quips.

'Now you're testing me,' I reply. 'No, I don't think we know each other. Unless you've been in hospital lately with a heart problem, which I sincerely hope you haven't?'

She looks back at me and smiles.

'Thankfully I haven't been in a hospital since I fell off my bike and plunged into the river when I was ten years old,' she says. 'And I'm hoping it will be a long time before I'm back there. Are you a doctor?'

'I'm a nurse,' I reply. 'NHS.'

'Fantastic,' she says. 'I hope you have a lovely Christmas. Safe trip home.'

She flashes me a dazzling smile.

'And you too,' I reply.

She goes back to her notebook and back to her thoughts. I can't help but watch as she holds her pen ready as if she's miles away, then writes a little more. She looks up, catches me watching, and smirks before looking away again.

'What?' I ask her. 'What's so funny?'

She leans forward in her seat.

'Did you know,' she asks, 'that hundreds of thousands of pints of the famous Irish black stuff are lost in men's facial hair every year?'

Ah.

'Did you Google that?'

'I may have done at some stage.'

'So, I have a Guinness moustache?'

'You have a Guinness moustache,' she confirms.

She hands me a fresh napkin. I dab the creamy gold off my upper lip.

'That's a lot of wasted pints caught up in stubble.'

'Too many,' she says. 'A terrible waste of an Irish national treasure in my opinion.'

She fixes her hat and pushes her curly hair off her face. Her cheeks are pink against pale skin, and I'm not sure if I've ever seen anyone as beautiful in my whole life.

'Derry?' I suggest, guessing her origin by her accent.

'Tyrone,' she replies. 'And you're Donegal through and through.'

'Correct,' I reply, sipping my pint very carefully this time. 'Thanks for the heads up on the Guinness moustache, by the way. I've had a very long night at work so I'm not exactly firing on all cylinders right now.'

She smiles and sets her pen down, then leans forward a little more with her hands under her chin. She has a very endearing heart-shaped face. She has nice hands too, which is a funny thing to notice but I do. They are delicate but smooth and her nails are—

I feel my face flush. I shuffle in my seat and try to dart my eyes anywhere but on her. I pick up my phone from the table but set it straight back down again.

'I too have put in a very long *morning* at the office,' she tells me. 'Never thought I'd say it, but I'm glad of the flight delay.'

'Me too.' I yawn to prove my point. 'I'm just off a ten-hour night shift at the hospital so I'm running on less than an hour of sleep.'

'I can't possibly beat that.'

'You'd be surprised how many people think they're having a heart attack at this time of year when it's really too much beer and sprouts,' I tell her, 'but it's always best to get checked. I'm exhausted.'

If this was a game on who was most tired, I've just won hands down.

'That's a long shift for sure. So, you're heading home to your family for Christmas?' she asks.

'Yeah, you?'

'First time in several years.'

'First time in ages for me too.'

She lifts her teacup with both hands and puts it to her lips.

'Gosh, there really isn't enough room here for so many people, is there?' she says, looking around the cramped airport bar. 'Do you have enough space? Sorry if I'm taking up too much of the table.'

She reshuffles her phone, her notebook and pen to try and create a bit more room, but since it's only me and my pint of Guinness sat across from her, there really is no need.

A young couple with a crying toddler in a pushchair squeeze through the crowds to the table next to us which makes it even more claustrophobic. The two young parents are frazzled as they work together to balance food, drinks and the baby who is arching her back to be set free.

'Thank you,' I say to my company when she's finished

organising her belongings. 'More room for me to spill my drink now. I hope I'm not distracting you.'

She shoots me a shy smile, which I'm not sure how to interpret. If this was someone else, if I was looking on, I'd almost think we had chemistry.

Should I introduce myself properly? Or is that overstepping the mark? Is this just usual 'cramped table sharing' small talk between strangers which will fizzle out now we've exchanged pleasantries, or—

'I'm Bea,' she says, beating me to it.

'Sorry?'

'Bea,' she says again. 'As in honeybee, bumble bee, Bea.'

'I'm Ollie.'

'Nice to meet you, Ollie from Donegal.'

I'm just about to launch into a bit more conversation, but she goes back to her book and her scribbling, so I go back to my pint and people watching.

Some people get bored at airports, but I never do. I enjoy the time to just read something, scroll through my phone or sit and wait. It's a good excuse to slow down and absorb your surroundings, as the option to do anything else is totally out of your hands. You just have to wait.

Bea, it seems, likes to write as she waits.

I deliberately avert my eyes to give her some privacy, but the more I try to make it look like I'm not looking the more my eyes are drawn towards her.

I wonder what she's writing that's so important. Surely it's not work-related on Christmas Eve, but who knows.

'It's eleven-eleven,' I say out loud.

'Sorry?'

'Nothing, it's OK, please just ignore me. Sorry.'

She glances at her phone.

'You're right, it's eleven-eleven,' she says, looking at the time. 'Make a wish.'

The way she says it is like she speaks with her eyes. I make a wish, then we both break into a giddy smile. I wish for the first thing that comes to my mind and if she could read my thoughts, she'd probably run a mile.

She goes back to her writing. I play a bit with my beermat, then realise that's probably very irritating so I stop. I play a game on my phone, but I can't concentrate when she's beside me. Then I hum along with the music that can just about be heard below the din of what sounds like white noise around us. Another Christmas song. *Wham!* this time, singing about last Christmas.

When I dare to glance back in Bea's direction, she is watching me with an amused smile.

'You're a good singer,' she says.

'Was I singing?' I reply. 'I thought I was humming quietly.'

She shakes her head.

'You were totally singing.'

'You mean you don't feel the need to sing in already super noisy airports?'

We both shoot a glance towards the crying baby and I wonder if she's thinking what I'm thinking . . . no, there's no way she could be thinking the same as me.

'Do you have children?'

'No,' I reply. 'You?'

'No, but I'd like to one day,' she says. I shift in my seat.
She was thinking exactly what I was thinking.

'How many?'

'Three would be nice.'

My God, I really like her already. I glance at her hands
again. She isn't wearing a wedding ring, so that's a good start.

'Triplets?'

'That's not exactly what I have in mind, but who knows,'
she replies, slightly recoiling but still flashing her gorgeous
smile.

'Who knows,' I echo. 'Well, I'm very sorry to disturb you
with my singing and spilling. I guess I'm a bit excited to get
home.'

She doesn't take her eyes off me.

'I think I'm done anyhow,' she says, holding her pen as
well as my gaze. She closes her notebook, and her face brightens as if she's just had a weight lifted off her shoulders. 'Yes,
there's nothing more I can do. I've written it all out, I've
memorised it, so Jesus, take the wheel. I can do no more. It's
all in the hands of fate.'

'Sounds important.'

'Oh, it is,' she says, her forehead wrinkling in thought.
'But I'm on top of it, so I'm going to order a sandwich, even
if we're practically in recession and airport prices might push
me further into an overdraft. Yes, I need food. I'm dwelling
on this no longer.'

I've no clue what she is talking about, of course, but her
energy is palpable. I find myself grinning in her direction.

'Go for it,' I reply.

She stands up, or at least she does her best to. It's not easy with so little space around us.

'Actually, sod it. I know it isn't even eleven-thirty, but I'm going to go all out and try the Christmas dinner,' she says, standing on her tiptoes now to look across to the bar where the menu specials are on a huge blackboard. 'It's almost lunchtime. I've had my cup of tea so I'm also going to have a gin and tonic this time. Or a nice glass of wine. Are you hungry?'

'Me?' She hands me a menu from her side of the small table. 'Well, I wasn't, but I . . . I am, now that you've mentioned Christmas dinner.'

'A man can't survive on Guinness alone, can he?' she declares, shuffling around to squeeze past me. 'So, turkey and ham, stuffing, veg and roast potatoes. *All* the trimmings? It's Christmas Eve after all. What do you say?'

She looks me right in the eye, my stomach leaps and I'm not sure what is happening, but I agree with every word that she says. For some reason with Bea, I imagine that most people do.

'Why not?' I reply. 'That sounds really good, actually.'

'Cranberry sauce?'

'What? Yes, yes, I'll come with you to order.' I do my best to stand up but it isn't easy with a child's pram parked right behind me. 'I'm not sure if they do floor service.'

She thinks for a moment.

'No, you wait here and mind the table or we'll lose it,' she suggests and before I can argue she's already zig-zagging past chairs, tables, bulky hand luggage and weary travellers to make her way to the bar to order.

I watch her excuse herself, squeezing through until she is just a red hat bobbing along across the surface of the crowd.

What on earth is going on? Whatever it is, I can't help smiling, that's for sure. I can just imagine Scott scratching his head and asking how, of all the people in a crammed airport on Christmas Eve, I end up beside a beautiful stranger while drinking Guinness and now she's bringing me Christmas dinner?

It's unexpected, it's fun and as quickly as it all just happened, it somehow feels like the most natural thing in the world to have happened today.

And who knows? Maybe it is.

Chapter Five

Bea

My only brother Peter, who was an old soul according to everyone who knew him, used to tease me about how I trusted people too easily. He'd often remark how I thought everyone in the world was nice and how I should really be more cautious, especially when I left home to work in big cities where most people preferred to mind their own business rather than be everyone's best friend.

'City folk aren't like us. They don't like to be told by strangers that their outfit is nice, or their hair is sitting well, Bea,' he'd joke with me at the kitchen table back home where we'd all have dinner together. 'Just don't think everyone is as open as you, because Benburb is not a city. And cities are not Benburb. Be careful, won't you?'

I can still hear the sound of his young voice, deep but velvety in tone, and how his eyebrows would scrunch up when he was making a point he really believed in.

My God, I miss him.

So now, as I sit here about to tuck into a turkey and ham dinner in this bustling bar in Heathrow on Christmas Eve during a flight delay, I can't help but giggle at how our Peter would be shaking his head if he could see me now.

I can talk ten to the dozen, he'd tell me, but it's always about other people's happiness and comfort while often sacrificing my own.

Is your room to your satisfaction, Ma'am? Is there anything else we can do to help your stay be more comfortable? No, it's OK, I can stay an extra hour. You go home early. I don't mind if I'm absolutely hammered with tiredness and can barely keep my eyes open. You go ahead.

I told him it was the nature of my job. He'd tell me it wasn't always good to be so selfless. He'd tell me to consider my own feelings. I think again of what Sita said.

'You are important too.'

So, with my script written in my notebook, that's exactly what I'll do when I get home. I'm going to take the bull by the horns. I'm going to say my piece to Sean once and for all. I'm going to stand up for Bea Malone's feelings instead of putting everyone else's first.

Ollie hasn't said much since we started eating except a very appreciative thank you. Not that I expect him to. We are simply two strangers sharing a table.

I hope I didn't force him to eat something, though he does seem to be enjoying his food.

'It's a bit of a step up from hospital dinners,' he says eventually. 'Are you sure I've given you enough cash to cover what you paid at the bar? I never usually carry cash so that was lucky.'

'I'm sure,' I tell him. 'You've given me more than enough,

even the tip which I hope you don't mind me having added on?'

He nods with enthusiasm.

'Not at all – this dinner is five star compared to my recent diet,' he replies. 'I mean, Christmas dinner *and* Guinness? Who would ever complain about that? This could be the best Christmas ever.'

He winks at me and I do my best to ignore how attractive he is. Early thirties, I'm guessing, dimples, sparkling eyes and almost cheeky looking but in a very endearing way.

I watch him tuck in, still wearing his heavy coat even though the heat in here is stifling by now. He is very cute to watch even when he's eating.

'It's warm in here,' I say out loud, not really meaning for him to hear or respond. He doesn't.

I take off my red bucket hat and smooth down my hair, then slip off my yellow coat and fan my face with a paper napkin. I focus on my plate, urging my tongue to stop the chatter that could quite easily spill out of my mouth. I can't help but think again how he looks almost familiar, yet I've probably never seen him before. And although he joked about *Vogue* magazine, there's undoubtedly something unforgettable about Ollie.

He's funny, he's very sweet and he has an ease about him that makes me want to know more.

Does he enjoy his job at the hospital? Did he always want to be a nurse? Does he like living in London or is it a temporary arrangement like mine was supposed to be? Does he have a wife? Or a girlfriend? Or a boyfriend for that matter? So many questions, but I do my best to hold back.

I mean, why am I so nosey? Why am I even wondering about this stranger's personal life when I've a mountain to climb at home with my own long-term boyfriend?

'You look like you've a million thoughts going on in there,' he says, catching me mid-stare. 'You know, I've been told I've a very good bedside manner, so I'm used to listening. I'm a very good listener.'

I jolt out of my bubble as the reality of facing Sean at home comes back to haunt me.

'Unfortunately, I do have a million thoughts going through my head,' I reply. 'Sorry to flatten the mood, but I'm dreading some parts of my short trip home.'

He sets down his cutlery and leans in to listen with a look of concern on his beautiful face. He has strong shoulders and a jawline that certainly wouldn't go amiss on the cover of a magazine.

Truth is, he's pretty gorgeous in every way and I could easily sit and stare at him for hours.

'You can talk it out if you want?' he suggests. 'I mean, the chances of us ever meeting again are so slim that even if I did tell ten other people it won't really affect you or your decisions.'

I take a sip of my cold, crisp wine. Its tartness catches the back of my throat. I'd better not think too much about my forthcoming conversation with Sean or I won't eat a bite, so I do my best to focus on the present instead.

'I wouldn't want to put you off your food,' I reply.

'It would take a lot to put me off my food,' he responds. 'And that's a fact.'

I laugh at his honesty.

Ollie is a good distraction from all that's been going on in my head all week.

As well as chatty and fun, he is attractive beyond measure with his thick dark curls, light stubble and dashing blue eyes with lashes I'd exchange a limb for. Well, not quite, but they're very impressive. His coat has seen better days, but it suits him too. I could never wear black, not without layers of make-up to avoid looking like a Goth gone wrong. His smile is infectious, his lips are full and—

'So, do you make a habit of this?' he asks.

'Sorry?'

'Ordering Christmas dinner with random strangers in an airport?'

I shake my head. He does have a point though.

'No, I don't actually, but I've worked in hospitality since I was basically a child, so asking if you'd like some food probably came without a second thought,' I do my best to explain. 'And even though I'm dreading parts of it, I suppose I'm in a celebratory mood because I'm going home. I'm full of nervous energy, I guess.'

He seems to accept that, which is a relief. It's the best I can come up with.

'Nothing like it, is there?' he says. 'Christmas at home. It's a nostalgic one for me this year . . . yet I'm . . . yeah . . .'

He trails off. I wait for the rest. Should I ask him why? Is that too much?

'I hope it's nostalgic for good reason?' I say, as if my voice box has gone into autopilot. How does that happen? How do words come out even when I'm not wanting them to? 'Sorry, you don't have to answer that. My brother always said I asked far too many questions.'

Ollie leans back in his seat and laughs.

'Your brother is right. You do ask a lot of questions.'

It's strange hearing Peter spoken of in the present tense but I'm not going to even go there.

'I'm kidding,' he says, as his eyes crinkle up with laughter. 'It's nice to meet someone so open and chatty instead of everyone being stuck to their phones. Christmas can be the happiest time and the saddest time for sure. It's not all jingle bells and tinsel, is it?'

I tilt my head to the side and allow myself a moment to take him in.

'I mean, look around you,' he continues. 'Imagine that every single person we can see is going somewhere different for Christmas. Imagine how every single one of them is facing different situations when they arrive at their destination. Happiness, sadness, everything in between. Who knows what they're all set to face up to over the festivities?'

I stare at the young couple whose baby has now stopped crying, much to everyone's relief, thanks to what I've overheard as something called *Cocomelon* on an iPad. There's an older man on his own staring at an empty pint glass, deep in thought. A couple with two young adult girls laugh as they clink glasses in the air while one of the girls takes a selfie. It's like we're surrounded by a rainbow of emotion.

'Do you mind if I write that down?' I ask him. 'Sorry, that's another question.'

'You can ask me anything,' Ollie replies. 'I like your questions. And yes, of course, do write it down.'

I open my notebook and quickly scribble his observations.

'You are encouraging me to be extra nosey,' I reply, touched by his depth of conversation. 'I'm very conscious of how I teeter on the borderline of annoying and friendly, especially when I'm nervous.'

'Why are you nervous?'

'I'm nervous about going home.'

'I understand,' he says, so much more in agreement than I could have expected. 'I'm nervous too.'

He comes closer again but drops his voice, which means I'm basically lip-reading now with all the background buzz, including the flustered parents beside us who, after a false surge of confidence, are battling round two of the screaming child when the iPad hits the floor.

'My dad is . . . my dad's very sick,' Ollie tells me, his blue eyes strong and firm on mine now. 'Like, he's *very* sick. So, while I'm really looking forward to seeing him, I'm also dreading it equally if that makes sense?'

'I'm so sorry.'

He sucks on his bottom lip for just a second.

'Yeah, it's probably going to be our last Christmas with him,' he tells me. 'Tough one for sure.'

I set down my knife and fork now, my face crestfallen.

'Your last Christmas with your dad?' I sigh. 'Oh my goodness, that's heartbreaking. Are you OK?'

My own troubles over my impending break-up with Sean seem so superficial now. Ollie shrugs. Of course he's not OK. What a silly question.

'I'm doing my best to just take it one step at a time and not look too far ahead,' he explains. I strain my ears to take in his every word. 'I go from that to reminding myself that saying goodbye to the people we love is part of life.'

'Which is very easy to say.'

'Exactly, but there's no way any of us can escape that unless we shut ourselves off from other people, and if we do that, we miss everything,' he says. 'All the good stuff. Every day is someone's turn to get sad news. And it's going to be my turn soon. Again.'

I want to write that down too, but instead we each go back to our food, our eyes darting towards each other every few seconds. Of all the times I've travelled back and forth from England, I don't think I've ever had more than a few lines of conversation with anyone at an airport, yet here I am beside him totally mesmerised.

'That's a – that's a very humble way to look at loss,' I tell him eventually.

'I'm doing my best to look at it from all angles, but no matter how I do, deep down it's a nightmare watching him slip away,' he says in return, fidgeting now with his napkin. 'It's totally awful, it's anger-inducing, and it feels terribly unfair.'

My big break-up plans with Sean really do feel very insignificant now.

'But don't get me wrong, we *will* have a festive time,' he

says, flashing a bright smile again before going back to his dinner. 'I'll make sure of that, plus my dad's in high spirits all things considered, so we'll make it a good one.'

'I've no doubt you'll make it very special,' I say, nodding in agreement. He is trying to play it down, but the pain on his handsome face tells a different story.

He sure does seem hungry, which makes sense if he's been working all night, but I don't feel like eating any more.

I look around at all the hustle and bustle, the families pushing trollies and buggies with small children, the stern faces of concentration of everyone in such a rush. Like Ollie just said, every single face I can see, every person is going somewhere for Christmas, and who knows what they're individually facing. Good times, bad times and everything in between. I'm enthralled at the thought, yet in a selfish way it makes me feel a little less alone in what I have ahead of me.

Every single person in this airport has their own mountain to climb, and every single person will have their turn at both celebration and heartache over the coming days.

I watch Ollie for a moment. His words have struck a chord with me.

'Time becomes more precious when it's short, doesn't it?' I mumble. He nods in agreement. 'And in a twist of fate, it seems to go faster when we'd love it to slow down.'

'Exactly,' he says. 'It always flies when you're in a hurry, or as the saying goes, when you're having fun.'

I glance at the clock on the wall and then check my phone to make sure it's telling the right time. Our one-hour delay is going so quickly now. Funny that.

I snap out of my brief haze when I see Ollie look at me with concern.

'I hope I haven't upset you with all that last Christmas with my father talk?' he says. 'I didn't mean to be all melancholy at what's supposed to be the most wonderful time of the year.'

There's a longing in his eyes, like he isn't just paying lip service. He is looking at me like he really does care.

My throat goes dry.

'It's not you, it's me,' I say.

'Sorry?'

'I mean . . . I'm going home to break up with my long-term boyfriend,' I blurt out, feeling a weight lift when I say it out loud. 'We've been together for seven years, three long-distance while I've worked over here, but it's all gone so stale and quiet lately.'

'Ouch.'

'Yeah, it's sore, but break-ups, just like death, are a part of life too, yeah?' I suggest, knowing I'm now the one trying to look at it from all angles. 'Most of our time lately has been spent apart. We've just become two very different people.'

Ollie isn't giving away much.

'We've drifted apart,' I continue quickly. 'We have very little in common any more. We feel more like friends than lovers. I'm not looking forward to it at all and . . . Say something, please.'

We both burst out laughing. Me with nerves, and Ollie, I'm guessing, at the desperate look on my face which begs him for some sort of comfort.

'Yes, break-ups are a part of life,' he agrees. 'Horrible, too. And after seven years it will probably involve some element of grieving, won't it? Almost like a death.'

'Not helping!'

'Gosh, you *are* nervous,' he says, 'but like I said, I'm a good listener if you want to get it all off your chest.'

I can tell that he is.

'I'm terrified, but there's no big story and no big drama that has led to this,' I tell him, feeling strangely defensive of my seven-year relationship with Sean. 'There's no one else involved, he didn't do anything wrong, he's a really sweet guy.'

'And that's what makes it even harder, eh?'

'In a nutshell, yes,' I agree. 'Before you joined me, I was writing out my thoughts to try and process it all.'

'Does that work?'

'It does for me,' I say, much to his amusement. 'I write everything down to help me figure stuff out. Work decision? I write it out. Birthday gift needed? I make a list then tick it off. Having a good day? It's all going to go in here.'

I tap my notebook as he watches on in wonder.

'Memoirs of an Irish Girl in London. You should start a blog or a vlog or whatever is coolest these days.'

'Something like that,' I say, my eyes widening. 'Actually, that *would* make an interesting read now you mention it. I work in hospitality and have had some wonderful encounters with guests down the years, especially the famous people who aren't always as confident as you'd think they might be.'

Ollie raises an eyebrow.

'Is this where you name-drop about the time you met Taylor Swift?'

'Taylor and I go back a long way,' I jest, and for a split second he believes me. 'I've never met Taylor. OK, random question, since we're essentially killing time here during an airport delay on Christmas Eve.'

'Go for it.'

'If you were really famous and you were to check into a hotel under a quirky pseudonym, what would it be and why?'

Ollie looks suitably puzzled. He thinks for a moment.

'I'm now under pressure to come up with something that's intelligent and humorous on the spot,' he replies eventually. 'You'll have to leave that one with me for now.'

'Fair enough,' I reply, glancing up to check the departures board. Our gate has been announced at last.

'Looks like it's time for me to face the music,' I whisper.

'Poor guy,' says Ollie, his head tilted to the side as he looks my way. 'Does he have any idea what's coming?'

'No idea.'

'Maybe you'll change your mind when you see him.'

I swallow hard. The thought had crossed my mind, but no, I must stay strong and see this through.

'I'm afraid of that too,' I murmur.

'Well, I hate to say it, but you'll have to hurry and finish up your food,' he tells me. 'We both have a plane to catch.'

I let out a long, deep sigh as reality creeps closer.

'I'm done,' I tell him, pushing my plate to the side. 'Heart-ache has no appetite.'

'Oh, and don't I know it,' he says with a nod.

I've a feeling that, like most people around our age, Ollie may have had his own fair share of love's ups and downs.

I gather my phone, notebook and pen. A weight returns to my stomach.

'You OK, Bea?'

Hearing him say my name brightens me up for a moment. I know we've only spent a short while together, but I feel like we've connected. There's something about Ollie that makes me feel like I've known him forever, but maybe that's just another distraction.

'I'll be fine,' I reply.

'You will,' he tells me confidently. 'Can't say the same for . . . what's his name again?'

'Sean.'

'Poor Sean.'

I shoot him a glance. He smiles.

'Now you're *really* not helping,' I smile in return. 'OK, I'll make more notes on the plane to be totally sure I avoid all clichés, prevent all possible arguments and prepare myself for every conceivable reaction.'

Ollie reaches out and lightly pats me on the shoulder, which makes me shiver. He's very handsome and ever so sweet, but even thinking that way makes me feel guilty when I picture Sean and the conversation I have to have when I get home. We stand up face to face, as crowds rush and push past us.

'It will all work out in the end, you'll see,' he assures me. 'Now, come on or we'll miss our plane and that would be an absolute disaster.'

I follow Ollie through the masses until we get to the gate where a snaking queue has already formed for the short flight across to Derry. I check my phone for messages from Sean, but there's nothing.

I swallow hard as tears sting my eyes.

No message to see if I've boarded the plane yet. No 'I can't wait to see you.' No plans for when I do get back home. Just a 'thumbs up' emoji when I told him earlier there was a one-hour delay.

But then again, he isn't really into texting. He's way too preoccupied with running his business.

'Cows don't stop needing to be milked just because it's Christmas, Bea,' he'd joke if I ever thought of doing something spontaneous that would mean he'd have to leave the farm for more than a couple of hours at this time of year. 'And hens don't stop laying eggs.'

I need to be brave. I need to stay strong. Sean is a sweetheart, but our relationship is going nowhere, and it's time we both admitted it.

'Just think, every step we take towards this awaiting plane is another step closer to a big moment for each of us,' Ollie says, leaning close, almost whispering into my hair as we wait in line.

I don't know whether to laugh or cry.

'That's very profound, Ollie, but true. I like that.'

I'm strangely sad that we're almost ready to head off in

different directions. We stand for a few moments in contemplative silence.

In another world I'd ask him for his number to keep in touch, but I wouldn't dare do that to Sean. I've never asked for another man's number before and I've no intention of doing so for quite a while until I know I've dealt with our impending break-up.

'We're both going home to a lot of change,' I whisper. 'Change can be very frightening. I'm sorry your dad is so ill.'

I tuck my hair behind my ears and let out a long, deep breath.

'You know, he doesn't say much these days,' Ollie tells me as we shuffle along slowly towards the airline staff with our boarding passes ready, 'but my aunt who lives next door says he's been singing "White Christmas" since yesterday because I'm coming home.'

'Ah.'

'Yeah, I know, isn't that so sweet? He used to sing that song from the first of December right through until the big day came round. He hasn't done so in years.'

I bite my lip and look up at my new friend. His eyes sparkle.

'That's beautiful.'

'I thought so too,' he whispers as the stewardess, who is wearing a Santa hat and rather fetching Christmas tree-shaped earrings, checks his boarding pass. 'I could dread this visit, but instead I'm going to embrace every single moment with eyes wide open.'

'You're so philosophical.'

We both burst out laughing again.

'I read that online somewhere,' he admits. 'So, what's your seat number?'

'Thirteen B.'

He takes a step back. He makes hand gestures that any onlooker might fear meant he had been shot or needed treatment for some sort of major shock.

'No way!' he exclaims. 'Ah come on, you're not in thirteen B? For real?'

'Yes way and yes, for real,' I reply. 'Why? You know, thirteen is said to be unlucky but it's always been the opposite for me.'

He stares at his own seat number on the boarding pass on his phone.

'Wow. No, I mean . . . well, it looks like we're not meant to say goodbye just yet then,' he says, showing me how we're in the same row. 'I'm in row thirteen too. So does heartache have an appetite for dessert?'

My eyes dance in response. I can't deny it. I'm glad Ollie is still close by for this last leg of my journey home.

'It does, actually.'

'Good answer,' he says, and before long we're ready for take-off, closer to reality, and closer to home and a very different Christmas for each of us.

Chapter Six

Ollie

Christmas Eve

Bea and I certainly cover a lot of ground throughout our short flight into Derry. There was an empty seat right beside her, so once we took off, I slid across so we could chat further.

There's a very jovial atmosphere onboard this small aircraft which, despite the mania back in Heathrow, is only half full. Children watch Christmas movies on devices, and there's a group of younger passengers singing 'Santa Claus is Coming to Town' away up at the front of the plane.

Bea and I play random question games, debating extensively over answers.

'Best drink at Christmas?' I ask her.

'Baileys Irish Cream on ice for sure,' she says with confidence. 'You?'

'*Not* Baileys Irish Cream on ice for sure. I like a Dark 'n' Stormy cocktail.'

This keeps us in conversation for quite a while.

'Ooh. One thing you can't stand at Christmas?' she asks next.

'Airport delays,' I say. 'Except this time, of course. You?'

'Surprises,' she answers straight away. 'Gosh, I really can't cope with surprises. I'd rather crawl into a corner and cry.'

'Me too. Biggest turn-off in a man not only at Christmas, but anytime all year round?'

She scrunches up her nose and mock shivers.

'This is easy. Laziness. Lack of empathy. Communication blocks. Huffing. Poor hygiene. Bad breath.'

'All right, all right, I meant just one. Don't be greedy.'

'Best Christmas ever?' she asks me.

I break into a wide grin.

'So many in childhood,' I say, my eyes glistening at the memories that flash by. 'You?'

'Same,' she whispers. 'I sometimes wish I could experience that Christmas magic just one more time, don't you?'

I turn towards her more.

'You know, when I was a boy, at around seven on Christmas Eve, one of my parents would knock on the front door. I'd race to open it, petrified that it might be the big man himself calling early, but too excited not to go and see. And when I'd open the door, there'd be a big red box with a huge matching bow, and inside the box would be some of my favourite things. Some candy canes, hot chocolate and marshmallows in a Christmas mug, new pyjamas, woolly bed socks, and favourite CDs. To me, that's when I knew it was Christmas, and that little surprise on the doorstep every single year is what made it the best Christmas ever.'

We reminisce about how we both grew up in a family where money was sometimes tight at this time of year, but love was always on tap. She speaks of how she can't think of ever leaving London, whereas I can't wait to get back to Ireland for good.

'I've been applying for jobs closer to home since my dad got sick, but no luck so far. They don't come around very often where I'm from, but I'd move back in the morning if I could.'

She seems to understand perfectly.

'I think I've travelled so much with my job I don't know where would tempt me to lay down roots for good,' she tells me, her eyes dancing as she drifts away somewhere in her mind. 'I believe I'm a city girl now, but at the same time I am quite tempted with the dream of finding somewhere off the beaten track where I could explore my inner Sister Parish with romantic, quirky décor and cosy nooks, somewhere where the locals are eclectic and that's only because they're mainly sheep and cows.'

I could easily launch into telling her how she's basically just described Oyster Cottage where I grew up in Donegal, and where I'm returning now. Or that I know of Sister Parish, a New York interior designer, because my mother was a fan too, but she probably wouldn't believe me.

My parents created a cocoon away from the rest of the world with Oyster Cottage, and best of all they shared it with travellers from every corner of the globe by turning it into a B&B. My vision is to go back there for good when I get the right job, and to do my best to create that same magic.

My dad and my elderly aunt Nora do their best to keep it going, but it needs some new energy, and fast.

'So, what does a cottage-by-the-sea gal from Tyrone see in London, then? I don't think there are too many cows and sheep there. Well, not of the animal kind anyway.'

'Work,' she answers immediately. 'I adore my job, and that's putting it lightly. You?'

That's an easy one.

'I flunked my A Levels so didn't get into my first-choice place to study in Belfast for nursing,' I explain. 'Went through the clearing system, which was basically like sticking a pin in a map, but I ended up in London. My dad always says if I fell in shit, I'd still come up smelling of roses. He has a point.'

She giggles at that.

'I think I'd like your dad.'

I take a drink of the beer in front of me as too many images go through my head, of what I'd love to say to her if things were different on her relationship front.

'I think he'd like you too, Bea.'

We skirt around various subjects without giving away too much personal information.

We crack jokes, we laugh out loud and at one stage my hand skims hers accidentally, which makes me feel like I've been hit by some sort of electric current. And when we land in snowy Derry, we both exchange a glance and a smile, that only people like us can understand when you live away from home at this time of year.

It's so good to be home.

'Never change,' I say to her as we wait at the carousel for her luggage. 'It was incredible to meet you. Good luck with everything.'

'And you too, Ollie,' she tells me. She looks at me like she is inhaling every tiny moment we've left together, just like I am. 'Enjoy your precious time with your dad at home. Meeting you made a somewhat difficult journey a whole lot easier.'

'Likewise,' I say, placing the handle of her brown suitcase into her hand when I lug it off the carousel. 'Go easy on the big guy, eh?'

'I'll do my best.'

'And remember it's OK to change your mind when you see him. Long distance is hard. Maybe you just need to see him to ignite the spark.'

The softness of her skin lightly brushes against mine for the second time, before we hug each other tightly, and for perhaps a few seconds too long.

'Thank you for distracting me at Heathrow,' she whispers before we let go.

'So, I *did* distract you?' I ask, feeling my heart skip a beat. 'I knew it.'

'In the nicest possible way,' she replies with tears in her eyes.

And just at that moment, I have an idea.

'Regarding your question from earlier about an alias name: I think I've got one.'

'Go on . . .'

'If I were rich and famous, I'd check into a hotel under the name Doctor Distraction. What do you think?'

Her eyes crinkle as she smiles.

'I think you were the most perfect distraction,' she replies, blowing me a kiss. 'Maybe our paths will cross again one day, Ollie.'

'Maybe next Christmas?' I suggest. 'Same time, same place.'

'You never know,' she shrugs, then points upwards as if she's wishing on a star. 'Goodbye, Ollie.'

'Goodbye, Bea.'

She turns around one last time to wave to me before she pushes through the swinging doors that lead to Arrivals, like an enigma I'll never come across again.

Christmas songs belt out loudly as passengers eagerly make their way along the last leg of their journey, to wherever they might be going on this cold Christmas Eve.

I try not to stare when I see Bea walk into Sean's warm embrace.

Sean looks just as I'd imagined he would: a big bear of a man, with a ruddy face and hands like shovels, but a gentle giant at the same time.

A nice man. A kind man.

He touches Bea's face with his fingertips and kisses her full on the lips with a hunger I recognise instantly, because I'd felt it too when I was in her company. I look away quickly.

My stomach is in knots, because for a fleeting second before we said goodbye and after only a few hours in Bea's company, I almost believed that part of her was mine.

But she wasn't. And by what I've just witnessed when she's reunited with her boyfriend, I don't think she'll ever be with anyone else but him.

'There he is! And you look even happier to see me than you usually do,' says Aunt Nora when she greets me at the front doors of the airport, a little bit later than expected.

She ruffles my hair like I'm a teenager when she pulls me in for a tight squeeze.

'I'm always happy to see you,' I tell her. 'Well, except when you used to wake me up for high school on winter mornings. How are you? You look—'

'Not just yet, Ollie,' she giggles, putting one purple-leather-gloved hand in the air. 'Let me get us to the car before you comment on my new hairdo.'

She links my arm as we scurry along the snowy pavement to find wherever she's abandoned her vehicle. Aunt Nora is known to break every parking rule and get away with it.

'I have absolutely no comment on your hair. Did you get it done especially for my grand return?'

'Ollie!'

'All right, I'll save it for later,' I joke with her. 'So how are you? How's the gammy leg? And the tooth extraction plans? And the blood pressure?'

She playfully taps my arm. Aunt Nora loves the banter between us and always has. It's what she misses most, she tells me. Well, that and having someone to fuss over who isn't my dad. Though she does fuss over him too, thank goodness.

'Oh, I'm fine, Ollie. I can't complain,' she says. 'Apart from the weather. I can always find a complaint about the Irish weather, especially when it snows. Is that a good enough complaint for you?'

'That's more like the good old Aunt Nora I know and love,' I tease. 'Now, you have ten minutes max to get all of your moaning out of your system then the complaints department is closed for Christmas. Officially.'

'No, no, I'm not complaining one bit. I'm seventy-eight years of age, I've all my bad habits intact and they've served me well,' she giggles. 'I'm just terrified of falling in this weather. Oh, your dad is beside himself with excitement to have you home for Christmas, Ollie. It's so good to see a smile back on his handsome face.'

Aunt Nora, my late mum's older sister, is decked out in her hand-knitted bright green mohair Christmas jumper which is almost as old as I am. I can tell by her tight, fluffy curls that she's been to the hairdresser's, but then she always does sport a new 'do' for the festivities. She smells of mints and lavender, two scents that whisk me back to the safety of my childhood in an instant.

'Honestly, he's been singing that song on repeat just like he did in the good old days at this time of year,' she continues, gripping on to the inside of my arm. 'It's almost like he knows we need to make this a good one. It's almost like he knows . . . well, you don't need me to say it out loud.'

Aunt Nora chokes up, and I feel a lump form in my throat. I need to change the subject pronto.

We make our way out to the car park, across the zebra

crossing and into her trusty black Polo which has seen better times. In fact, it's so old that it rattles but she insists that with age comes experience, so it suits her better than a fancy new model.

'You do look well, dear old aunty. Are those new glasses? Or, come on, *is* it a new hairdo? Something looks different.' Aunt Nora pauses, pulls her glasses down to the end of her nose and raises a thin, pencilled eyebrow.

'Go on, say what you really think, Oliver,' she says, fastening her seat belt with gusto. 'I know something cheeky is coming and I've heard it all before. I can take it. Who do I look like now? The last time it was Dame Edna Everage. Go for it. I'm all ears.'

She can barely speak for laughing.

'No, no, it's Christmas so I'm being kind,' I tell her. I push the buttons on the radio to change channels, but she lightly taps my wrist and puts it back to her favourite local country station which blasts out some Daniel O'Donnell. 'I mean, I could say you remind me of a prize—'

'No, no, we can leave it at that,' she giggles. 'So, what's got you so chirpy? A new girlfriend at long last?'

I love that Aunt Nora can give as good as she gets.

'Ooh, touché,' I laugh. 'No, no new girlfriend at all. I'm chirpy because it's Christmas and I finally get to see you.'

'As if,' she replies, rolling her eyes. 'You know, I hate to state the obvious, but even before what happened, I never did like Monica.'

I let out an exaggerated groan, but I know she won't stop until she gets it out of her system. I don't think she'll ever get her distaste – and distaste is putting it mildly – of my ex-fiancée fully off her chest.

'Which is fine for me to say now, of course,' she continues, waving one hand for effect as she drives, 'but even before she was exposed as a heartless, lying harlot, I just knew there was something about her that didn't add up.'

I cover my ears and hum loudly.

'Anyhow, I'm so glad she's history and safely back home across the Atlantic Ocean, even if it is with Foxy.'

Ouch.

'Can we please not talk about Foxy?'

Aunt Nora clears her throat. That stung and she knows it.

'Sorry. So, what about Buster? Is he still in touch? And Simon?'

I don't think I'm ever going to get away from this conversation totally. Well, not until Aunt Nora has had blood or some other sort of meaty revenge on my ex-fiancée running off with my former best friend.

'Buster is still very much a good friend, as is Simon,' I reply, hoping to nip it in the bud now. 'We can't blame Buster and Simon for what happened. Blame Foxy, blame Monica, but not Buster. Buster didn't know.'

Aunt Nora sticks her chin out and purses her lips. I can tell she is dying to let off some steam about it all, but as my dad says, there's no point walking down memory lane to feel bad when you could walk into the future and feel better.

No wonder I'm full of one-liners. I've had them drummed into me all my life.

'Oh, they will both eat humble pie one day,' Aunt Nora says, not quite ready to let it go. 'Pardon the pun, but long runs the fox . . . just you wait and see.'

I pretend I'm pulling my hair out, which makes her laugh as she drives.

'I'm not waiting to see anything. It's fine. And I'm sure *they're* fine back in New York or Rio de Janeiro or whichever city they're polluting these days,' I say. 'We're all fine. It's water under the bridge, it's in the past. I'm totally over it.'

'Good,' she says, but I can see tears in her eyes behind her blue rimmed glasses. 'Foxy was such a likeable boy growing up in Teelin. His dear old father would be disgusted at his behaviour if he was still alive. I do often wonder where it all went wrong.'

I raise an eyebrow.

'When someone like Monica gets under your skin, she gets under your skin,' I remind Aunt Nora. 'Foxy thought he'd died and gone to heaven when she turned her attention to him only months after she conveniently called off our wedding. Foxy never got the girls when we were younger, but a bulging wallet is sometimes more attractive than a bulging you-know-what.'

'Ollie!'

'I feel sorry for him at this stage,' I continue. 'He must be almost skint now that she's got her claws so well into him.'

Aunt Nora's eyes widen at that possibility. I've no doubt that Foxy will be cleaned out by Monica, who once had long-term visions of selling up my parents' B&B so we could live in sunnier, more exotic climates. In a way I should be thanking him for allowing me to dodge a bullet.

'He was your friend,' she says more seriously now. 'Monica did what she had to do by calling off the wedding, but Foxy was your friend.'

She wipes a stray tear from her eye which makes me briefly look away.

As much as I've moved on from what happened, I can understand why Monica's flit to the USA closely followed by a hook-up with one of my best friends is still a sore point for those who love and care for me.

I watch my dear aunt as she drives, the transparent skin showing blue veins on her liver-spotted hands as they move the gearstick, knowing that to see me struggle after the whole sorry mess had taken its toll.

She is the closest thing I've had to a mother since I turned sixteen, while I'm the child she never had.

And as the years tick by, I'm reminded now and then of how any type of pain I feel is her pain, just like she told me it would always be when we propped each other up through loss all those years ago.

As we drive away from City of Derry towards my home county of Donegal, I try to make her feel a little bit better by giving her the short version of how I met the beautiful stranger, Bea, at the airport. Even though I'm taken as always by my aunt's company, Bea hasn't left my mind for one second.

'Oh, now *she* sounds lovely, Ollie,' she says. 'Not full of her own self-importance at all.'

We both burst out laughing.

'She really was,' I agree. 'Next thing we're having a turkey dinner in a cramped airport, then we're swapping life stories and *then* we end up right beside each other on the plane. Mad weird, isn't it? Of all the people on that flight I end up in the same row as her, meaning we got an extra ninety minutes to chat to each other . . .'

I trail off, unable to stop smiling as I remember the past few hours.

'It was meant to be, you mark my words,' Aunt Nora declares, squinting through the squealing windscreen wipers as snow drifts down on the green fields in the distance.

'You think so?'

'Oh, I'm sure of it,' she says. 'That's your beautiful mother guiding you from above, Ollie. I mean, what are the odds of that happening? It's one thing to bump into someone and make idle conversation at an airport, but to eat together and talk for so long and then to be seated right next to each other on the plane? That's fate.'

She's on a roll now, and thankfully off the subject of Monica and Foxy, whose name I can barely say out loud to this day. I can talk about Monica, no problem, yet even hearing of Foxy's existence stings and burns in a way I wish I could extinguish forever, even if he did do me a massive favour in disguise.

I chuckle as Aunt Nora talks with her hands, displaying her huge belief in 'the man above' working his magic. I'm doing my best to interrupt her flow with the big 'but' of the situation, which is the fact that Bea has a boyfriend of seven long years – albeit one who could be getting the chop right now as we speak – but still.

She has a boyfriend.

'I always knew you'd meet a nice girl from Ireland, London or no London,' continues Aunt Nora. 'Monica was never right for you. I mean, it was interesting at first that she was American—'

'Brazilian, actually.'

'Well, yes, so . . . are you getting my point, Ollie? You'd have disappeared away to live in Brazil, which would have broken your father's heart with all those miles between us. It's hard enough that you've upped sticks and gone to London, but at least it's only a couple of hours away on a plane. Brazil, on the other hand . . .'

I can't help but chuckle at my aunt's latest, ever so slightly controversial, views on life and travel.

'I hope you got her number,' she declares as we chug along at a snail's pace. 'You did get her number, didn't you?'

I bite the inside of my cheek and stare out the passenger seat window as flashes of green grass whirr by.

My silence says it all.

'I don't even think I got her surname.'

'Oh, I don't know what I'm going to do with you! Young people these days,' she scolds when I don't answer her straight away. 'You don't think she's just going to magically reappear one day, do you? That's not how it works, Oliver. You don't let opportunities like that pass you by. Are you listening? No, you're not listening, you're humming along to music like you've always done when you know you're wrong.'

She turns off the radio and I raise my eyebrows with a snigger.

'I'm thirty-three years old,' I remind her. 'I think if I'd wanted her number, I'd have asked for it, and vice versa.'

I wish I'd got her number.

I wish I'd got her surname so I could at least look her up on social media.

'And so that's that then?' she says, waving her hands up in the air so that she lets go of the steering wheel again. 'I thought you'd good news to share with us all for Christmas, but no. Just the usual doom and gloom about old people with heart problems in the hospital, I suppose. Where's she from? Please tell me you at least know that?'

'Can you please keep your eyes on the road?' I implore.

'My eyes are firmly on the road,' she replies, her voice going up an octave. 'You're as bad as your father, always telling me how to drive. If you'd listen more often it would suit both of you better.'

I lean my head back on the headrest and close my eyes.

'She is from Tyrone.'

'Sure that's only down the road!'

'It's potentially two hours down the road depending on where in Tyrone,' I remind her. 'Anyhow, she has a boyfriend.'

Aunt Nora goes quiet at last, but not for long.

'Ah for crying out loud, that's that then,' she mumbles.

She sits up straight in her seat, her back like a poker as she blinks back disappointment and does her best to focus on the road ahead. 'Why didn't you say that in the first place instead of getting my hopes up?'

'I could barely get a word in with you as usual.'

We drive along in silence for a bit until she reaches across and pats my arm like I'm still the sixteen-year-old boy who lost his mother suddenly to a massive heart attack all those years ago.

I don't think I'll ever be anything else in her eyes.

'Never mind,' she says, sounding way more upset than I am over my love life. 'You deserve the best, my darling. And it will come.'

'I'm not that bothered right now,' I say to her, 'so please stop worrying. Monica has no effect on me any more, none whatsoever. *And* I've the tattoo on my arm to remind me of the fun I had on what was meant to be our honeymoon, alone.'

She seems satisfied with my answer, if only for now.

'So, we'll go to Midnight Mass this evening and you know what we'll do?' she announces moments later with a new burst of spirit.

'What?'

'We'll pray for the two of them.'

'Who?' I ask her.

'We'll pray that those two, Foxy and Monica, get some sort of gruesome rash or repulsive food poisoning, or that they at least come out in hives. Nothing too bad or life-threatening, but something to make them itch like feck for days.'

She laughs and blesses herself at the same time.

'You'll go to hell, you know,' I tell her.

I love when she gets into fits of laughter, but I'm also thankful when she regains her composure and focuses on the road ahead.

'Can I ask you a question, Aunt Nora? And it's not about Mass or wishing rashes or food poisoning on anyone.'

I know she isn't sure if I'm serious or not. On this occasion I am.

'Go on, but I hope you're not winding me up, you rascal,' she says. 'God preserve us, I've days of this ahead. You and your father with your wit on full power and me the butt of all your jokes.'

'Ah. We'll go easy, I promise. It's Christmas after all.'

'I'm all ears,' she says, turning off the road on to the bumpy lane that further leads to Oyster Lane. My heart swells when I see the chimney pots of my father's cottage in the distance. 'Is this a deep question, Ollie, for you're taking a very long time to come out with it?'

'It's a deep question, yes,' I say, pausing again for effect.

'What is it, for goodness' sake?'

I take a deep breath.

'Do you believe in love at first sight?'

Her eyes almost pop out of her head. She stops the car outside her cosy home, which is just a short walk from mine, yanks on the handbrake and shoots me a famous Aunt Nora stare, then tuts and shakes her head.

'I can't for the life of me understand why you didn't get her number.'

Chapter Seven

Bea

It's a ninety-minute drive from City of Derry Airport to my home village of Benburb in County Tyrone, during which I should have plenty of time to open a conversation with Sean about our future. But so far, the words won't come out, no matter how hard I try to find them.

I open my mouth to speak, but my throat goes dry at the very thought of it all, and when Sean reaches across the car to take my hand as he drives, I know I'm going to have to leave it until later.

'Did I tell you about our Paddy's new girlfriend?' he asks me, half an hour or so into our journey which has been a mix of random updates and lengthy silences, with seasonal music on the radio filling in the gaps in our conversation.

'Which one?' I joke, which makes Sean laugh. My heavy topic of breaking up seems even harder to raise. 'Paddy isn't wasting any time since his divorce, that's for sure. Your poor mother must be saying decades of the rosary that he'll settle himself soon.'

Sean's laughter has always made me smile, and his

humour is so familiar it temporarily distracts me from the task ahead as he launches into an entertaining account of his older brother's new fascination with online dating.

With every mile that passes on our journey, so too does my courage to bring up the subject of our own relationship which has slowly drifted on to this plateau where it feels more like a friendship than anything else.

The past few months have been the worst. I counted three full days of no communication from him, just because I didn't instigate it, and when I did eventually call he hardly seemed to notice there had been a gap. And the last time he came to London was a disaster, the whole time spent arguing about everything from what to eat to where to go to what to watch on TV.

'Maybe it's just the seven-year itch?' Sita said to me when I first told her how jaded I was feeling after Sean's last visit to London. 'Don't rush into anything, Bea. That way, when you do make the decision you know it's for the best and not just some knee-jerk reaction to familiarity. He sounds like a lovely guy in general.'

'He is a lovely guy in general, Sita. That's what's making this even harder. Seven years is a long time to throw away.'

Even if most of that time has been long-distance, shopping online for bargain flights and fleeting visits that didn't disrupt either of our hectic working lives. Even if most of that time lately has felt like a whole lot more effort than it should.

There have been fun times too, of course.

I know every crevice of Sean Sullivan's body, every turn of phrase he uses, how he acts when he's angry, and all the things that make him belly-laugh too. I know his favourite foods and favourite colour, I know his favourite band and the type of music he can't stand. I know he enjoys a simple way of life that was once so familiar to me, but which now feels like it's locked away in some foggy dream, a closed chapter I'll always look back on and read with fondness.

We'd been classmates all through school, and while Sean was always on my radar as a fun-loving local it wasn't until I came home at the age of twenty-five after a disastrous stint in Australia when I broke up with my first real love that he came to my notice.

It was shortly after my brother died when we eventually clicked. Sean came into the bar where I worked for a drink late one night after a date that had gone terribly wrong. I listened to his tale of woe, we ended up in stitches laughing and he kissed me on the doorstep of my family home when he gave me a lift rather than let me walk in the rain.

I used to live for Tuesday nights back then, counting down the hours until Sean and his football buddies would come into the pub for a cold beer after their training with our local club. His hair would be still damp from the shower after a gruelling session on the pitch, and he'd smell so fresh and clean, his eyes dancing when he'd catch mine behind the bar.

We'd spend weekends snuggled up on the sofa in his living room, watching movies and stuffing our faces with Chinese takeaway and popcorn, without a care in the world. I found solace from my grief in his arms. He'd sit in silence just holding me for hours while I cried over Peter and the cruelty of the illness that robbed him of his young life.

Peter would have turned thirty this year, a milestone most of us take for granted. I sometimes wonder if knowing this has instilled a need for change in my own life as we move towards that date.

A job at Ashford Castle in County Mayo just before Sean and I were due to move in together brought an opportunity I could never have turned down. It also took me away from home at a time when deep down I knew I needed a fresh start, away from the pain on my mother's face, away from the memories and the knowledge that Peter was never coming back, and sadly away from Sean who could never up sticks and leave his life to join me, as much as we'd talked about it.

And when I said I was being transferred temporarily to The Carnation in London, his words were of the utmost support, but the look in his eyes told me that he knew it could be the beginning of the end for our relationship. Just as we both feared, the hurdle of the Irish Sea between us has created a big obstacle, even though we've both been too frightened to admit it.

My work life in London is all-consuming, as is his back here in Ireland, where everything revolves around their thriving farming business and rural way of life. Days are spent ploughing the land, herding cattle and keeping on top of administration which is literally a whole family affair. Houses are built on plots of land handed down from generations before, meaning most of Sean's neighbours are related to him, and there's nothing that can't be discussed over a cup of tea and warm soda bread.

Sometimes I wish I had that same contentment in my own

heart, but our family life will never be the same since losing Peter. Everything changed when we lost him. Sean eased that pain for quite a while, but now I need to face up to the reality that our long-distance relationship was only ever like a sticking plaster over a broken bone.

Until today.

Typically, today it feels like Sean knows what I've been thinking. It feels like he's clutching on to straws as he knows we need to up our game before it's too late.

He watched me so tenderly as I walked to greet him earlier at the airport, with a longing in his eyes that stopped me in my tracks. Lately we've managed to leave the look of love behind, no matter how much time passes between visits, yet there he was watching my every move with an intensity I haven't seen in a long, long time.

'Welcome home, honey,' he called to me, his arms widespread as I made my way towards him. He wore his usual jeans and a plaid shirt under a heavy padded jacket, and his smile made me feel like someone had rewound the clock back to when we first got together seven years ago, on that cold winter's night when I was so engulfed in grief and he made everything seem so much better.

'How was your flight?' he asked me, his unknowing smile ripping my heart inside out. I want to shake him. I want to ask him why he's upped his game suddenly with the pleasantries. Is it just because it's Christmas? 'Pity about the delay, but I got your text just in time before I left the house. At least the weather is settling down.'

I couldn't help but notice the many happy families around

me, bouncing into each other's arms with hugs and kisses in true festive spirit.

And here we were talking about the weather.

'The flight was fine, just the usual. Thank you for picking me up. I know it's a bit of a trek to Derry,' I tell him, almost choking on a mixture of emotions which range from fear to guilt to sadness about what's to come.

'Ah, it's grand. The delay gave me an extra hour to get a few bits done round the farm,' he replied.

'That's good.'

'Of course my ma is cooking like it's the end of the world ahead of tomorrow, bless her, but then she does that every weekend, never mind on Christmas Eve.'

He cupped my face in his hands, kissing me firmly in a way he hadn't done in years and almost taking my breath away.

'Everything OK?' I asked him, more than a little bit puzzled.

He at least had the decency to laugh at the look of shock on my face.

'It's Christmas,' he said, pulling me into a lengthy embrace. 'Let's make this the best one ever.'

As Sean hugged me, I spotted my new friend Ollie walk away in the distance, and I felt like I'd done something terribly wrong, like I'd cheated on Sean by being so focused on Ollie all morning. I've never been a good liar. I've never been one to hide my emotions, always wearing my heart on my sleeve, yet there I was already struggling with honesty when it came to telling Sean the truth of how I really feel.

I searched my mind for something more to say, but he got in first.

'You look beautiful,' he told me, taking my suitcase easily in one hand and grasping my hand in the other.

'Seriously, are you feeling OK?' I joked. 'It's been a while since I've heard such terms of endearment. Was it something you ate or drank maybe?'

He threw his head back and laughed.

'I'm on top of the world, Bea. I'm just glad to see you. I might have forgotten to say it sometimes this year, but I'm always glad to see you.'

Despite my inner despair, being with Sean always does feel safe and familiar, which does nothing to convince me that I'm ready to break the news to him that I think our relationship has run its course.

'Old habits die hard,' was Leroy's comment when I asked him for some friendly advice a few months ago just after Sean had left London and I was feeling empty and numb inside. 'You and Sean have fallen into a pattern of accepting the distance between you, getting used to the different paths in life you're slowly taking, and feeling that you've been known as a couple for so long it's hard to make the changes you both deserve. You think it's a waste of all those years to throw in the towel now. How about letting it be a lesson that you don't want to waste the years you have ahead, for none of us know how many of those we have?'

My heartbeat settled as we marched through the airport. I was glad that Ollie was no longer in my vision. Sean leaned down and kissed me on the cheek as we walked, which again took me a little by surprise. We always greet each other with a kiss, but after so many years we are way beyond the gushy, touchy-feely stage. It almost seemed like Sean had had some sort of personality change. Maybe he'd been in Patsi and Jacques' company and was taking tips from the young lovers. Or maybe, after our last fairly bland meet-up in London, he was doing his best to remind us both what we used to have.

I'd glanced out the side window as we drove off from the airport, and in the wing mirror I saw Ollie walk along with an older lady I guessed was his Aunt Nora who he'd told me all about during our journey home.

Seeing him again while in Sean's presence made my stomach flip.

Something has changed after spending time with Ollie. It's like my head has been turned to another man, and that has never happened before, like something has awakened that has lain dormant for far too long. My decision to break up with Sean wasn't triggered by anyone else, but Ollie has stirred something deep inside me.

And now I feel guilty, like I've cheated on Sean by spending those few intimate hours with Ollie – and more to the point, for enjoying it so much.

I haven't cheated, have I?

The tiny village of Benburb comes into sight at last, and my heart lifts at the thought of spending Christmas with my family. Snow-topped houses with smoke billowing from their chimney pots are dotted beneath the dusky afternoon sky, and the warm glow of festive spirit fills my soul like only being here can. Twinkling lights dress shop windows and misty clouds peep out above the castle.

It's so good to be home, even though I know that after just a few days I'll be missing my own space back in London.

I yearn to sit by the wide waterfalls of the Blackwater River down by the priory, watching the foam smother the rocks below me and letting the pure, unspoilt sounds of nature calm me from the inside out. There's a serenity there like nowhere else, a sense of spirituality and comfort in the shadow of the priory where Servite Friars live in a community that welcomes anyone and everyone.

It's a million miles away from the bustling streets of London. In summer I like to picnic with Mum and Dad amongst the bluebells that cover the grounds like a beautiful blanket, and in winter I find the fast-flowing waters so soothing, like they can wash all my troubles away, even for just a fleeting moment.

This was our playground growing up, where Peter, Patsi and I would spend hours down by the gorge picking wildflowers, watching anglers and canoeists on the river, and sunbathing by the reeds in a world that felt so safe and calm. Now the castle ruins in the valley's park sit alongside a wealth of arts and crafts businesses, and there's a delightful coffee shop where I love to run into locals on my brief visits to see Sean.

'Home sweet home,' says Sean when he pulls up alongside my family's modest but cosy riverside bungalow. I turn to face him, unable to ignore the sparkle in his eyes since he picked me up at the airport earlier.

'Sean – I, I was wondering if we could—'

'Ssh,' he interrupts. 'Sorry, just let me go first before I forget.'

He is smiling from ear to ear as he leans into the back seat and pulls through a small gift bag, then takes out a parcel immaculately wrapped in gold foil paper.

'Will I open this now?' I ask, somewhat puzzled. We never usually exchange gifts until Christmas Day after dinner, once we've gone through all the formalities with our own nearest and dearest.

'Go ahead,' he says, talking non-stop as I tear open the paper. 'Remember when I was in London and you spied a red leather purse you really liked at Camden Market? I saw a similar one in Belfast at the weekend and thought you might like it.'

I swallow hard as tears prick my eyes.

'It's beautiful, thank you,' I whisper, stroking the soft leather. This all feels so out of character, so late in the day. I don't know how I'm going to do what I intended to.

'It's not your real Christmas present. Just a token gift to welcome you home,' he tells me, taking in my every move with glee as I examine the soft leather purse. 'So, what were you going to say before I interrupted?'

I bite my lip, hoping he doesn't notice the tears in my eyes.

'It doesn't matter,' I tell him.

'No, go on, tell me,' he insists, turning off the ignition. 'I shouldn't have jumped in like that. I meant to give you the gift when I saw you at the airport, but I left it in the car.'

I want to scream right now. I long to shout and cry that

this new, tender, attentive behaviour should have been happening months ago, years ago, even.

'It's . . . not to worry, I'll tell you later,' I reply, unable to meet his eye in case I burst into tears of frustration. 'Let's go and find everyone. It's Christmas Eve after all.'

Chapter Eight

Ollie

Oyster Lane, County Donegal, Ireland
Christmas Eve

I see him.

He doesn't hear the car door shut. Nor does he notice Aunt Nora's chatter, nor did he turn his head at the car tyres slushing through the melting snow on our way up Oyster Lane.

He doesn't seem distracted by the whipping wind or the chill that breezes off the Atlantic Ocean in the near distance.

Bunches of holly and mistletoe hang over the front door which has been freshly painted the brightest sea blue. It was yellow the last time I saw it, and pale green in the more recent photos Aunt Nora sent my way. She has always tried her best to experiment with colour, but I know she is only ever doing it to hold on to memories of my mother who had the most vibrant ideas and taste.

My father stands slightly stooped on the far end of a narrow, winding pathway, lost in a world of his own, with bare hands dipped in soggy soil beneath his favourite ash tree which has been here even longer than he has, his baggy dungarees splashed in paint, his gaze far away from reality, yet I know he is loving what he does best.

I reach into my coat pocket and grab my phone to capture the moment, then I zoom in to picture him.

He is luminous as he holds up a string of what look like tiny fireflies twinkling above his head.

I stand with my rucksack on my back, watching him as tears fill my eyes with the thought of what is to come.

He hasn't been quite as chatty lately as he once was, but that's to be expected, I guess.

His phone calls have become a lot less frequent, more to the point than ever before, and our conversations have become stilted and paused as he searches for the words to say, knowing his time with me and Aunt Nora is ticking away.

He always loved his garden. It reminded him of his happiest times with Mum, he'd say.

Rain, hail or snow, ever since I was a small child, I'd find him talking to plants, flowers and insects like they were his best friends in the world.

'It's way cheaper than therapy,' he'd joke if I ever caught him talking to himself. 'I've solved most of my problems in my one-way conversations with nature, Ollie. You should try it for yourself. It works and it's free.'

A tug of guilt claws my insides for all the days he may have talked to his garden while I've been living my best life in London, caught up in an opposite realm of sunshine and cocktails, so far away from rainy, wet, cold Ireland.

'Don't be silly. I have Aunt Nora living next door, and she'd talk the leg off a stool,' he'd tell me in his deep, Donegal lilt if I'd ever fussed or bothered. 'I've friends now from every corner of the world thanks to this little haven by the sea. Living here is like an all-year-round holiday. It was your mother's dream come true, so you go ahead and live out your own dreams. You deserve to.'

I close my eyes for just a second, the flakes of fresh snow falling on my face and the sound of Aunt Nora's country music still ringing in my ears from the car, but it fades away as my senses are filled instead with wind chimes that harmonise with the song of the breeze bouncing off the cliffs of Slieve League, some of the highest and most majestic in Europe.

The wind whistles louder and the sound of the waves crashing nearby fills my heart with joy. I'd forgotten how much I missed it here. There's something about the bitter cold Atlantic sea air in December that can make you feel alive like no other element can.

I go to call his name but no . . . not yet. I want to savour every moment of seeing him in real life for the first time in so long. It's been too long since we last embraced, since I last ate with him, laughed with him . . . all the little daily things we take for granted when we are with the people we love.

He wraps the fairy lights around a holly tree and stands back to look upon his work of art, his head tilting to the side before he tweaks and fixes it again.

The garden wind chimes jingle in the breeze and the white metal sign that stands by the picket fence of my childhood home squeaks when an ambitious gust catches it. I reach up to touch it, running my fingers along the blue letters that mark the place that will always hold my heart.

Oyster Cottage – Eleanor's B&B.

'Build it and they will come. Your mother told me that when she shared this dream of hers way back then,' he'd often tell me. 'And she was right.'

Oh, and they did come. In fact, for years they came from all over the world to this cosy little home outside the village of Teelin, tucked away on the edge of the sea, like a hidden gem off the beaten track. Lately though, it's been looking and feeling a lot wearier, a lot more tattered and torn, dying slowly on its feet just like its owner, no matter how much he tries to keep it going.

'Dad?' I call him. 'It's me. I'm home for Christmas.'

'My darling boy,' he says softly, shuffling back as his hands go to his face. My stomach swirls.

I hold my arms out to him as I walk up the long path, every word choking me as my eyes sting. Murphy, our Irish Red Setter, joins in by bounding around the side of the house, nuzzling his nose into my leg. I reach down and pat his silky fur, marvelling as always at how he recognises me no matter how long it's been since I've seen him.

'My boy,' Dad whispers, his tired, sunken eyes dancing now with delight. 'It's so good to see you.'

'Happy Christmas, Dad,' I call as I quicken my pace to greet him. I fall into his hazy warmth, the scent of every ounce of my childhood filling me from head to toe.

I never want to let him go. Aunt Nora watches on from

the bottom of the path, wiping tears from her eyes as the reality of this holiday and what it means sinks into all of us.

But we will make it a good one.

There's no place like home at Christmas.

Chapter Nine

Bea

Benburb, County Tyrone
Christmas Eve

After a shower and a quick change of clothes into a new green shoulder-padded jumpsuit topped off with a sweep of red lipstick, I head off with Sean, straight to the local pub in Benburb where my family have already migrated, having apparently become fed up waiting on my delayed flight according to the text my sister had sent me.

We'll head on and keep a seat. Don't leave it too late. Everyone is mad to see you and the music finishes early in time for Santa coming!

God forbid that anything should come between the Malones and their traditions on Christmas Eve. Even when we were children, the three of us – me, Patsi and Peter – would be decked out in our best attire and treated to a lemonade and crisps in the bar as the whole village crammed in to celebrate the birth of the baby Jesus a day early, but in truth we all loved it.

Sean is chatty the whole way as we walk past the gates of the famous priory on our way to meet everyone. I don't think I've heard him talk so freely in a very long time.

The stars twinkle above us in the dark sky and the moon sits right over the castle in the distance. It's a sight I've dreamed of. It's a walk I've dreamed of for so long. But not like this. Not with all this heaviness on my mind.

'And the way things are going, I'll have the site cleared in no time,' Sean tells me, 'so I'll have so much extra space to work around. Honestly, it was a real gift, Bea. You'd nearly think it was all meant to be. I'd seriously consider building us a house there one day. Only if you like it there though. What do you think?'

I can hear the noise from the local pub in the distance, and with every step I take I wish I could get there sooner. I can't answer questions like this right now. It's too much. It's too unexpected. It's too late.

'Most people say every year it doesn't feel like Christmas, but this year I think it does,' he tells me, draping his arm along my shoulder as we walk along the pathway past the castle gates. 'What do you think, Bea? Are you glad to be home?'

'I am,' I reply, finally managing to get a word in edgeways. He is full of nervous energy in a way I've never noticed before. 'To me, Christmas is always like Christmas, but maybe that's because we start the season very early at the hotel. Even

Nana gets excited when she sees the tree going up. She's such a clever dog.'

Sean's strides are long and fast as I teeter beside him in my heels which are hardly ideal on this cobbled pavement.

'Ah, she's a cutie, that's for sure. But I've a feeling this Christmas is going to be one to remember, that's all,' says Sean, gently pulling me in from the outside so that I avoid a splash from an oncoming car.

I've no idea what to say.

He finds my hand to hold as we walk closer to the pub.

'I was talking to Christine and she's mad to spend some time with you, maybe Boxing Day?' he suggests. 'We could go and meet her and Johnny? What do you think?' Christine is my best friend, and Johnny is Sean's best buddy.

'Yes, that would be nice. I'd love to catch up with them both.'

Oh God, I can't do this. I can't rock his world, not now.

He is on top form. He's excited to have me home. More excited than usual, more conversational than usual and looking so handsome and sweet too, even if he's making me nervous with all this chit-chat.

He pushes the door of our local pub open and steps aside to let me in from the cold.

'There she is! The pride of Benburb!' says PJ the barman when he sees me. The warm air is a stark contrast to the bitter cold evening outside, and PJ's smile would light up a whole village for Christmas. 'And Sean, you're right. Our very own London lady gets more beautiful every time she comes home.

97

It must be the big-city air and the cosmopolitan lifestyle, eh? Suits you, Bea.'

'Thanks, PJ,' I reply, blowing him a kiss as a chorus of 'hellos' echoes around me.

PJ gave me a summer job here in the pub way back when I was just a teenager, with no idea that it would send me off on a journey where I'd end up managing the front of house of a London hotel.

The dancing fire inside is welcome to my cold hands and toes, but maybe it's the sight of so many familiar faces that makes me glow from the inside out.

'I love your jumpsuit,' a girl whose name I can't place says to me on the way past. 'The colour suits you.'

'That's very kind,' I say in return as she looks up at me with wide eyes. 'And you look lovely too.'

At least half our village seems to be crammed into this pub as if it's the last Christmas Eve we'll ever experience. The atmosphere is familial, like a warm hug on a cold day like today. I feel my shoulders drop. Despite my inner anxieties over what I need to discuss with Sean, it feels so, so good to be home.

I look around me, waving at faces I haven't seen in forever.

There's the Mackle family who are wearing Santa hats and dangling bauble earrings in their usual pew by the fireplace, and the Dalys who have downed tools in the nearby restaurant for the festive break. They've brought a feast of sausage rolls and vol-au-vents which they've displayed on a long table with enough to feed a nation. And just as I'd predicted, a local lad is strumming a guitar in the corner by the open turf fire, while my sister Patsi commands the crowd with her lilting voice.

'You'd nearly think they all knew you were coming home,' says Sean with a wink. 'Half the village must be here.'

'I was just thinking the exact same,' I tell him. 'Not that they were here for me! I mean that half the village must be out for the night. It's so good to see everyone enjoying themselves.'

Sean puts his arm around me and despite all my bravado, despite all my speech writing, I still can't bring myself to tell him how I really feel.

'It's Christmas and she's finally here!' my sister squeals from across the pub when she sees me. 'Mum, Dad, she's here! My big sister is here, everyone!'

My parents smile and wave in my direction, but Patsi goes all out with her effusive welcome. She bounds towards me like a leggy gazelle followed by a merry Jacques who looks like he's settling in very well with his bottle of beer and Christmas jumper.

Patsi squeezes me tight, rocking left to right until I'm almost dizzy.

'*Bonjour, ma sœur*!' she says on repeat. 'How's London?'

'A lot quieter without you and Christine there to keep me company in the flat.'

'You'll get used to it! And I love, love, love the funky jumpsuit! Are those new shoes too? Mum and Dad wanted to wait back at the house for you, but you were taking *ages* so I convinced them to come straight here.'

'It was just a one-hour delay, Patsi,' I remind her.

'Felt like so much longer,' she says, taking my hand. 'Sean, I'm stealing her for a minute. Come and tell us all the craic about London – I want to know everything. And *voilà*, I've already got a drink waiting so you don't even need to tackle the crowd at the bar. One vodka tonic just for you, sister.'

Sean is engrossed in conversation with Mick who runs the Post Office, so I follow Patsi and her pink hair to a bustling corner where she and Jacques have set up camp with my parents. Dad looks a bit jolly already too, while Mum sips on a Baileys with ice, her head tilted to the side, almost lost in a daze. She is smiling at me, but her eyes are full of pain, just like they've been for years since we lost Peter.

'Welcome home, my love,' she says, giving my hand a squeeze. My God, I wish I could take it all away and make her feel better, but even my grand arrival isn't enough to shake her out of her agony. 'How's Leroy? And the lovely Nana? And all at The Carnation?'

I reply with the usual chit-chat, not going into the detail of how I'm slightly worried about Leroy as he's been taking time off like never before, or how Sita has made a final audition for a well-known musical so I'm afraid we might lose her soon, or how Nana the dog fills my soul when bouts of homesickness threaten me so badly I want to jump on the first plane home.

'You're starting to dress like a Londoner,' my dad quips,

not that he would even have a clue of what a Londoner would dress like these days, and not that there's a generic London look either. I see every style imaginable on my daily commute from Notting Hill into Kensington.

'Patsi is like a head-turning, Parisian punk, while Bea is a burst of London glamour,' says Jacques, and we all 'woo' at his observation.

'And your mother is the epitome of a red-haired Irish colleen,' says my dad, which makes us all laugh out loud, except Mum who rarely breaks a smile these days. She tries, she really does, but the pain inside her is just too much to bear. 'An authentic Irish beauty who we all adore.'

My eyes prick with tears as I'm reminded how much my dad tries to keep our family's spirits up by always looking on the bright side, even in difficult times. I've noticed as the years roll by how he props Mum up at every opportunity, putting on such a brave face, though I've heard him sobbing in the bathroom often enough before coming out to face us with a clap of his huge, safe hands and a valiant smile.

'There's no place like home though, is there girls?' he says, raising his whiskey with tears in his eyes. 'It's so good to have you both here at the same time, and although he isn't here to celebrate this evening, he isn't too far away. And that I truly believe. To Peter.'

My father's early 'celebratory' toast to my dead brother almost takes my breath away.

'To Peter,' we say together, except for Mum, who can barely bring herself to say her late son's name out loud, at least not in this joyous way.

Even the new addition of Jacques hasn't managed to distract her so far with his presence, though he's doing his best by singing along and swaying to the pub singer's rather splendid rendition of 'Merry Christmas Everyone'.

I settle into the snug beside my parents, my sister and her boyfriend, feeling a rush of nostalgia which almost chokes me up, but in the nicest possible way. Flashbacks of our childhood warm me from the inside out, and I am once again reminded that I'll never feel safe anywhere in the world like I do here.

'Being here with you all feels so cosy,' says Jacques when I ask if he is enjoying his new Christmas experience in Benburb so far. 'I see Patsi smile so much since we got here yesterday. Everyone is so kind. So welcoming.'

And it's true, it really is how I remember Christmas at home.

'Patsi Malone for a song!' someone shouts from the bar. I clap my hands in agreement, and as I do, I notice that Sean's brother Paddy has arrived. And his parents John and Briege. And so has my best friend Christine and her husband Johnny, who I haven't seen in so long. That's strange. Christine, who used to live with me in London, loves to take a spin out to beautiful Benburb when I'm home, but she lives miles away and is usually forced to spend Christmas Eve with Johnny's parents in Belfast.

I'm almost dizzy as I take everything in around me. Couples young and old kiss under the mistletoe, some have tinsel draped around their necks and some have it tied around their waists too. There's a true feeling of celebration in the air, but it's more than I've ever remembered it to be.

'I think I know what you mean when you say it really does feel like Christmas,' I say to Sean when he eventually pulls himself away from the Postmaster, who was bending his ear for quite some time. 'Everyone's on great form, aren't they? Isn't it lovely to see?'

Sean looks smug.

'You wouldn't get that in London, would you?' he says, before putting his arm around my waist when he squeezes into the snug beside us. 'There's no way a Christmas in London could ever compare to what we have here.'

I shoot him a glance. Maybe this is the opening I need to start our conversation, or at least hint at it.

'Look, I know you love it there,' he says quickly, putting his hands up in surrender. 'I'm not knocking it at all. London is a great city. It's just not home, that's all I'm saying.'

Every time I open my mouth to speak, Sean gets there first.

'In fact,' he says, 'I've come to accept that you'll always love your job there. And I wanted to tell you tonight that I'll support you fully if that's where you want to be for now. No matter how long you stay there for, I'm right behind you, Bea.'

Oh.

'Really?'

'Really,' he says with confidence. 'It doesn't have to come between us at all, if that's what you want to do for now.'

For now . . .

'I know you love that hotel and all its character,' he continues. 'So rather than fight against it, from now on I'm behind you every step of the way.'

I feel a little bit sick. I swallow hard.

'You've changed your tune,' I tell him with a laugh of disbelief. I take a drink of my vodka tonic, wishing the alcohol would kick in quickly to give me some Dutch courage. 'You always said you hated me being so far away. You hate coming over to London to see me. You said it costs a fortune too, all this back and forth on aeroplanes, trains and buses. And you know I've no intention of making a move anytime soon.'

'Ah, I wouldn't say I've totally changed my tune,' he says with a shrug. 'I've just tried to change the way I look at it, you know. It's like . . . well, I suppose you could say it's all in the mind. So, let's call it the best of both worlds instead. You have your space for now, and I have mine here. And as a bonus, every time I see you it's like a mini honeymoon until the time is right for you to move back home. Absence makes the heart grow fonder and all that.'

Oh God.

'A mini honeymoon,' I whisper. 'That's a very interesting way of putting it.'

'A mini honeymoon, yes,' he repeats, giving my shoulder a squeeze. 'I think if we want to make it work, we can and we will. I'm busy here, you're busy there. So, we meet up when we've some time out and we'll get on like a house on fire until the time comes when we want that to change. No panic. No hurry. We can do it our way.'

I feel so dizzy.

If it wasn't already sweltering in here I'd think I was having some sort of hot flush at the sound of Sean being so bloody understanding.

Why can't he start giving off about London like he used to? Why can't he tell me again how he's fed up with me being away for most of the year? Why can't he start a row by saying that he hates big cities, that he hates leaving the farm to travel on monthly flights to see me, and that he can't stand London with all its pushing and shoving and noise?

Why can't he give me something, *anything*, to spark off a debate on where I feel I need to be just now, so I can deliver the speech I'd planned in some shape or form to end things?

Or even give me an ultimatum? A really tight one, like making me choose between life at home with him or life in London without him.

But no. Instead, he looks like he has never loved me more, and I feel as if everyone is staring at me while I'm sweating like a pig in a blanket.

My eyes fall closed to take some quick space to think, and when I open them I see that my mother is looking my way again, her head still tilted to the side like it seems to be all the time now.

Something has briefly replaced the usual agony that has taken up residency in her eyes, and I see for the first time in forever a glimmer of happiness, a tiny glimpse of a smile. It's a look that sends me into the past before her whole world came crashing down.

She looks . . . *happy?*

For just a fleeting moment I see the woman she used to be. My heart lifts at the tiny sign of hope that she might have turned a corner. But then she nods at Sean, and I realise it's all because from where she sits, he and I probably look completely loved up on the outside, whereas on the inside I am so nauseous I could easily throw up.

Am I imagining it that every single person is looking my way now? It's as though they've formed some sort of layered circle, holding drinks and grinning like they know something I don't.

Patsi taps the microphone.

'One two, one two. OK, so I'm meant to be singing,' she says in her best telephone voice while the pub singer sits poised with his guitar in the corner by the roaring fire.

Everyone is looking her way now. Thank goodness for small mercies, but what the hell is she up to?

'Now, before I share with you all my dulcet tones, I want to dedicate this song to my big sister,' she says. My stomach leaps.

'What?' I say out loud. First an early toast to Peter and now I'm the centre of attention with a song dedication, and I've barely thawed out or finished my first drink.

'You're the glue who keeps our family together, Bea,' she continues to a sound of 'aah'. 'You're the one we all know we can lean on when times get tough, the one we all look up to. You are quite simply the rock of our family.'

Everyone breaks into applause. My mother bursts into happy tears. What the hell is going on? Is this my funeral and

I'm floating around in some daze of in-between worlds? People only say nice things about you like this when you die, which I've always felt was a terrible waste, but at the same time it's totally cringeworthy.

'And when you met the handsome Sean Sullivan, not long after we lost our Peter . . .'

Oh no.

'Well, we all knew that Sean would love you just as much as we all do,' says Patsi, speaking right from the heart. 'So, tonight on this cold, stormy Christmas Eve, I want to dedicate this song—'

Oh no.

'To my big sister and to Sean. It's one of their favourites. And it goes like this.'

Sean takes my hand and leads me to the front of the pub's hearth, smiling like I've never seen him smiling before. As Patsi sings 'Merry Christmas Baby' in her signature, raspy tone I think I'm going to faint.

No, I think I'm going to die. Please, please don't let this be what I think it might be.

Our neighbours and friends sing along, arm in arm, to the Otis Redding classic as Sean twirls and spins me around in a space not big enough to swing a cat.

I'm so dizzy from all the fussing and twirling that I can't even see the door. Could I make a run for it? Is this why Christine and Johnny are here instead of being with Johnny's parents like they usually are? Is this why Sean's parents are here too?

And then I spot my own parents, their arms around each

other with tears in their eyes. My mother looks like she's pressed rewind, that she's right back to before she suffered the loss no mother should. And oh my God, now she's clapping. My parents are singing along, smiling and clapping. This is a big first. Mum looks incredibly cheerful right now. I wish I could stop and take a picture, but I needn't worry as everywhere I look someone is holding a phone up in the air, recording everything.

Patsi winks at me as if she's some big superstar on stage, and not like she's my little sister in our local pub on Christmas Eve where it feels like I'm stuck in some sort of twilight zone of existence.

But when the music fades eventually to a gentle hum, so does the noise of the crowd. Then, my biggest fears for this Christmas come true right before my eyes.

Sean drops down on one knee.

He wipes his misty eyes and looks up to me with a sincerity that comes right from his big, generous heart, in his new outfit and new haircut.

It all makes sense now. I should have known this was coming. Why didn't I stop it before it got to this stage? But at the same time: how could he? He knows I hate surprises.

'Bea Malone,' says Sean out loud so that everyone in the bar can hear him. His voice cracks and he almost breaks down in tears. He takes a deep breath. 'I've asked your father, who said to ask your mother.'

Cue laughter and cheers from the gathered crowd.

I might cry, but not in the way I'd ever imagined I would in this moment.

'And she said yes,' he continues. 'So, I'm hoping that you say yes too.'

The whole room is spinning.

My hands go up to my face and now I *am* crying. Tears are streaming down my cheeks, though I'm not sure if it's shock or panic or a mixture of the two.

'You're the most beautiful girl in the world by far. You *are* my world,' says Sean. You could hear a pin drop. 'Bea Malone, I knew it from the first day I met you.'

'Hurry up and ask her, you lucky devil!' shouts a heckler from behind the bar who I realise is PJ.

I feel the weight of a hundred pairs of eyes on me.

'Bea Malone. I should have asked you this question a long time ago. Will you marry me?'

Chapter Ten

Ollie

Teelin, Donegal

The snow glistens on the bare ash tree outside and the wind chimes ring in the porch of Oyster Cottage while Dad and I have playful debates over games of Scrabble that last into the wee hours when neither of us can sleep over Christmas.

Murphy lies right across Dad's feet, moaning in contentment by the blaze of the open fire. He's such a regal dog with his grace and his flashy auburn coat.

'A redhead with a heart of gold', as my father would often say.

It's a cosy cocoon here, but every minute that ticks by is also tinged with a tug of fear that I'm never going to get this chance again with him. This time next year will be a very different Christmas, but for now I'm going to absorb and enjoy every single second without thinking too far ahead.

We watch black and white movies under a patchwork blanket on the sofa each evening, and I try to get a blast of fresh air into his lungs at least once a day with a walk outside. On St Stephen's Day afternoon, when he isn't feeling so strong, we wheel him into the garden in his chair where he watches with glee as Aunt Nora and I build a snowman whose head is far too big for its body.

'Oh for goodness' sake, Nora, and you call yourself a sculptor,' Dad pipes up playfully from his perch beneath the silver branches of the ash tree as Aunt Nora stands with hands on hips, her head tilted to the side in bewilderment.

'I beg your pardon, Jack Brennan!' she exclaims, scratching her head under her woolly hat. 'I'm simply taking on a supervisory role here as my winter ailments are playing up. Ollie, how did that happen?'

'Don't blame me!' I laugh as Murphy does his best to topple over our efforts, barking at the topsy turvy snowman. 'It was a joint attempt so equal responsibility. We've built him upside down!'

'I've seen better snowmen when you were a kid, Ollie,' Dad chuckles. 'Tighten up, boy. We have high standards here at Oyster Cottage.'

But it's our evening conversations that I'll really treasure forever.

'Any nice girls in London these days, Ollie?' he asks me over a hot whiskey at the kitchen table on St Stephen's Night. 'There's a glint in your eye I haven't seen before. A twinkle of some sorts. C'mon, you can tell me who you've your eye on. Tell me all about her.'

For some reason I immediately revert to a pre-pubescent

112

teen in my head and feel embarrassed at the question. I'm thirty-three years old. I was meant to be married by now but it all fell apart in front of my entire family at the eleventh hour. I feel stupid talking to my dad about girlfriends when he'd been hoping for grandchildren, had it all worked out with Monica.

'Oh, here we go with the matchmaking.'

'I liked Monica, just for the record,' he says sternly. 'Let me say that once and for all. She did you wrong, but everything in life happens for a reason, you'll see. And life's too short to bear a grudge.'

His bushy grey eyebrows meet when he frowns. He looks up at me with his hands clasped beneath his chin.

'Dad, you don't have to have any opinion on Monica at this stage,' I reply. 'And be careful around here coming out with things like that. Do you want Aunt Nora to have a stroke?'

We both burst out laughing, but I am somewhat serious. There's no need for my own flesh and blood to feel like they must always take a view on Monica as a person just because we didn't see our marriage plans through.

She showed me a lot about life in the long run, and although it ended up in carnage, we had some good times too. We spent months in her native Rio de Janeiro with her family, who treated me like one of their own. We danced the night away in London clubs, we partied like we were teenagers and we made plans for marriage and children, but it wasn't meant to be.

Getting cold feet before a wedding is one thing. Hooking

up with one of my oldest friends a few months later is a very bitter pill to swallow, but it's water under the bridge now. I've spent a fortune on counselling to help me think this way, so I don't want to open up those old wounds.

'You know, Ollie, there are some people in life who are sent to teach us,' my dad tells me in a more serious tone. 'I've said it before and I'll say it again. Try to look at what happened with Monica as a lesson on what you don't want from a relationship, if that's at all possible.'

I watch the flames dance in the hearth as he talks, savouring the sound of his voice. I notice how he crosses his legs at his ankles and wiggles his toes in his new cotton Christmas socks as he speaks. I take in the way his hands move through the air when he wants to make a point, like he is doing at this very moment.

I try to record it all in my memory. I don't want to miss a thing.

'I think you may have told me that before, yes. Now, you and Aunt Nora need to chill when it comes to orchestrating my love life,' I remind him. He is as frail as I expect him to be at this stage of his cancer battle, but still full of spirit and with the look of someone who is well looked after in his tartan pyjamas and furry slippers. There are some days still when he can walk and talk easily without losing his breath, and other days when he has to stay in bed, but he's never lost his humour or his wisdom. 'You're just looking for a grandchild, admit it. You were hoping for Jack or Eleanor Brennan Junior, isn't that right? Go on. Admit it so.'

His eyes sparkle as he laughs. Then he clinks glasses

with me and flicks the TV over to a rerun of *Only Fools and Horses*, both of us knowing he'll never live to see his grandchildren now.

'Murphy is like a child to me,' he says, reaching his big, generous hands down to pat our dog's silky head. Murphy takes that as an invitation to jump up on to his lap which is far from ideal, but Dad welcomes him anyhow and he folds in like it's where he belongs.

We sit for a moment in silence as the clock ticks, the dog groans and Del Boy and Rodney joke ironically about this time next year on the telly.

How many times do we wish and plan for next year with the very best intentions? 'I'll be back to see you in just a few weeks, so it won't be long,' I remind him the next morning when I notice his mood drop. We look out over the horseshoe-shaped Silver Strand Beach, which is off the beaten track, but well worth the drive from our cottage a few miles away. With one hundred and seventy-four steps leading down the steep cliff face to the sand, we have only come for the view from the car park today, but just looking out on to the vast greens and blues of the ocean and the sweeping cliff faces of Slieve League is enough to top up the soul at any time of year.

'One hundred and seventy-four steep steps,' he says to me as we look out over the ocean in the near distance. 'Not for the weak-hearted, but worth every single one if you're brave enough. A bit like life and love in general, Ollie. You'll know when you find the one who's worth the climb.'

I've suggested I take time out from work to be here with him, but he won't hear of it, agreeing instead that I pop back and forth as and when I can around my commitments at the hospital.

'Don't worry, son. I'm not afraid of where I'm going next,' he tells me, then gives me a watered-down version of the handshake we used to call a Jack Brennan Classic, which came in the shape of a whopping big bear hug, complete with a few slaps on the back for good measure. 'And when the day comes, I want celebrations and laughter about all the good times, do you hear?'

I squeeze my eyes shut.

'You mean singing and dancing?' I suggest.

'If you want,' he says with a smile. 'But there'd better be music and smiles for the days I've lived, the nights I've loved and the joy I'll have when I see your mother's beautiful face again.'

I give him another hug for good measure as the rain falls on our shoulders, so grateful to have had this conversation with him in such a spectacular location with the wind on our backs and the lapping of the sea close by.

Aunt Nora claims she was chopping onions which is why her eyes are watering when I find her in the kitchen when we get home.

'I'm happy, Ollie, that's all,' she says when she admits she's been crying. 'Having you here just lights up his whole world and mine. This has been a wonderful Christmas to remember.'

'It really has,' I agree with her.

She turns towards me, her lips tightly pursed. I can see in her eyes just how frightened she is beneath the façade.

'This is really happening, isn't it Ollie?'

I can't answer her.

Instead, we hold each other for probably longer than I realise as Irish country music plays from her tiny pink radio on the windowsill, a Christmas present from my mum that she refuses to upgrade.

'He wants a fiddle player,' I tell her. She folds her arms and stares at me.

'A fiddle player?'

'When we scatter his ashes.'

She covers her mouth with her hands.

'Do you fancy a mince pie and clotted cream?' she asks, taking her glasses off to wipe them with her apron.

I turn up the radio, take her hands and waltz with her around the kitchen to the sounds of her favourite singer crooning in the background.

'Of course I do, but before that is there any chance of a turkey and ham sandwich before I've to go and fend for myself in cold and lonely London again tomorrow?' I say when we finally let go of our impromptu dance. I wish I could stay longer, but the scramble for annual leave at Christmas time is always a battle and I'm already looking at flights for my next visit home once the festive madness dies down.

Aunt Nora playfully swipes me with a tea towel in

response, but within minutes she has conjured up a feast from Christmas leftovers like only she can.

Some of my lifelong friends, including Buster and Simon, call for drinks with Dad in the evening which lifts all our spirits on my last night here at Oyster Cottage. Aunt Nora is in her element hosting the lads, saying it reminds her of the good old days when we were all at school in the nearby town of Carrick.

'Every day of the week, Ollie would land home from school with one of you on his tail,' she says when she finally sits down to join us with her favourite Christmas tipple, a good old sherry. It always makes her cheeks pink when she's had one too many, and she's known to burst into song, too. 'I used to always put extra potatoes on knowing either Buster or Simon or Foxy would be here for dinner. Those were wonderful days. I'm so honoured to have been part of them.'

She seems lost in thought as Buster and Simon stare at the carpet on the living room floor at the mention of Foxy. It's always going to be an elephant in the room when we get together. Foxy's betrayal has had a ripple effect on our friendship, and as much as I want to hate him, I can't help missing him, too.

'Are you expecting guests to stay here in January, or will it be quiet until Easter?' Simon asks my dad, doing his best to swiftly change the subject. 'The place is looking well. I always loved coming here as a boy.'

Aunt Nora and Dad explain how although they've one or two bookings from regulars in the coming weeks, it's no longer a priority to keep Oyster Cottage as a bed and breakfast.

'Ah, that's a pity,' says Buster. 'We had the best of times here as kids, didn't we lads?'

'We really did,' I agree, wishing we didn't have to brush those magical memories under the carpet now just because we're all afraid of offending someone by mentioning Foxy.

Our youthful summers here were bursting with adventure, exploring beaches, fishing down by the pier, meeting girls who spent weeks in our village as guests of the Irish-speaking college known as the Gaeltacht, with kisses stolen down an alleyway known as Lover's Lane. Before my mother died suddenly, we would skip down to the college with a bottle of Coke and a Twister ice lolly in hand, guessing who would end up with who.

Between that and the eclectic mixture of visitors from Europe and the USA who descended on our B&B all year round, it was a childhood of dreams. I learned how to speak French one summer when a group of teachers from Lyon stayed so long in our home, we thought they'd never leave.

'Do you remember the time your mam treated a young couple who stayed with us on Valentine's night?' Dad chuckles when it's just the three of us later in the evening. 'She put so much effort into it all with soft music, chilled wine, rose petals, chocolates – the works – and the young lady appeared in a beautiful red velvet dress to say thank you, like something from a movie. They still send me a Christmas card, you know.'

He nods towards an impressive collection of Christmas cards from all over the world that sit on the mantelpiece, most of them mentioning memories of the best times here with my mother at the helm. A true testament to how many lives they touched when the guest house was in full force.

Aunt Nora stares with a faraway look in her eyes. She and Dad have done their best to keep Oyster Cottage going down the years, but we all know that it's never been the same since Mum died, and probably never will be.

We've made memories to treasure this Christmas, even if it does go way too quickly for my liking. All too soon, it's time for me to head to the airport again, but Dad insists on one final beach walk with Murphy before I leave for London, even if his first attempt a day or two before was a disappointment.

This time we go to Fintra, which is much more accessible and equally beautiful, with clear waters that sweep into a lagoon. Dad sits on the edge of the passenger seat and leans down to untie his shoelaces, which is no mean feat in his condition.

'Hang on, Dad. It's Baltic out here,' I say, holding Murphy's lead. The dog is bouncing with excitement but I don't want to let him off the lead just yet.

'I want to feel the sand in my toes,' he says, looking up at me with yellowing, sad eyes. 'It's little things like this that remind me I'm still very much alive. Can you help here, Ollie?'

I let Murphy go, doing my best to ignore the lump in my throat. I kneel down on the sand and untie my father's shoelaces, then scoop off his brown leather brogues by the heel and his socks one by one, glad of the excuse that there might be sand in my eyes.

He reaches his hand up, his head bowed, and I help him out of the car and he stands with his eyes closed as the cold sensation of wet sand hits within. I quickly take off my own trainers and throw them in the backseat of the car.

'That's more like it,' he whispers gruffly. 'There's no better way to feel peace than to walk in nature and feel the beauty of the world around us.'

'You always did lead by good example,' I say to him. He seems to like that, even though I'm so choked up I can hardly speak at all.

He links my arm as we tread barefoot on the sand, leaving sunken footprints near the water's edge, father and son arm-in-arm with the wind in our hair and our cheeks ruddy from the cold as our dog bounces around in the distance, wrestling with seaweed, sticks and whatever else he can get his paws on.

'I don't think there's ever been a day when I don't think of her,' he says as he bends down slowly to pick up a cluster of seashells. 'It's a great test, you know, Oliver. It's a great sign that you really love someone when you can't stop thinking about them, no matter how many times the earth moves around the sun. Your one true love will never leave your mind for long when you're apart.'

He studies the shells in the palm of his shaking hand, then offers me the nicest one, just like he used to when I was a boy. Its pink, rainbowed surface feels so thin in my hand, a reminder of how fragile life is.

I put it in my pocket.

'Delicate like life, love and serendipitous connections,' he tells me. 'Never to be taken for granted.'

He winks at me with a smile.

'Who are you talking about?' I ask him.

'I think you know who I'm talking about,' he says, linking my arm again. 'The one you can't stop thinking about. The one who hasn't left your mind since you first set eyes on her.'

I see flashes of Bea's smile play back like a movie in my mind. My father, as usual, is right. She has been the first thing on my mind every morning when I wake up, and the last thing at night, but I don't want to look too closely for her in case she worked out things with her boyfriend. Having been on the other side of infidelity, I'd never be the one to instigate a relationship until the coast is clear and all wounds are fully healed.

'You'll look after Aunt Nora when I go, won't you, son?' Dad says when we get to the car. 'Even if it's from across the water, don't forget about her.'

'You know I'll be right home as soon as I can find a job here, Dad,' I reply, my voice carried away by the wind. He feebly kicks the tyres to get the sand off his shoes before he gets into the car, again just like I always remember him doing when he'd take me to the beach almost every day. 'And I'll look after Oyster Cottage too for you and Mum. I promise you that with all my heart.'

He takes a deep breath, looking out on to the miles of ocean in front of us, then up at the sky with tears in his eyes.

'Your dear old aunt will be waiting to take you to the airport,' he reminds me. 'We'd best get a move on, son. Come on, Murphy. It's time for me to go home.'

We drive back to Oyster Cottage in a comfortable silence, both content with our few precious days together and magical moments found in the simplest things. I pack my bags and say a quick goodbye to Murphy, to Oyster Cottage and to my father who I plan to see again as soon as I can get my shifts at the hospital rearranged to do so.

He doesn't see me to the door. I think the beach walk took more out of him both physically and emotionally than he's letting on, or else he has said all he needs to say to me for now.

Aunt Nora does her best to keep both our spirits up as we drive back to the airport. She drops me off at the same spot where she picked me up just a few days ago in the airport car park.

'Imagine if your friend Bea is on the same flight again, now wouldn't that be just the icing on the cake,' she says, her eyes dancing behind her thick glasses as she fights through her real emotions. 'And if she is, Ollie, I mean it, you better get her number, boyfriend or no boyfriend.'

'If only life was as simple as that,' I say, kissing my aunt's powdered cheek. 'Let me know immediately if anything changes with Dad. I'll be on the first plane home.'

She tries to distract me again by talking about Bea.

'I know you're going to cross paths again, just you wait and see,' she tells me, fixing my jacket like she's sending me off to school. 'You're a good lad, Ollie. A precious, sweet young man who deserves the very best. Make sure you eat well over there. And text me if you see her again, won't you?'

She watches me from her car window until I disappear into the small Departures lounge at City of Derry Airport, and as soon as the blast of warm air hits me in the doorway, I stop and breathe in the enormity of what I'm leaving behind.

I close my eyes and pray to my mother that I find a nursing job close to home soon. I enjoy London, but my heart is in Donegal and always will be.

As I walk through the tiny airport, I can't help but feel the ghost of Bea everywhere. I hear our last conversation echo in my mind.

I scan around for reminders and signs of her, even though I knew she won't be here. Her trip home to Ireland is for a full week, whereas I was lucky to have been able to book a few days off from the hospital.

Nonetheless, I imagine I might still see her in the distance, lugging her giant case in her bright yellow coat, a true burst of colour on the greyest of days. I even walk over to Arrivals just to be near the last place I saw her when she hugged me tight and kissed my cheek.

I look for her in cafes and in bars, I close my eyes and hear her voice. I think I catch the scent of her perfume when I walk through Duty Free, and I smile as I recall the facts and figures she gave me about Guinness froth and men's facial hair.

And then I wonder if Aunt Nora was right. Will I see her again? Who knows?

London is a big city, it's not like home, so the chances of me just bumping into Bea again are very slim. I have no idea where she lives or works, and I don't even know her surname to look her up online. I wouldn't want to do that anyway, in case I'm met with crushing disappointment that she's still with her long-term boyfriend.

At least this way I can still dream.

I close my eyes briefly as the plane takes off, leaving Ireland and a precious last Christmas with my father behind.

The woman beside me tucks in her earbuds and scrolls through her phone. A man in front coughs and splutters into a handkerchief. A baby cries somewhere in the distance.

Life goes on.

Everyone on this plane is going somewhere, to someone, after Christmas. I feel very blessed to have spent mine with my wonderful father who has taught me everything I know in life, including how to live without him.

I drift off to sleep, wishing Bea was beside me again so I could tell her all about it.

I wonder what she's doing now.

Chapter Eleven

Bea

Benburb, County Tyrone

It's another one of those long, lazy blissful days with no name between Christmas and New Year and all we seem to do is eat, drink, watch TV and, in our case, talk about churches and dresses and whether Sean and I should get married at home or abroad.

It's also my dad's sixty-first birthday dinner, but he has escaped to the sitting room to watch *A Wonderful Life* on his own with a beer, having almost fallen asleep into his birthday cake at all the wedding chat.

I can hardly blame him. The chit-chat in the kitchen is non-stop, and all centring on the same subject.

'Well, it will all be happening at home, naturally,' says Mum, almost spitting at Jacques' act of blasphemy when he made a genuine suggestion that we could get married somewhere like Italy or Spain and the whole family could make a holiday of it.

'My sister got married in Morocco,' he tells us, as Patsi

looks at him with adoring eyes. 'It was so wonderful, wasn't it Patsi? The sun was shining high in the sky, the drinks were cold and flowing, and the sea was a magnificent turquoise blue. I highly recommend.'

It never ceases to amaze me how much Patsi and Jacques have packed into their short relationship so far. Despite both having demanding work lives and numerous hobbies between them in Paris, they seem to travel from glamorous weddings to spontaneous city breaks at the drop of a hat. In the meantime, I can't even get Sean to join us for a family birthday dinner this evening as he's too busy waiting on a vet to call out to the farm.

I know his job is important to him, and I know it's an important job to do too, but it also means he's never there for family get-togethers like this one. I've hardly heard from him today at all, apart from a brief reply to my text asking if he was still alive, and since the big public proposal on Christmas Eve I calculate that we've spent a grand total of twelve hours together, eight of which we were both sleeping.

'I'm not so sure about a wedding abroad, but Patsi and I will come to London to do some shopping,' Mum suggests, which almost makes Patsi choke on her wine.

I tune back in to this latest epiphany.

'What?'

'We'll all go wedding shopping together on Oxford Street and stay in Bea's fancy five-star hotel,' she announces. 'Or maybe you'd rather have your dress made locally, Bea? I know your fashion taste is years ahead of what Mrs Tate down the road might design, but you could guide her? What do you think? If I'm totally taking over, just tell me. Sorry!'

Patsi glances my way across the table and flashes me a smile now that she's got her breath back.

It's as if someone has replaced Mum's batteries after she's been tossed aside like an old forgotten toy for seven long years. Her energy is palpable as she talks about everything from venues to cars and who should be my second bridesmaid, or my third, or my fourth. With so many cousins, the options are endless, or so she says. I even caught her cuddling and smiling with Dad in the kitchen when they thought none of us were looking, which made me glow from the inside out.

And now she's suggesting she come to London to go shopping? My mother has never left Ireland. Well, except for once on her twenty-fifth wedding anniversary when we saved up and sent them both to Santa Ponsa for a week in the sun. She hated every minute of it, even though she tried to tell us different.

Now she seems to have caught some sort of travel bug, planning a trip down Oxford Street and a stay in The Carnation as a treat. I can barely keep up.

Everyone – from close friends and family to strangers I've never met before – is full of congratulations and good wishes on my surprise engagement, while I feel like I've been blindfolded, spun around and pushed forward into an abyss of some sort.

I've no idea where I'm going or who oversees my life

any more. But my mother is so happy she could burst, and that's what has stopped me from blowing up and calling it all off.

I have been on autopilot, drifting in and out of conversations like I'm only a fly on the wall and not the actual subject. It's like everyone around me is a million miles away, whereas I'm frozen in a state of shock, unable to speak up and tell them that although I've a ring on my finger the size of the rock of Gibraltar, Sean and I haven't even properly discussed a wedding date yet, never mind all the gory detail. Plus, I've absolutely no intention of leaving London for at least a few years.

I was so looking forward to a whole new chapter when I got back to my city life, but instead it's like I've pressed rewind and landed in even more hot water than I'd been in before.

'Patsi,' I call out, trying not to draw too much attention to myself.

'Yes?'

'Can you come with me a second?' I say, doing my best not to sound frantic or desperate in front of Mum or Jacques. 'I'd love to show you something I had in mind online. It's much better on the laptop screen in our bedroom than on my phone.'

My poor mother's mouth drops open at being left out. She looks like she might cry now.

'I want to keep it as a surprise, Mum. Don't worry, it will be all worth it, you'll see.'

That seems to work. She goes back to her fizzy wine and

her debate with Jacques, who is still trying to sell the benefits of getting married abroad while stuffing his face with shortbread. He's been obsessed with shortbread and sausage rolls since he got here.

Patsi takes the bait, so we go down the hallway, past the almost life-size Nativity crib which takes up most of the space and into what used to be our shared bedroom in our three-bedroom bungalow. My palms are sweating. I can barely control my breath, but the sparkling French wine we had at dinner is giving me Dutch courage to say what I've been dying to for far too long now.

I close the door behind her and hold it as if I'm keeping her to ransom. She stares at me, puzzled, her own glass of wine still in her hand.

I know my eyes are wild and desperate, but I can't keep this in any longer.

'Why are you going along with this?' I ask her.

She takes a step backwards, frowning as if I've just sprouted an extra set of limbs.

'Going along with what? What are you talking about?'

I look behind me as if to make sure no one is listening, even though the door is shut tight. I point at my ring finger.

'This! The surprise engagement!' I hiss. 'You know I bloody hate surprises. I've barely slept a wink since!'

'I'm totally lost. I—'

'You know Sean and I haven't been exactly getting along lately, and you know I've no plans to leave London, so what the hell was he thinking dropping that bombshell in front of the entire village?'

'Did I know all of this?' She looks up at me from beneath a perfectly arched eyebrow.

'Well, no, you probably didn't because you're in Paris and I'm in London and I sometimes forget to tell you absolutely every single detail of my life, but you do know I hate surprises,' I tell her. 'I've been working up to this trip home for weeks. I even wrote out my own script on how I was going to do it. Patsi, I was planning to . . . I was planning to . . .'

I can't say it. Even trying to say it out loud to my sister feels cruel after all that has happened. I picture my mum in the kitchen with Jacques, no doubt designing wedding dresses on paper as we speak. She's already chosen the bridesmaid's colours and has scoured the bible for her favourite readings for the service.

Patsi's pretty face crumples. Tears well slowly up in her eyes like they used to when she was a little girl. She's always had a look that pulls you in, so if she cries you do too. Therefore, it's no surprise that I feel my own eyes sting.

'You were planning to break up with Sean?' she whispers.

Gosh, she really has had no idea – but then why would she?

'Well, yes I was,' I admit, 'but then he proposed in front of everyone, and I haven't been able to get my breath back since.'

Patsi looks like she's been shot. She puts her hand on her chest, touching the red Christmas jumper that clashes with her hair. Then she sits down on the edge of the bed, a million thoughts racing through her mind, no doubt.

'Is there – is there someone else in London?' she says a

little too loudly before hushing her voice down into a whisper again. 'Bea, have you met someone new?'

'No.'

I shake my head, wondering how to explain that as much as I love Sean Sullivan, I am no longer in love with him like I should be.

'Swear?'

'I swear,' I reply. 'No, it's not like that. It's never been like that. Oh Patsi, we've simply outgrown each other, and I think that deep down Sean might feel that way too if he could just admit it. We've only been seeing each other once a month lately and that's at a stretch. I don't know what he was think-ing. He *wasn't* thinking!'

But my sister is having none of it.

'Sean is part of our family,' she whispers. 'You can't break his heart at Christmas. You can't humiliate Mum and Dad after such a big engagement party on Christmas Eve in front of the entire village!'

'A big engagement party on Christmas Eve in front of the entire village that I'd no idea about!' I tell her hotly. 'I'd no idea what was waiting for me when I came home. You could have told me. You *should* have told me.'

'And ruin the surprise?'

'Yes, exactly! You all know I hate surprises! Did anyone even think of me in all of this?'

She has the grace to look a little guilty.

'But – but I thought you and Sean were solid,' she cries. 'You're like the foundation of our family, or whatever's left of it. If the two of you crumble, we all crumble. I can't believe this. I really can't. I'm in shock.'

I bite my tongue and count to ten inside.

Maybe if Patsi wasn't so wrapped up in her own world in faraway Paris, she'd know a little more about mine. Maybe, if she'd just pause for a second, she might realise that I have feelings too, and that I can't exist just to make other people happy. I've done it for far too long since Peter died. I must stay strong so that the others stay strong. I must put on a brave face for fear that if I don't, then everything will fall around us like a deck of cards. As Leroy once told me, I've been setting myself on fire to make sure others are kept warm.

And then I say it out loud.

I didn't intend to, but as always, words seem to find their way off my tongue, especially when I feel it's the truth.

'Patsi, me marrying Sean is not going to fix or change anything.'

I sit down beside her on the bed. I take a deep breath.

'Sean is not Peter,' I whisper.

She looks at me like I've stabbed her in the heart. Maybe in some way I have. I tread a little more softly this time.

'Sean Sullivan is a wonderful person. He's strong, he's reliable, he's steady and he's safe. But he isn't a replacement or a filler-in for the brother we've lost,' I explain. 'He isn't our Peter. And nor would he want to be seen as the answer to all our grief.'

Patsi stares at me for what feels like forever but then, as if the penny has just dropped, she falls into my arms and hugs me like she hasn't done in a very long time.

'Oh my God, I'm so sorry.'

She says this on repeat as hot tears fall on to my shoulder. I stroke her hair and hush her, just like I've done so many times before. I know how much she looks up to me and Sean as the relationship she always wanted. I know how having a big brother-type figure in Sean has sometimes eased her pain, even if it's just for a fleeting moment when she misses Peter. But I also know that Sean could never, and would never want to, be in our family to ease a pain he can never take away. That no one can ever take away.

'You're just like Mum,' I tell my little sister. 'God knows we all deserve something to look forward to, especially at Christmas. Especially so close to Peter's thirtieth birthday. But this isn't the answer to our grief, Patsi. I only wish it was different, but I just can't do it.'

'What are you going to do?' she asks when she finally lets me go. We sit side by side on her bed, just like we used to do when we were getting ready for a night out when we were younger.

She looks so young and innocent in this moment and, despite her twenty-eight years, I realise how much she still has to learn about life, love, and all its ups and downs.

'I've no idea,' I whisper, wiping the tears off her face first, and then dabbing my own. 'I'm mostly worried about Mum, to be honest, but I'll figure it out, don't worry. I always do. I'll take my time and speak to Sean first, then I'll deal with our parents. But I'll wait for a little while longer. I can't bear to break their hearts all over again before we get past Peter's birthday.'

She nods in agreement, then downs the remainder of her wine.

'That's only a few weeks away,' she says, taking a deep breath. 'OK, let's get Mum through that first and then I'll be there for you every step of the way afterwards. Plan?'

'Plan,' I say, feeling a bit more in control now that I've got a navigation out of this mess.

'And who knows, maybe you'll change your mind when you get back to London,' she says with just a glimmer of hope in her eyes.

I touch the engagement ring on my finger, my heart bleeding for Sean already.

'I don't think so, sis. I've made my decision, but I can't ruin everyone's Christmas by going through with it now,' I reply. 'I'll dust myself off and I'll tell Sean how I really feel when I'm home in a few weeks for Peter's birthday.'

Chapter Twelve

Ollie

Royal Elizabeth Hospital, London
January

With Christmas already a memory which is fading like an old but precious photograph, I throw myself into work at the hospital where my patients never fail to take my mind off the two things that keep me awake at night.

One, my father's illness which almost stopped me from returning here in the first place, and two, the longing for the most beautiful person I've ever met who haunts my mind day after day and night after night.

But hospitals have a way of keeping us humble and strong, and today, Monday, has been one of those where I've barely had a chance to pause for breath. Heart trouble is a year-round problem, and it certainly doesn't stop for someone like me who is licking my wounds after finding the woman of my dreams and letting her slip through my fingers on Christmas Eve.

'Good morning, Mr Gates. I see no one had the sense to buy you a new hat since I last saw you?'

As a former in-patient now making an unexpected return to our daytime cardiac rehab clinic after having stents put in a few years ago, I know Mr Gates will have arrived to see me armed with quips aplenty, so I decide to hit him with one first, knowing it might make a difficult morning a little bit brighter.

As expected, he comes back at me without pausing for thought.

'And I see no one has yet had the sense to show you the way to the barber's either, young Oliver,' he replies, taking off his fetching grey trilby to reveal his wiry silver hair.

At sixty-four years old now, he is a dapper man with the quick wit of someone who has travelled a lot and witnessed many chapters in a life well lived.

And now, although I'm devastated to see him returning for new health tests which might indicate further surgery, I know his way of coping is to keep the chat light-hearted and to never dwell on what might be around the corner for him.

Mr Gates takes a seat in the waiting room and I join him with my clipboard to go over a few bits of paperwork before I take him through for his appointment with the consultant.

Mondays at the cardiac rehab clinic are a nice break away from the main hospital ward. This afternoon session is where our patients sometimes end up when complications kick in that don't need immediate treatment, so it's usually a slightly more pleasant shift.

The bright and airy glass-fronted building where I'm

working today always holds a reflection of hope in my eyes. Here, it's often the early days of someone's journey, or a relief to find things aren't as bad as they could have been, and as terrifying as it can be, most people I see can still hold on to hope for a future without illness once they get a diagnosis and a treatment plan.

Mr Gates, like so many others who walk through those doors, is a walking definition of hope, spirit and humour.

'Remember we don't even have running water in Ireland. We all live with leprechauns at the bottom of our garden, so I couldn't find a barber, especially not over Christmas,' I reply, which makes him chuckle. 'But I'll have you know that the ladies love my unruly curls. I'm a walking aphrodisiac.'

He lets out a raspy chuckle. I've missed the sound of his laughter.

'Did you have a nice Christmas?' he asks me.

'I had a lovely break,' I reply, even though my own heart hurts with worry about my father. I miss him already. 'Now, how have you been? Fancy meeting you here again . . .'

Patients like Mr Gates could easily get under my skin emotionally, so I've always had to work hard at not taking my work home with me. He reminds me of my dad with his sharp wit and banter, not to mention his stiff upper lip when it comes to telling anyone in his world how sick he might be.

I'm doing my best to keep everything upbeat, but we both know he isn't here for a good reason.

'I'm keeping the sunny side up as always,' he replies heartily. I can see from the look in his eyes that he means it.

My good friend and colleague Jane walks past us, not missing the opportunity to welcome back one of our old favourites.

'Good afternoon, Mr Gates,' she calls out. 'We were all fighting over you this morning, but Ollie won as usual. You're looking as smart and handsome as always.'

Mr Gates straightens his tie and flashes a smile in Jane's direction. It's evident he's never lost his charm.

'All right, cowboy, come on this way,' I say, watching as Jane checks in another patient near the doorway. It's blowing a gale outside and, just three days into January, I've already slotted back into my rhythm of work, daily gym sessions and the odd evening out with Scott and the lads when we can all manage a time when we're off shift together.

Jane catches my eye again. She waves and walks away with her hands in her pockets, her face downcast. She's having a tough morning, I can tell.

I know that expression as I've seen it so many times before on my own face when I look in the mirror. Working in a hospital on the front line can be the emotional equivalent of experiencing four seasons in one day. You could start a shift signing someone out after a full recovery, much to the delight of the patient and their family, and in the next breath you could be consoling someone who has just received the worst news possible.

Which is why I look forward to seeing people like Mr Gates, who never fails to act like a burst of sunshine, no matter what is going on beneath the surface of his life.

'I think I'd better grow my hair like yours after all,' he tells me as we walk down the corridor. 'Maybe those curls do attract the girls.'

'Of course they do. Can't you see the effect I have on women?'

'Oh, I can indeed,' he says in earnest. 'A blind man could see it. I think I'll ask you for some more tips, Ollie. Do you have any for an old guy like me?'

We reach the triage room and Mr Gates sits in a leather armchair where I begin to prep him for his appointment. I check his details – his name, date of birth and address – out of routine, even though I can almost remember them off by heart from the last time he was here.

I tear open a cannula and sit on the edge of the hospital bed beside him, pondering my answer to his question about relationships.

'My biggest tip is this,' I tell him as his eyes widen in anticipation, hoping to distract him from needle I'm about to draw blood with. 'Even if the likelihood of someone giving it to you is nil, even if you think there's no point in asking, even if you think you're punching above your weight and you're going to make a fool out of yourself . . . my advice is that you should always, always ask for someone's number if you think you'd like to see them again.'

Mr Gates looks at me from the side of his eye.

'Now, that's rookie stuff,' he laughs with confidence, which doesn't make me feel better at all. I picture Bea in my head, walking away from me with her boyfriend just over a week ago at City of Derry Airport. 'Didn't they teach you that in school, Ollie? That's the first thing we all learn when it comes to the law of romantic attraction. Any old fool knows the phone number rule.'

I purse my lips together in thought for a few seconds, then get on with the job at hand. I do feel very regretful, and I'm sure Mr Gates is lost in the calamity that is my non-existent love life by now.

'You aren't helping at all,' I tell him, to which he guffaws in reply. 'Right now, you're looking at the biggest fool in London.'

'No, the biggest fool in the whole of England,' says Mr Gates, holding up his free hand to emphasise his point.

'Gee, thanks. Ah, one day I'll listen to my elders, isn't that right, Mr G? Now, sharp scratch coming up.'

Mr Gates closes his eyes.

'Tell me all about her,' he says as he winces. 'Where did you meet her?'

'At the airport,' I tell him, feeling fuzzy and romantic already as I think about the girl who, quite literally, got away.

'Interesting,' he replies. 'On your way home for Christmas?'

'Yeah. Ah, she was like no one I've ever met before,' I tell my patient, who feels like an old friend. 'She had the most captivating smile, but she also had the huge obstacle of a boyfriend back in Ireland.'

Mr Gates's huge brown eyes open wide again. He stares up at me.

'Go on.'

'She works in a hotel here in London.'

'Which hotel?'

'I've no idea,' I continue. 'Again, big mistake. But she's got the most wicked sense of humour. And I know this is really clichéd and romantic, but after spending just a few hours in her company on Christmas Eve, I felt like . . . I felt like something happened between us. Does that sound crazy? Don't even answer that. I know it's crazy. I don't even know her full name.'

As I carefully remove the needle, I wipe Mr Gates's skin with some cotton wool, bend his slender arm, then press on the tiny puncture with some gauze.

'Crazy, yes, but now I'm crazy too as I'm already invested and I'm waiting on the punchline,' he says. 'I'm waiting to hear about your next move. There'd better be a punchline, something like you're both escaping back to Ireland where you'll live together happily ever after.'

'I'm afraid that's where my story ends,' I tell him, anticipating an Aunt Nora style lecture. 'Like I said, she has a boyfriend. One she was planning to end things with over the holidays, but that's not how it looked when I saw her greet him on the other side. The way he kissed her when he saw her . . .'

Mr Gates looks almost as disappointed as I am.

'A boyfriend is a very serious problem, yes, but there's a glimmer of hope if she wanted to end things on the other side,' he agrees. 'So, you don't know if she's broken up with him then?'

'I've no idea,' I reply. 'Nor do I have a way of finding out. I mean, I probably could – let's face it, I could spend hours Googling or searching her first name on social media – but I prefer to hold on to the tiny possibility that one day I'll see her again, when she's free and when it's meant to be.'

For a moment I hear her voice so clearly in my head once more. And even though I know it's highly unlikely, I get a real rush that somewhere in the vastness of this city of London, she might be thinking of me too.

'We have to be brave, Ollie,' Mr Gates whispers. 'Fortune favours the brave, don't ever forget it.'

'What do you mean?' I ask him. His dark skin is cold with goosebumps, so I fetch a blanket and tuck it in around his waist. I wish I could take all this pain away from such a wise, endearing gentleman.

'Be bold, be brave. Go find her, Ollie,' he continues. 'Because only then will you know that you've tried your very damn best. Always, always try your damn best in life and then you'll have no regrets when you're a sick old man like I am, afraid to tell even the people you love the most because then that will mean it's really true.'

I stop and stand back, wondering how Mr Gates and I have gone from light banter to such a deep, meaningful conversation.

'You haven't told anyone you're feeling unwell again?'

He shakes his head. Tears form in his eyes which hits me in the heart.

'I don't want this to be real,' he whispers. 'Like you, I prefer to dream, so I should really start taking my own advice, eh? I know. I'm a fool, but it's worked for me before.'

I think of my dad tucked up at home in Ireland, surrounded by such warmth and love in his illness. Aunt Nora looks after him like an egg, I phone at least twice a day to check in and hear his voice, and the whole village rallies round with news, visits and conversations over a cup of tea to show how much they care.

Mr Gates has no one. Not even a dog like Murphy to keep him company.

He may not have terminal cancer like my dad does, but he is back with us as an outpatient because his heart isn't working the way it should, and that's a worry that shouldn't be carried alone.

'Maybe you'll find the courage to speak to someone close to you soon about what's really going on,' I suggest. It's the best I can think of. 'A wise old man once told me that a problem shared was a problem halved.'

'Was that me?' he asks, his cheeky smile showing again, thank goodness.

'That was you, Mr G.'

'Aha, well, since you seem to heed and remember what I say, can I tell you something I really love to do to take my mind off things these days?'

He has my full attention now.

'Go on.'

His tired old eyes are misty in reflection.

'In the late afternoon, round about four, just after I've downed tools for the day and before it gets too dark, I fully enjoy a leisurely wander through Kensington Gardens.'

I'm listening.

'I like to stroll across west by the Long Water, then stop by the Peter Pan statue for a while where I'll admire the little

145

squirrels, mice and fairies by his feet. I always enjoy that, Ollie,' he says, then as if he's sprung back to life, he smiles at me. 'There's a sprinkle of magic there in the early evening light, especially when there's frost on the ground and dusk is preparing us for the mystical dawn of a new day. It's hypnotising. You should do it too.'

I'm more relieved at the upturn in his tone of voice than what he has to say right now.

'Is that it? I'm waiting on the punchline. There'd better be a punchline, Mr G.'

'That's it, that's the story.'

'And here I was all ears, waiting on the big moment when you'd say fairies would appear or there was a money tree or something.'

He laughs again, then coughs out a splutter and his thoughts are far away once more.

'Are you OK, Mr G? If you're worried you can always talk to me,' I tell him. I dart a glance over to the consultant's office door where he'll go in a few moments to learn of his fate, which is often as terrifying for me as it is for the patient, especially when it's second time round like it is for my friend here.

'Ah, I don't need to burden you or anyone,' he tells me, just like he did those few years ago when we first met. 'There's no point breaking someone else's heart just because mine doesn't work properly. When I am sick, I don't want anyone to know.'

I feel a sense of déjà vu. We've had this conversation before, and I know a change of subject is swiftly on the way.

Of all the times I've met him, I've never seen Mr Gates accompanied by anyone to an appointment, which has always made me sad. He has no next of kin, no emergency contact, no one. I don't even know what he does for a living these days, but I've always assumed he took early retirement due to his heart condition.

'Do you have regrets?' I ask him, hoping I'm not probing too deeply.

I resist glancing at the clock. I've another patient to check on but like always, I never want to leave Mr Gates alone for long.

Just like I remember him, he fetches his novel from his leather satchel and places it on his lap to pass the time while he waits to be called.

He clutches it in both hands and thinks for a moment.

'Life's biggest lessons are learned by looking in the rear-view mirror,' he tells me, then clears his throat to make his point. 'I have many regrets, especially when it comes to my love life. I did have a love life, once upon a time, believe it or not, but the man above had other ideas. My heart was broken. It has healed a little over time, but I've never forgotten her. She's never left my mind.'

I glance at the ring he wears bearing two initials. I've always wondered what the story was behind it but knew he would take his own time to tell it.

'I'm so sorry to hear that,' I whisper, thinking of how my father said a similar thing to me on our beach walk. 'Maybe you'll tell me about her one day.'

He taps his nose and lets out a burst of laughter.

'I think I'd rather hear about your future love life than my past,' he says. 'I've always been a sucker for a good old love story.'

It's like someone has rewound the clock having these conversations again, and although I hope his check-up appointment today brings him good news and he doesn't have to come back here for another long time, it's been so nice to see him once more.

'Now, go and do some work, young Ollie,' he tells me with a wide, gummy smile. 'I'd like to read my book in peace while I'm waiting to be seen.'

Chapter Thirteen

Bea

The Carnation Hotel, London
January

I've always enjoyed taking down the hotel's Christmas decorations.

I adore putting them up to make the place look colourful, bright and cosy, but I also love the cleansing feeling of a new year and a new start. It's like hitting the refresh button, which is something I need to do in my everyday existence as much as I do at the hotel.

Be it at home or here at The Carnation surrounded by the grandeur of the hotel foyer in all its glory, I make a ceremony of undressing the tree, with music playing to reflect a new start, a new year and a new beginning.

My soundtrack of choice as I dismantle the fairy lights, the baubles and everything else that brought our guests Christmas cheer, is some retro Irish with U2's 'Angel of Harlem'. It always gets me singing along at the top of my voice, and I can almost *feel* Sita's eyes rolling.

She isn't a fan. She thought Bono was a dog's name.

Speaking of dogs, Nana seems to share my excitement as she watches me from where the huge Christmas tree used to sit in the foyer.

'I know, Nana, I know,' I say to my canine companion. 'I'm almost done and then I'll take you out for your afternoon walk, I promise.'

Preston, who shares the concierge post at the hotel with Leroy, comes to my aid by carefully lifting boxes of baubles and tinsel to the beat of the music once I have them suitably packed.

'It's so good to be back here,' I say to him as he shimmies past. 'Please don't break anything!'

'I won't,' says Preston, making me laugh as he two-steps across the marble floor. 'I wouldn't have put you down as a U2 fan, Bea. Aren't you too young?'

'I beg your pardon,' I say in mock horror. 'They're classic! Larry Mullen has been my idol ever since I first saw him beating those drums. He's very sexy.'

I stand up and dust off my uniform, take a quick look around to make sure I haven't missed anything, and then make my way to the staffroom to get changed.

I pull on some cosy black leggings, a few layers on top as well as my faithful yellow padded jacket, and with my trainers on I already feel like I've a new spring in my step. Peter's thirtieth birthday is just weeks away. I'll return home for our celebration dinner as planned, and after the formalities I'll sit down with Sean and we'll have a long overdue heart-to-heart.

'Come on, Nana, let's go get some of that crisp air into our lungs,' I say, rattling our resident dog's lead, which always makes her bounce like she's on springs.

'Are you staying for dinner?' Sita asks me from reception as I wrestle with Nana, who would rather lick my face than sit still. 'Chef was asking if you'd like him to keep you some of your favourites for later.'

One of the best things about working here is that we are all treated like one big family. Even though we don't like to take advantage of the generosity shown to us staff, we know that there's always an offer of a hot meal or a warm drink on a cold winter's day like today.

'It's Wednesday, so I've a very important date,' I say to Sita. 'I'll take Nana for a quick jaunt in the park, then I'll be on my way.'

'Oh, that's right,' she says with a smile. 'Wednesday Supper Club with Leroy. You two are the cutest.'

I make a funny face to break the atmosphere when I see Sita's sympathetic look of concern as she tilts her head to the side.

She was astounded when I told her of the engagement, but she understands why I've played along, too.

'You don't need to look at me like that. Nobody died, for goodness' sake.'

Sita bursts out laughing, which is a reaction I much prefer to any one of my friends here feeling sorry for me.

'Your ring is beautiful,' she tells me for at least the tenth time today. 'Is it OK to say that? Sean has excellent taste.'

I hold out my hand, noticing how the teardrop of diamonds sparkle under the hotel chandelier, then I let out a deep sigh.

'It really is stunning,' I agree, moving my hand so the light dances off the precious gems that make up the cluster. 'I'd make a joke about Sean having excellent taste in women too, but I don't think that's very appropriate under the circumstances. Right, I need some fresh air and so does this girl. Come on, Nana. Let's go and put the world to rights before it gets too dark.'

Nana barks in delight and tugs on the lead, much to the amusement of a very cute older couple who come in from the bitter cold outside, bickering over dinner plans but still wrapped up in each other's arms.

I notice how Sita looks at them, starry eyed, and I know that she is thinking exactly what I'm thinking as we watch how they interact.

The chance to grow old with someone you truly love must be the most beautiful thing in the whole world.

I hope to realise that for myself one day. And that Sean finds the same happiness too.

Kensington in the snow is a true winter wonderland.

As Nana and I stroll through the resting gardens, it's like someone has thrown a delicate veil of magic over nature.

'OK, you lead the way as always,' I say to Nana, wishing I'd brought some walking boots instead of these trainers which are already soaked through with sludgy snow.

I'm not thinking straight. I haven't been since I got back to London after my eventful seven-day break.

Sean couldn't take me to the airport in Belfast due to a last-minute emergency at the farm, so instead I spent the journey with my parents, who declared it to be the best Christmas they'd had in a very long time.

'I know it's early days, but have you thought any more about a venue yet, Bea?' Mum asked from the passenger seat as Dad drove on the motorway at what felt like a snail's pace. Her voice was full of joy in a way I'd almost forgotten it used to be. 'Your Aunty Briege says the Four Seasons Hotel is hard to beat for a big wedding. They've even got a huge marquee if you need it. Will you invite all your cousins though, darling? I think the eldest from each family is more than enough, but it's up to you and Sean, of course.'

Patsi had offered to drop a few gentle hints on my behalf after I'd gone but no, that would be a real cop-out and would only leave them stewing over everything around the kitchen table. I couldn't bear to think of that, especially with Peter's thirtieth birthday just around the corner. Plus, I can't say a word to anyone until I talk to Sean, and he is harder to pin down than ever before.

'I'm so sorry I lashed out at you,' Patsi whispered to me when we said our farewells. 'You hit the nail on the head as always when you said we might be looking at Sean as a sticking plaster to heal our grief over Peter, but that's not fair on anyone. Least of all Sean. I hope you get to sort this out sooner rather than later, for both of your sakes.'

'Don't worry, I will. Now, you take good care in Paris,' I said, kissing her forehead. She looked as funky as always in her silver tulle skirt and Dr. Marten boots. 'Let's keep in touch a bit more, eh? A sister is for life, not just for Christmas.'

'Love you,' she'd said, waving me off from the doorstep. 'I do miss you, Bea, and I'm sorry for getting carried away with wedding excitement.'

'So you should be, you old romantic eejit,' I joked, then gave her an extra hug for good measure. 'You'll probably be married with children well before I am at this rate.'

I miss her already. I miss Benburb too, but London is where I'm meant to be for now. This is where I can be myself. And I can't change that for anyone.

Nana leads me down to the Long Water, the magnificent lake in Kensington Gardens which is almost frozen under the hazy blue January sky, all framed by a midwinter fine dusting of snow.

Herons, coots, ducks and geese fly overhead while the tranquillity of the bare-limbed trees and the peace the lake offers to brisk walkers or casual strollers never fails to take my breath away.

I fix my scarf up over my mouth and nose as a blast of bitter cold air stings my face. I've spent hours by myself here on spring and summer days, scribbling in my notebooks and diaries, watching the world go by. And now in winter, even though the wind is whipping through my coat and tingling my skin, there's something refreshing about being by the water. It helps me think more clearly.

'Ah, look, it's Peter Pan,' I hear an attractive young woman say when she and her boyfriend approach the famous statue erected by J. M. Barrie himself, in memory of the little boy who never grew up, and my favourite story of all time.

I do my best not to stare at the couple as they chat, but I always take great delight when I hear a child or a tourist discover my favourite spot in Kensington Gardens for the first time. I always find comfort by the Peter Pan statue. It's the place I go to when I need to think of my own little brother who didn't get to grow fully into manhood. At least, he didn't for long.

Nana, who has walked this way with me since she was a puppy, sniffs the ground and takes me across the crunchy grass towards the statue like it's second nature. She even pees there to mark her territory, as if she knows where she got her name from.

The couple are both bundled up for their winter walk in hats, gloves and scarves. I feel a twitch of excitement as I watch the woman's reaction of wonder when I get closer. She pushes her blonde hair off her face against the wind, taking in every second of seeing this monument for the first time.

'Don't tell me you've never been here before, Jane?' I hear the man say to her.

Jane looks up at him with admiration, but I'm frozen on the spot and it's nothing to do with the weather. His voice catches me right in the heart. He sounds like home to me. And strangely familiar.

'So, it takes an Irish man to show you Londoners what's on your very own doorstep,' he continues. 'Sacrilege, that's what I say. Sacrilege and blasphemy.'

I know that voice. I'd recognise that voice anywhere. And I know that sense of humour and turn of phrase too.

Sacrilege and blasphemy.

I take a step backwards, almost tripping over Nana, which does nothing for my intention to remain incognito while I catch my breath.

'What do you mean, you *Londoners*?' Jane jokes back at him. 'I'm not from London originally, and you know it. I'm a northerner through and through.'

She leans across and tenderly fixes his hat while he stands with his hands in his pockets.

'I'm teasing,' he says in return. 'Northerners are the best. Still can't believe you've never been here before though.'

My heart is thumping.

I don't know where to look or what to say or do, but Nana barks, interrupting what appears to be a private, romantic moment – and totally blowing my cover.

'Come on, Nana,' I whisper, doing my best not to make a fuss, but it's too late. They've noticed me. Well, they've noticed the dog.

'What a gorgeous dog!' says Jane, looking right at me now. 'Just look at those big eyes. Ah, she's so beautiful!'

Nana pants and barks more at the chance of some attention from a pretty stranger. She bounces and pulls on her lead, but I'm locked in a stupendous haze of disbelief. Someone could come and easily knock me down right now with a feather.

'She's a – she's a good girl.'

I don't even recognise the sound of my own voice. Ollie

watches on, smiling as Jane pats Nana's head. I want to say hello. I need to say hello.

And then I go for it.

'Ollie?' I say, pulling my scarf down around my neck again to show my face.

His ridiculously handsome face crumples in confusion and surprise.

'Yes?' he says cautiously.

'You don't remember me?'

He takes a step closer, doing his best to see me properly in the dim light of dusk on this snowy late afternoon. He almost staggers in return.

'What the—?' he gasps. 'Oh my God, Bea! Is it you?'

I nod and smile.

'It's me.'

The world seems to move in slow motion. His hands go to his face. Mine do the same.

It's like time has stood still as our two worlds collide once more, but I'm not sure if this is real or some illusional dream.

'Wow! It *is* you!' he says, coming towards me like he's going to take me in his arms, but he stops abruptly as if he's had second thoughts.

'It's me.'

My stomach leaps into my mouth. I feel dizzy and confused at the same time. How can this be happening?

'Oh my goodness! What brings you here? Do you – wow. Sorry, this has caught me totally unawares.'

We stare at each other for what feels like an eternity. It's like the earth is still moving but we are the only two people who matter right now.

Jane looks from one of us to the other in equal surprise.

'Do you two know each other from home?' she asks, her eyes widened in anticipation. 'You have very similar accents.'

I'm conscious of her getting the wrong impression, but I feel like my heart might explode. I feel tears sting my eyes, and a longing to reach out to him, but I know again that I can't for so many reasons.

'It's so good to see you again,' he whispers.

'It's so good to see you again too.'

We haven't answered Jane's question, and the truth is I don't know where to start.

For once in my life, I simply cannot find the words.

Chapter Fourteen

Ollie

Kensington Gardens, London
January

I walk towards her just to be closer to her, forgetting for a brief moment about Jane, who I invited to walk with me after an emotional shift which saw one of her patients take a turn for the worst.

She'd cried it out in the staffroom when our shift was over and I'd made her a cup of tea. Then I remembered Mr G's suggestion about the clarity and healing he found by walking in Kensington Gardens at this time of day when the light was dropping, and the air was still. Maybe it would help Jane too.

And now here we are, face to face with Bea and her dog, in what suddenly feels like the most magical winter wonderland on a cold, crisp January evening.

Bea is wearing the same yellow coat and red scarf and hat as before, and just like the first time I laid eyes on her, her smile stops me right in my tracks, catches my breath and almost makes my head spin when I look at her.

'Er – sorry, Jane, this is Bea. Bea, this is my colleague Jane,' I explain, hoping she doesn't get the wrong impression of what it may look like on my part, in case it makes a difference. 'We're just out for a walk after our shift at the hospital. Jane had a tough day.'

'I'm sorry to hear that,' says Bea.

'Thank you,' Jane responds. 'All part of the job, but Ollie was kind enough to talk it through with me.'

'It's lovely to meet you, Jane,' she says in return. 'There's nothing better than talking things through with a good friend. It's sometimes the best medicine.'

This is incredibly awkward. My palms are sweating. I have so much to say, I've spent hours upon days imagining what I would say if I ever bumped into Bea again, yet now that it has miraculously happened, I'm lost for words.

She looks slightly stunned, or maybe she's like me . . . Maybe she had imagined that one day our paths would cross again, and maybe she'd gone over a range of different scenarios of how amazing it would be. How we'd marvel at the chances of it all. How we'd slip off immediately with a sense of urgency to spend time together at last. She'd tell me all about how she ended things with Sean. I'd listen intently and sympathise. I'd praise her for her honesty.

Then we'd have a drink or go for dinner, and it would be the beginning of something so wonderful, so meant to be. We'd tell the story for years to anyone who would give us an ear.

Yet here we are and it's not like that at all.

'Oh, I totally agree. And Ollie is a very good listener, aren't you Ollie?' smiles Jane.

'Sorry?'

'Jane is saying you're a very good listener,' says Bea. Her voice sounds lower than when we first met. She isn't as bright and bubbly as she was before.

'Just one of those days that come around much too often in our line of work,' says Jane. In a way I'm irritated that she's here, but also grateful for her filling in the gaps in our conversation. 'By the way, your engagement ring is simply stunning, Bea. Congratulations.'

The lift in Jane's voice brings me right back to my senses and my eyes drop to Bea's left hand where a dazzling cluster of diamonds glistens in the early dusk.

Wait a minute.

My stomach drops to my feet.

'Oh, thank you,' Bea says swiftly, before reaching into her pocket and finding some fine black leather gloves which she quickly puts on her hands. 'I totally forgot I'd these in my pocket. It's cold, isn't it?'

I feel a lump form in my throat.

'You're engaged?' I say, feeling like my eyes might pop out of my head. My insides go queasy. 'Wow.'

'Wow indeed,' she says, shoving her left hand into her coat pocket. She can't meet my eye at all now.

'Congratulations,' I say, the word sticking on my tongue. I try to swallow but my throat is dry. 'That's . . . that's great news. Must have been a nice surprise?'

I have no idea why I'm asking her that. I remember her saying how she hates surprises, but it's absolutely none of my business. This is a person I spent no more than a couple of hours with on an emotional Christmas Eve, so I've no right to feel anything more than delight for her happiness.

But she doesn't look very celebratory.

'Yes, it was very much a surprise,' she says, her eyes skirting around so they land anywhere but on me. 'I – I had no idea it was going to happen.'

Cue a lengthy silence.

I can feel every breath I take like ice cutting the back of my throat. I can see every breath she takes too in the sharp, cool air. My stomach is in knots.

'How – how is your dad?' she asks me, as if she's just been struck by divine inspiration on something to say. 'Did you have a nice Christmas with him?'

Jane looks on from one of us to the other and I realise I haven't explained how Bea and I know each other. Not that I have to. Not that we even really *do* know each other very well.

'My dad, yes, he was very glad to have me home,' I stutter. 'He . . . he's coping well. It was tough but good. A very emotional trip, but that's what was to be expected.'

'That's so good to hear,' she whispers, looking at the ground now.

Jane is staring at us, drinking in this very surreal moment.

'Sorry, Jane . . . um, Bea and I met at the airport on the way home to Ireland on Christmas Eve. Our flight was . . . our flight was delayed. It's crazy we've just bumped into each other here.'

This is all very uncomfortable, but I want to ask if Bea lives nearby.

I want to ask if she works nearby.

I want to ask if she comes here often, as clichéd as that may sound. But it doesn't feel right to ask anything when she is wearing a dazzling engagement ring on her now-covered-up finger.

There was a chemistry, an attraction, a connection. Call it whatever you want, but there was something that day. I felt it and I know she felt it too.

But now she is engaged. I feel like I've been gut-punched. My legs have gone to jelly.

'And you remember each other from the airport?' asks Jane, puzzled.

'Yes, I remember it well,' says Bea. Her beautiful forehead is creased. She is holding on to the dog's lead like she's holding on to her sanity. 'It was a very – it was a lovely afternoon. I think we're both in shock at seeing each other again so soon.'

I gulp like I'm swallowing razor blades.

'Yes, that's exactly it,' I reply, but everything is different now. Like my dream is over. Talk about a complete one-eighty turn-around. How could she have gone from wanting to break up with her boyfriend to agreeing to marry him? I have so many questions but it's not my place to ask them.

'Doesn't the universe work in marvellous ways,' laughs Jane. 'Nothing is ever a coincidence – that's what I believe, anyhow. I do love meeting new people in unexpected places. So, is this your dog? She's very friendly.'

I take by her changing of the subject that Jane is feeling a bit awkward too.

We all focus on the dog, who is the distraction we all need right now as we stand in the cold in this picture-perfect London park. I hear children's laughter in the near distance, the roar of red buses rushing by from Kensington High Street and the faint scream of a siren in the background. My mind flashes back to how Sean kissed Bea with such passion when he saw her at the airport.

How could I have been so foolish as to think that I ever stood a chance? I don't even know her. We are strangers. How can I have feelings for someone I don't even know?

'Nana lives at the hotel I work in,' Bea tells Jane, but her voice is shaky. 'She's very used to people so she never makes a fuss with strangers, do you Nana? She's such a good girl. We have the best of times, but I'm glad that she can't speak human. She knows all my secrets.'

Bea glances up at me as she reaches down and pats the dog's damp black and white fur.

Her eyes are fixed on mine. I can't hide the pain I'm feeling inside or the shockwaves that hit every nerve in my body. Maybe she's thinking the same as I am? Doesn't she feel there's something between us? She has the same longing in her eyes as I have from every inch of me. I know everything changed on Christmas Eve. I haven't been able to shake it off since.

Or am I just seeing things the way I want them to be? I think back to Monica and wonder how I could have read this all so wrongly once again. Am I really so clueless when it comes to interpreting signs?

'So, when is your wedding?' Jane asks, which only serves to drive a knife further into my already suffering heart just as I was about to suggest an escape so I can lick my wounds in peace.

Bea fixes her scarf with her free hand, loosening it quickly. She laughs nervously, looking up to the darkening sky. I can see her breath in the air. Her nose twitches. She rubs it with her gloved hand.

'We don't have a date just yet,' she replies, taking a few steps in the opposite direction, looking like she now wants to escape too. 'Look, I'd better be off. It . . . it was nice to see you again, Ollie. And lovely to meet you, Jane. I'd better keep going. It's a cold evening.'

Awkwardly we almost dance around each other in the snow.

'Yes, it's cold indeed. I guess we'd better get going too,' I say after another few seconds of forced smiles and silences. 'Congratulations to you and Shane.'

'Sean,' she corrects me.

'Sorry, Sean, of course,' I say, pointing to my temple as if I'd lost my memory.

I hadn't. I knew it was Sean, but I don't want her knowing that I've been pondering over her love life enough to remember every detail.

'Happy New Year, Ollie,' she says, tilting her head to the side. 'And you too, Jane. Come on, Nana. Let's get you home and warmed up by the fire.'

I pull my coat up under my chin, feeling the weight in my stomach settle into an uncomfortable mound of sorrow and longing that takes me right back to the last time we had to say goodbye.

'Happy New Year to you too, Bea.'

I watch her walk off into the distance under the early evening moonlight, her footprints in the sprinkle of snow, until she disappears into the darkness which is dropping down fast.

I long to have had more to say to her, but I don't. Not right now.

Right now I'm stunned. I'm lost for words.

If there is such thing as love at first sight, then my heart has already broken in two.

Chapter Fifteen

Bea

Notting Hill, London

For as far back as I can remember I've always found comfort in making a curry from scratch when I'm confused, in a tizzy or when I simply need to feel grounded in my thoughts.

Music helps too, so, when I get home from work after safely delivering Nana back to the hotel, I find myself chopping chicken, peppers, onions, garlic and mushrooms at lightning speed while thoughts of seeing Ollie again so unexpectedly spin through my mind.

Taylor Swift playing in the background helps. I turn her up louder and sing along with gusto at a volume that makes me glad I live alone.

I had no idea what to say to him.

I was flustered and stunned, like a rabbit in headlights, and I could tell that he was too.

And what gives me the right to have felt a twist in my gut when I looked back and saw him walk away with Jane in the opposite direction?

She leaned closer to him under the lamplight and linked his arm, almost snuggling against him as they strolled to God knows where. A pub maybe? A restaurant? Or maybe they were going back to his place to watch a movie and eat pop-corn on the sofa. He said they were friends, but the way she tenderly fixed his hat and the way they looked so good together gave me a very different impression.

Taylor knows. She totally understands. I turn up the volume just a little bit more.

Poor Nana had to listen to the sound of my rants of dis-belief all the way back to The Carnation where I spilled my guts out to Sita, who was just finishing her shift.

'Are you sure you don't want to go for a quick drink and talk it over?' she'd asked, but no, I couldn't do that. I already felt silly enough having let someone who is practically a stranger knock me off my axis.

'I'm still officially engaged, so whatever I feel doesn't really count, does it?' I reminded her. 'Oh my God, how did I let this happen? Why did I say yes to Sean? What have I done?'

'You said yes because you're human and you were caught unawares. You said yes because you have a heart and you didn't want to cause a scene in your home village. Come on. Let's get it all out of your system over a cocktail. At least you have a plan made for after Peter's birthday.'

Sita is a sweetheart to offer to hear me out, but I feel fool-ish and embarrassed for telling her this much. I'm supposed to be her senior at work, not someone who comes to her for relationship advice.

'I have to get back to cook for Leroy,' I explain to her. 'I'll do my best not to bend his ear too much, poor thing.'

I add some extra veg to the curry to bulk it out, with one eye on the clock as I stir up a storm in the kitchen. Leroy will be here any minute, so I need to shake it off, pardon the pun, and pull myself together. We haven't had a good old heart-to-heart in ages. I'm so looking forward to catching up with him.

I set my kitchen table for two, grab a bottle of my favourite New Zealand Sauvignon from the fridge, then select two of my finest goblet glasses from the cupboard.

The phone rings. It's Leroy at last, returning my call. I turn the music down, imagining that he may be running late due to the horrendous weather outside. January is showing no let-up for storms, and we're already facing another week of snow and hailstones in London.

'How's my girl?' he asks. He doesn't sound as if he's even left his flat yet.

'I'm fine, but why aren't you here, darling?' I ask him, glancing again at the time. 'It's Wednesday. Have you forgotten?'

I look across at the small Ikea kitchen table which is looking impeccable as always for our Wednesday Supper Club, with fresh seasonal flowers – in this case winter ber-ries, foliage and some of my favourite pussy willow – matching placemats, and dark green napkins. But I know by the sound of Leroy's voice that something is up with him too.

'I've got a problem. I'm sorry, Miss Beatrice,' he tells me, sounding breathless. 'I'm sorry for such short notice but I'm not going to make it.'

'Gosh, Leroy, what is it?'

'A water leak in my flat,' he tells me.

'You scared me there! I thought you'd been hurt.'

'Sorry, no, no. It looks like a burst pipe, which is unsurprising in this weather. I've called a plumber, which was a challenge as they're all out on call it seems, so I can't leave until he gets here.'

'I will come to you then,' I tell him, scouring the flat for where I need to start packing everything up. 'I'll bring you some curry. Do you need anything from the shops? I can stop off at the Tesco Express en route.'

He takes his time to answer.

'You'll do nothing of the sort, my love, but thank you as always for looking out for me. You are so kind to me, Miss Beatrice,' he says with a raucous laugh that is so Leroy. 'You take care and enjoy your evening. I'll see you at the hotel in the morning, bright and early.'

I tap my foot under the table. I hate the thought of Leroy being in any sort of bother, even if it's only a burst pipe.

Ever since I started working at The Carnation, I've adored him. He is almost retiring age, and he only works on a casual arrangement now, but he is one of those people who can brighten my whole day with just a smile or a few words of wisdom. He tells me stories of how he met the love of his life, Coral, at The Carnation when he was treating his elderly mother to a fancy dinner there for her birthday. Leroy's mum was a nurse in the NHS while Coral was a merchant's daughter from Belgravia, and her parents did everything in their power to keep them apart. They had plans to elope, which only Leroy's mother knew of, but Coral never lived to see it happen when she was knocked down on a busy London street on her way to meet him. Their love story brings me to tears no matter how many times I hear it.

In return for his stories of immigration and forbidden love, I like to cook for him once a week in my flat, or if we're feeling fancy we go to a movie and grab something tasty like a Chinese or an Indian curry in town.

He tells our colleagues Preston and Sita that it's his favourite day of the week, so I know that it's a big deal for him to miss it.

'Maybe I could eat some of it tomorrow if you bring it to me in one of your fancy lunchboxes?'

'Yes, I'll bring you curry for lunch, that's a promise. But can you promise me in return that you'll call if there's anything I can do?' I say, feeling torn between my own inclination to go to him and his insistence that I don't.

'Are you any good with burst pipes?'

I roll my eyes. I can just see his face when he says that.

'No, I'm not,' I reply in defeat. 'My DIY and decorating skills are second to none if I do say so myself, but I think we should leave a plumbing problem to the experts. OK, keep in touch and I'll see you tomorrow.'

The rich waft of savoury spices in my flat makes my own tummy rumble when I hang up.

Leroy named our weekly evening together the Wednesday Supper Club, which began one Wednesday in summer when I met him in Marks and Spencer on Kensington High Street buying a TV dinner for one. I convinced him to come to mine for dinner, and it soon became a regular occurrence.

Our shifts at the hotel are mostly daytime through the week, so unless something major crops up like a special function or a trip home to Ireland for me, we manage to make it happen most Wednesdays.

We eat together, we drink some wine, he fills me in on some behind-the-scenes gossip at work or tells me about Coral or adventurous stories of his childhood in Jamaica. He lights up with tales of how he travelled to many places with nothing but the clothes on his back, before coming to London with his mum in search of his uncle, as well as to try and make a better life for all of them.

I share my own anecdotes of home in Benburb and my huge extended Irish family which always make him laugh out loud. His favourite is the one about my Uncle Gerry who fled to Mexico when he changed his mind about his lifelong ambition to be a priest, got married to an exotic dancer and became a professional matador instead.

My own appetite has waned, but I've been losing weight lately through what I can only assume is stress, so I go to the cupboard, take out a plate and spoon some fluffy rice on before topping it with curry. I'd better try and eat something, even if my heart isn't in it.

I pour myself a large glass of wine as the snow falls softly on to a street lantern outside my first-floor window. I watch it for a moment, its fragility somehow soothing my weary mind. I flick on the TV and stare at the moving images on the screen without really taking anything in. Everyone on *The One Show* is talking about diets and exercise, so I quickly switch it off and contemplate listening to more Taylor instead.

With every mouthful of food, the diamonds on my engagement ring catch the light that hangs above me.

I'm just about to instruct Alexa when a loud ring on my doorbell brings me back to my senses. It's after seven on a cold winter's evening in January. Who on earth could it be?

I rarely have visitors. Unless it's a neighbour who's lost a key? Or someone with a wrong sense of direction? I'm baffled, but I guess I'll soon find out.

'Hello?' I say into the intercom, thankful for this layer of security on our flat, which is a far cry from the one I rented when I first arrived in London – so wet behind the ears about living in a city as opposed to the middle of nowhere back home.

The line crackles as I wait for a response.

It comes eventually.

'It's me.'

'Hello?' I repeat, thinking I must be imagining things.

It couldn't be.

'Sorry to surprise you like this,' says a familiar Irish accent which almost knocks me off my feet. 'I know by now you don't like surprises, but it's me. We need to talk.'

What the . . .

'This *is* a surprise.'

'I – I just had to talk to you in person, Bea,' he says. 'We need to talk this over.'

Moments after I've pressed the entry buzzer, Sean makes his way into my flat. He doesn't take off his coat despite being soaked through from the sleet and snow outside.

'You've come all this way?'

'You bet I did,' he tells me. 'I think you know why I'm here. It's not exactly a conversation we can have over the phone, is it?'

I do my best not to burst into tears at the thought of him travelling for hours on a plane, train and Underground to face up to the reality of what has become of our relationship.

'Would you like a beer or some curry?' I ask him, my voice shaking, not really knowing what else to say just yet. 'I made some for Leroy but he's had a burst pipe at home.'

I know I'm rambling. I can't help it.

'It's the weather for burst pipes, yes,' says Sean. He doesn't even sit down. 'I'm not really hungry, but thanks anyway.'

He glances at my left hand. I feel very raw and exposed.

'Sorry I didn't get to see you much over Christmas,' he says, still standing in the middle of the kitchen floor.

I pull out a chair for him at the table.

He sits down eventually.

'I know it's not easy being with someone in my line of work,' he continues. 'There's no such thing as regular hours or shifts to plan around, and it can seem like work comes first all the time, which I suppose in a way it does.'

I push the plate of steaming curry and rice away from my placemat. A brief silence follows before we both speak at the same time, our words tumbling out of our mouths and mixing in the air in a desperate flurry of frustration and sorrow.

'I'm sorry.'

'No, I'm sorry.'

'I tried to talk to you.'

'You were never around.'

We stop again. I catch his eye and put my hand across to touch his, but he pulls it away.

'Please don't,' he whispers, staring at the table where Leroy should be sitting now, tucking into my food. 'Let's not make this harder than it already is.'

'Sean—'

'Please let me finish,' he says. 'I've travelled six hours to say this. I know we've been drifting apart lately. I know I'm not the best at communicating most days, and that your life here and mine back home are just so . . .'

'Different?' I suggest when he trails off.

'That's one way to put it.'

'We've been so disconnected lately, Sean,' I tell him. 'We used to be so close, but things have changed with my job commitments here, the distance, the lack of conversations. I don't know that we've a great deal in common any more.'

He stews on this for a moment, staring out the window where the snow is still drifting down through the yellow light of the lamp-post, a picturesque contrast to the pain we are both feeling now.

'I guess I could feel you slipping away,' he says, his voice breaking. 'And I panicked.'

'I'm sorry.'

'I took it too far.'

More silence.

'I thought a sign of commitment from me might change things,' he says, 'but I know now that it would only do the opposite . . . now that I've had a few days and more to think about it. I'm never going to move to London, and I don't want you to leave a job and life you love. There's too much that needs to be fixed between us. Things an engagement ring can't fix, unfortunately.'

I reach out once more to touch his hand, just to hold it in agreement with everything he has just said.

This time, he doesn't pull away.

'I'm catching the last flight home tonight,' he says. 'But I thought it best we talked in person. And I also knew the longer we left it, the harder it would be to face up to the truth. I don't want to be anyone's burden, Bea. I'd rather we both faced up to the truth that what we had just isn't there any more. Do you agree?'

I nod my head and bite my lip.

'You were never a burden, Sean,' I tell him softly. 'You are a wonderful, funny, handsome and strong man. I'm sorry we've come to this, but you're right. It's time to face up to the truth once and for all, because we can fool the world around us, but we can't fool ourselves, and we both deserve better.'

'I totally agree,' he says, staring at the wall now.

I have so much respect for him right now. He is much braver than I've been. I slide off the stunning platinum ring he gave me and place it in his hand. He doesn't flinch, but I'm struggling to hold back tears.

'We can still be—'

'Don't say friends,' he interrupts, closing his eyes tight as he puts the ring in his pocket. 'Maybe one day we can be in touch again, but for now I just want to close this chapter and do my best to move on. I'm sure you do too. Do you mind if I do have a beer? I could do with one now if the offer is still there.'

I get him a drink with a mixture of huge relief and deep sadness. It's never easy to end a relationship, it's never easy to know you've broken someone's heart, but somehow, I think that when the dust settles, Sean will know that this big change will be the best thing for us both.

I believe he may know that already as his mood changes within minutes, and we're chatting with a whole new lightness in the air, almost like we used to do.

'Thank you for coming to talk to me,' I say as we stand in the doorway just over an hour later. 'Can I walk you downstairs to the main door?'

'No need. It's freezing cold out,' he says, unable once more to hold eye contact. 'I've probably stayed too long, but it was well worth the journey.'

'Thank you.'

'I'd better make tracks.'

I want to say sorry once more, but I think we've both said all we had to for now. So instead, I close my flat door and walk to the window from where I watch him walk across the street towards Notting Hill Underground station.

With my hands shaking, I pour a hefty glass of wine and then call Patsi for some comfort. Sometimes even Taylor Swift can't do what a sister can do. Sometimes we need the power of real-life sisterhood to see us through.

Chapter Sixteen

Ollie

Royal Elizabeth Hospital, London

On a crisp, cold February afternoon we celebrate my father's beautiful life with the sweet sounds of an Irish fiddle and the scattering of some of his ashes on Slieve League cliffs, just like he had requested. The rest will be buried with my mother in our local graveyard.

A lot sooner than expected, Aunt Nora and I, together with a small handful of neighbours, family friends and distant cousins, gather on the magnificent Irish landmark for our small but poignant farewell, taking turns to set him free like speckled dust into the wind sweeping far across the Atlantic seas.

It is as uplifting and special as he wanted it to be. And of that I'm so very proud, yet also stung by the irony that at last I have an interview for a job at a recently established heart unit back in Donegal next week. I'm glad I got to tell him that on the phone before he deteriorated so rapidly. He was elated, knowing how much I've always wanted to come home. Aunt Nora said it was almost as if he let go once he knew I was making my way home to Donegal at last, as he knew how much it meant to me. I, on the other hand, felt he was holding on until he knew there'd be someone here to keep an eye on Aunt Nora. Whatever way it happened, my father left the world with grace and dignity, and it fills my heart to believe that he and my mother are reunited at last somewhere out there.

There was no open coffin at the wake like we have in some parts of Ireland, just three smiling photos on display from happier times: one of his wedding day, another one of an early family holiday with Mum, and a third one with me and Aunt Nora on my graduation day from medical school when I qualified as a cardiac nurse.

I was mid-shift on Ward 3 when I got the call with the news, only a few weeks after my return to London after Christmas.

It's a moment in time that will now be etched in my mind forever, in the same way everyone remembers exactly where they were and what they were doing when they hear life-changing news.

I'll never forget it.

Right before I got the call that changed the whole direction of my day and subsequently my life, one of my patients, an eighty-two-year-old doll-like lady called Mary Doris, had been admiring my new white trainers.

As she lay wired up to a monitor and still in a hospital gown, she was keeping me entertained with her quips and comments about how wonderful it was to be so well looked after in hospital after her valve replacement surgery.

Miss Doris, as she liked to be addressed, spoke in a shrill but timid voice, and she had a compliment for every single one of us who tended to her needs.

'Ah, they're just plain, comfy trainers for work, Miss Doris. Nothing fancy, but thank you for the kind words,' I said with a smile. 'And I have to say you're looking very perky today too. You've a fine colour in your cheeks, which is very reassuring only two days post-surgery. You'll be back playing bridge with the ladies in the WI in no time.'

Miss Doris seemed to be searching for something nice to say in return, even going so far as to say I suited the blue colour of my uniform as it matched my eyes, and then she wrote down my name in a little red notebook – '*Nurse Ollie – sparkling blue eyes, curly hair, nice shoes, no girlfriend, sadly.*' She referred to this notebook to remember staff names, which was very endearing, but there really was no need to add the part about my romantic status.

'Ouch, Miss Doris, thanks for the reminder that I'm *sadly* single,' I quipped. 'So, what did you write about my friend Scott who you met in A&E on admission? Big feet? Laughs at his own jokes? I bet he doesn't have as fine a description as I do.'

She scanned her own looped handwriting with the tip of her pen until she found him.

'*Nurse Scott – tattoo on hand, calm in a crisis, bleached hair but kind face. Laughs a lot. Big strides. Liverpool.*'

'Big strides? That's very polite, but is that it?' I asked her, folding my arms. 'Nothing about his love life or lack of it, then? Scott hasn't had a girlfriend in five years, but you let him off with that and slammed me, eh?'

Miss Doris giggled, but then her laughter turned to a splutter and a cough which made me glance around to make sure no one else was looking. It wasn't really advisable to make fragile elderly patients laugh out loud when they were in recovery from major surgery.

'You won't be single for very long, Ollie,' whispered Miss Doris when she finally got her breath back after a glass of water and a raise of her pillows. The twinkle was back in her eyes too, thank goodness. 'You come to my house some day and I'll read your tea leaves to tell you all about the girl of your dreams. I'll write down my address for you.'

Again, I glanced around to make sure I wasn't being watched.

'No, no, it's fine,' I told her quickly. 'I'm not sure I'd be allowed to visit, but thank you for the kind invitation nonetheless.'

She looked up at me in wonder.

'What do you mean, not allowed? Why ever not?' she asked. 'I love visitors, I always have. And I'd love to tell you all about your Irish rose. You've already met her, but she'll cross your path again very soon.'

I did a double take.

'What do you mean, Irish rose?'

'Well, you're Irish, aren't you?'

I laughed at my own wishful thinking.

'Oh, OK, it's my accent, isn't it?' I said, rolling my eyes. 'Irish boy most likely to meet Irish girl and all that. Hardly need tea leaves to come up with that.'

Miss Doris looked offended. This conversation was going downhill.

'You know, my Aunt Nora believes wholeheartedly in the power of reading tea leaves too, so don't mind cynical old me,' I whispered, moving her tray closer to her so she could sip on some more water if she needed to. 'I'm just being silly. I'll keep my eyes and ears open for a nice girl from home. Thank you, Miss Doris.'

She burst into a smile, much to my relief. I could have kicked myself for almost upsetting her. And it was only a tiny white lie that saved the day. Aunt Nora doesn't believe in tea leaves, but she does in all the signs that come from 'the other side', as she calls it.

'Maybe you could bring your Aunt Nora when you come to visit,' chirped Miss Doris, a lot happier now as I was about to move on to my next patient. 'If I write down my phone number, can you ask her to give me a call? I'd love to meet her. I'd bet we have lots in common.'

'You do that, Miss Doris,' I said with a wink and a nod. 'I'd better go and see what needs doing round here or I'll be accused of favouritism again and we don't want that.'

'You're my favourite, Ollie,' she said, and I watched as she added that to my bio in her notebook, scoring out the 'no girl-friend' part which strangely healed my slightly wounded ego.

I wondered how Scott would feel when he read his. Big strides. Now that was a new one.

I was still smiling as I left my quirky patient's bedside, but I had no idea my whole world was going to change. Jane was approaching me from the nurses' station, but she barely had to say a word.

She looked pale, shaken. I stopped dead in my tracks. My blood ran cold.

I knew. I just knew.

'I – I was looking for you, Ollie. I'm so sorry,' she murmured.

'It's OK,' I whispered, closing my eyes. 'He's gone, isn't he?'

It was a call I'd known would come one day soon, but not this soon. It was a scenario I'd played over and over in my head. Where would I be when I heard the news? Would I make it home in time to say one last goodbye? Would I get the news directly or from a friend? Would I be at work or at home?

'That was quick,' I said, my eyes locked into a stare at nothing as my mind went into overdrive.

'Your Aunt Nora called the ward just now,' Jane continued, her warm hand on my bare arm. 'She couldn't get through on your mobile. You'd better make your way home, Ollie. I can help you with flights. Or anything you need. Ollie . . . ?'

I swallowed hard as Jane's words echoed in my head, then for just a few seconds, the world around me went into slow motion. Everything became a blur.

The sounds of phones ringing on the nurses' station faded into the distance as if they were miles away. A row of blue and green uniforms walking past me in the corridor became a whirl that made me dizzy, and the smell of disinfectant that I'd grown so used to seemed suddenly overpowering, almost making me choke.

I dropped everything at work right there, and went straight to the airport to catch the next available flight home, not even taking the time to go via my flat to pack a bag.

'I'll get you there, I promise,' said Scott softly as he helped me put on my coat in the staffroom. 'I'm so sorry, man. This is incredibly cruel. I'm so sorry.'

With a sense of déjà vu, Scott was my wingman once more, driving me through the wintry elements on that Friday afternoon to make sure I made my flight – only this time there were no festivities to look forward to, no random meet-ups with someone like Bea to make my heart sing.

This time I charged through the airport, knowing I hadn't got the chance to say goodbye to my father before he closed his eyes forever.

I wiped my eyes going through security without caring who saw me cry. I wanted to shout it from the rooftops. I wanted everyone to know that even though their world was operating in business-as-usual mode, mine had just collapsed because my dad, my hero, my all-time best friend Jack Brennan was gone only weeks after the most magical Christmas spent together.

I got home to our cottage to find out that everything for the funeral had been planned in writing well in advance. He'd made sure we'd no big decisions to make, nothing to ponder or wonder, nothing to ever regret. He'd even left a bottle of his favourite gin, the locally made An Dúlamán from the local Sliabh Liag Distillery, and he'd asked us to toast him on the steps by the front door – the same doorway where he'd carried my mother over the threshold when they'd married some thirty-five years before.

I was impressed by his choice of music in the local chapel (a *lot* of Bob Dylan, my mother's favourite hymn 'Lady of Knock' and a satirical blast of 'Don't Worry, Be Happy' to finish). He'd asked his beloved Gaelic football team to act as pallbearers on the day and he'd left instructions for a small celebration of his life to be held after Mass at a nearby hotel which had more laughter than tears, exactly as he would have wanted.

Aunt Nora was told in a letter to take a well-earned long holiday to Spain to see her sister which, again, was paid for, and in a move that almost broke me but also made me smile, he'd left verbal instructions for me to get right back to work with no hanging around.

'Don't stop saving lives just because this one is over, Ollie,' were the exact words he'd asked Aunt Nora to pass on.

He'd also left a letter to each of us which he'd written on Christmas Day. I'd no idea he'd done so until my darling aunt gave it to me once the formalities were over, and the house was quiet again.

My last words from him were handwritten inside a snow-white card on which he'd drawn three delicate snowdrop flowers, painted in watercolours from a small collection he'd created in his younger years and saved for 'only very special occasions'.

I guess this was one of those occasions. His words, as always, packed a punch.

My dear son, Ollie,

It's Christmas Day, I'm by the fire and I can hear you and Nora singing that annoying Band Aid song in the kitchen.

You're laughing, but she is laughing louder, which is music to my old ears.

I've always said laughter warms a home, and you have brought us so much warmth and joy this Christmas by spending it here with your family. Thank you.

You'd laugh more if you knew I am writing with my 'good pen'. You remember that, don't you? My good pen always meant business.

I do mean business today, my son.

As you know, I'm sick, so sick, but my heart feels like it could burst with pride right now so even though I've been putting off writing this note, I feel that it's now or never.

I need to tell you how you've always made me so proud, Ollie. I need you to know that first and foremost.

I am proud of absolutely everything you do, of everything you stand for and every decision you make – even the wrong ones from time to time. But I'm mostly proud of how you make others around you feel.

You take time for other people no matter who they are, no matter what age they are. You make us all laugh, you go the extra mile, and you care. My God, you care so much, my darling boy.

To top it all off, you've chosen a vocation that changes the world. You heal broken hearts just like your mother always believed you could. Although I know you'd love to one day return to live in Oyster Cottage, please don't ever forget the truly special job you're doing. Think hard before you ever give that up.

To help those suffering from ill health is a gift from God. I've always believed that nurses are walking angels who soothe frightened patients and ease worried loved ones.

It's surprising how in our final hours we cling to hope and comfort from the simplest places.

Just a few moments with someone special can feel as good as a whole lifetime. Just a few words whispered when you need to hear them can sound like a whole symphony. And just a brief touch of a hand when you're frightened can reach right inside and hold your whole heart to keep it beating for a little while longer.

Look after Aunt Nora for us, won't you, Ollie. Keep making her laugh when you can, and lean on her when you must. She's a lot stronger than she looks. She also loves you as much as your parents did, so consider yourself lucky to be loved unconditionally by so many.

Your mum and I were always your biggest cheerleaders from day one, and we will continue to be just that, even if it's from up above, or alongside, or in front, or behind, wherever and whenever you need us to be there.

I'm sorry we have both left you so young. But we'll only ever be a whisper away, forever.

And by the way, I can hear you two talking now in the kitchen about love, so my view is this – in case you need it.

I believe in love at first sight with all my heart, and do you want to know why?

Because I loved you at first sight, and I always will.

Your dad, big Jack Brennan xo

I have re-read his letter at least a hundred times, lingering over each sentence and absorbing every precious word. Every time I read his words or touch the swirling letters he wrote with the 'good pen' I now keep close to me always, I absorb something new.

Grief stops us in our tracks. It puts the real world on pause as we reverse into a corner, so far from the reality we can't face just yet. We cushion our broken hearts, we build walls to protect the people in our circle and we lick our seeping wounds in the darkness until one day we are able to face the bright light and take that first baby step towards the sun again.

I've seen so much grief in the hospital, and I've seen how, although it may feel impossible, life around us doesn't stop just because we have lost someone. More people need help, more people need love and more people need to feel less lonely through a kind word or a sprinkle of humour to brighten their day.

Don't stop saving lives just because this one is over, just as my father said.

Life continues to go round and round like we're all on a

carousel, and that's what keeps those of us left behind going on too.

Soon, I'm back at work again in London where new families pace the corridors with tentative footsteps and hushed voices, new names roll off our tongues becoming part of our daily conversation in the nurses' station, and new faces full of fear stare up at us from beneath crisp white sheets – all searching for a glimmer of hope.

Life is fast; you can blink and everything changes. Nothing ever stays the same.

'They need you downstairs in Emergency, Ollie,' says the ward sister on her way past at what feels like lightning speed. 'Sorry, but Tina just called in sick so we're down cover until at least lunchtime. It's manic but I know you can handle it.'

I make my way down three floors on the lift and get stuck into the change of environment where Scott is knee-deep in paperwork.

'Welcome to the mad house,' he says, without lifting his head.

'I'm here until lunchtime. Use me and abuse me as you feel necessary, pal.'

You see, the thing I love about working in a hospital is that there is never time to feel sorry for yourself or to dwell for too long as there's always someone needing your help. There's always someone worse off, or weaker physically, or with a bigger fight on their hands than you have, and that's what keeps you humble. That's what keeps you showing up.

No two days are the same on the cardiac ward, or in the

rehab clinic, or in the Emergency department. No two patients are the same – and while few of them will remember your name, they'll never forget how you made them feel. And every one of them wants only one thing: to survive.

'You're quiet,' Scott says as we devour a sandwich on our thirty-minute break after a crazy but manageable morning.

Despite the dropping temperatures and the frost on the ground, we eat outside while leaning against a brick wall just to reset our brains – or at least that's how Scott has convinced me to do so.

He's barely recognisable in his dark green jacket which goes up over his mouth and nose on top of his uniform. He unzips it slightly between bites of his home-made ham and cheese sandwiches, which makes for comical viewing, and if it wasn't for the tufts of his bleached hair showing out beneath the fur-lined hood, he could be anyone really.

Meanwhile I'm wrapped up in my trusty black overcoat and an ancient grey monkey hat that comes down over my ears. We both share a steaming flask of tea which is at risk of sliding off a sloping, icy windowsill, all while walking on the spot as we eat to keep our blood circulating in this freezing weather.

'I'm OK,' I tell him, even though he won't believe me. 'If I zone out, just know I'm probably taking a walk down memory lane in my own head, but it's nothing to worry about.'

He stares at me as he chews his food beneath his hood.

'It's all part of the process, Scott, so no need to overthink it,' I try to explain to him. 'Thank God I love my job. Thank God he told me to get back here straight away, or I'd be stuck in bed over in Ireland overthinking around the clock while Aunt Nora sips sangria with her sister at a villa in Málaga.'

Scott raises an eyebrow.

'You still looking for a job over there?'

'In Málaga?' I tease.

'No, in Outer Mongolia,' he says back to me. 'You know what I mean. Donegal. Home. The back of beyond by the sea.'

I can't hold it from him any longer.

'I've got an interview soon for a post in Letterkenny University Hospital. I'm trying not to get my hopes up, but boy, I'm excited.'

I half expect Scott to be horrified at the very idea that I might up sticks and leave London for good, but he knows I feel the calling of home, and I imagine he'll end up moving closer to Liverpool one day, too.

'That's bloody amazing, buddy,' he says wholeheartedly. He is rubbing his nose now, which is a rather fetching bright pink colour, though I'm sure my own could give his Rudolph look a run for its money. 'I'm happy for you, genuinely so happy for you. I know this has been on your radar forever, but it can take a good whack of grief sometimes to put things into perspective and make us see what we really want in life.'

I kick a stone and let out a long, deep breath of gratitude for how my father had the chance and time to plan his last wishes. He'd never want me to change career, but he'd also want me to follow my heart, which lately has been calling me back home to Teelin and to Oyster Lane. Now it looks like that chance is finally coming my way.

'On a different subject,' says Scott, 'when were you going to tell me about seeing the mystery lady you met at the airport? And what if you bump into her again? What would that do to your big plans to move home?'

I almost choke on what's left of my sandwich.

'What are you on about, monkey brain? I did tell you all about her. I remember exactly where we were when I told you, and you said—'

'No, no, I mean about you meeting her at Kensington Gardens with Jane. Before . . .'

Before my dad died.

Scott can't say it out loud, which is fair enough. I can't really say it either.

'Gosh, news travels faster than lightning around here,' I reply. 'Does Jane tell you everything?'

'I can't believe you didn't tell me about meeting her again, that's all,' he replies, talking as usual with his mouth full even though I can't even see his mouth. 'If a girl as much as glances my way in a nightclub, I tell you all about it, down to the last detail.'

I change my walking-on-the-spot pace to a light jog.

As much as it's nice to get some fresh air to break up our shift, I'm not sure the risk of hypothermia is worth it today.

So, Jane has blabbed all about my stammering and stuttering over Bea in the park and how I turned to mush afterwards and couldn't even finish my drink when we went to the pub on the way home to thaw out.

'There's no point talking about something that's never going to happen,' I say to my colleague and friend, trying not to seem miffed that my supposed tête-à-tête with Jane has already taken wings.

'So, it wasn't love at first sight like you first thought it might be?'

I don't know whether to laugh or scream.

'Is that what Jane told you?'

'More or less,' says Scott.

That probably means 'less', then.

'She's engaged. Didn't Jane tell you that?' I remind him in my defence. 'So despite my initial romantic notions about the whole situation . . . she's engaged. Lights out. The End.'

Scott is just about to make a smart comment or offer more words of wisdom, but our conversation is interrupted by the screaming blue light that screeches to a halt by the Emergency front doors just a few feet away from where we've set up our winter picnic.

'I've a feeling that's one for us,' Scott announces, as one hand quickly unzips the front of his hood to take the last bite of his sandwich.

'For you, you mean,' I tell him. 'I'm off back to Ward Three where I belong. Time for you to work your magic, Scotty boy.'

'Magic or the morgue,' says Scott, and I shoot him a glance as we walk underneath a blast of heat at the hospital doors just ahead of the ambulance crew. That's a new one, even by his standards.

My pager bleeps to indicate a major cardiac arrest has arrived on site, so I'm not going back to the main ward as quickly as I thought I might. I'm here now, so I may as well take one for the team.

I look behind me to see the uniformed paramedics race towards us, pushing a patient on a trolley.

'A neighbour called the ambulance at 13.07,' the paramedic calls to us when we meet them on the far side of the swinging doors inside that lead to Resuscitation. 'Poor old guy was calling out for help in his ground-floor flat before he collapsed. The lady next door heard the crash through the slightly open window. Blood pressure was eighty over fifty, pulse is faint but he's still with us.'

Scott and I follow as the paramedics wheel the patient through the corridor towards the resuscitation room where the rest of the cardiac team are already on standby.

'CPR performed at the patient's residence followed by ECG en route. Sixty-four-year-old male, South London . . .'

My skin goes clammy as we march along, but I do my best to ignore it.

South London address. Sixty-four-year-old male.

I've goosebumps, and I can't think straight. What's going on?

I'm used to emergencies. I've learned to switch into autopilot and let adrenaline take over as I default into a robotic state of what has to be done, but something feels different this time.

Maybe I've come back to work too soon after losing Dad. I can't think straight.

But when I see the man's hands clasped together on his chest, my eyes widen, my heart rate rises, and I snap right back into action. Mr Gates needs me. I'd recognise that initialled gold signet ring anywhere.

'Let's go, Ollie boy,' says Scott, without noticing the look of recognition on my face right now. 'And let's try and make sure it's magic and not the morgue for this poor soul.'

Chapter Seventeen

Bea

Brixton, London

Sean's arrival into London was a bolt from the blue and although the outcome was everything I'd wished for, the reality of being single, of not hearing his voice when I need to, or the knowledge that I've always someone glad to hear from me, takes a lot of getting used to even now we're a few weeks into our break-up.

'Mum's a whole lot stronger than we think,' said Patsi when I filled her in on how I broke the news the morning after Sean's impromptu visit, and how smoothly she sailed through Peter's birthday party which I managed to get home for, even if I did act like an undercover agent in Benburb in case I bumped into Sean or any of his family.

Leroy has been a rock and a shoulder to cry on when the tsunami of fear overcame me during the past few weeks, but since he didn't turn up this evening for our Wednesday Supper Club and isn't answering his phone, I thought I'd bring my humble offerings to him to make sure he is OK.

'Leroy! Leroy, it's me. I hope you're hungry!'

I call through the letterbox of Leroy's ground-floor flat, balancing a tin foil-covered saucepan of now lukewarm Irish Stew in one woolly gloved hand, with the other holding up the tiny letterbox to try and see inside after ringing the doorbell to no avail.

'You're allowed to feel it all,' he told me the last time I was here at his tiny flat. 'Let it all out, Miss Beatrice. Just because it's what you wanted, ending a relationship with someone you care for deeply still brings a rollercoaster of emotions that can change from one minute to the next. You're allowed to miss him, you know. You're allowed to grieve for the plans you'd made and the life you'd been given even a tiny glimpse of. Let it all flow, let it all go.'

His deep Jamaican drawl always soothed me from the inside out, whether it was in person when I called on him here, or on a random phone call when I was feeling sorry for myself in my newfound loneliness.

No matter what time of day or night since I first moved to London, Leroy has been there for me, especially on Wednesdays when we'd get together for just a couple of hours.

We've played vinyl records and sung along as we enjoyed bangers and mash balanced on a tray on the sofa. We've watched game shows on telly as we munched our way through a pasta bake, and since last week's Jamaican Jerk Chicken was a challenge with just a little bit of pressure for me to get it right, we agreed it deserved candlelight at the kitchen table.

I'm much more confident this week in my Irish Stew offering, which is a recipe I put together myself, but one that's always a winner with Leroy.

Potatoes, slowly cooked steak pieces, carrots and onions, all merged like a hug in a bowl. But now I'm confused as to whether I've got our plans wrong. No, I'm almost sure we discussed this. Yes, we did, because he said he'd get some crusty bread and Irish butter to top it all off. He said he'd have to go easy on the salt and patted his chest for effect.

Oh Leroy.

'Are you there?' I call out again into the wind and rain. It's always quiet around here, apart from perhaps a few children kicking a football against the huge gable wall which bears a famous mural called Ride of the Apocalypse. Leroy loves the artwork and would never hear of it being referred to as graffiti.

I stand on tiptoes, trying to see inside the small front window of his home, imagining and hoping he may have fallen asleep.

'Leroy,' I whisper, hugging the saucepan to my chest.

My stomach sinks and my eyes fill with tears when I see his empty armchair, a blanket strewn over the side where he'd sit by the electric fire.

A mug sits on the coffee table by a bundle of newspapers and magazines I brought him earlier, and a book – Leroy always has a book – is open where he's left it, with his reading glasses on top.

My heart skips a beat at the scene before me.

I don't like what I see, but I'm repeating the possibility that he's gone to bed extra early this evening, perhaps having forgotten what day of the week it is.

'It's Wednesday Supper Club time,' I mumble to myself, gripping the handles on the saucepan as I will him to come to the door in his checked pyjamas and slippers, his dressing gown tied loosely on top and his wiry silver hair standing up as if something has given him an electric shock. 'Come on, Leroy. You don't want to miss this stew, it's a really tasty one.'

My voice is trembling. I don't know what else to do.

He didn't answer his phone today when I called to confirm like I do every week since we started our Wednesday Supper Club. And now I'm here at seven on the dot as usual, I'm wondering if I've forgotten a change of plan he may have told me about. My head has been in such a muddle lately, so there's a chance Leroy has told me of an appointment or a trip away and I wasn't listening.

But Leroy doesn't go on trips away. He doesn't have appointments outside of his work schedule at The Carnation, and he's always told me that alongside Nana our rescue dog, I'm his best friend in the world. My breathing quickens. I blow out a long, straight flow of mist to try and keep calm.

My mind goes into overdrive when I think of all the worst possible scenarios that could have led to this. Should I bang on the door harder? Why didn't I ask him for a key in case anything like this should ever happen? For months now I've been quizzing him at every opportunity on his health, on his dwindling days at the hotel – a place I know he adores like a second home.

He's been peakier than usual recently, but no matter how much I've skirted the issue, and no matter how many times I've asked him straight up for the truth, he refuses to give me any medical updates, claiming he's 'fine'. I should have pushed harder.

I don't think he's been fine for quite a while now.

I pace the pathway that runs parallel to the block of flats which has been Leroy's home for as long as I've known him. We've put the world to rights in this dark grey building where, alongside the murals, pops of winter colour in flower-pots brighten up doorsteps and windowsills in the drizzling rain.

I check the time again on my wristwatch. It's well past seven-thirty. I'm cold to the bone. I'm shaking inside with worry, and I don't know what else to do.

By the time I get to the hospital entrance I'm soaked right through to my skin, my face – which I caught in a window reflection – is flushed and my hair is dripping wet, but none of that matters at all.

I just need to see Leroy.

The thought of him being alone, so worried and afraid wherever he is now in this huge hospital, is giving me more shivers than the cold and rain outside ever could.

The man at the hospital reception scrolls down on his computer while munching on an apple, so far removed from the urgency I'm feeling inside right now as he looks for Leroy on the system.

I think of my dear old friend's sad, lonely eyes, darting

around a room looking for a familiar face but finding no one he knows to comfort him.

I want to tell the man on the desk to hurry. I want to ask why it's taking so long to find Leroy. Am I at the right hospital? Maybe his neighbour Anne got it wrong when I knocked on her door to ask where he might be? Or does the fact he can't be found mean that something awful has happened?

'Can you give me his date of birth, please?' asks the man as he sinks his teeth in and takes another bite of his crunchy apple. 'He may not have made it on to the admissions ward yet.'

I do my best to work out Leroy's date of birth in my head but the numbers won't register. I can't count right now.

'It's the seventeenth of April but I'm so sorry I can't think of the year. 1960? 1961?'

He looks up at me beneath his glasses.

'And you are?'

'Look, I know I'm not family,' I tell him. 'But please believe me when I say I'm all he has. Leroy doesn't have any family left here in London so he'll want to see me. I know he will. So, if you could, please just tell me where he is so I can go to him. I just need to go to him quickly.'

The man sighs behind the desk and fixes his eyes on his computer screen again. I lean on the counter, my head in my hands as a million scenarios go through my mind. I can't bear to imagine life in London without Leroy. I can't bear to imagine never seeing him again on the door at The Carnation or hearing his laughter or his voice when he calls me Miss Beatrice, even though I've told him a million times my name is just Bea.

A nurse brushes by in a hurry, meets my shoulder in a light clash and drops a bundle of files at my feet.

'Clumsy me,' he says, bending down to pick up the files.

I bend down too, in sync with his swift movement, my instinct to help kicking in. It might take my mind off things for a split second as I wait, if nothing else.

The nurse mutters about how he didn't see me, how it's been a long day and he's not so good at multi-tasking, which his female colleagues like to tease him about, but I'm barely listening as my head is so full of Leroy.

I blink back tears as we both rise from the floor to stand face to face with each other, and I hand him some sheets of paper he dropped.

I look into his eyes. A shiver runs right to my bones.

I push strands of wet hair off my face and let the tears that have threatened to push through fall on to my cheeks.

'Ollie?'

His mesmerising blue eyes that look like home to me stare into mine and a wave of release floods through my body like a touch from heaven.

'Bea,' he whispers, his frown dissolving into the smile I've dreamed about every single day since I last saw him in the park. 'What are you doing here? Are you OK?'

I crumble.

Without another word, Ollie sets the files on the counter

beside where we stand, shakes his head in disbelief and pulls me close to hug my soaking wet body like I've never been hugged before.

'Mr Leroy Gates is on Cardiac Three North,' says the man behind the desk at last. 'You can go ahead when you're ready.'

Chapter Eighteen

Ollie

I'm not sure which I'm in more shock over – Mr Gates's arrival at the Emergency department with a massive heart attack or seeing Bea so unexpectedly in the hospital reception.

Or realising that all along we've had Mr Gates in common.

We sit outside on a sheltered memorial bench in the hospital gardens.

The rain has stopped, giving way to a cold and frosty evening, but despite the cold, I felt it best to take Bea outside for some fresh air after finding her some clean, dry clothes from my locker to wear.

We don't talk too much.

Instead, we sit side by side under the black sky which is dotted with bright stars, a world away from the reality we are living through down here.

'I've always loved the sky in winter,' Bea whispers. 'I could stare at it forever. You know, when I was a little girl back in Ireland, I used to sit outside at night for hours by the castle where I lived. I'd pretend I was a princess who had the power to change the world.'

I watch her face under the moonlight as she speaks. She is as beautiful as the first time I saw her. As cheesy as it sounds, I could easily stare at her forever.

'I've no doubt that you've the power to change the world, Bea.'

I want to tell her that she's certainly changed my world since we first met on Christmas Eve, but that's probably far too much, too soon.

'Do you believe in heaven?' she asks me, then turns to meet my eye. 'I like to think there's something out there waiting for us when this is all over, though I'm not exactly sure what that might be.'

That's a pretty loaded question, but straight away it makes me think of my dad. I think of how lately I've heard his voice in my ear when I'm feeling low or lonely, or how I'd smell his tobacco when there was no one else around to explain where it was coming from. Or when I'd see his name, Jack, on a patient's bed just when I was thinking of how much I missed him or even when I'd hear a song he loved on the radio.

'I think there are little signs of heaven everywhere,' I tell her. 'I know that's hardly a scientific reply, but that's really what I believe. You?'

She tilts her head back so that the nape of her neck leans on the back of the wooden summer seat we're sitting on.

'I think heaven is near too,' she whispers to the sky.

'Little signs everywhere. A rainbow or a shooting star. I like to think they're signs that someone's up there looking out for us.'

'Yes.'

'I really do believe that.'

Bea smiles for the first time since I laid eyes on her this evening. She still looks so frightened, so pale and gaunt having heard the news of Mr Gates, but it's good to see her smile. I'm relieved I could take a short break on my shift to spend this time with her.

'I can't believe you and Leroy have known each other all this time,' she says, shaking her loose curls. 'Who knew we'd this massive connection between us? It's a lot to take in, isn't it?'

I haven't even paused long enough yet to let that sink in.

'Mr Gates and I go back a long way,' I explain to her. 'He's a tough old cookie in many ways. And I know we're both worried, but he's in very good hands here. We'll all take the best care of him.'

I look up at the lights in the rows of windows that dot across the hospital building's third floor where I work, mesmerised as always at how behind the pane of glass of every single window in the cardiac unit lies a person holding on tightly to life.

Meanwhile, down here, under a tiny shelter on a little summer seat erected by a patient's family, Bea sits close to me as we both cling on to the hope that Mr Gates will make a full recovery.

'I had an awful notion something had happened to him,' she tells me softly. 'I quickly handed his neighbour the Irish Stew I'd cooked. When she told me he'd called out for help, and how she'd luckily been outside at the time to hear him, I had this overwhelming feeling of hope. That the world was on his side. And then I get here and find out that you were his nurse when he arrived at the hospital.'

'It's strange because I don't normally work in the Emergency department,' I tell her. 'I work on Ward Three, but I was asked to cover for someone who'd gone home sick.'

'You know I never fly into City of Derry Airport, always Belfast, apart from that one time on Christmas Eve?'

'Maybe it was meant to be,' I whisper.

We sit so close, side by side on this little bench where hundreds of others have sat praying for a miracle.

'Is he going to be OK, Ollie? Please tell me there's still hope. I'm so scared for him.'

Bea looks up at me in a way I've never been looked at before. There's a mixture of sorrow, regret and fear alongside relief and trust in her eyes. I glance quickly at my phone to check the time.

'He's as strong as an ox,' I reply, glad I don't have to fill her head with empty promises. 'And he called for help just in time, it seems. Would you like to see him now?'

She sits up straight, then stands up as if she doesn't need to be asked twice.

'Yes, I'd really love to. Thank you.'

Her eyes travel to the small gold plaque on the bench where we've been sitting for the past ten minutes or so.

She runs her fingers along the text, reading aloud even though I know it word for word by now. I've found many moments of solace on this bench since I first came to work at the Royal Elizabeth five years ago.

'*So come with me, where dreams are born, and time is never planned. Just think of happy things, and your heart will fly on wings, forever, in Never Never Land.*'

Bea's mouth drops open in awe.

Peter Pan! 'Little signs everywhere,' she says with wide eyes.

'Let's go find Mr Gates,' I say, putting my hand on her shoulder. 'He'll be so glad to see you.'

'There you are,' says Scott, greeting us as the lift doors open. 'I'm gagging for a cuppa, mate, so good timing.'

He doesn't remark on my company, assuming, it seems, that Bea was a stranger sharing the lift with me.

'Sorry, Scott. I'll explain later,' I say with a wink.

'No worries, it's all good,' he replies, just as the lift doors close over. 'Mr Gates is awake, by the way. He's asking for you.'

With Scott out of sight, I turn towards Bea and let out a sigh that comes from the pit of my stomach.

We don't say a word, but I up my stride as Bea comes shuffling beside me.

It's a busy part of the ward, adjacent to the watchful eye of the nurses' station. I scan the board to find his bed number and lead Bea straight towards where he lies slightly propped up with pillows right beside the window.

'I see they gave you a room with a view,' I quip, the relief changing the tone of my voice instantly. 'And look who I found.'

'Miss Beatrice,' he croaks. 'My forever ray of sunshine.'

Bea rushes to Mr Gates's side and lifts his hand to her face. All the build-up of the day rises to the surface as she cries and kisses his forehead.

'Thank goodness,' she says on repeat. 'I thought I'd never see you again.'

A tear rolls down his face. I dab it with a soft tissue, then hand one to Bea who is finally getting her breath back.

As always, when a patient has emotional overwhelm after a cardiac arrest, I go into my default mode of doing my best to distract their mind a little by lightening the mood.

'Well, besides your unexpected check-in at Hotel Royal Elizabeth, who knew that we had this beautiful friend in common, Mr G?' I say to him. 'You kept that quiet, you old dark horse.'

I help him drink some water again when he reaches his hand out for more. Bea barely takes her eyes off him.

She's still wearing the spare sweater I found in my locker and although it almost drowns her, it makes her look even more adorable if that's possible. It's red, which against her dark curls reminds me of the hat and scarf she wore at the airport on Christmas Eve. She sits at Mr Gates's bedside, stroking his hand as she stares at his frail face.

'Don't even think about attending any appointments alone ever again,' she scolds, albeit in a gentle tone. 'Now that Ollie and I know we share you as our dear friend, you won't be getting away with suffering in silence any more. Thank goodness your neighbour heard you when she did.'

Mr Gates looks at me with a familiar look of panic in his eyes. But as private as he always has been when it comes to his personal life, I can sense that somewhere in his mind he is relieved to have this all out in the open. Relieved and scared as to what might have been if his neighbour hadn't come to his rescue and called an ambulance when she did.

'My reading glasses are still where I left them in the sitting room,' he says. 'I was enjoying that book a lot, not to mention looking forward to your Irish Stew, Miss Beatrice. I'm so sorry about all this trouble I've caused.'

'You've caused no one any trouble whatsoever,' whispers Bea. 'I just hope you know now how important it is to tell someone when you're as poorly as you were.'

'I've been telling him that for quite a while,' I add.

'You know, I had a feeling it was more than a burst pipe that last time you cancelled our plans,' says Bea, glancing my way. 'You've been sick all along and you've been hiding it. I should have been pushier, but you're a tough old nut to crack when it comes to it. No more secrets, you hear?'

'I hear,' he tells her. I do believe he's turned a corner when it comes to keeping everything so close to his chest. 'I consider myself well and truly told off in the nicest possible way, and by the nicest possible person.'

I can't help but smile when I see her light up as he says that.

The way she looks at him, the way she cares so much, makes me fall in love with her just a little bit more and tells me that my father was right. There is such a thing as love at first sight. The way my heart feels right now, the way she glances in my direction and our eyes meet for just a fleeting second, makes me want to believe that this was all meant to be.

'So, Miss Beatrice is the girl from the airport you were telling me about,' Mr Gates says with a light chuckle. 'You met on Christmas Eve.'

I have one hour left on my shift and for the first time in my life, I wish it would last as long as possible.

Bea's eyes light up in amazement.

'Wait a minute. You told Leroy about how we met?' she says.

'I did,' I admit.

I put a blood pressure cuff on Mr Gates's arm and pump it up until the machine bleeps for my attention. His rate is high, but that should improve with rest now that he's over the worst. With two new stents in to keep the first two from his last stay with us company, some medication, and some tender loving care, he'll be back on his feet in a few days, we hope.

'Well, I don't want to talk out of school,' Leroy replies, tapping his nose. 'But I did kind of play a part in it all.'

Both Bea and I are equally puzzled.

'I recommended that Ollie should go for a walk in Kensington Gardens at a certain time of day. I told him to pay particular attention to the Peter Pan statue where I know a certain young lady likes to walk a boisterous dog called Nana on occasion.'

'You rascal!'

I throw my hands up in disbelief.

'My old ticker might be dodgy,' he says, 'but it doesn't mean I can't do my best to play Cupid every now and then.'

Bea stares at me open-mouthed and we both laugh in disbelief at our discovery. Not only did we have this fateful link in Leroy Gates all along, but the old guy was doing his best to make sure our paths crossed again without making it seem deliberately so.

'So, you've been coming here for appointments, not telling me you were poorly and at the same time scheming so that Ollie and I would meet again?'

'I have to say I didn't expect for it to happen so soon, but yes, that's what I was hoping for,' says Mr Gates. 'And I didn't bargain on being in here in this condition, but seeing how you two young lovebirds can't keep your eyes off each other is probably the best medicine for my old ticker. It does my heart good, as the saying goes.'

Bea has tears in her eyes again.

'You're wonderful, Leroy,' she tells him softly. 'I'll pack you a bag including your book and your reading glasses. Is there anything else you'd like me to fetch for you? I'll bring a few healthy treats in too, of course.'

I fill out Leroy's latest medical information on a sheet that hangs on a clipboard at the bottom of the bed and slip off to see to my next patient as they chat, unable to wipe the smile from my face.

What a rollercoaster of a shift it has been. One minute I was reflecting with Scott on my father's passing and how much I miss him, then I was delivering CPR on a patient I've grown to know and love, and now I'm only a few feet away from the girl of my dreams who has barely left my mind since I spent those magical few hours with her on Christmas Eve.

She hasn't mentioned why she isn't wearing her engagement ring yet, and I haven't had the courage to ask her. Instead, I'll allow myself to dream that maybe, just maybe, this third meeting might be the lucky one for us both at last.

Chapter Nineteen

Bea

Ollie was not only kind enough to get me a dry sweater to wear earlier when I came in here soaked to the bone, but he also went out of his way to find a pair of fresh, clean pyjamas from the lost and found section which fit Leroy like a glove.

That, I admit, kind of stopped me in my tracks. The way he so tenderly held me in the hospital foyer, the way he explained everything to me as we sat under the stars in the garden, and how he talked to me while we made our way to where Leroy lay following the heart attack that could very easily have ended his life. And the way he brought me a cup of hot, sweet tea for shock before he left us to see to his other patients.

I watch the clock as Leroy rests. I hold his hand. I tell him how loved he is, and how much we adore him at the hotel. I tell him stories of our friendship, like the day we found Nana so cold and hungry on the streets and how much joy she has brought us both, even though he had his own reservations at first.

I remind him of the time we welcomed his all-time musical hero Tom Jones to the hotel, and how for once Leroy was lost for words when Tom broke into song after dinner in the restaurant, much to the other guests' delight.

He keeps his eyes closed as he listens. Sometimes I think he is asleep, so I'll stop talking and he'll open one eye and tell me to keep going.

And so I do.

I talk to him about how I love to see him play around with Nana at work or when he joins us on our daily walks in Kensington Gardens, and how much we both look forward to our Wednesday Supper Club nights.

I tell him how I simply can't imagine being in London without having him there to call my friend. I remind him of my very first day on the job when he lit up my heart the moment I saw him in his smart top hat with his wide, friendly smile and a hug that made me feel like I was home.

I always believe there's a comfort in hearing old stories when you're feeling vulnerable. I've always believed in the power of words to heal and help us through the toughest times.

'I'm so glad you're here,' he whispers.

His eyes are heavy now, so I slowly stroke his forehead to encourage him to sleep.

'What is the cure for a broken heart, Miss Beatrice?' he whispers. 'I would really like to know what it is.'

I'm choked, but I won't show him so. He needs us all to be strong.

'You go to sleep now, Leroy. Don't worry about a thing.

I'll be right back in the morning with your book and your reading glasses.'

'Thank you, Miss Beatrice.'

My voice breaks as I speak, and when I look away from Leroy I see Ollie standing at the foot of the bed, watching us with a tender smile on his face. I'm not sure how long he's been there for, or how much of my ramblings he may have overheard.

'You're amazing,' he whispers.

I don't think I know how to reply to that. I don't feel very amazing. I feel like I need a shower, some food and a good rest – in that order.

'He must be exhausted, poor thing,' he says to me. 'And you must be too. It's been quite a day all round.'

I watch Leroy for just another moment as he drifts into a deeper sleep.

'I'll be fine, Ollie, just as long as Leroy gets strong again,' I reply. 'He's in the safest of hands here. You guys are the best.'

Ollie is wearing his black overcoat and carries a khaki-coloured rucksack. He has finished his shift, which gives me a strange feeling of panic that I'll have to temporarily say goodbye to him again.

'I can't thank you enough for everything you did for my friend today. And for me. You've been even more wonderful than I could ever have guessed.'

He takes a deep breath in and then out again.

'Me and Leroy go way back too,' he explains gently. 'I think we first met over three years ago, so I'm quite attached to the old guy and have been for a while now. I thought of him so many times, but never wanted to see him in here again. But today I was just doing my job.'

I gather up my belongings and switch off the little night light that is attached to the wall beside Leroy's bed.

'No, you did so much more than that,' I tell him. 'You made him feel at ease, you took away a lot of his fears and you made sure I was well looked after too, even getting me some warm, dry clothes.'

'Suits you better than it does me.'

He nods at the sweater I'm wearing. I wonder should I give it back to him now or take it home and wash it first? I imagine I'll be seeing a lot more of Ollie over the next few days, which excites me despite the life-threatening circumstances that have thrown us together.

'I've never stopped thinking of you, Bea. Not once,' he says.

His words take my breath away.

'No matter what has happened in my life since – and believe me, there's been quite a bit going on, there was never a day that passed when you didn't cross my mind a million times. I just needed to say that out loud in case, in some twist of fate, I never see you again.'

I swallow hard. Ollie's words make me catch my breath.

'Same,' I tell him.

He takes a step back.

'All the time,' I whisper. 'Ollie, Sean and I . . . we broke up. Just in case you're wondering. I'm not saying that's going to make a difference now, but—'

'I'm so sorry to hear that,' he says. 'Are you OK?'

I nod. I get the feeling he can't wait to get out of here, so I put my coat on as we talk, taking one last look at Leroy before I leave for the evening.

Ollie and I walk away in step, side by side until we are out of earshot of his colleagues and the other patients who are all drifting off to sleep. There's a sense of peace on the ward as the lights go down, a feeling of calm and safety, of everything being under control.

'I was hoping to talk more,' Ollie says when I turn to face him again. 'To you. Tonight.'

I think my heart might explode when he moves closer to me.

We are on a busy hospital ward where his colleagues are tiptoeing around as the mood on the floor silences around sleeping patients. I can smell his aftershave, which brings me right back to Christmas Eve at the airport when I first knew my whole life had changed for having met him.

'I was hoping for that too,' I tell him, unable to ignore how fast my heart is beating right now.

We walk side by side until we get to the lift.

Every step feels like I'm walking on air. Even though my head is full of what could have happened to Leroy, being with Ollie means my insides are dancing with excitement at the prospect of spending some proper time in his company. I want to reach out and touch him so badly. I want to feel his fingers intertwine in mine, I want to link into his arm. I want to rest my head on his shoulder.

The lift dings and the sliding doors open. We step inside

and as soon as the doors close, it's like the rest of the world has disappeared and it's just Ollie and me in existence.

We stand side by side, unable to disguise the huge smiles that have taken over both our faces.

'So, would you like to go for dinner? I know it's late but we could grab something and talk some more?'

'Are you asking me on a date in a hospital lift?' I joke.

He pauses and I wait for a smart return.

'Don't knock it,' he says. 'These lifts are a great pick-up joint. In my spare time I like to spin up and down for hours, hoping some random member of staff or a visitor will say yes to my dinner date suggestions.'

I meet his eyes in the mirrored walls as my stomach leaps. I'm so filled up with nerves and excitement, but the slightest suggestion of a date makes me want to run for the hills. It's much too soon.

'That was my poor attempt at a joke,' he whispers, staring at the floor now. 'I'm not asking you for a date in a hospital lift.'

'Good,' I reply.

'Glad we got that cleared up,' he says. 'Though I do think it was you who mentioned it first.'

He's right. I did.

'I'm not quite sure I'm ready for dating yet, Ollie,' I tell him. 'But I'd love to get to know you better for sure.'

He shakes his head in mock horror.

'We ate together on Christmas Eve and that wasn't a date,' he reminds me, nudging me playfully. 'No need to jump to any conclusions, Miss Beatrice. I thought I heard your tummy rumbling, that's all.'

I can't help but beam from ear to ear when he calls me by the same nickname as Leroy does. He really doesn't miss a beat.

'Chinese?'

'I quite fancy sushi,' he quips in return.

'Are you serious? At this time?'

'I'm very serious,' he replies, flipping a coin. 'Heads or tails?'

'Now you really must be joking. There's no way I'm going to end this crazy day on the flip of a coin, especially when food is at stake.'

When Ollie raises an eyebrow and leans closer, smelling so fresh, I feel like my heart might explode.

Leroy, with his delicate and broken heart, has no idea what he may have started.

Chapter Twenty

Ollie

We are seated right by the window in one of my favourite Chinese restaurants in South East London.

'So, do you always win arguments, or do you let others win sometimes?' I ask Bea, who is not letting it go that she got her own way after she agreed to flip a coin to choose which type of food we'd dine on. When it came to it, Bea took the challenge very seriously, insisting it was the best out of three turns.

'I'm not usually competitive at all,' she pleads. 'I mean it. I'm normally a bit of a walkover when it comes to decision-making on a social level, but sushi on an empty stomach is no way as good as these steaming hot noodles and spicy sauces.'

'Sacrilege.'

'Come on, Ollie. You have to give me that one. My choice was better.'

I'm glad to have had time to quickly shower at work and change out of my uniform, but never in my wildest dreams did I think I'd be having dinner with Bea sitting opposite me, wearing my red hoodie and looking as beautiful as ever.

I can't take my eyes off her, nor do I think I'll ever grow tired of hearing my name on her lips.

We chatted like old friends all the way here and I don't think there's been room for a gap in our conversation since we sat down at the table. The restaurant is quiet, it's just past ten-thirty on a Wednesday night, and as the wind howls and rain lashes outside on the windowpane, there's simply no place I'd rather be.

Bea is entranced by the décor and can barely concentrate on her sizzling beef and noodle dish as new elements of the restaurant keep catching her eye. I chose my usual satay chicken but we agreed to share, which is just the type of company I enjoy best when it comes to late night Chinese food.

'I'll give you full credit though for suggesting we come here,' she says, taking in her surroundings in minute detail. 'And look, they even have a tropical fish tank.'

'A sign of abundance and prosperity,' I inform her, 'so having ornamental fish in water at the front of the restaurant symbolises wealth and draws good luck to their business.'

'Not just a pretty face,' she says, holding her chopsticks in mid-air. Because she won the toss, I challenged her to be authentic and eat with chopsticks rather than a knife and fork. So far, she's playing a blinder.

But she's right. This restaurant has a very eye-catching interior, which is exactly why I chose it.

Wooden tables and chairs are separated by carved dividers for intimacy; bamboo and cherry blossoms decorate the walls and the room is lit by real Chinese lanterns in reds and golds, while soft Asian music plays in the background.

'Look at the dragons, Ollie,' she squeals, noticing how the walls have the faintest outline of tiny dragons drawn in what looks like gold leaf. 'They're hand-painted, I can tell.'

She runs her fingers delicately over the fine gold paint on the wall beside her, taking in every exquisite detail.

Now that I know exactly where she works, her passion for interiors doesn't surprise me. I've never been to The Carnation, but from what I heard from Mr Gates, it sounds like something from the pages of a very high-end, boutique magazine with every room a masterpiece in design.

I wonder how I hadn't made the connection between Leroy and Bea before. I suppose a patient's job is the last thing on my mind when we're dealing with life-or-death conditions, though I know Leroy did tell me at least once that he worked in the plush surroundings of a five-star hotel which overlooked Kensington Gardens. And if I'd told him her name, he'd have been able to direct me right into her path, which is exactly what he did anyhow using his own intuition.

Clever old Leroy.

'I hope Leroy's OK tonight,' Bea whispers like she's just read my mind. She looks out through the rain-splattered window on to the puddles that splash beneath cars and buses as they race by on the busy street. 'I know he doesn't like sleeping anywhere but his own bed. He doesn't even stay in the hotel when he finishes late and the manager offers a room.'

I want to hold her hand to reassure her, but I'm doing my best not to come across too familiar. She's made it very clear that she is nowhere near ready to jump into the dating scene, so I'll fully respect that. Just being in her company and connecting with her again is more than enough.

'I can text one of my colleagues on the ward if you'd like some reassurance,' I suggest, lifting out my phone. She nods in appreciation, so I send a quick text message and within a few minutes I've got an answer from one of the team. 'Sleeping and comfortable. He's in the very best hands, Bea. Please try not to worry.'

'Thank you.'

She lights up at that and tucks into her food, so I do the same as we talk about everything we've lived through since that Christmas Eve at the airport, which in many ways feels like a lifetime ago.

'And how's your Aunt Nora managing back at home?' Bea asks me when we talk about my dad. I told her of his passing on our journey to this restaurant, determined not to load her with heavy conversation but still feeling it's something she should know. 'You did say she lives close to you guys over there, didn't you?'

'Yes, she does, that's right,' I tell her. 'She lived with us for years after we lost Mum but eventually bought a cottage on the same lane. She's still more or less part of the furniture at Oyster Cottage. I think she's the opposite of Leroy when it comes to sleeping in her own bed.'

'Ha, really?'

'Oh yeah. Aunt Nora often jokes she likes to sleep around.'

'What?'

'Not in that way,' I say swiftly. 'She loves to travel when she gets a chance, that's all. She's in Málaga at the moment.'

'Good for her.'

'I totally agree,' I reply. 'She spent years looking after me and then cared for my father when he took ill, so I'm delighted she's able to go and have some fun in the sun. She may as well. As she keeps reminding anyone who will listen, she's only seventy-eight.'

Bea looks impressed.

'She sounds like an absolute whirlwind,' she says, twirling more noodles on to her chopsticks. 'And hang on, did you say Oyster Cottage? Is that the name of your family home?'

I lean back to take a break from eating. Of the two separate dishes in front of us, I think I've already wolfed down at least my fair share, so I need to slow down.

'Yes, it's a bed and breakfast,' I tell her. 'Well, it used to be a full blazing bed and breakfast experience and visitors flocked to it from all over the world, but in the past year or so my dad and aunt began to run out of steam.'

'That makes sense, I guess.'

'They've kept it open for selected loyal guests. It was a very exciting, unique playground to grow up in, that's for sure.'

Bea is now taking a break too, it seems. Either that or I've totally captured her attention now by talking about my home across the sea.

'Next you'll be telling me there's a beach and a pub and

lots of wild walkways to get lost in,' she laughs. 'And I suppose there's a garden too and a host of bedrooms with creaky taps and squeaky floorboards that ooze character. Wait. You're nodding. Does such a place really exist?'

'You've just described it to a tee,' I say, moving closer to the table again. I lean my elbows either side of my plate and clasp my hands, which I know my late mother would have tapped my wrists for. 'It's in a village called Teelin in an Irish-speaking region of Donegal, very close to the cliffs at Slieve League, and yes, a choice of blue flag beaches within a very short driving distance. There's a job for you there if you want.'

Bea stares at me with her mouth open.

'Don't tempt me! Can I please just ask why the hell are you in London?' But before I get a chance to explain that I might not be for much longer, she keeps talking. 'I mean, I'm not for one second suggesting you ditch your career in nursing. I've seen you in action and they don't make people like you every day. But it sounds like a heavenly place to live, it really does.'

I want to tell her about the job application and the interview at Letterkenny Hospital next week. I want to tell her that this is an opportunity I've been watching out for since I first got here. I know she'll understand exactly why I want to go back – especially now she's heard more about my homeplace – but I don't want to tell her just yet. I don't want to cut our friendship short before it's properly started, and I'm afraid if I do tell her then she'll go her way and I'll go mine again.

'Aunt Nora is going to keep an eye on the place for now,' I explain. 'Obviously, the bed and breakfast in a traditional sense will stop for a while, but now that Dad's gone and Nora has her wings back, I might look into an Airbnb approach in the meantime, maybe hire someone in to help run the place like it should be.'

Bea seems enthralled.

'Why did you want to be a nurse?' she says. It's a question I've been asked so many times I could recite my answer in my sleep, but when Bea poses it I know she isn't asking me with the usual thought in mind.

'You mean why didn't I train to be a doctor?' Bea opens her mouth to answer but I step back in quickly. 'I'm kidding, you know I am. Here's the short, easy answer. I wanted to help bust the myth that caring professions are only for women.'

She seems impressed by that, but as always with Bea, there are more questions.

'Interesting, but can you give me the harder, longer answer too?'

I pause and take a deep breath, as if Bea has opened Pandora's box.

'You sure? No one has ever asked for that before.'

'No one else is as nosey as me,' she replies. 'Well, I like to say interested rather than nosey . . .'

I'm not sure why I've never told anyone this before, but I imagine it's because most people are satisfied with the first answer.

'OK, here we go,' I say, taking a deep breath. 'It's kind of a tip of the hat to my late mother. Like something I could do in her memory.'

She sits up straighter in her chair across from me.

'Oh?'

'She was an artist who was very in touch with nature and spirit, but she also had a deep respect for those in the caring professions,' I explain. 'She fought a fierce battle to get pregnant and lost four babies before I came along, so when I did, you can imagine how elated she was. It was what she wanted more than anything in the whole world. And then, as I was growing up . . .'

I stop for a moment, as an unexpected grip of emotion chokes me.

'Anyhow, yes, when I was a little boy, she'd hold me at night and tell me that I'd the charm to mend a broken heart, and that I'd fixed hers,' I explain.

'Oh Ollie, that's beautiful.'

'So, when she died, I decided I wanted to see if she was right. I wanted to see if I can fix broken hearts quite literally, and I trained to be a cardiac nurse. I'm not sure it's the type of fixing she meant, but in a practical sense it was the closest thing I could think of.'

Bea rubs her arms and shivers.

'That just gave me goosebumps,' she whispers.

'That's what all the girls say,' I reply, then quickly jump in again before she gets the wrong impression. 'I'm kidding. I don't think I've told anyone that before in so much detail. Thank you for asking for the long answer.'

She breathes out long and slowly, as if I've just knocked her for six.

'Wow, Ollie, that's really beautiful.'

'Just a wee memory I like to hold on to. Kind of means that she didn't die in vain.'

'What type of artist was your mother?'

The brief claw of grief has passed as quickly as it crept up on me, and I'm now at ease, delighted to be able to share stories of my mum with someone who seems genuinely interested.

'She was insanely talented,' I say, feeling a deep glow inside as I speak of her. 'She sold paintings all over the world, she loved interiors and everything about the world of hospitality, too, which Dad later believed was a work of art in itself.'

'I suppose it is when you think about it,' Bea agrees. 'Everything we do in life has an artistic side, I believe.'

'Yes,' I agree. 'Yes, it does.'

I'm on a bit of a roll now as I go down memory lane in my head, talking like an excited teenager about my childhood.

'Our guests at Oyster Cottage were treated like royalty and Mum had it down to a fine art,' I explain. 'She'd a knack for making every single person feel totally unique and welcome, always going that extra mile to make Oyster Cottage an experience and not just somewhere to rest your head for the night.'

Bea tilts her head to the side, drinking in every word I say with eyes full of wonder.

'It sounds like she was well and truly ahead of her time,' she says softly.

'She most definitely was,' I tell her. 'My Aunt Nora tried to keep it going at the same level, bless her, but she never had the flair or patience or commitment that her younger sister had. And I mean that with the greatest respect.'

'What was your mother's name?'

I swallow, feeling a pull of emotion once more.

'Her name was Eleanor,' I croak. 'Eleanor and Jack Brennan. Two beautiful people inside and out.'

I picture my parents together again now in some other realm, and it makes my stomach lift in the way it used to when Dad would drive over a hill too quickly in the car. Then in a heartbeat I'm a boy again, opening their bedroom door in the middle of the night and crawling in between the two of them where I snuggle into the safest place in the whole world.

I don't know where that thought came from, but it hits me hard.

'Ollie?'

'I'm talking too much about myself now,' I say quickly.

'No, you aren't, I promise,' Bea reassures me.

'I am,' I reply. 'Tell me something about you, Bea. About where you come from and who you are. Why did you come to London?'

She tucks her dark hair behind her ear and looks away fleetingly.

'A happy accident brought me here and opened my eyes to a whole new world, but like you I think of home always.'

The enthusiasm in her voice is a welcome contrast to where I was heading in my thoughts, which I'm grateful for. I haven't failed to notice how Bea picks me up instantly with the energy she radiates, even when she's sad.

'Go on.'

'I feel incredibly lucky to come from a very beautiful place, too,' she continues. 'It isn't a cottage by the sea, but an ancient little village in Tyrone called Benburb. The river, the people, the walks amongst the bluebells, the rolling green fields, the memories of more innocent times keep me going when I get pangs of homesickness, which I do on occasion even though I love it here in London too.'

'Do you still have family there?'

'I do,' she says, but she doesn't go any further, at least not for now. I fear that I may have said something wrong, so I go back to the rice and chicken on my plate. 'A sister . . . and . . .'

When I glance back towards Bea again, she is staring out through the window into the rain.

'Are you OK, Bea?'

She turns and smiles, then reaches across and takes my hand for just a second.

'I'm so glad we found each other again, Ollie,' she says, her eyes fully engaged as she looks into mine. 'I can't wait to get to know you more. You're one in a million.'

I'm a little confused at how a question about her family brought this on, but I don't need to ask as she continues.

'My only brother, Peter, died of leukaemia seven years ago when he was only twenty-three years old,' she tells me. 'Losing a sibling leaves a massive, gaping hole inside, much

233

the same, I imagine, as losing a parent when you're young, like you did. He was my very own little Peter Pan and I've been nursing a broken heart ever since we lost him.'

'That's incredibly tough,' I say. 'I'm so sorry to hear about your brother.'

Peter.

So that's why she likes the walk in Kensington Gardens and why the memorial bench at the hospital earlier this evening stopped her in her tracks. Her own Peter Pan.

'It catches my breath every day,' she replies. 'Anyhow, I hope that one day you can come to Benburb and meet my parents and see it all for yourself. My sister Patsi lives in Paris now, but my mum and dad are still there in a little bungalow by the river. I'd love to show you around.'

She takes a drink from her glass of water and sniffs, then finds a tissue in her pocket and gently dabs the insides of her eyes.

'For someone who didn't want to call this a date, we're moving pretty fast with an invitation to meet your parents,' I say, hoping to make her laugh again.

It works, but there are still tears in her eyes as she giggles at the suggestion of this being a date, when she's so adamant that it's not.

'Sorry, I'm just tired and emotional,' she says, then perks up a bit. 'My goodness, Ollie. What a day! I certainly wasn't expecting all of this when I woke up this morning.'

'Me neither,' I say, eyeing up the leftovers on the table, hoping that we can at least get a doggy bag. I don't think I could eat another bite. 'You finished? I'll get the bill if so.'

'Yes, that was just what the doctor ordered. Thank you.'

'You must be exhausted.'

'I'm shattered, totally wiped, but thank you for a very special finish to a strange day,' she says. 'You've been amazing, really. But I'd a feeling you would be.'

'Right, let's get you home to your own bed,' I say, noticing how her eyes are getting heavier by the minute. 'But first of all, can I please have your number so we don't need to depend on fate or Mr Gates ending up in hospital before we can cross paths again?'

Bea puts her yellow coat on over my red hoodie. She rattles off her number which I punch into my phone, then I send her a WhatsApp with a smiling emoji.

'I hope you didn't send me a thumbs up,' she says, shooting me a side eye glance as she fixes her coat. She has the most engaging eyes. 'Number one rule. Never, ever send a thumbs up.'

I lean forward and whisper to her.

'You really are tired and emotional.'

'I am. Now, let's get out of here,' she says, waving across with a smile to the waiter, who brings the card machine our way. 'Let me get this. You can pay next time.'

'Next time?'

'Yes, next time.'

She catches my eye and we both light up at the very idea of a next time.

This has been a tough day, but it's also been the best day. I'm already looking forward to tomorrow, which is something I haven't felt in a very long time.

Chapter Twenty-One

Bea

Kensington Church Street, London
April

One of my very favourite things to do on my days off in springtime London is to wrap up warm, take Nana on the lead and spend hours browsing along the wide range of antiques and fine art on Kensington Church Street.

Many of the dealers who exhibit at prestigious antique fairs like the world-respected Masterpiece London, Olympia, Maastricht and New York Armory have their showrooms here, so walking along this historic street is like stepping into a treasure chest, with everything from Asian art to antique furniture, clocks and jewellery.

Nana loves it too. She likes to follow her nose as we walk from shop to shop, sniffing the ground as if she too is hunting for gold. I often wonder if it's the smell of the old furniture or the fact that some of the dealers know us so well by now that they always have a tasty little treat ready for her in case we pop by. A few welcome Nana into their showroom, while most prefer if we look through the window from outside due to the value of their stock, but either way it's my favourite way to browse with a coffee in hand, and Nana by my side.

I can rarely afford to buy anything on Kensington Church Street, but it's food for my soul to window-shop and dream of one day being able to fill my home with precious objects like I see every day at The Carnation.

'You have an exquisite eye, Bea,' says Victor, one of the friendly dealers who I've got to know from my regular visits here. Victor, who is delightfully flamboyant and as tea stained with fake tan as some of the furniture he sells, catches me staring at a writing bureau which is quite like one that sits by the window in one of our suites looking out on to the palace grounds. 'This style of desk became very popular when it was purchased by the Prince Regent for Carlton House, his palatial London home. The desk was synonymous with the Prince's taste for not only French furniture, but for fine English furniture too.'

'How much?' I ask, only out of curiosity and wonder.

'Twenty-four thousand,' he replies with a polite nod.

'I'll take two, then,' I joke. 'You can deliver to my usual address in Mayfair.'

Victor and I have become good friends over the years. He often boasts how he managed to sway my taste in theatre from jukebox musicals to classics and opera, and I guess that's true. We've had many great evenings out ever since we first hit it off when we met at the hotel, where he dines often with his partner Terence.

'I like to take in every crevice on these pieces of furniture and try to imagine who may have sat at this desk and what type of letters they wrote,' I say to him in awe as he ruffles Nana's fur, much to her delight. 'Your customers, I mean your real customers as opposed to bluffers like me and Nana, must have lived the most exquisite lifestyles.'

Victor glances around to make sure a very ordinary-looking elderly couple who are also browsing don't hear him.

'Old money mostly,' he whispers with a wink of his eye. 'And none of them are remotely as charming as you and dear Nana. Now, how's Mr Gates? I hope he's still on the mend after being so poorly?'

I'm very touched at Victor's kind comments and his enquiry about Leroy's health. It's been a long few weeks for all of us, especially Leroy, as we waded through a wide range of emotions, going from the elation of him surviving his health scare to the realisation of how terribly wrong it could have gone.

'I think the nurses at the hospital miss his wit and joviality,' I tell Victor. 'But it's good to have him home and settled in his own environment again. He's reading a new book every few days and his neighbour Anne checks in on him when I'm at work, but all he wants is to get back on his feet so he can join us again at The Carnation in time for the summer season.'

'I can imagine he's had quite a scare,' says Victor. 'And I don't blame him. I'd miss The Carnation too if I couldn't pop by as often as I do.'

'Yes, but I keep reminding him to be patient, as has Ollie,'

I tell him. 'We all only want the best for Leroy, and we don't want to risk any more heart problems. He's a very special person.'

Victor raises an eyebrow playfully at the mention of Ollie.

'And speaking of special people, I can't help but notice how you talk about this Ollie person quite a lot lately,' he says. 'Has anyone else remarked how you light up from the tips of your toes to the top of your head at the mere mention of his name?'

I roll my eyes, though there's no point denying it. Ollie and I have both been enjoying each other's company for six whole weeks now since that fateful day when Leroy was unwell. Finding time to get to know each other around our working hours is sometimes like trying to choreograph a rigorous ballet, but we text constantly in between and have managed to walk in Kensington Gardens with Nana at least twice a week, as well as eating out together as often as we can.

I still won't call it dating though.

It's too soon after seven years with Sean for me to jump straight in, so I'm very lucky that Ollie is giving me the time and space that I've asked him for.

'Ollie and I are getting on like the proverbial house on fire,' I say to Victor, knowing he would love to hear much, much more juicy detail. 'He's very funny, very caring, and if I do say so, very easy company.'

Victor almost does a jig on the spot with excitement.

'Handsome too,' he says, clasping his tanned hands together. 'Oh, you two seem like a match made in heaven,

Bea. Please don't let him slip through your fingers – he sounds like one in a million. Now, I'd better get back to Madame and Monsieur Arnault over there. They have their eye on a very fine set of bronze statues bearing the Val d'Osne Foundry Inscription. You two have a lovely day. Please pass on my regards to Mr Gates when you see him next. And bring Ollie here one day. I'd love to meet him.'

Nana wags her tail as we leave Victor to his paying customers, and we head off to browse around some more shops along Church Street, which is a great distraction from my tendency lately to check my phone every few minutes, knowing there'll be some sort of communication from Ollie, be it a funny photo of something going on in his day, or a cheeky-faced selfie or an enquiry as to what I'm up to.

I'm enjoying every moment of this whole new world with Ollie, and I often think back to that moment when he joined me at the table in Heathrow on Christmas Eve. Who would have thought back then that we'd be so inseparable now, even if we've resisted any physical touch yet. But not for much longer. Like Victor said, I can't let him slip between my fingers and I know Ollie has been super patient as I detach from my relationship with Sean on every level.

Ollie messages just as I'm examining a rather delightful, and of course high-priced, gold Italian tea-set in a shop window at the far end of Church Street. I open his text with my usual anticipation and excitement.

Swim done. Sauna now then gym session. Any plans later? Dinner?

His message is accompanied by a rather eye-watering photo of him, bare-chested after his swim and looking very buff and almost edible with wet hair and a sexy dark stubble. My heart skips a beat, reminding me how I just can't resist him physically, and although I'm doing my best to go slowly, my insides leap when I see him, every single time.

I'm hooked. And it feels so good to know he is too.

So, it's time for me to step it up a gear at long last. We usually grab a bite together somewhere in town, but tonight I think we need to try somewhere more intimate and see where it takes us.

Dinner at mine, six p.m.? I suggest. I'll cook some pasta. You bring the wine.

He messages me straight back with another photo showing a very puzzled face, which makes my stomach do a somersault. Is it possible for him to get more gorgeous by the second?

Wait a minute – you're inviting me to your flat? Not to a restaurant or a pub?

Yes.

Is this a date?

Maybe, I reply, smiling ridiculously as I stare at the screen, waiting for the usual string of emojis to come through as I hold off on labelling our growing connection.

My eyes water when I scroll back to the photos he sent post swim. How the hell have I resisted him for so long? I deserve a medal – or else a kick up the backside for being so stubborn.

'We need some cooling down,' I say to Nana, who as

always shows her full support by doing exactly as I ask her to. 'I think it's time for a Sunday treat, what do you say?'

She wags her tail with just the appropriate amount of enthusiasm, so we make our way to buy some gelato to finish off our day. I choose a calorific salted caramel delight and its flavour pops an outrageous silky experience for the tongue, while Nana gives her full four-paws approval to a whipped cream 'puppuccino'.

'Here we go, Nana,' I tell my furry friend. 'Let's find a place to sit and watch the world go by. What do you say? Yes? That's a good girl.'

We stroll along the street until we find a bench just across from the Churchill Arms, which is famously dripping in flowers on the outside, and crammed with memorabilia once you step inside its doors. Ollie and I had lunch there one day recently. My eyes glisten at the memory of some of the insightful conversations we've had about life and love and everything in between.

Nana lies on the pavement by my feet now, her long pink tongue making sure there isn't one dribble of her well-earned treat left, while I watch the famous London red buses rush past and listen to the flurry of accents that linger in the air with tourists and shoppers posing for photos at every turn.

I close my eyes for a moment and take in the sounds and smells of this culturally rich side of London. Sundays can be a lonely day for me when I'm not working, but today my heart is full of springtime joy as I count my blessings for all I have.

I have a good life here, one that fills my soul every day

when I get to do a job I love every single second of. I have my crew at The Carnation who are more like family than colleagues, a warm and cosy flat all to myself which I've decorated to my own taste. I have Nana, I have Leroy, Sita and Victor and of course now I have Ollie.

Sweet, funny, beautiful Ollie.

I also have butterflies every single time I think of him, which is more or less every waking moment of my day.

I can't wait to see him this evening.

'Come on, Nana,' I say when we've both finished our treats and rested a while. 'Let's get you back to The Carnation where Preston will look after you for the evening. I'm cooking for a very special guest tonight. I just need to figure out what I should wear.'

Later in the evening, my flat smells like an Italian dream with a blend of fresh tomatoes, basil, garlic and red wine sauce simmering on the stove, and a feast of peppers, mushrooms and courgettes slowly roasting in a drizzle of olive oil in the oven.

All I need to do when Ollie gets here is throw some pasta into a pot of boiling water and we're all set for an evening together where there's no waiter checking in on us, no pub landlord calling last orders and most importantly, no closing time, meaning we can stay together as long as we want to.

Patsi calls me just before six to hear how my preparations are coming along.

'Are you going to jump his bones, or what?' she asks me. 'It's been six whole weeks now of hearing how mad you are about him. Oh, I hope this evening goes well for you, sis. You deserve all the happiness in the world.'

I laugh at her enthusiasm, but she's right. Every time I think of Ollie arriving here this evening, I can't fathom how I'm going to resist touching him, kissing him and holding him any longer. I've been skirting the issue for long enough now.

Tonight's the night – if he agrees, of course. I've a feeling he might.

When my intercom buzzes to tell me he has arrived, I take one last look around to make sure everything is as perfect as it can be. I've lit candles, I've blasted the heating system so the flat is warm and cosy, and I've asked Alexa to play some easy listening music to make sure the mood is calm, romantic and relaxed.

'Am I early?' he asks, kissing me lightly on the cheek when I open my door to him. 'Wow, look at you.'

I do a twirl in my casual but subtly sexy, I hope, pale blue tea dress.

'Come in, come in. You're very welcome.'

'I won't lie. I asked my Uber driver to do an extra lap of the neighbourhood so I wouldn't seem too keen by coming at six on the dot, but it's six on the dot and I couldn't wait any longer,' he says.

He looks and smells delicious, even more appealing than the dish I've prepared for us to eat. His wavy dark hair is swept back off his face and he is wearing a black T-shirt under a soft bomber jacket with blue jeans and trainers. I do my best not to drool.

'I've been watching the clock too,' I say, unable to hide my delight to see him. 'Come and make yourself at home. It's so nice to have you here at last.'

I take his jacket and hang it up on the cloak stand I keep by my door. My flat reflects my taste in design, with lots of green potted plants and white walls, and a faded tan leather sofa sits by a low table where I keep my collection of interior magazines. In the tiny but compact kitchen area, which looks out on to the sand-coloured tower of St Peter's Church in Notting Hill, I've set the table impeccably with tall, elegant crystal glasses and my best vintage crockery.

'You've gone all out,' Ollie says when he sees my table display. 'You've got an admirable style, Bea. I mean, I always knew you did, but this place is very impressive. Very chic.'

'Thank you,' I reply. 'I aim to please.'

We hold each other's gaze for a few seconds, but there's something different about him this evening that I've noticed already. Something that spells there's more than dinner on his mind, and I don't mean anything romantic. He seems a little distracted, or nervous.

Maybe it's just because I've invited him into my home for the first time.

'Have a seat,' I suggest. 'Everything OK?'

'Everything is fine,' he assures me, but I'm not quite convinced. 'Relax. I'm looking forward to our evening.'

'Can I get you a drink while I serve up? I have beer, wine or—'

'A beer would be perfect, thank you,' he replies. 'Bea?'

'Yes?'

'Have I ever told you how beautiful you are?'

I stop in my tracks, then look over my shoulder to him with a smile.

'You have,' I whisper. I don't know why but I feel tears sting my eyes.

I can feel him watching me from where he sits at the table, then I see his eyes darting around the walls where I have framed posters on display of some of the iconic imagery I've collected during my years living here in Notting Hill.

'Those pieces are all I can afford for now when I go around the markets and antique fairs,' I tell him. 'But one day I'll have my own hotel to decorate. Now, wouldn't that be the ultimate dream.'

We eat and talk like we always do, catching up on every minute detail of our lives since we last saw each other, which was a grand total of three days ago when we went to the cinema to see a re-run of the Cohen brothers' classic, *The Big Lebowski*.

'Have you always lived here alone?' he asks me. 'It seems a nice neighbourhood.'

'It is. I like it, even though it's quite a lot to keep up with since my sister and another friend from home left for pastures new,' I explain. 'Patsi is loved up in Paris as I've already told you, while Christine went back home to Ireland to marry her childhood sweetheart.'

'Like you thought you would do too some day?'

My stomach leaps at the thought of it.

'Like everyone else thought I would.'

He nods knowingly. 'How is Sean?'

'I think he's doing fine,' I tell him. 'It's hard, but we both know deep down it was the right decision.'

He asks me about my parents, and in turn I ask him about his Aunt Nora who has returned from her lengthy stay in Málaga and is now adjusting to life without his dad on Oyster Lane.

'She's finding it all very strange, but I guess that's to be expected,' Ollie explains, his face scrunching up at the thought. 'When I went back on my flying visit to see her last week, I was shocked at how frail she looked. I was expecting her to be full of chat after visiting her sister for two whole months, but I think Dad's passing has had a bigger effect on her than I could have imagined. She's very lonely.'

I offer him some seconds, which he takes with gratitude, and I pour some more wine for both of us.

Ollie brought a woody, deep Malbec which goes impeccably with our tomato pasta dish. I couldn't have chosen better if I'd tried.

'I'm sure she was very glad to see you, even if it was only a quick hello,' I say, still unable to shake the feeling that there's something else on his mind. I want so badly to sit closer to him, to reach out and hold him tonight – and in the back of my mind, I know I'm going to want him to stay with me.

'She was very glad to see me,' he says, then he sits back

in his chair and closes his eyes. 'And she was very sad to see me go.'

He plays with his food for a moment. Then he sits back and lets out a long, deep breath.

'Bea, there's no easy way of saying this.'

Oh God.

'I knew there was something,' I whisper. 'What's happened? Are you all right? Is it Aunt Nora?'

He nods his head slowly, as if he's willing himself to just spit it out once and for all.

'I've had something on my mind for a few days now, and I've wrestled with how to tell you,' he replies. 'The timing of it all couldn't be more ironic. I swear I've hardly slept, wondering if I'm doing the right thing, but I hope you understand.'

I have no idea what's coming.

'And maybe you won't care so much,' he continues. 'Maybe it's me who will have to learn to live with it, but it's just so damn typical that after looking for you and wishing for you and hoping that one day I'd bump into you again . . . these past weeks have been incredible, Bea. The happiest days I've ever had here in London, no competition. I couldn't have asked for any more after Dad died, and I don't mean that to come across like you've been some sort of crutch because you haven't. You're so much more than that.'

I take a sip of my wine. It doesn't taste so good any more and the tangy tomato sauce from my cooking feels wrong in my mouth now too.

'I don't blame you if you've grown tired of waiting for me,' I tell him, hoping it might make it easier for him to tell me what's on his mind, but my heart is thumping with fear that I've pushed him into the friend zone for too long. Has he met someone else?

I hear Victor in my head, warning me not to let a good person like Ollie slip through my fingers. I get fast-forward images and sounds of all our conversations where I put him off any notion that we might be any more than friends, no matter how I felt inside. I hear Patsi's words of wisdom telling me to hurry up and go for it, and Leroy's matchmaking efforts when he said he knew if I met Ollie again something magical would happen.

'Never,' he says, staring at the table. 'No, it's not that at all.'

'Tell me, Ollie.'

He reaches across the table and takes my hand.

'I know you've done long distance before and it didn't work out.'

Ah.

'I've made it no secret that I've always been searching for a job closer to home, ever since I got to London,' he tells me. I can feel my lip quiver, but I can't make this harder for him than it evidently is. I need to stay strong. 'I've finally been successful after a lot of searching.'

'You've got a job in Ireland?'

'Yes. I've accepted a job at Letterkenny hospital in Donegal.'

He takes another deep breath.

'I'm going back home to live in Oyster Cottage,' he continues. 'Aunt Nora needs me there, and as wrong as the timing feels now, I know it's the right decision. London has never felt like home to me.'

I force a smile, but beneath my own disappointment that I'll no longer be able to see him when I want to, deep inside I'm bursting with happiness for Ollie. I know how much this means to him.

'I'm so happy for you,' I whisper, wiping tears from my eyes. 'That hospital will be very lucky to have you on their team.'

He stands up from the table and puts his hands in his pockets, pain etched all over his beautiful face.

'But what does this mean for us?' he asks. 'Will there ever be an "us" at all, Bea?'

I push my chair back and stand up just opposite him. I can barely breathe. All I want to do is run into his big, strong arms and lay my head on his chest and tell him that yes, there will be an 'us'. There has to be an 'us'. It's what we both seem to want more than anything.

But I know better than anyone that Donegal and London are like two parallel worlds. It will take flights and even more difficult choreographed meet-ups around two jobs that require very antisocial hours.

'I'm so, so happy for you, I really am,' I say as tears run down my face. 'But you're right. I can't do long distance again – not in a romantic way, anyhow. It's too hard. It's lonely and it's—'

He looks up to the ceiling.

'I don't expect you to,' he whispers.

'I'm so proud of you, Ollie,' I tell him. 'And I know your mum and dad would be too.'

He nods and manages a faint smile, then he looks right into my eyes. We are breathing in sync in the middle of my tiny kitchen, where earlier I'd imagined we'd be laughing and making plans for a very different future.

'My feelings haven't changed for you. I hope you know that. They never will.'

I bite my lip. I want to turn away from him and cry, but I'm doing my best to stay strong.

'So, when do you go?' I ask him. I'm almost afraid of the answer. The past six weeks have been a non-stop high and now, just like that, it seems like it's over.

'I should have told you earlier, but I couldn't find the words,' he replies. 'I leave on Friday.'

'This Friday?'

'Yes, this Friday,' he says, with his eyes closed again. 'I travel home by boat from Liverpool to Belfast this Friday. You will keep in touch with me, though?'

'Always,' I tell him.

'Does heartbreak have room for dessert?' I ask eventually.

I have absolutely no appetite left, but I've a light lemon cheesecake in the fridge and it may as well be eaten.

'I can give it a try,' he says with a smile. 'I'm going to miss you so much, Bea.'

'Likewise,' I tell him, doing my best to stay calm and composed after his shocking news. This is not how I'd envisaged our evening together at all. I'm happy for him, of course, but like he said himself, the timing is far from ideal.

I serve up the cheesecake then I watch him eat it in front of the television. He puts down his plate and stretches out his arm for me to come closer. I hesitate at first, but his smile and the look in his eyes brings me to my feet. I sit beside him, rest his head on my chest and then he holds me on the sofa until I fall asleep in his arms.

I'm lost in some sort of a hazy dream when he kisses my cheek, puts a blanket around me and then tiptoes out of my flat, taking my heart and all my hopes and dreams with him.

How can something so beautiful have to end already when we've only just begun?

Chapter Twenty-Two

Ollie

Oyster Cottage, Teelin, County Donegal

I'd no idea how much I needed the time and space to grieve for my parents until it hit me like a freight train one morning as I was walking on Silver Strand on a hazy August day with Murphy.

Unlike the rest of us, old Murphy seems oblivious to any change after a long spell in the local doggy hotel while Aunt Nora was away.

It cost a small fortune to keep him there for so long, but it was another thing Dad had thought of in advance and had set aside money for to make sure Nora got a much-deserved change of scenery.

All of my memories, all of my precious days with each of my parents, are steeped in the rocks of Slieve League cliffs, in the sound of the gulls in the air as they sweep across the Atlantic, in the mist of the majestic waterfalls and in the smell of seaweed where it clings to the sands of the beaches around my home turf in Teelin.

Even though the rain pelts off the ground here and the wind howls sometimes as if it's winter rather than summer, we made the most wonderful memories walking along beaches with shimmering waters, tasting oysters for the very first time and dancing together on the sand.

It was just the three of us and it was heavenly. Dad used to call us the three bears. Mum believed we were untouchable.

I feel so close to them both here, and as the weeks and months go by, I know I'll never want to live anywhere else in the world.

And yet, even though I know this is where I truly belong, I miss Bea with every single beat of my heart.

Time and space can't and won't ever change that.

The expanse of the Irish Sea makes it feel like there's half a world between us, but on the upside we've found a rhythm to our days and kept our promise to stay in touch.

We communicate by text and FaceTime between my shifts at the hospital and her shifts at the hotel on a level that has never faded or waned. I always like to make sure to wish her a good day first thing in the morning and sweet dreams at night, but I'll never lose the longing to hold her and have her here with me in person.

We are closer than friends, which leads to great confusion sometimes. It also leads to rows where we argue like an old married couple who are deeply in love despite words of anger that just come from frustration.

'I love the lifestyle here in the city, Ollie,' she reminds me from time to time. 'I get such a buzz from working in the hotel, from walking in the parks and all the shops and streets and places to explore. I need the space away from home and from all the pain of losing Peter too, and being here gives that to me.'

'Well, that's that then,' I reply when I'm finding the distance between us tough. 'I hope you meet someone there who gives you all the love you deserve, because it doesn't look like I can from here.'

'It was your decision to move, Ollie! OK, just stop. We're going round and round in circles. I know I'd rather have you in my life than not, but if this ever gets to the stage when one of us feels it's too hard, or it's holding the other back, then we say it, deal?'

I agree, but it doesn't make it easier when we both know we don't want to be with anyone else.

Aunt Nora watches my every move here on Oyster Lane with such care and attention, knowing I'm not only missing Bea and my father but also slowly adapting to this much slower pace of life in the wilds of Donegal. I look after her too, with grocery runs into the town of Carrick as well as keeping her entertained with stories of my new job at the hospital.

'And then he shouted at me, in front of all the other patients and visitors and my new colleagues, that I'd never be a real nurse because a real nurse would let him light up a cigarette on the ward,' I tell her over dinner one evening. 'The man was just out of major heart surgery and was dying for a smoke, quite literally. He'll thank me one day, I hope.'

I watch as Aunt Nora clucks about her kitchen, building her nest with food and warmth now that I'm here for her to fuss over again. Oyster Cottage next door feels barren and empty without Dad and the buzz of the bed and breakfast which we've had to close temporarily, so I spend a lot of my time in my aunt's kitchen where we set the world to rights.

I already feel the pressure of opening the doors of Oyster Cottage to guests again, but it's something I'll address in the New Year after we see through our first Christmas without my father.

'We all need a purpose in life, Ollie,' Aunt Nora reminds me on occasion. 'Even the simplest purpose can change someone's life and make them a lot less lonely. I'm so used to having your dad and the B&B to keep me busy, but now they're both gone, my days are very long and quiet. If it wasn't for our Murphy, and making you lunch and dinner each day, I don't know what I'd do to keep busy.'

'You need a new hobby,' I tell her. 'You need to start cold water sea swimming with that group in town. That would soon wake you up in the morning.'

She glares at me from over her glasses.

'I can think of nothing worse.'

'Well, you need to do something exciting or new.'

'And so do you. You need to invite Bea to stay – that might put a smile on your face,' she reminds me, even though she knows I've made it very clear to Bea that she will always be made welcome if the time is right for us both. Working in a hospital and working in a hotel can be quite the juggle for a phone call, never mind an overnight stay.

'I know I do.'

'How is she these days? And her mum and dad up in

Tyrone? Did her dad's throat infection clear up? I must get you the number of that lady in Killybegs with the cure for a sore throat. You can pass it on to them.'

Aside from fussing over me like I'm a teenage boy again, Aunt Nora is also slightly obsessed by the Malone family, and that's putting it mildly. She enjoys weekly updates (at least) of what's happening in Benburb, as well as what's happening in London at The Carnation Hotel, not to mention Patsi's life in Paris. That's her favourite part to hear about. I think she secretly fancies Jacques even though she's never set eyes on the alluring Frenchman.

'I'll do that, yes,' I reply, not knowing if Bea's father's throat infection has cleared because I'd totally forgotten all about it. 'Now, let me see what else I've to fill you in on . . . well, Patsi and Jacques were home in Benburb for a week at the end of July, but with it being high season at The Carnation, Bea couldn't up sticks and leave London to see her as much as she'd have liked to.'

Aunt Nora tut-tuts and shakes her head in sorrow.

'That girl works way too hard. I hope they appreciate her.'

'They do – and before you shed a tear, in a swift turn of events, Patsi took Jacques and both her parents to London to see Bea.'

She puts her hands on her hips.

'To London? Both Mam and Dad? Seriously?'

'Very seriously,' I tell her. 'They all went shopping on Oxford Street and they even went to see *Hamilton* in the West End. Well, the girls did while the boys found a pub nearby, but they'd all a super time. So, it was a case of moving

Mohammed to the mountain or whatever way that saying goes. You get my drift.'

Aunt Nora looks like she's been hit by a bus.

'You mean Mrs Malone got on a *plane*? Now there's a turn up for the books!' she says. 'Fair play to them all. I hope they enjoyed it. Ah, I'm sure Bea was thrilled to have them. It must be lonely for her over in London now that you're back here, eh?'

This is major news and will keep Aunt Nora's mind busy for the rest of the day. She has never met any of the Malone family. She hasn't even met Bea, but she's fully invested like they're some sort of reality TV show family she thinks she knows inside out.

I do have other news for her that I think might make her spontaneously combust, so I'm saving it for closer to the time or she'll be like a child waiting for Santa.

'Bea seems very happy in London. She adores that hotel, and it's even better now with Mr Gates back in action, even if he's only there now and then,' I say to Aunt Nora, leaving out the fact that last night on the phone she broke down and cried for an hour saying she wished she could jump on a plane and come over here, but her work is insanely busy with bookings right up until the end of the month. 'She is very much embedded in the way of life in London and has made it clear that she has no intention of moving back to Ireland anytime soon. But yes, a visit from her would be nice for both of us.'

'I'd love it too,' says Aunt Nora dreamily.

'For the three of us,' I add on. 'Yes, a visit from Bea would be very nice for you too.'

It's on the tip of my tongue to tell her the news, but I urge myself to wait, because I feel just like a child waiting for Santa myself every time I think of it.

'I hope I get to meet her soon,' says Aunt Nora, filling the sink with hot water and washing-up liquid so high that it almost bubbles over. 'And I hope you two work out a way of being together properly. All this Zooming and FaceTiming and Snap-shopping can't be healthy. It's real-life interaction people need, not screens or phone calls. It isn't good for the soul.'

'Snapchatting,' I correct her, even though Bea and I have never communicated that way.

'Snapchat, Facebook, it's all the same to me,' she mutters. 'Do you think I'd have met your late Uncle John if I hadn't gone to the dance hall that Midsummer night in Boston? Do you think your mother could have had a proper relationship with your father if there was a big lump of land and sea between them? It's not natural. Relying on technology is the ruination of us all. The ruination.'

'She's coming over here next weekend,' I blurt out, realising immediately that my timing may have been too out of the blue as Aunt Nora, in her excitement, sprays the entire kitchen with soapy bubbles that fly away from her waving hands.

'You're joking!' she says. I'm terrified she's going to slip on the now damp tiles, so I get up and fetch the mop before there's an accident. 'Oh Ollie, I could cry with joy! Well, if it isn't about time. But what about The Carnation? Or will Sita manage things while she's away? Gosh, isn't it great that

Leroy's back and enjoying his new love life with his neighbour Anne? That was a nice bit of news. I like Leroy.'

I mop round her feet, giggling to myself as she talks about everyone in Bea's life like she's their best friend. As well as being a little bit in love with Jacques, Aunt Nora also has a very soft spot for Leroy, she adores Nana the dog, and she thinks it's only a matter of time before Sita gets her big break in a West End show.

'So, our mission now is to get Oyster Cottage warmed up and ready for her arrival,' I say as her eyes dance with excitement. 'The rooms are a bit musty upstairs, so will you help me give them a clean? And out the back is still a bit of a mess as I haven't taken the time to clear up properly over the summer. I've built Oyster Cottage up so much to Bea that I don't want to disappoint her.'

Aunt Nora is already head deep under the sink, pulling out cleaning liquids, bleach and rubber gloves, even though I already have it all next door.

I've barely digested my dinner, so I didn't exactly mean we needed to make a start now, but I suppose there's no time like the present.

And if it makes time move faster towards the weekend, I'll more than happily get stuck in.

Bea is coming to see me at last. I simply can't wait to hold her, to show her my home and to feel her close to me in person. Aunt Nora is right. There's nothing like real human connection.

I've been waiting on this moment forever.

Chapter Twenty-Three

Bea

Teelin, Donegal

Early September in County Donegal is like a dream.

I am instantly reminded of childhood summers and how the colours in the sky change by the hour, from golden sunrises to shimmering blues in the afternoon to pinks and golds in the evening as the sun goes down in the distance.

It's almost like time has stood still, and it's a beautiful reminder of how spectacular the Irish landscape is as well as reminding me of everything else I miss about Ireland, no matter how much I enjoy the fast-paced ways of city life across the Irish Sea.

Just when you think you've seen the best of the best part of my homeland, another winding, stone-walled road or a shimmering seascape falls into view, stopping you in your tracks and taking your breath away.

And the people are unique here too, just like they are in my sweet Benburb.

Joe the taxi driver talks to me like he's known me forever,

calling me by my first name from the moment he picked me up from Donegal town for the short drive out to Teelin.

'So, it's your first time here, Bea?' he says when I ask him to bring me to Oyster Cottage. 'Ah, it's a different pace of life altogether. We have two speeds – "go slow" and "stop". It takes a wee while to get used to, but once you do, you'll never want to go back to the way you came from.'

I think of Ollie's stories so far about his new job at the hospital and how he too said it's like stepping into a parallel universe in so many ways. The expertise and skill there is second to none, but the patients are much more easy-going about procedures than what he remembers in London.

'Just four months in and I can't relate to that fast pace of life in London at all any more,' he told me on a recent phone call. 'It seems like a different lifetime in many ways.'

I'm happy that he's fitting in so well at home, even though we've missed each other terribly.

'Just for a change it's raining,' laughs the hearty taxi driver. 'People come to Donegal for the feeling, not the weather. You can never predict the weather here on the west coast of Ireland.'

Ollie was on a long shift last night so I've told him to sleep it off while I make my way from City of Derry airport, and while Aunt Nora offered to pick me up, I wouldn't hear of it, even if she is *only* seventy-eight.

I'm used to public transport from living in a big city, and the anticipation of seeing Ollie in person after so long is enough to put a fire in my belly which means I'd have walked if I had to.

'It's pretty wet up the road where I'm from too,' I tell him.

'Let me guess? County Derry?'

'No,' I say with a smile, remembering how Ollie thought the same when we first met. 'I'm from the green fields of Tyrone. God's own country.'

He smiles at me through the rear-view mirror and turns up the radio, makes a throwaway comment about Gaelic football then mutters how he loves the new song by some native country singer and sings along like he's on stage at the Grand Ole Opry.

I sit back and relax to take in my surroundings, which is just the distraction I need as I make my way to Teelin. It's been a hectic summer with The Carnation bursting at the seams with visitors from all over the world, and although I've thrived on every single moment, I've spent far too many long, lonely nights wishing for a time when I could see Ollie in person again.

We've talked on the phone into the wee hours, leaving us both exhausted and frustrated, we've fallen out and fallen in again, and we made a promise that one day we'd get to see each other once more.

And now that time has finally come.

I point my phone out through the windowpane of the car, doing my best to capture some moments to send to Patsi who is waiting on tenterhooks for updates in Paris. She has listened to my longing for Ollie on more phone calls than I can remember, and it was her, my dear sister, who urged me to pick a date, book a flight and stick to it.

Leroy and Sita have been encouraging me too, mostly fed

up, I can imagine, at catching me staring into space, lost in thought when days without him became all too much. I've painted on a face for our guests, I've thrown myself into work, taking on extra shifts to fill my time, and I've spent long summer afternoons down by the Peter Pan statue where I'd talk to my brother, urging him to give me signs that I'm doing the right thing by staying in London so far away from the one man I can't get out of my head.

And now, with every turn of the wheel of this taxi as we drive over bumpy roads and through winding valleys, I'm getting closer and closer to him at last, already lost in the beauty of this part of the world he calls home.

Tiny sheep dot the rolling green fields that frame one side of the vast ocean, and chocolate box white-washed cottages with thatched roofs are scattered along the coastline with tufts of brown smoke billowing from their chimneys.

The smell of turf seeps into the car and fills my senses. I feel my eyes well up and my heart soar. I want to close my eyes and savour this moment, but at the same time I want to keep them open wide so I can drink in every single moment of the beauty that surrounds me.

'This looks heavenly,' I whisper, already wishing I'd been able to come here much earlier in summer to lap it all up with Ollie by my side. We drive past Teelin Pier where Ollie spent his childhood fishing and jumping into the cool Atlantic waters. We pass signs for the majestic cliffs of Slieve League, and Joe waves to locals when we slow down to let a herd of cattle cross the road.

'The best time to do something may have been yesterday,'

said Leroy when I felt I couldn't wait any longer for this day to come. 'But the next best time is today.'

Then I see the chimney pots of the houses on Oyster Lane and my heart lifts at the sight of it all. I sit up on the edge of the seat as far as the seat belt will allow me to.

'Nearly there now,' says Joe as he turns to the left then trundles up a narrow lane, past a cottage with no lights on as if no one is home, but beside it sits the pièce de résistance in all its glory.

'I feel like I should pinch myself,' I say out loud. 'It's so beautiful.'

'It sure is that, Bea,' says Joe, with such pride you'd almost think he owned the little B&B himself. 'Oyster Cottage on Oyster Lane, place of dreams and where wishes come true.'

He turns down the radio as if it might let me see it all more clearly.

'My wife often says how she'd love to stay here someday, even though we only live a stone's throw away,' he tells me. 'Enjoy yourself and remember to take a photo beneath the ash tree in the garden. It's kind of a tradition, or at least it was when old Jack Brennan was alive. Meant to be a sign of healing, magic and life, if you believe in all that airy fairy stuff.'

He laughs at his own remarks as I pay him the fare, then I climb out of the taxi and breathe in the sea air which is almost a shock to the system compared to the smog of London.

'Oyster Cottage,' I whisper in disbelief. 'I'm here at last.'

Twinkling lights draped over an evergreen holly tree glisten on the winding pathway and ivy hangs loosely over the front door. A sign which has seen better days creaks and groans on a metal bar, and the sea-blue door has a mat at its feet saying '*Céad Mile Failte*' – a hundred thousand welcomes. It greets me like a warm hug.

And then I see him through the rain. He stands in the doorway with his Irish Red Setter dog, Murphy, who I've heard so much about, by his side.

'Ollie,' I whisper.

'Bea,' he says, walking towards me as the cool rain dances on the path and off his shoulders. He's wearing a vintage grey T-shirt which is soon soaked through, but he doesn't seem to care, and neither do I.

He takes me in his arms and holds me so tightly I don't ever want him to let go.

We don't utter another word, as there's nothing more we need to say right now. And when I finally look up to meet his eyes, we both lean into each other's mouth with a hunger and passion I don't think I've ever felt before in my whole existence.

His kiss is as electrifying as I'd imagined it might be. He rests his hands on my face and we make up for all those lost days and weeks and months apart with a first proper embrace that takes both our breaths away. I feel his hands move down the sides of my body until they reach my waist, then he lifts me up slightly and I kiss him again.

'I've been kissing you forever in my dreams,' he says when we manage to pull apart in the pouring rain. 'But that beats every single way I'd imagined it. I'm so glad you're here, Bea.'

'Me too,' is as much as I can muster.

I'm dizzy from his kiss, from his touch and from just being so close to him physically again. I'm already left wanting more.

He takes my bag and then my hand and leads me in through the front door of Oyster Cottage where I stop in the hallway to take it all in. Murphy sniffs around the floor, eager to figure out who I am and where I've come from.

'Now, now, Murphy, you should be used to greeting guests with decorum and respect. Remember your manners, that's a good boy.'

I look up to see the famous Aunt Nora hold her arms out to meet me like she's known me all her life. She looks exactly as I'd imagined her, slim and small with candyfloss curls and winged glasses, just like Ollie described her.

I give her a hug while Ollie makes comical faces behind her back. I know how much he idolises her, even if he does wind her up as much as is humanly possible every day.

'How's Patsi's new job coming along? I can't wait to hear about the music scout, too, who spotted her singing in the jazz bar! I'm sure Jacques is bursting with pride.'

Ollie puts his hands on his face and shakes his head.

'Give Bea a chance to get her bearings before you give her the Spanish Inquisition for goodness' sake, dear old aunty!'

We all share a giggle and make our way into the kitchen where I can see she has been hard at work baking an apple pie. The smell of home cooking makes my stomach growl.

I already feel at home. I already could easily stay here forever.

'Before you sing her praises, she burnt the first two,' Ollie tells me, which triggers a playful and well-deserved swipe from Aunt Nora.

'I've never burnt an apple pie in my entire lifetime, and he knows it,' she tells me, laying the kitchen table with some teacups and plates. 'Now, let me get you some refreshments while Ollie shows you to your room, and then you can tell us all about your journey. How's Leroy? Isn't it just fabulous that he's back at the hotel, even if it's only at his own pace.'

I can't help but smirk as I reply in detail about all the goings-on at The Carnation as well as all the latest news from my family in Benburb. Ollie has told me many times how Aunt Nora is obsessed with us all, which I find very endearing.

'Aunt Nora! How can I show her to her room when you won't stop talking?'

We leave her to it in the kitchen, muttering and mumbling to herself even though Ollie isn't taking in a word she says.

'She is absolutely fabulous and I totally love her already,' I say as he shows me first into a cosy living room decorated with family photos. I stop and stare at the family portrait that hangs so proudly above the mantelpiece, allowing myself to absorb the beauty of Jack and Eleanor Brennan, and all they have created here at Oyster Cottage. It's a joyous photo in every way, bursting with smiles and happiness. The way Ollie's mother rests her hand on her little boy's waist and leans her head towards her husband's strong shoulder almost brings a tear to my eyes.

We climb the stairs and on the way I marvel at Eleanor's artwork that lines the walls. Her style is impressionist mixed with a traditional take on many of South Donegal's most loved landscapes – the lighthouse at St John's, the horseshoe-shaped beach known as Silver Strand, and the bobbing fishing boats of Killybegs.

'And this is your very own boudoir,' he says, opening a heavy wooden door at the top of the stairs. 'I wasn't sure how you'd feel about sleeping arrangements, so I've prepared this room for you.'

'I love how unassuming you are,' I whisper. 'But I think I might get cold in here all alone.'

'I was hoping you'd say that,' he says, putting his forehead against mine. My heart is racing. We both breathe out, doing our best to control our urges with Aunt Nora downstairs whipping up a feast in the kitchen.

The generous-sized room smells like fresh lavender, and I notice sprigs in a vase which add to the character. It has lemon and white floral wallpaper, gingham matching curtains and is clean, cosy and ornate in every way with a high, antique brass bed that calls out for me to touch it.

'Is this all your mother's design and taste?' I ask him, looking around in wonder. 'Gosh, she really was creative if so.'

'Everything you see is hers,' he tells me. 'We've redecorated the walls and updated the paintwork, of course, but we've never replaced any of the furniture, ornaments or art on the walls. That was Dad's promise to her, and mine to him. Oyster Cottage will always be a reflection of the passion she poured into every single corner.'

I marvel at every tiny detail. Its quirky interior, with no room the same, reminds me in many ways of The Carnation. Oyster Cottage will never be a cardboard cut-out place to stay. It oozes warmth and character, and everything from the clocks on the wall to the old-style furniture could tell a thousand stories.

I inhale it all, much to Ollie's delight. All the pubs, bars, restaurants and five-star hotels I've worked in have made me appreciate just how wonderful a little nook like this can be. I've never been drawn to large chains or corporate hotels, always preferring the more individualised quirks of boutique or family-run establishments.

I want to tell Patsi all about this place immediately. I want to whisk my mum and dad away here, to give them a new lease of life. I want them to take their time, to wander around the narrow country roads, to listen to the lilt of the Gaelic language that rolls off everyone's tongues in a way I hope I can one day learn to imitate, and to savour the sounds of the lapping waves that can take all your cares away.

I want them to fall in love with Ollie and Oyster Cottage just as much as I already know I have.

Our weekend is spent roaming around the beaches by day and spending cosy evenings by the fire in this wonderful safe haven that fills my soul with every minute and hour that chimes on the clock in the hallway of Oyster Cottage.

We eat and drink our fill in pubs where lilting music fills the air, we burn it off with some surfing and hiking in the morning, and we picnic with Aunt Nora on top of Slieve League at Bunglass viewpoint, which gives panoramic views of the magnificent cliffs with a sense of solitude and peace.

We take photos amongst purple heather that has burst into life over the summer months. We scramble down steep slopes and look for seashells through tangled seaweeds while Murphy bounces in the ocean waves. And at night, when the world outside is silent, we climb into my bed together, afraid to sleep in case we miss a moment of this snatched weekend of bliss.

'Do you ever wish we could stop the clocks?' he whispers on our last night together as we lie naked beneath the covers.

I'm just about to reply when my eye is drawn to a rather unusual ornament which distracts me. It sits on the windowsill beneath the net curtains that block out the early autumn sun.

'Is it just me or is that little wooden elephant on the windowsill staring at us?' I joke.

Ollie cranes his neck around to follow my eyeline.

'That's one of my mum's random ornaments,' he says with a smile. 'No doubt it comes with a story of its own but I've no idea what that might be.'

I can't help it. I keep looking at it over his shoulder. Its eyes are fixed on us both in return, and its stance is bold and deliberate, as if there's a lot on its mind.

'It almost looks like it wants to say something to us,' I muse, loving that I already know how Ollie is playing along with my wandering train of thought.

He eases his body away from mine, then leaps off the bed and fetches the shiny wooden elephant which looks like it has come from anywhere other than Donegal. I like to think of his mum browsing around a market, somewhere wild and wonderful in Asia or Africa, and then bringing back this elephant to her home here on the edge of the ocean. It feels like everything here has a history which totally intrigues me and ignites my senses.

'I think I know what it's trying to say to us,' he says, holding the elephant gently in his hands. He puts on a deep voice, holding the wooden elephant up to his mouth in his best effort to act like a ventriloquist. 'I'm telling you both to never forget, Bea and Ollie.'

'Forget what?'

'This. Us. The feeling we have right here, right now,' he says, still in the elephant's voice.

'You're a very wise old elephant,' I reply, patting the bed for him to come back to me. He does, making my eyes drop at the familiar smell of his skin and the warmth of his touch.

'I want us to always remember how totally wonderful it is to be here, just the two of us in this warm, cosy cocoon with the sea in the distance and not a care in the world,' he says as he kisses my forehead. 'Old Nellie the elephant is reminding us now to never forget the little things in life. The moments that we'll one day treasure the most.'

'I'll never forget this,' I reply, impressed at Ollie's quick invention with the elephant on the windowsill, even giving her a name. 'I'll never forget us and now.'

'And neither will I,' he says with a sparkle in his eyes.

I notice how he has put the elephant back on the window-sill so that it's now looking out through the window instead of towards us like before. He slinks his arm around my waist until his fingers make me lose my breath in anticipation of what's to come.

The cool of his fingertips on the top of my thigh makes me curl into him like nature intended, and as the clock chimes midnight we make love on top of the patchwork quilt, slowly and easily.

He spoons me from behind, so warm, so secure. I feel warm, safe and loved like never before. There can never be anything more wonderful, more blissful than this.

'I'm missing you already,' he whispers as he nuzzles into my ear.

My stomach churns slightly at the thought of it too, but I also know I'm needed back in London in the way a mother knows she needs to get back to her child.

'What are we going to do, Ollie?' I ask him, seriously now. 'The thought of a long-distance relationship again is enough to make my head spin, but at the same time I don't want to say goodbye to you.'

He wants me to do the impossible. He wants me to pack up my life in London and come here to live with him forever. But he is too polite, too respectful and too kind to put me in that position. I don't want him to ask, as I know what the answer to that question will be, at least for now.

I love it here, but I still love my life in London too. This weekend has not been real life, in which he has to work shifts in the hospital day and night, and where I'd have to find a job nearby to make ends meet.

This is us in a hazy holiday mode, a honeymoon period where every colour is enhanced, every sound is at full volume and every word spoken is significant.

Yet as we lie here together, I know that London is beginning to feel further and further away from where I want to be.

I want to be here like this in his arms forever.

I want to be where he is, always.

But does he want that too?

'My friend is getting married on the second of December,' he says, brightening. 'Would you come with me to the wedding as my plus one? Aunt Nora is going too, just so you know.'

I turn around to face him, feeling his warm breath on my face.

'Like, on a date?' I ask him playfully. He kisses my forehead. He kisses my temple. 'I'll see if I can get the time off work.'

'Work, work, work,' he teases.

'Real life,' I remind him. 'Are you asking me to be your date?'

'Yes, I'm asking you to be my date,' he says with determination. 'I'm asking you to be my date at long, long last, Bea Malone.'

I don't leave him waiting for an answer. It's just September now, so a date in December will give us both something to look forward to, and I've always loved a winter wedding.

'And I'm saying yes at long, long last, Ollie Brennan,' I

tell him as he pulls my waist closer into him. 'I'm saying yes, yes, yes.'

We have eight hours left until I have to leave for London again, so I imagine we'll stay in bed until it's time for me to go.

I'm already dreading saying goodbye to Ollie, but as painful as it will be for both of us, duty calls.

I need to get back to my own life in London – back to Leroy, Nana, the hotel and all my realities, and back to a place where I'll pine for moments like this every single day, even more than I've ever done before.

Although I'm trying my best to deny it, the lights of London are slowly dimming in my mind, and I'll be leaving a huge piece of my heart here in Teelin with Ollie.

December cannot come quickly enough.

Chapter Twenty-Four

Ollie

Being with Bea for that wonderful weekend in early September kept me glowing for weeks after, but as the autumn winds blow in and the bite of winter lures us into darker mornings and evenings, I long for something to change between us, so that we can find a way of spending more time together.

The high of our time together gives way sometimes to moments of frustration when our rotas clash, our social lives go in different directions and the tension between us means that conversations can be stilted for days.

But we always go back for more, and she never leaves my mind.

Although we haven't put a label on our relationship, the weekend at Oyster Cottage changed everything on so many levels. It gave us the confirmation of how deeply we have fallen for one another, but it also heightens the levels of tension that linger across the miles between us.

I miss Scott too, and Jane, and I'm always grateful for a catch-up with one of them where I hear all about work life and the nights on the tiles I'm missing out on – a far cry from my very slow pace here in Donegal. Scott calls at least once a week, while Jane's check-ins are mainly a quick text or a funny meme about hospital life, which always brightens up my day.

Out for some well-deserved after-work drinks tonight. Missing you, was the latest on WhatsApp from Jane, accompanied by a very happy-looking photo of my two London besties holding a cocktail each in our favourite pub. They look very cosy, and though I wish I was there beside them, I have a strange feeling that they're doing OK without me. There's a twinkle in Scott's eyes and the way Jane is resting her head on his shoulder makes me wonder if they've grown a lot closer now that three is no longer a crowd, but I won't pry. At least I won't just yet. Their happy faces warm my heart and that's the most important thing. Maybe my own loved-up existence is making me jump to conclusions I've never even contemplated before.

Scott and Jane, romantically involved? Who knows? I suppose stranger things have happened at sea.

I sent Jane back an equally cosy but a lot less romantic picture of myself and Murphy snuggled up on the sofa, to which she replied with a flurry of hearts in appreciation. Jane is a true dog lover and always enjoys a Murphy update, so I try to keep her stocked up with funny encounters, be it a sandy run on the beach or the time he greeted me at the back door with one of my muddy trainers which had been missing for days. He'd made mincemeat of it and wasn't one bit bothered.

Scott seems to have some sort of intuition which means

he calls me just when I need to hear from him, and the lilt of his familiar Liverpudlian accent always raises my spirits.

This time, I'm just in from a very challenging shift where one of my patients received the worst news about his heart condition, so the sound of Scott's voice when he calls just before bedtime is a welcome balm to my weary mind. As an A&E nurse, he sees the fine line between life and death on a daily basis, yet he never takes any of it for granted, always thinking of the person and the family who are in his care.

'We always wish we could do more, Ol,' he tells me as I take solace in a hot chocolate in front of a roaring fire, which was kindly lit so it was ready and waiting for me on this cool autumn evening by my ever-caring aunty. 'But unfortunately we can't save them all. We're not God. We can't fix everyone.'

I think back to the fateful day Mr Gates was admitted to the Royal Elizabeth, and how I overheard him asking Bea a question about how to cure a broken heart. His frail voice, the quiver in his tone and the fear he must have felt in that moment has never left me. It reminded me, of course, of how my mother used to tell me I'd fixed her broken heart, and the reason why I went into this job in the first place. I'm aware that sometimes I take it too literally, and I find it hard to switch off after a heavy shift like the one today.

I also know there are many ways to interpret Mr Gates's question. He has told me stories about Coral on many occasions since I first got to know him, and I can only try to understand the pain of such a young life being stolen from this world, as well as all the hopes and dreams they had for a

future together. She was quite simply the love of his life until
the freak accident that stole her from this world in the blink
of an eye. It unnerves me to think of how we never know
what's around the corner for any of us, which only makes me
want to spend more time with Bea as soon as possible.

'Jane and I talk about you all the time, mate,' Scott tells me,
which brings a smile to my face. 'Jane says the cardiac ward
is very solemn without your bad jokes, and the little old ladies
are not so keen to hang around now that there's no eye candy.
She mentioned a returning patient, Mary someone . . .'

'Ah, my old friend Miss Mary Doris,' I say with a smile.
'Now that *has* cheered me up. She will be delighted to hear
I've stepped things up in my love life, even if it's only a little.
She has a very revealing notebook which helps her remember
the nurses' names. She probably still remembers you from
A&E as having big feet and bleached hair. She liked you all
the same.'

Scott spends way too long laughing at that one, but I must
admit, Mary Doris was a patient I'll never forget because of
her notebook, her observing ways and quick wit. It takes my
mind briefly off the poor old man in Letterkenny University
Hospital this evening who is facing his last few days with his
family.

'Just shout when you're ready for me to come visit,' Scott
told me at the end of our call, like he usually does. 'Let's hook
up really soon, buddy.'

'Yes, soon. For sure,' I replied. 'Please know you're welcome here anytime.'

*

I spend my days here when I'm not working slowly bringing Oyster Cottage back to life, and with every milestone reached I feel my parents smile down on me. I paint the walls in the same timeless colours my mother chose many years ago; I match up wallpaper with modern versions to reflect her eclectic taste of stripes, checks and floral prints, with each room a deliberate opposite to the one next to it.

The bathrooms spring back to life with a facelift, the hallways and doorways are welcoming and refreshing, while the kitchen slowly bursts into colour with an autumn glow. I play music to keep me company as I paint and decorate, and in the evenings I look forward to a catch-up with Bea when it suits us both to have a lengthy chat where I'll update her on my DIY and hear all about her latest news from The Carnation.

'The new logo is really fitting,' she tells me, always on hand with encouraging tips on how to get Oyster Cottage back on the market for the next season. 'I didn't know you had a creative side, but it makes sense when your mum was so artistic.'

I like that Bea never fails to bring my late parents into our conversations, even though she never met them. Talking about them always makes me feel a little less lonely now that I'm beginning this new chapter here without Mum and Dad.

'I don't think I'll be starting a side hustle on graphic design just yet, but I'm quite proud of it, yes,' I reply. 'It has a special meaning with the three purple cowslip flowers found here mostly in late summer, and it's from the heart, which is most important, I guess. My mother used to draw cowslips a lot, so I scanned one of her paintings and simplified it until it felt right for the new logo.'

'She would be very proud of you and everything you're doing to make Oyster Cottage as beautiful and vibrant as she once had it.'

'I really hope so, Bea,' I tell her. 'I hope I've made the right decision by coming back here. Sometimes I do wonder if I'd be better making a new start elsewhere, but there has always been a tug to come back here. I feel like it's where I'm meant to be.'

A brief silence falls between us as once more we both realise that if we do want to be together, one of us is going to have to make a very big decision, and that it won't come easy. I know Bea is far from taking a different direction in her chosen path, and there's no way I'm ready to give up on what I'm building here.

'We'll find a way,' she whispers. 'I know we will, Ollie.'

'I really hope we do,' I reply, then we talk as usual until we're almost asleep. I like when that happens.

The days tick by, with Aunt Nora never far away, and when I'm feeling like a change of scenery out of the hospital or away from the cottage, I fill my senses by walking with Murphy along Pilgrim's Path, a challenging, rocky walk that isn't for the faint-hearted. But most of my time is taken up with home improvements and I'm enjoying the transformation already.

'Oh, I'm not sure about that wallpaper in the main bathroom at all. It's very—'

'Loud?' I suggest.

'Vulgar,' replies Aunt Nora.

'Vulgar?' I echo as she repeats it in a singsong voice at the same time.

'I think I might be losing the plot,' I say after a few moments of deliberation. 'Thank goodness you're here to keep me right.'

'But I like it,' she says eventually. 'No, don't change it. Leave it so. It will be a talking point, I'm sure, and you know what's worse than people talking?'

'No, but I'm sure you're about to tell me.'

'When they're so bored they've nothing to say. That's what's worse. It's always good to get them talking. Let the vulgar stay. I quite like it, really.'

When I'm not taking notes from Aunt Nora on my interior design efforts, I join the lads for a few cold pints down at The Rusty Mackerel, where we always put the world to rights. I've taken Bea's advice on writing down my feelings in a notebook she sent me in the post, and it helps when the nights are long and when grief gets a grip on me.

My life here is simple. It's quiet and it's what I've always imagined it might be, even if I don't have my father's words of wisdom to drive me forward like they used to. I visit his grave sporadically, only when I feel in the mood, and I take strength from talking to them both there. It's a frosty autumn morning when I find myself there on my way to the hospital, and my breath is almost taken away.

Because right by the gravestone which bears the names of my beloved mum and dad, Jack and Eleanor Brennan, is a little clump of wild purple cowslip, just as I've featured on our new logo for Oyster Cottage. It has sprouted, off season, up through the white marble stones on the grave.

I stare at the flowers, almost afraid to count them but knowing already how many there are. I reach into my jacket pocket, my hands red with the early morning cold that seeps into my bones.

'One, two, three,' I say out loud before I take a quick photo, almost afraid that my eyes are deceiving me. I send the photo to Bea, then to Scott and to Jane who I know will appreciate just how much this will mean to me.

Scott and Jane both send me emojis only seconds apart to show their support, and I smile as I imagine them rushing out to perhaps start their own morning shift on the wards. It's Monday, so Scott is most likely nursing a hangover while Jane will be juggling a run with her little daughter's drop-off at nursery before she gets to the Royal Elizabeth.

But it's Bea's response I look forward to most and, as usual, she doesn't disappoint. She sends me a photo, her hands covering her mouth in awe and tears filling her beautiful eyes.

Little signs everywhere, she reminds me. I wish I was there to give you a big hug, Ollie. I can't wait to see you again. Keep looking for the signs.

I hold my phone to my chest, longing for the day I get to hold her for real again. I know I'm on the right path.

I know now that I've chosen wisely to come back here.

This is exactly where I'm meant to be.

Chapter Twenty-Five

Bea

Leroy is in his usual position at the front door of The Carnation, his top hat in hand as he nods to greet our guests on arrival, or wish them well on their way home after a splendid visit with us, while Sita is behind the desk doing her best to stay calm as we await a very special person into our reception area this morning.

I do my best to stop yawning, but no matter how tired I feel I can't wipe the smile off my face, knowing it's because Ollie and I sat up way too late last night talking on the phone, both falling asleep at around the same time as we were unable to say goodnight. My heart glows every time I think of him, and we are both counting the days until his friend Buster's wedding when we will see each other again.

September feels like a lifetime ago, and although I did pay a flying visit to Benburb in between times, it was just for an overnight stay as my mum had a brief health scare and Ollie wasn't able to get time off work to join me at such short notice.

Mum's fright wasn't anything serious, thank goodness,

and her blood pressure has since settled, but she has been doing her best to keep her spirits up lately which is such a joy to see. She has joined a fitness class at the local community centre, she has enjoyed a few evenings out with Dad for dinner and they have even gone dancing, which made my own heart sing.

The day after I arrived back in Benburb, I took my notebook down to the river and wrote out my thoughts.

I wrote about Leroy and how I was taking so much joy in seeing a new spring in his step now that he and his neighbour Anne had found a blooming friendship. He had told her all about Coral, and how her parents never contacted him after her death, preferring to ignore their thwarted elopement. He told her of the guilt he has lived with ever since, and how he knows that if they hadn't planned to run away together, she never would have died so tragically. I was glad to hear he'd been so open and honest with Anne. I was even happier to hear that she had told him that if Coral's parents hadn't been so snobby, he and Coral would never have had to go to such drastic measures to try to be together. I like Anne. She is so good for Leroy and if she makes him smile, then I could never ask for anything more.

I wrote about my conversations with Patsi, which have become much more frequent now. I check in on her as much as I can and she shows more interest in my life than she had been doing before, admitting she was so wrapped up in the lovely honeymoon period with Jacques that she couldn't see the wood for the trees. But now that they've moved in together, she's beginning to get to know him as a real person and thankfully she is still madly in love with him even though he snores like a pig at night or, as she says, *'comme un cochon'*, then backs it up with sound effects in case I didn't get the picture. I can't wait to tell Aunt Nora all about that!

I wrote to Peter, of course, wishing he was still with us to get to know all these wonderful new people in our lives. I imagine he'd have a lot to say for himself, and I often think that he'd have found someone just as special to share his life with now that he'd have turned thirty. He was so focused, so entrepreneurial, so determined to make a difference to the world he was brought into. He'd have chosen wisely, someone to light up his life and stimulate his senses. As I sat on a bench by the gushing River Blackwater with my feet crunching on the autumn leaves, I asked him to continue guiding me on my way here without him. Seven years have gone in a blink, and although time is a great healer, my younger, wiser brother never leaves my mind. He was my go-to person, my first sibling, and even though I was a little older than him I never stopped looking up to him.

'What is the cure for a broken heart?' I found myself scribbling down as I thought of him. Leroy's question has never left me, yet I'm not sure I've ever really tried to find the answer.

'One caffè latte made with oat milk,' I heard a familiar voice say behind me. My eyes widened when I looked up to see Sean holding out a takeaway coffee cup in my direction. 'I thought I might find you here.'

Astonished, I moved across on the bench and closed my

notebook. I hadn't even heard him approach me and it took my breath away.

'Sean? Th-thank you, but—'

'Don't freak out, I wasn't following you,' he chuckled. 'I was out for a walk and I saw you in the distance, your head buried in your words. I thought rather than disturb you I'd go get us both a coffee to warm you up and come back this way again to say a quick hello. So, hello?'

'Hello,' I said, blowing on the coffee through the hole in the lid. The warmth of the cup gave a welcome heat to my cold hands. 'Thanks for this. Sorry, I'm just a bit taken aback, I wasn't expecting to see you.'

He shifted slightly away from me on the bench so we were more face to face, and a wave of feelings rushed through me on seeing him again. A pang of guilt at first, then sorrow for how it all ended, then, dare I say it, relief that we're able to do this with no hard feelings. Well, not on my part anyhow, and his olive branch of a coffee to warm me up told me he might feel the same.

'I heard your mum had a bit of a scare last night,' he told me. 'News flies quickly around here. How is she?'

'She's fine, thank goodness,' I replied, grateful for his caring ways when it came to my mother's health. 'It was a false alarm, but she did right to get it checked out. I fly back to London tonight, so I thought I'd pass some time here down by the river. This place gets into my soul. It always will no matter how long I stay away.'

Sean leaned back again on the bench and we both stared at the racing, turbulent water. A heron landed on a rock and drew our attention, its wide wingspan so elegant and regal almost, reminding me of the power of nature and the wonder of the world.

'Do you think you'll ever settle for a life like this again, or will you forever be chasing rainbows, Bea?' Sean asked. 'I hope you find what you're looking for in London.'

I almost choked on my coffee. All of a sudden it tasted bitter.

'Chasing rainbows? What's that supposed to mean?'

'I dunno, chasing something out of reach, chasing the impossible?'

I sat up straight and faced him head on.

'Sean Sullivan, I have a career and a life over there that I happen to love and enjoy!' I told him. 'I'm very proud of all I've achieved in my job and I will continue to be so. Why do you think I'm chasing rainbows? That's very insulting.'

He laughed a little, which made me wonder if he had any idea of just how cutting his words were. Was this an attempt to make me feel guilty for not jumping to his commands or his surprise proposal when we hadn't been getting on well for months beforehand?

'We could have had a good life together, that's all I'm saying,' he told me, then he stood up and nodded at my notebook. 'Still writing away until you figure it out, I see?'

I rose from the bench and handed him my cup, then gathered up my notebook and pen, holding them to my chest.

'You know, Sean, the coffee was a lovely gesture. Seeing you here could have been a really nice end to my short but rather traumatic visit home, but you've blown it. I'm as sorry we didn't work out as you are, but I don't want a good life. I intend to live my best life, and if I have to write it out to figure it out, I'll keep doing that. But when I decide on my next move, it will be my decision, not anyone else's. And certainly not yours.'

I stomped away, leaving him aghast with his mouth wide open. I don't think I've ever raised my voice to Sean. I don't think I've ever told him how suffocating he sometimes could be with his bull ignorant plans that never really did involve me. Maybe if he'd taken the time to let me have a say in our future, I might have felt a bit more part of it.

He called out after me, but I just waved to him and wished him well. What really irritated me was that deep down I couldn't help wondering if he was right. Was I chasing the impossible? What exactly *was* I chasing? I haven't been able to get it out of my head ever since.

'Psst! She's here! Miss Beatrice, she's here!'

Back in the present, our special guest is about to descend on The Carnation Hotel and my stomach twists as always on the announcement of her grand arrival. She would be disappointed if she thought any of her staff were nervous or making a fuss at her popping by, but it's always out of respect and awe that I feel this way when the ninety-two-year-old owner and founder of The Carnation, Alice Charles, drops by.

She was a style icon in her day and she still turns heads now with her epic glamour and the way she enters a room. I do my best to strike a balance of being busy while giving her space to take in her surroundings before I make a move to greet her. As always she goes to greet Nana first. Nana lies brazenly by the fire, unaware of just how important Alice is to us all here, and she even lets out a groan of pleasure when Mrs Charles strokes her head.

'What a beauty you are, sweet Nana,' I hear her whisper. Sita and I share a glance of admiration for the lady who created such a wonderful place for us to work. As far as hospitality goes, she will forever have set goals for people like me to look up to and I can never thank her enough for all I've learned during my time here at her hotel.

'You have this place looking and, more importantly, *feeling* impeccable as always, Beatrice,' she tells me, planting an air kiss at both sides of my cheeks. Her dainty hands are gloved as always in the softest leather – purple, of course, no blacks or navy or browns feature in the palette of Alice Charles. She wears a clashing blue floor-length velvet coat, with pink boots peeping out from beneath it, and her lipstick matches them to perfection. She takes off her sunglasses, pushes them back on to her snow-white hair and beams a smile in my direction.

'I'm glad I can keep it in line with your expectations,' I tell her, clasping her hands in mine. 'We adore this place as much as you do, if that seems possible.'

'I can tell,' she assures me. 'I believe I have afternoon tea ordered. You'll join me, perhaps?'

I look at Sita who nods and shoos me away, then across to Leroy who is too busy charming a new resident to notice. Not that I was ever going to turn down her offer. In all my years here, I've never had the opportunity to spend one-on-one time with Alice Charles, and there's no way I'm giving that up for love nor money.

I follow her and her chauffeur into the restaurant where a sumptuous display of dainty rectangle sandwiches – no crusts, of course – sit on an elegant white tiered plate, with a variety of home-made cream delights decorated with a rainbow of seasonal berries on the layer above, and the top layer features a mouth-watering array of macaroons and cheesecakes. We are seated by the window, the best seat in the house and no less than I would have expected.

'Your hands are shaking, darling,' she says with a light smile. 'I hope I don't make you nervous. I just fancied some company and thought you might enjoy a break away from the front line. I know Coral always did. She and I became great friends. I'm not sure if Leroy ever told you that.'

I swallow hard, doing my best to stay cool and collected. Truth is, I'm shaking on the inside as well as on the outside. I'd never have expected to live up to Coral in anyone's eyes around here. To everyone who has been here long enough to remember her, Coral Williams was the poster girl of The Carnation who fell deeply in love with the lowly concierge, but whose life was cut short before they could find their happy ever after.

'Her parents haven't crossed the doors of this place since, but I don't feel their loss, I'm afraid,' she explains, raising a delicate hand to say she has had enough tea poured into her cup already by our waiter. 'Thank you, George. This looks absolutely delightful as always.'

The young waiter, who is only a recent recruit, beams

widely at her greeting him by name. He blushes and walks away with his head held high, even though it's most likely because she could read his name badge discreetly rather than that she remembered him personally. I like her little touches like that. Alice Charles makes everyone at The Carnation feel special.

'I've heard so much about Coral,' I say with a smile. 'Leroy talks about her as much as he can to anyone who will listen. To me, it's the most beautifully tragic love story, if that's even a thing.'

'Oh, it's a thing,' says Alice with a twinkle in her blue eyes. 'They were so in love. I knew of their relationship, you see. I watched it bloom with my very own eyes and I saw how Coral lit up when he was close by. It was like something from the movies back then. Leroy was so handsome in his uniform, and she was like someone who belonged on a red carpet. This was only supposed to ever be a summer job for her, a favour from me to her parents who were our good friends, but she rose to the challenge perfectly. She had an instant flair for hospitality. My guests adored her, and I've never seen anyone have that effect on them since.'

'I can imagine.'

'Until now,' she tells me.

I pause, my teacup in hand.

'Until now?' I repeat.

'Until you, I should have said, perhaps. Until you, Beatrice.'

My skin prickles with goosebumps. I do my best to absorb her words without stammering or stuttering out a response.

I take my time to reply, but I don't have to as she continues before I get the chance to catch my breath.

'I always knew that, if she had survived, Coral would go on to run her very own place, her and Leroy together,' she tells me, her eyes dancing with delight at the thought of it. 'Now imagine that for a dream team! She used to pick my brain on how she could get started. She'd lay out her plans to me in a way she couldn't do with her own mother. Susan wanted Coral to use her university degree and become a doctor, but Coral had no interest in medicine. She was a performer, a magnet for people, a charismatic beauty who had the public eating out of her hands with a pleasant word or a compliment. She would always go that extra mile to make them feel like they were the most important people in the whole hotel. You do that too, Bea. You have a flair for this industry that I haven't seen here in a very long time.'

I manage to settle my breathing and do my best to take in what she has to say. I'm not sure how or why I'm sitting here, but it's making me more nervous than any celebrity guest ever could, or any VIP who I'd been told about in advance of a high-end stay in our penthouse suite. Is this her way of letting me know she doesn't want me to leave? I know how rumours start. Has she heard about me and Ollie and my deepening feelings for him?

'I'm not going anywhere, don't worry,' I tell her quickly. 'I adore this place as much as you do.'

She squints at me now, like she is somewhat lost in our conversation.

'I think you already told me that,' she says, 'but I also think you're not hearing me properly.'

I gulp rather noticeably, knowing I'll go over and over this conversation later in the most minute detail and torment myself for every breath I took, never mind every word I said.

'I – I don't understand.'

'Let me tell you something, Bea,' she says, nodding at the salmon and cucumber sandwiches in front of us. I take one and nibble on it, only out of politeness as my stomach is swirling right now. 'I wasn't born with a silver spoon in my mouth. Nor did I marry a rich man and live to regret it like my old friend Susan did.'

I couldn't like this lady more if I tried.

'I made my way up, every single step of the ladder, at my own risk. I took gambles. I borrowed and scraped and saved and sacrificed everything to make this work. My husband met me at my darkest hour, but he loved me deeply and he stuck around. He was like my backbone. I believed in The Carnation. He believed in me. And most importantly, we believed in each other.'

I feel myself relaxing at last like a deflating balloon. I take another sandwich, still listening in awe.

'You have, I hope, as many years ahead of you as I have behind me now,' she tells me, before dropping her voice down to a whisper. 'But the thing is, my darling, none of us know our own fate. None of us know if we're going to live until we're in our tenth decade like I am, or if we're going to be taken out in a heartbeat in our youth like Coral was on that horrid day in 1996.'

I think, of course, of Peter. I think of Ollie's mum Eleanor, whose life was taken far too young, too.

'You have to follow your own dreams. You have to chase your own—'

'Rainbows,' we both say at the same time.

She smiles.

'Now you've got it,' she tells me. 'The Carnation. This was my dream. Now what's yours?'

I am astounded at the second reference to chasing rainbows I've heard recently, but I much prefer Alice's positive approach to Sean's scathing remarks that day by the river.

'I – I suppose I've always dreamed of having my own place where people would want to stay,' I say, unable to stop the words from tumbling from my mouth. 'I've worked hard to get where I am, but yes, that would be my ultimate dream. But I do love it here. I've loved it from the day I first met Leroy on the steps outside. I've loved it ever since I first saw you in person. I've—'

'In your own time,' she says, interrupting my flow, but I'm somehow glad she has, as I've no real idea as to where I was going in my train of thought. 'I think you already know your own destiny, don't you, Beatrice?'

'Do I?'

She nods, her eyes never leaving mine.

'Listen to your heart,' she tells me, lightly tapping below her dainty collarbone. 'That's where you'll find the answers to all your questions, and the way to fulfilling your wildest dreams. It's all in your heart.'

I don't know why but I feel all afluster.

All I can see in my head right now flashing before my eyes is a future with Ollie at Oyster Cottage. But Oyster Cottage is not mine, it's his. That's his legacy from his parents, from his mother and her own style. I can't imagine it ever feeling like mine.

George the waiter comes back to top up our teacups at exactly the right moment. I feel tears sting my eyes. I feel confused and uneasy. I feel a little bit sick, if the truth be told, because every single word Alice is saying to me is true.

As much as I love it here at The Carnation, I see life moving on very quickly while mine in some ways is staying still. I see Leroy growing closer to Anne, I hear of Sita's latest auditions in the West End and I know she is close to success. Life is moving fast. I'm very comfortable and could easily see another ten years pass me by.

And then what? Am I just kicking stones here? Am I doing exactly what I said I'd never do and settling for a good life rather than my best life? How do I know if I'll be blessed with another ten years? What do I know? What am I waiting for? Or am I content? Is that what this is? If I am, why do I feel like I'm killing time until I can be with Ollie again?

That's not contentment, that's torture.

'Eat up and drink up, my dear,' Alice tells me gently. 'I think we've covered enough ground for one day, don't you?'

I nod graciously, glad of the break in conversation to do my best to find an appetite for the exquisite food that sits before us. I know how much this all costs and I couldn't bear to send it back without making a good effort.

'You've given me a lot of food for thought, pardon the pun,' I say to her, relaxing a little.

'I'm glad,' she replies, nibbling on her sandwich before reaching for a cream bun with a huge smile on her face. 'You know, Leroy has often asked me what the cure is for a broken heart, and do you know what I've always told him?'

My eyes widen now. 'He asked me that too when he was in hospital. I had no idea what to say.'

'My answer is to love harder,' she tells me. 'When you think you've loved enough, love harder. It will get you through everything you need to in life, believe me. And I'm living proof that it works. Always stay in the here and now, not the past or the future, and love with all your heart, as hard as you can. And then it will heal. I see him healing now, don't you?'

She nods to her driver politely, which attracts a flurry of staff to her side, and even though I'd my eye on a second cheesecake for myself, I dab my mouth with my napkin and stand up to see her off.

'You finish up, there's no rush,' she tells me. 'Same time next week, then? And you're allowed to use that love for yourself too, don't forget. In fact, it's the best place to start.'

I can barely reply, so I just mutter in agreement.

'Thank you, Mrs Charles. I will certainly have a lot to think about now.'

'You can call me Alice,' she replies as she puts on her own coat with confidence. 'I hope you know you're appreciated here, but never stop chasing your own dreams. This was my dream, Bea. I can't wait to hear more about yours.'

Chapter Twenty-Six

Ollie

On the morning of the wedding in December, Aunt Nora sits proudly and protectively beside me and Bea in the church pew in her brand-new navy dress, a fancy net headpiece and with rosary beads clasped around her fingers.

Bea looks stunning in her long-sleeved red velvet dress which her friend Sita helped her choose in a charity shop in London, knowing today was a big occasion for us both in more ways than one. It's our first official outing together, even though we've known each other in some shape or form for almost a year.

As always, she is taking in the surroundings as if she's seeing things through the eyes of a child. Winter-themed blooms have transformed the altar of our local church with an arch of crisp foliage and neutral-coloured dried flowers, while tall, almost life-size candelabras fill the church with romantic flickering light.

'It's all so dreamy,' Bea whispers, resting her head on my shoulder. 'It's like a true winter wonderland, Ollie. I love it.'

'Aren't you delighted there's no sign of them?' hisses my

aunt when the church organ strikes up the entrance hymn to announce the long-awaited arrival of Buster's bride. She blesses herself as she speaks in case that makes a difference. 'I don't know about you, Ollie, but I can breathe now. Thank heavens for small mercies they're not here.'

My old friend Buster, looking dapper in black tie, cranes his neck around to see his stunning wife-to-be walk towards him. He catches my eye from the front pew of the church, so I give him a thumbs up.

'Best of luck,' I mime to him, as an unexpected wave of emotion surges through me when I think of how things should have been. My dad should have been here for a start. He would have enjoyed today.

He loved weddings and he adored Buster. He adored all my friends, even Foxy, and when the dust finally settled after I got back on my feet in London, he predicted one day I might forgive Foxy for affording me a blessing in disguise.

Dad would have loved Bea too, and all her family. He would have enjoyed how her father and sister sing together in perfect harmony, which I can't wait to hear for myself one day, and how they never forget to raise a toast on every single occasion to young Peter who left them all too soon, even keeping an empty seat at the table every Christmas in his honour.

I wipe a tear that appears unexpectedly in my eye, which Aunt Nora notices, but I shake my head in case she thinks I'm worried that Monica might show, which is so far from my own train of thought right now.

It's not every day you see your best friend get married,

and although in a different life it would be the three of us friends – Simon, Foxy and I – standing by Buster's side up there at the altar as his best man and groomsmen, I'm relieved he chose to avoid any awkwardness by going with just Simon instead. As kids we always said we'd be all together on our individual wedding days, but that was before my best man ran away with my bride-to-be.

'She's beautiful,' whispers Bea as the bride, Deanna, leaves her father's arm to be welcomed by Buster, who is beaming like I've never seen him smile before. 'That vintage cream dress is sensational. Look at the detail on the back. Wow.'

Just as I'd expected, Aunt Nora is weeping into a tissue like she does at every wedding. Bea is emotional too, which is endearing, especially since she's never met Buster or Deanna before.

'I don't know why I'm crying,' she sniffles as the happy bride and groom walk hand in hand back down the aisle to a booming string quartet rendition of Elbow's 'One Day Like This'. 'It's all just so touching and romantic.'

And it really is. I can breathe out now. I'm glad I came today, and I'm also secretly glad Foxy and Monica stayed away so we all can enjoy our day.

'What a stunning bride Deanna is,' Aunt Nora enthuses as we shuffle behind the other guests down the aisle. 'Unique, classy and so, so elegant. Buster looks like the cat that got the cream, and rightly so.'

After the Mass we make the short journey to the reception full of chat and reflection.

The music was uplifting, the bride and groom were on top of the world, the style was outrageously glamorous and even the priest was funny as he joked and quipped about turning water into wine and how it would come in very handy as Buster was known to be tight with money.

But this is all put to rest when we arrive at the venue, where it seems like no stone has been left unturned by the new bride and groom. It's stunning, with scenic views of nine counties of Ireland and across the breathtaking, choppy shores of Donegal Bay.

'Let's go inside and have the most wonderful day together, all three of us.'

I'm just about to open the car door when I turn to see that Aunt Nora's face has turned to stone.

'What's wrong?' I ask her. 'Aunt Nora, what is it?'

She tries to speak but can't, so she just nods towards the windscreen, then points her finger towards the hotel's main doors. When I look in the same direction as she does, I see exactly what has caught her attention.

Monica stands posing on the red carpet which has been laid out for the bride and groom in front of the beautiful hotel.

'Jesus,' I whisper.

She wears a figure-hugging red velvet dress almost identical to Bea's charity shop find but no doubt at least three times more expensive. She has her hand on one voluptuous hip, her head is thrown back so that her long, poker-straight black hair reaches her waist, and her full lips are painted the same colour as her dress. Her photographer, my former best friend Jimmy Fox, snaps her in different poses as she laughs and seduces the camera.

'Ah, I was sure they would have the grace to sit this one out,' I say, a lot louder than I intend to.

'Are you OK, Ollie?' asks Bea from the backseat.

'Of course I'm OK, Bea. It's fine.'

I just need to take a minute to breathe. My palms sweat as the day my former life fell apart flashes before me like a black and white movie. Voices echo in my head, overlapping with each other.

I hear Foxy plead innocence, that it wasn't as it seemed.

I hear Monica crying in deep sorrow one minute then finally confessing her undying love for my best friend, doing her best to explain how it 'just happened' and how they were going to tell me when the time was right.

I hear my father mutter expletives about humiliation and trust and brotherhood and how he'd always treated Foxy like one of his own.

I hear Aunt Nora slam the door in their faces, telling them never to cross our paths again.

But the one voice I don't hear is my own. Why didn't I speak out?

I barely said a word because I couldn't think where to start. I got drunk, very drunk indeed. I went on holiday alone and even though my heart and my pride was in pieces, I threw myself back into work at the hospital, which became my saving grace.

But I still said nothing. Which makes me believe that the person I'm most annoyed at now over all this, is myself.

'Utterly shameless,' says Aunt Nora, unable to look in their direction any longer. 'Oh, I'd rather just go home if you don't mind, Oliver. I can't be responsible for what I'll say or do to those two, especially after I've had a few sherries. I'm sorry, but no.'

She folds her arms and stares out the passenger side window on to a magnificent view of Benbulben mountain, but there's a new fire in my gut that makes me want to rise above their audacity to show up here today.

I hear my father's voice in my head, his gentle tone tinged with hurt and sadness, yet also with a sense of deep strength and pride.

Their actions say more about them than they do you, son. Never, ever forget that.

I turn around from the driver's seat to check on Bea. As flashbacks played in my mind for the last minute or so, I didn't think to see how she would be feeling.

But she simply shakes her head and laughs it off, just like I hoped she would. No drama, no fuss, no overwhelm – just logical, practical, strong and beautifully Bea in every way.

'It doesn't bother me in the slightest,' she says. 'And I mean that sincerely; however, I'll go with the flow if it's uncomfortable for you, Ollie. Do whatever you feel is the right thing to do.'

'But what about you?' I ask, just to be sure.

Bea flashes me a smile that warms my heart and fills me

up with a reminder of just how blessed I am to have her in my life.

'Personally, I think the girl is a sorry fool to have let someone like you go,' she says, reaching out and squeezing my hand in support, 'but I'm glad she did, because I wouldn't be here otherwise. I'm the lucky one in all this. We both are. It's her loss, and Foxy's.'

Aunt Nora glances at me, her eyes wide and her mouth open.

'Well, that's another way of looking at it, isn't it?' she quips in amazement. She takes off her glasses and quickly cleans them with a hankie. 'Bea, I think the world could do with a lot more people like you. Why didn't I think of it that way? Gosh, I could kick myself for letting them get under my skin for so long!'

'The world could absolutely do with more people like you, Bea,' I agree, lightly kissing the tips of her fingers in appreciation of her wisdom and support. She always has the words to ground me when I go off kilter. Right now, I don't think I could fall for her harder if I tried.

'It's a Leroy thing,' she explains with a smile. 'Following in the footsteps of Michelle Obama, he always taught me there's a lot more mileage in taking the higher ground. When someone treats you low, you rise up and go high. I've tried it, and although it can be hard and although it can sting, it always works out the better option.'

Aunt Nora clasps her hands tightly together as if in prayer for a second.

'I've always loved Leroy,' she says, undoing her seat belt with gusto. 'Right, let's go and celebrate the joy of love and marriage with our dear friends Buster and Deanna in the style that they deserve. I hope they're serving Killybegs salmon for dinner. My mouth is watering already.'

Bea gets out of the car first, looking radiant in red as the cool winter sunshine reflects off the bay in the distance. I follow next, fixing my jacket and bow tie in the car window's reflection. Aunt Nora, after topping up her lipstick which she once told me gave her superpowers, takes my arm, as we walk towards the hotel's entrance.

This could be brilliant.

Or it could all go horribly wrong.

Chapter Twenty-Seven

Bea

With a warm, spiced glass of mulled wine in our hands, festive tunes tinkling on a harp and a cosy corner by the open coal fire in the luxurious hotel lobby bar, the mood in our small gathering is what I would describe as bold and brave yet tinged with the slightest air of tension.

'Keep smiling, it will confuse them,' I say to both Ollie and Aunt Nora. 'Gosh, have you ever seen such sparkle and glamour? I could sit here and people-watch forever.'

I know this is hard for them. I know how much it must hurt despite so much time having passed, but I also know that no one has the power to make you feel bad unless you give it to them.

'It's a top-class location,' says Ollie, taking in the huge Christmas tree and sea views from the floor-to-ceiling windows. For a day in December, the sun is shining high in the sky even if the air is biting outside.

I always feel instantly at home in hotels, no matter where I am in the world, so for just a moment, I allow myself to take in my surroundings, watching the impeccable staff cater to every single guest's needs with care and attention.

Sparkling champagne is poured into tilted glasses with raspberry frosting, while the sound of laughter mixed with festive songs and clinking cheers fills the air. The smell of seasonal foods wafts through the warm air from the kitchen, and a show-stopping harpist in a sparkly black ballgown tinkles gently in the background, playing Christmas carols which sound like balm for the soul.

Dainty festive canapés are laid out on the tables, a treat we are all very ready for after the moving church service which set the tone for the day. There are Bloody Mary prawns with lettuce scoops, chopped egg salad on salt and vinegar crisps, brie and cranberry twists and good old-fashioned pigs in blankets alongside mini sausages smothered in a sticky honey and mustard dressing.

'This food is delicious,' I say, tucking into the prawns and lettuce scoops to begin with. I offer Ollie some pigs in blankets, but he politely refuses. Aunt Nora doesn't seem to have much of an appetite either. She taps a packet of cigarettes on the table as she glares into space, a million thoughts racing through her head, no doubt.

'I think winter weddings always top the polls in the fashion stakes,' I say to them both, still doing my best to keep the mood up. 'There's something about all the glitz that sets them heads above weddings throughout the rest of the year.'

Yet despite my efforts to crank up some conversation by admiring the style of the ladies' winter fashions, or remarking how the men all look so dapper in their tux and tails, or wishing I could see Buster and Deanna on their wedding photoshoot down by the cliffs, nothing I say or do can break the undercurrent of frosty air that lingers around our small table by the fire here in the corner of the vast lobby bar.

'At least it's stayed dry so far,' Ollie says eventually, gulping his glass of mulled wine. 'Nothing as bad as rain on your wedding day, is there?'

More silence follows, so I turn to the harpist for conversational inspiration.

'Is that "Silent Night" I hear?' I ask.

' "Mistletoe and Wine",' Aunt Nora replies. 'Christ, I can't stand Cliff Richard.'

'Sounds like "Silent Night" to me,' Ollie agrees.

'It's Cliff Richard,' she insists.

I'm not quite sure who is right, but the mood isn't set up for debates right now, so we leave it at that, though I'd put money on it that it's 'Silent Night'.

Monica and Foxy mingle in the distance, but I can't help but notice how their conversations seem staged and exaggerated, like they're trying too hard. She looks like an iconic movie star, he is like some sort of seventies rocker, and together they ooze confidence and audacity like I've never seen before.

I wonder what Ollie is really thinking when he looks at them. Is he angry? Is he sad? Is he still hurting? Does he still *care*?

That makes me feel very wobbly, but rather than tell him how I feel, I'm more focused on making sure Aunt Nora doesn't break character. The last thing we want is a scene at someone else's wedding.

'Our Bea could defuse a bomb in less than sixty seconds,' my brother used to say when I set out to settle a row. He called me the peacemaker, a default role I'd adapt when as kids we argued over the pettiest everyday issues like who got to sit in the front seat of the car with Dad or who had the best taste in music or fashion – or anything really. I would always solve the row. I'd always give in or give up to avoid confrontation.

But Ollie and I have no secrets, so I've no fear of confrontation when it comes to him.

He's sworn to me that he is over the trauma and all that stemmed from his messy break-up from Monica.

He told me about the effect it had on all his friends, how he had to let his wider family circle know that the wedding was off, even though the news had travelled around them all faster than the speed of light.

He also told me how his father assured him afterwards that one day he'd be thankful for the whole sorry situation. He may have lost an old friend, but he'd dodged two bullets for the price of one, and that was worth any heartbreak for sure.

I wish I'd met Jack Brennan. I'm sure Ollie could do with his fatherly ways and words of wisdom today.

'I have to say, those decorations must have cost a small fortune,' I say in a bid to lift the long silences that hang in the air between us, masked only slightly by the harpist and the humdrum chatter in the room. 'It's unusual to see golds and silvers mixed, but I like it. I must keep that in mind for The Carnation next year. What do you think, Ollie?'

Ollie smiles at me in appreciation of my efforts to keep the conversation flowing, reminding me of how much I feel for him. He is painting on a very brave face, but I know he's finding this just a little awkward.

'I think they're beautiful, just like you are,' he replies.

He looks so handsome today in his black and white tuxedo, and the huge Christmas tree that twinkles right behind where he sits makes a beautiful backdrop.

'If we do cross their paths at any stage of the day,' I whisper to him, 'just be polite but walk away. Rise above whatever they have to say and walk away.'

'I've no intention of crossing their paths,' he tells me in return. 'I don't care, I promise. I'd much rather focus on the important people in my life, which includes you by the way. You are the most important.'

He leans across and kisses my cheek, which makes me shiver. He holds my hand and his eyes light up and then fill with emotion. It feels like everything around us has stopped, frozen in time. My hands are shaking. His are too. He puts his finger lightly under my chin and looks into my eyes.

'My God, I'm the luckiest man in the world,' he whispers, laughing a little in what seems like disbelief.

We stare and smile by the warmth of the turf fire, then he lifts his glass and clinks it on mine. I'd love to freeze this moment for real, to capture it forever, as I don't think I've ever felt so much for one person as I do for him. It's times like this when I wish I could write it all down or photograph it or record it in some physical way, yet I know deep down that I don't need to because I'll never forget this feeling.

It's too intense, too high, too much like pure love to ever fade away. I also know that tomorrow we will have to say goodbye again, and the thought of that already burns. But Christmas is around the corner, and another busy season awaits us both. I want to tell him I love him. I want to scream it from the rooftops. I want to do what I told Alice Charles I would when we last met and throw caution to the wind and come here to be with him, but is it too soon? Is it better too soon than too late, like she told me?

'Penny for your thoughts,' he whispers, still caught up in the bubble we just created around us. 'You look worried now.'

'You are perfect, that's all,' I reply. 'This is perfect. I want to enjoy every moment of this time with you before . . .'

'Before we have to say goodbye again,' he says, finishing my sentence.

The idea of goodbye hangs like an unwelcome stranger between us now. I close my eyes. No, I won't give in to thinking too far ahead. We need to stay in the moment and appreciate what we have in the here and now, no matter how tempting it is to worry about the future.

But it has already killed the mood somehow.

'I'll be right back,' he says, giving me a quick peck on the cheek. 'Bathroom, won't be long.'

I bite the inside of my cheek as I watch him walk away.

'You OK, Aunt Nora? Can I get you anything?'

Aunt Nora, bless her, is doing her best but can't hide her feelings about Monica and Foxy quite as subtly as she'd hoped. As soon as Ollie's back is turned briefly, she takes the opportunity to have another swipe at her sworn enemies who stand at the bar in the distance, both looking like they've stepped out of a blockbuster movie set.

'You'd think they'd have had the manners to stay in America or wherever they've been, knowing we'd be here today,' she whispers, shooting daggers with her eyes in their direction. 'I'm sorry, love. I know this is like picking at a scab and it's the last thing you want to be hearing about, but Ollie is like my own son and has been for many years. When my sister was dying . . . when . . . '

She reaches inside her sleeve to pull out a tissue, then carefully dabs the sides of her eyes, all the while making sure Ollie isn't yet within hearing distance.

'When my sister Eleanor was dying, I made her a promise that I'd look after Ollie in the very same way as she had hoped to do as his mother,' she tells me, her voice cracking with emotion. 'That boy has suffered enough heartbreak in his short lifetime by losing both his parents, so it eats me up inside to see people he counted as his closest inner circle disrespect him and try to ruin him in the way they did. How very dare they show up here today!'

I put my hand on her shoulder. This is perhaps much more difficult for her than any of us could imagine.

'I saw them together once,' she says.

'I'm so sorry.'

'They said I was crazy,' she sniffs. 'They said I was imagining things. They lied until their lies became so twisted and contradictory that they had to come clean and admit what they'd been up to in that room, but the bigger blow came when they told us they were in love, and had been for some time.'

I wave at Ollie, who is thankfully walking back towards us now but still out of earshot.

'Look at him, the handsome devil,' I say to Aunt Nora to lighten the mood. 'Was his father as striking at his age? Or does he get his looks and charm from his mother's side, Aunt Nora?'

She takes the bait and ponders my question for all of two seconds before bursting into a fit of giggles.

'He's the image of his grandfather, even in his swagger and the cool way he walks,' she says, sitting up straight now as if our previous conversation never took place. 'And he knows we're talking about him. Look at the smile on that face. Look at those dimples. The Brennans didn't have dimples like that, no way. He gets his good looks from my side.'

I reach across to sample another festive treat from a platter on the table in front of us, delighted to have made her laugh if only for a moment. Feeling like I've made some progress at last, I'm just about to offer Aunt Nora some when I feel my skin run cold as a voice calls out Ollie's name.

I look up. It's her.

Surely it can't be Monica approaching him casually, right under our noses? No, no, no. None of us were banking on this. How can any of us be cool and dignified when she is so blatant and insensitive?

She strides towards him like she's on a catwalk, dripping

with expensive jewellery and with a tan that's most definitely not out of a bottle.

'Oliver! My old friend! I'd know those strong, manly shoulders anywhere,' she calls to him, almost purring like an exotic cat. 'And those dimples. You look gorgeous, babe.'

Babe?

Ollie stops in his tracks and turns towards her so that we're looking at the back of his jacket. He puts his hands in his pockets. He knows we can hear her.

I put my hand on Aunt Nora's lap to reassure her it's best for her to keep the peace for now. Once again, I hear Leroy's words of wisdom echo in my mind. I also hear Peter's voice in my head, playfully teasing that if I always sit on the fence, I'll get splinters.

'He can handle her, I'm sure,' I whisper, even though it doesn't look that way so far. I take a long gulp of my champagne. Aunt Nora does the same beside me.

I try not to look at Monica, but I can't help it when she's so close. Her dress – so like my red velvet gown but much, much shorter – reveals never-ending bronzed legs which makes me tug at my hem, regretting why I thought it would be a good idea to wear tights. I feel frumpy, ordinary and quite small as she towers over us, ignoring our very existence.

'My God, you're still as hot as ever up close,' I hear her say to Ollie in a seductive tone, then she catches the glare of Aunt Nora and changes her tune. 'Whoops, I'm a little bit tipsy. I came over to say I'm sorry.'

I feel sick.

'You're sorry?' says Ollie.

'About your dad,' she tells him, stroking his arm. 'I just heard this minute. Simon told me. Gosh, I'd no idea he was so ill.'

I feel slightly nauseous.

'Well, I'm not going to stand here at a wedding and apologise for the rest, am I?' she whispers but we can still hear every word. 'Not the time or the place for that, but I did want to sympathise. I am so sorry to hear your dad has passed on.'

I count to ten inside my head, fully expecting Ollie to blow up at her horrible, patronising tone, but he stands there like a statue, letting her have her say. Is he afraid of her or is he just biding his time for the right moment? We agreed to be polite then walk away. Is this the polite part? If so, it's really running its course.

'Maybe you and I could have a word in private when the party gets started?' she asks him. 'I'd love to catch up for old times' sake.'

Has Ollie forgotten I'm right behind him? Does she know I exist?

My heart is thumping in my chest. I try to imagine what it might be like to be in Ollie's position right now as he faces an ugly episode of his past in real life after years of healing and acceptance, not to mention losing his father only earlier this year. But why doesn't he speak up?

Surely he'll take this opportunity to tell her to go to hell. Surely he'll say what he thinks of them both once and for all. Surely he'll speak up against all the hurt, the humiliation and the betrayal they brought his way.

I squeeze Aunt Nora's hand. I know she is about to explode, but the last thing we want to do at a beautiful wedding like this is make a scene. I feel eyes from every angle of the room darting in Ollie's direction, I hear hushed whispers as they look on, but my stomach really goes into overdrive when his so-called friend, Foxy, slides up behind his model girlfriend with two pints of Guinness in his hand.

'Peace offering?' he says, handing one to Ollie. 'You still drink the black stuff, Ollie? Look, I know this is incredibly awkward for all of us, but can we call it a day? We've all moved on. Feelings change. I hear you're doing well? New job in Letterkenny? New girlfriend too, I see? She's very pretty.'

I want to interrupt. I want to swipe the pint of Guinness out of Ollie's hands and pour it over Foxy's expensive suit. I want to get off the fence and tell them both just how much hurt they have caused to two people I love dearly, but just as I'm about to get up and say my piece, Ollie beats me to it.

He speaks up at last.

'Cheers,' he says to both Foxy and Monica, raising his pint in the air. They both look perplexed at his reaction, and they watch agog when he puts the pint glass to his lips and gulps it down in one.

'Cheers,' they both mutter as they wait for him to finish.

'Ahhh. You're right, I do still love a pint of Guinness,' he says, handing Foxy back the empty glass. 'Thanks for that, Fox. And thanks also for saving my ass four years ago when I almost made the biggest mistake of my life by marrying someone who was so wrong for me, a blind man could see it. You better believe I'm doing well. I'm on top of the world, *mate*. Now, you two go and have a good day together. I know we will.'

He turns away from them and comes back towards us with a cheeky smile and a walk that oozes so much confidence, I feel an urge to high-five him, but I won't. I need to play it cool. Aunt Nora clasps her hands and looks up to the heavens, then shakes her head softly with her eyes closed. I can almost guess what she is thinking, or at least who she is talking to in her mind.

'I know before you say it,' he says to me when he plonks down beside me.

'That you're awesome?'

'Well, that's very nice to hear, but I thought you were going to tell me I had a Guinness moustache, and that it's a terrible waste of a national treasure in your opinion.'

'You do have a Guinness moustache,' I smile as he licks it off then wipes the rest with the back of his hand.

As the bride and groom arrive from their photoshoot in a shiny silver limousine outside, Aunt Nora watches Ollie and me caught up in the most blissful moment.

'I'm so proud of you,' she says across to him. 'So proud.'

We make our way to the dining room for the wedding breakfast, where I marvel at the rows of chandeliers hanging from the ceiling, not to mention the burgundy blooms and greenery in bronze vases with white pampas grass giving the whole room a boho aesthetic.

'There's Killybegs salmon on the menu,' I tell Aunt Nora as we take our seats, guided by a detailed table plan and shiny grey pebbles from Fintra Beach, each bearing our individual names in fine white hand-painted lettering. 'They must have ordered it especially for you.'

'This day keeps getting better and better,' she says, as she takes her seat and marvels at the wedding favours, which are cute little clear glass Christmas baubles inscribed with the date and the name of the bride and groom.

I take a photo of the exquisite table setting and send it to my family group chat, knowing Mum and Patsi will appreciate the décor and detail as much as I do.

Hope you're having the best time, Patsi writes back. Try not to think too much about tomorrow.

Mum sends a love heart, and a follow-up to what Patsi is thinking. The very thought of tomorrow is already filling me with dread.

A painful goodbye is the price we pay for love, she types, which brings tears to my eyes. Your time with Ollie is precious. Don't let the thought of tomorrow ruin that, darling!

I hold Ollie's hand and make a silent wish that saying goodbye tomorrow comes easier than I think it might. I also know right now that I'll never feel for anyone else like I feel for him, but something is going to have to change very soon.

We need to have the conversation.

I need to decide if my life in London, where I've made a career and a reputation in five-star, high-end hospitality, is worth being apart from him for.

He needs to tell me where he sees our future. Is it back in London or is it here at Oyster Cottage? Or am I thinking too far ahead? Will he laugh it all off and tell me to relax and enjoy the ride?

Is that what I should do? I squeeze his hand again beneath the table, sweetly savouring how his fingers find mine and entwine so easily as he chats to his company. I rest my head on his shoulder, breathing in the dreamy comfort that only he can bring my way.

I want to press pause, to inhale this moment, to relish being with him for just a little while longer, but as I do, the pain of tomorrow creeps closer, suffocating me already.

It scares me to admit it, but I'm not sure I can live in this halfway existence for much longer. With Sean, the distance was like a safety net between us, but with Ollie it's a threat that pushes me into a corner, forcing me to decide on all or nothing.

Before I leave Oyster Cottage this time, I need to make the call on which of the two it will be.

Chapter Twenty-Eight

Ollie

Oyster Cottage, Teelin, County Donegal

I wake up the morning after the wedding feeling like I've been living a lucid dream. Yesterday was like looking at my life through a kaleidoscope, with so much colour and confusion to begin with, then what emerged to be a day full of love, laughter and closure on so many levels.

And it was all because of Bea. She is like my anchor on a stormy day, always there to keep me steady. I watch her as she sleeps soundly beside me here in the comfort of my own bed in Oyster Cottage. Her dark curls fall like a waterfall on her shoulders, and her soft breath sounds like a rhythm that soothes my heart. When she is here with me, it's like my family home bursts into life again, and I can almost feel my parents smiling down on us both when we're together.

She has lit up every corner of this cottage, gliding from room to room throwing out ideas like confetti on how I should revamp the vibe of the place while keeping with my mother's timeless taste. I try to imagine my life before she came along, allowing this moment of glorious in-between-day-and-night to bring me back to our very first meeting on Christmas Eve when she had her head buried in her notebook at the airport.

I remember how she told me that she found solace and clarity in writing stuff down, and how she recommended I give it a go. I did try it a little, but now with my head full of love for her as well as the dread of saying goodbye in a few hours, I lean quietly across my pillow and open the drawer of my bedside locker, where I find a pen and some paper.

Outside, a light fall of snow sits on the windowsill and a robin drops by to say hello, then flies off as soon as I start writing. It's gibberish at first, so I scribble it out and start again, wondering how many times she does the same. But then it flows. My heart swells when I picture her so strong and radiant, so loyal and fierce and so wise with words yesterday, and advice when those around her need it most. I write it all down, then I fold up the paper and tuck it into a side pocket of her suitcase which lies beside the wardrobe in my bedroom. I chuckle to myself, wondering when she'll find it and hoping that it might make her feel closer to me when we are apart. It's light, it's maybe a little bit funny, but I hope it makes her smile one day.

The clock on the wall ticks like a timebomb, reminding me that we are just hours away from saying goodbye. Bea's hire car is in the driveway. She will leave early afternoon before darkness falls and make her way to see her family in Benburb before catching the flight from Belfast to Heathrow.

I will occupy my mind with work this evening, holding on to the glow of her presence until it fades in a few days and we both feel so far apart, empty and bereft. I know she is struggling this time more than ever as our time together comes to an end. I've caught her staring into space when she thought I wasn't looking. I've seen the pain in her eyes as we grasp onto every precious second as time slips through our fingers. And I'm not sure how long we can keep this arrangement going before one of us, probably Bea, will explode with frustration.

Then Christmas will come, and who knows what that will bring. The hospital rota is being made up this week, and I'm torn between wanting to work so I can forget about it all until I can go to London to see her, and the need to be at home with Aunt Nora for Christmas, the first one without my father.

I've accepted that it will be impossible for Bea and I to spend Christmas together. With it being my first one on the new job and with her commitments at the hotel, it seems more and more unlikely as it creeps closer.

'Did I hear someone say bacon and eggs for breakfast?'

Bea's first words when she wakes up bring me back to the present. The room is airy and cool, but our clothes from the night before are draped over chairs and on the floor, a reminder of how eager we were to get under the covers and spend the night in each other's arms.

Now, a sense of dread lingers. One neither of us dare mention. And the clock on the wall keeps ticking.

'I do believe it's your turn after my MasterChef efforts yesterday morning,' I say with a long stretch. She turns around to me, draping her arm across my waist. I wish every morning could be like this. 'Bacon, eggs, toast, coffee, orange juice, the works. You know where everything is here by now. Go on. I'll time you.'

She snuggles in closer, wrapping her leg across mine so our bodies are entwined. Her skin is warm, almost hot to touch, and when she kisses me across my bare chest I know that breakfast, just like most mornings when we are together, is going to have to wait.

'How is she?' I ask when Bea comes back to Oyster Cottage after saying her goodbyes to Aunt Nora.

Bea has been quiet since breakfast, barely eating what we ended up preparing together and grabbing the excuse to say goodbye to Aunt Nora with both hands while I washed up. We're performing a tightrope dance around each other, skirting the issue that hangs like a dark cloud above us.

'She refused to admit singing Cliff Richard songs all the way home in the taxi and she's adamant she doesn't have a hangover. She's just tired, she says.' Bea laughs. 'I only hope I have her stamina when I'm her age.'

Bea, as always, has Murphy by her side in the kitchen. He seems to like having her around as much as I do.

I hand her a coffee. She uses it to warm her hands as her cold breath from outdoors mixes with the steam that rises from the mug.

'I suppose I'd better make tracks soon before the weather gets any worse,' she tells me, bringing up the inevitable as tears prick her eyes. Her voice shakes at the mere mention of leaving. 'Are you all set for work? Did you say it's a seven p.m. start tonight?'

'Yes, seven p.m. until seven a.m. I'll squeeze a gym session in before then to sweat out the toxins from all that food and alcohol yesterday.'

I flex my biceps and she rolls her eyes, then puts down her coffee and comes into my arms.

'Oh, Ollie,' she whispers. 'My heart is hurting, like I can physically feel it smashing into tiny pieces. Is that possible?'

I kiss her hair. I hold her tighter.

'Please don't say that,' I reply, but I feel it too. 'Every time we say goodbye it gets harder and harder to do, yes, but we'll find a way to see each other again soon, I promise.'

'When?' she asks.

I stare up at the ceiling. I don't have an answer to her question.

We stand there for a few minutes, our eyes closed as we sway gently from side to side. I do my best to enjoy the moment. I do my best to appreciate the experiences we've had over the past forty-eight hours rather than pine for the long stretch ahead until I see her again.

She pulls away gently and retrieves her coffee, then leans against the small island that sits in the middle of the kitchen floor.

A white blanket lies on the garden, glistening snow resting on the branches of my father's precious ash tree. Its blinding light makes the red berries on the holly tree pop, while the heat from the stove inside where we are makes it a cosy contrast to the outside winter wonderland.

'When are we going to talk about it, Ollie?' she asks me. 'I'm leaving today and I don't know what's next for us. I don't know when I'm going to see you again. I don't know if we'll even see each other at Christmas this year.'

'Really?' I ask. 'Surely we'll be able to see each other at some stage over Christmas?'

She blows out a long breath. I sit down across from her, glad in a way we're finally addressing the elephant in the room but afraid of where this conversation is going to take us.

'But how?' she replies. 'And every day that follows Christmas? This is agony. Absolute agony.'

I scramble in my head for some sort of solution, anything to smooth this over, if only for now, but dates, times, days of the week all blur into one.

'How about – how about we look at it from a different perspective?' I suggest. 'We could make it exciting. You know, the spontaneity of not knowing when we'll be together again could keep things fresh. It could . . . I'm grasping at straws, I know.'

Bea shakes her head.

'I'm sorry, but I can't see it that way. It's weighing me down,' she says with tears in her eyes. 'I miss you too much; it eats me up inside. I can't do this any more.'

Her words hit me right where it hurts.

'What do you mean, you can't do this any more?'

'I mean I can't do it.'

'Please don't say that.'

'But it's true, Ollie,' she whispers. 'It's getting harder

every time. I can't do it. I can't be with you but not be with you. It's too painful.'

My heart is beating so fast right now. As much as I was expecting a conversation like this to come up before she left, I didn't think it would be so extreme.

'Are you saying it's all or nothing, then?' I ask her, terrified of the answer already. 'Is that what you're saying, Bea, because I'm not sure I can make that choice right now and I don't think you can either. I'd never ask you to. I'd never ask you to make that choice.'

She shakes her head in defiance. Murphy tries to jump up on my lap, but I can't entertain him right now as my whole world is under threat of crashing down around me.

I search my mind for options on what to do or say.

'One of us has to make that choice,' she says, wiping tears from her cheeks. 'We can't even make any plans to keep us going through the days apart because our jobs don't allow it. I feel like I'm freefalling, Ollie. I've no control over any of this and it scares me.'

'But it won't be forever,' I insist. I want to hold her, to reassure her. I also know I don't have the answers we both need. And neither does she.

'I'm afraid of what it will do to us. I've been there before, remember?' she says. 'Distance soon becomes a poison that swirls into all the gaps that time apart allows it to. Please take it from someone who knows.'

I stand up and walk towards the window. My skin has gone cold, even though the kitchen is like a furnace in comparison to the icy conditions outside.

'But what about yesterday when you said everything was so perfect?' I ask her. 'Was that real, or were you just caught up in the moment?'

'It was very real,' she replies firmly, then stands up to face me.

'And how about when we lie in bed for hours without having to say a word? What about the fun we have, the laughter and all the understanding? That's not going to go away just because of distance and time, is it?'

She nods, crying still. I have a lump in my throat that I can't shift, but I'm too shocked and angry right now to shed any tears.

'Bea, please don't do this,' I plead. 'Tell me what to do to make this better and I'll do it. I'll do anything!'

She keeps looking at me like she's waiting for the penny to drop. Like I don't understand how the road ahead is so full of hurdles that we'll never make it to the other side.

'You're building a truly beautiful life here, the life you've always wanted, and I respect that,' she says. 'I love how passionate you are about your new job and your patients. I adore how much time you have for Aunt Nora and all the love you pour into Oyster Cottage too. But my life . . . my career, my whole existence isn't here, is it? It's in London.'

I want to say it. I want to ask her to be part of this life I'm building here.

'Forever?' I ask. 'Is your life in London written in stone forever? Or could it be somewhere else? With me?'

She takes a deep breath. She waits, as if there's more for me to say, but I don't want to pressurise her, or say too little, or not enough. Eventually she breaks the silence as if in defeat.

'Being with you here in Oyster Cottage has been the best time of my life, Ollie,' she whispers, staring at the floor. 'I will always remember these days as the best days ever. Thank you for having me here. It was magical.'

She lifts her car keys and pats Murphy on the head as tears stream down her face.

'Bea, what do you want me to say?' I call out to her as shock turns to panic and then anger within seconds.

She clutches the car keys in her hand.

'I'm trying to protect my heart from being broken,' she says without looking my way. 'Because every time I leave you, I feel like it's being chipped away at, and I can't go on like this any longer.'

I shake my head. There's no way it can be as cut and dried as that.

'Aren't we worth the sacrifice?' I ask. 'In a world of all or nothing, are you telling me you'd rather have nothing?'

She meets my eye this time.

'Maybe nothing will be easier on both of us in the long run.'

My eyes widen. My throat goes dry.

'Are you serious?' I ask her. 'Oh my God, you *are* serious! What the hell, Bea? Is this what you do?'

'What?'

She stops with her hand on the kitchen door handle and looks back at me over her shoulder.

'You heard me,' I say as frustration fizzles right through

me. 'Is this what you do? A man falls deeply in love with you, head over heels in love with you. So, you wait until he's totally smitten and, at the first sign of reality out of the big honeymoon bubble, you shove it all back in his face and run away because it's a case of all or nothing?'

Her mouth drops open. She shuts the kitchen door and marches back to where I stand by the sink.

'How dare you!' she says. 'How bloody *dare* you. You have no idea how hard this will be if we keep going this way. You're so wrapped up in life here that you've no clue how it feels to be so far away from the person you love long term. It's pain, Ollie. Real pain that hurts until it snaps and breaks. It doesn't work! I'm saving us some major heartache in the long run, believe me.'

I pace the kitchen floor, full of pent-up frustration. Murphy whimpers past me and finds a warm place in front of the stove while Bea and I battle it out like two gladiators in a ring, each as stubborn as the other.

'This is extreme though, isn't it? Is this the best we can come up with?' I ask her. 'Are there no ways to compromise, no meeting each other halfway?'

Our faces are so close they are almost touching.

'I don't want to do this, but I have to,' she replies. 'I can't concentrate on anything in real life any more. Work, friends, nothing fills me up the way it used to because every day I want to be with you, but now you're here and I'm there. This distance is only going to lead us to more heartbreak in the long run. Every single goodbye is killing me inside.'

My head is spinning so much it hurts. We breathe together.

I place my hand on her cheek, wanting to touch her just one more time.

'Don't do this,' I beg her.

She stares back at me, her eyes full of pain.

'I'm sorry,' she whispers. 'I can't think of my life without you in it, Ollie, but I can't live this way either. I ended up resenting Sean because we lived in two very different worlds, and I don't want to ever feel that way about you. I don't ever want to resent you. I have to go now.'

She wipes tears from her eyes with the back of her hand and makes for the hallway.

'I will wait for you,' I tell her. 'Take your time and think this all through, and when you're ready I will be here.'

She stares at me. 'You don't have to say that,' she says.

'I promise I will wait for you here. Forever. If that's what it takes.'

She leans in and hugs me quickly, but before I can say another word, she leaves through the front door and runs down the garden path to her car which is covered in a flurry of snow.

'Damn it!' I shout, kicking the snowy gravel on the driveway as she spins off down the bumpy lane, away from the cottage and out of my life as quickly as she came into it in the first place last Christmas Eve.

Chapter Twenty-Nine

Bea

The Carnation, London

London feels cold, hungry and empty on my return.

I wander from Underground station to station, feeling anonymous and small as strangers push by, each in a bigger hurry than the last. I try to indulge my senses in some shopping, but I feel no rush or excitement in anything I buy.

Being back at work in the hotel with everyone in high Christmas spirits has propped me up a little since I got back from Ireland. There's nothing like working on the front line and having to deal with the public to keep you bobbing along as if everything is well in your world; so as far as possible I've been painting on a smile, faking festive cheer and putting my best foot forward at The Carnation.

But inside I'm bleeding.

And as Christmas creeps closer and closer, no matter how many songs I hear on the radio, no matter how many fancy corporate parties we host at the hotel and no matter how many times my mother calls me to ask if I'm feeling

'Christmassy' yet, I feel like a dead weight is hanging over my shoulders without Ollie in my life.

'It was your choice to be so frivolous and call it quits like a spoilt child,' my sister reminds me on the phone, choosing to show me tough love instead of sympathy. 'He said he'd wait for you, but at the end of the day he'd be justified in licking his wounds and moving on if he wants to. I don't blame him for not being in touch. You should be grovelling to him, not the other way round.'

'Patsi, this isn't helping,' I tell her, hoping a pomegranate face mask and a citrus-infused foot spa will make me feel better this evening after a long day at the hotel. 'Oh Patsi, what have I done?'

I flick through Netflix as we chat on the phone, but every movie and every series I see triggers a memory of my time with Ollie. Songs do the same. Even if they're totally unrelated to our time together, I can still manage to find a link to our love which just drives the pain home further.

'He's a babe, Bea,' she continues, rubbing salt in my open wounds. 'And he works in a very female-dominated world, don't forget. Oh, I can't believe you were so flippant in your big "all or nothing" speech. Yeah, it will be no time before Ollie is swooped up by someone new. You snooze, you lose, sister.'

Patsi is never one to beat around the bush, so I'm not surprised by her approach, but the very thought of Ollie being swooped up by someone new is enough to make me almost physically sick.

'I can see exactly what you're trying to do and yes, it's

336

working, so you can stop right there,' I tell her. 'If you think I'm cruising along and loving life here in London, you're very wrong. I'm like a teenager checking my phone at every turn to see if he's messaged or called. I spend my days looking through photos of us together and at night I'm doing my best to ease the pain by drowning my sorrows in wine or popcorn or ice cream, whichever I can grab first. Even walking with Nana isn't hitting the spot any more because all I see is the ghost of him everywhere I go. This is purgatory but I can't see any other way round it.'

Patsi takes great delight in spelling out what she believes, and has always believed, to be the perfect solution to our great dilemma.

'If I were you, I'd have a good heart-to-heart with Ollie – a proper one this time – and discuss, like two consenting adults, how you could both merge your talents to make Oyster Cottage the success it once was for guests from all over the world,' she tells me. 'Bea, it would be a dream come true for you to live and work there. It's as plain as the nose on your face. And you'd get to be with him every single day just like you both want so badly. It's a no brainer.'

The very suggestion is enough to send shivers down my spine. Even though I'd never have contemplated a move to rural Ireland a year ago, the thought of being with Ollie at Oyster Cottage is enough to make my heart flutter nowadays, but even if I did decide I could up sticks and move to be with him permanently, it's not up to me to suggest it.

It's up to him.

And he didn't.

Or did he? Is that what he meant when he said he'd wait for me forever?

I visit Victor for coffee on days when I'm feeling really low, which is a lot more often than I'd like to admit, especially when I'm surrounded by the world in full jingle bells and festive mode.

He indulges me as I wax lyrical over Oyster Cottage and how wonderful it is, from the wild, rugged seascape views to the quirky corners and cosy bedrooms.

'It sounds like paradise to me,' he tells me with open ears and wide eyes. 'I can't believe you'd want to leave such a place, never mind the dishy owner who is head over heels in love with you. Are you sure you're thinking straight, my friend? Oh, Bea, what have you done? You belong together. You belong at Oyster Cottage if you ask me.'

And in the still of the night as I toss and turn, crying in the dark, I replay every moment of our final conversation, searching through the words we spoke for clues and signs on what the future might hold for me and Ollie.

Leroy taps his gold wristwatch, urging me to hurry along or I'll be late for our dinner date. It's Wednesday Supper Club night, but not as we know it, because tonight we will dine in style on the early bird menu at The Ivy before making our way into the West End to see our very own Sita on stage.

'We are going to be late, Miss Beatrice,' Leroy announces, rolling his eyes to the heavens. He looks very dapper in his deep grey suit, white shirt and Christmas tie, while I've chosen a little black dress for this evening's celebrations, even though I'm feeling anything but festive on the inside. 'I didn't get all dressed up to stand around my place of work seeing things that need to be done. Come on. There's a malt whisky with my name on it, so please hurry.'

The Christmas tree in the lobby of The Carnation is looking as festive as always but with a new look this year, all decked out in silver and gold just like the tree I saw at Buster and Deanna's magnificent wedding.

Every time I look at it I think of Ollie, and every time I think of Ollie my nerve ends tingle at the tough decision I've made.

'I'm on my way, handsome,' I say to Leroy, giving Nana one last snuggle before we head for dinner, but Nana doesn't seem too bothered that I'm leaving. She gets up and wanders behind the mahogany front desk where she pushes her nose into Tessa's leg, wanting more attention from the new girl. It comforts me to know that she's such a sociable dog, so placid and pleasant, and because she sees so many different faces every day, she's never shy.

'Give Sita my best wishes,' says Tessa from behind the huge bunch of red carnations that greet our guests all year round. '*The Sound of Music* has always been my favourite. She'll make a wonderful Baroness.'

'Oh, I will, thank you. And don't forget there are two pre-arranged early check-ins this afternoon,' I remind her as I pull on my new red woollen coat, flicking my dark curls so that they bounce just above my shoulders. 'It's on the house. It's almost Christmas after all.'

Tessa nods.

'You're very kind, Bea. But you *have* told me this at least five times,' she smiles.

'And I'm feeling a sense of déjà vu with all this fussing,' says Leroy, offering his arm to me to hurry me along.

I take one last look around the foyer of The Carnation before we go, doing my best not to feel emotional at all the change I've experienced here in a year.

Breaking up with Sean after a hasty engagement, Leroy's illness and heart attack which terrified us all, Sita's sudden recent departure from The Carnation for all the right reasons to follow her dreams, and mostly everything that happened between me and Ollie, who didn't even know each other this day twelve months ago . . .

It will be a whole year soon since we first met. A whole year since I last went home for Christmas, and now here we all are getting ready to do it all again, but in a very different way to last time.

I think of all the families who are facing changes on a much deeper level than I am, and I take a moment to count my blessings for having my own healthy family who are growing stronger as each Christmas without Peter passes by.

I think of the thousands of families facing an empty chair at the table for the first time tomorrow. There are far too many people who won't have enough money to put food on the table or to put presents under the tree. I think of all those who are facing up to Christmas in hospital, or who are living in unhappy or unsafe homes.

'Deep breaths,' says Leroy, reading my mind as always. 'Tessa has everything under control. This hotel doesn't crumble to the ground every time you leave it, you know.'

He has a point.

'You put your heart and soul into this place on every shift,' Leroy reminds me. 'Every single room, every single corner and crevice of The Carnation sings your name, Miss Beatrice. You should be very proud of all you have achieved since you first walked through those doors four years ago.'

He's going to make me cry. I don't want to ruin my make-up before we've even stepped out through the door.

'Alice was right to offer you a pay rise and a promotion, but if it were up to me, there'd be a gold plaque in the doorway stating your name.'

I lean down and pat Nana's dark fur for comfort.

'Isn't the lovely Anne from next door jealous that you're taking me out for the evening?' I tease, doing my best to shift the attention off myself. 'I hope I'm not stepping on her toes.'

Leroy zips his lips.

'I'll save all the juicy gossip on my love life for over dinner,' he says, then leans forward and whispers to me, 'Now, for the last time, come along.'

'Have a wonderful evening, Bea,' calls Tessa from the place where Sita used to sit and greet our guests. And here we are now, going to see her on one of the West End of London's most famous stages where she'll entertain a whole new audience in a world she once only dreamed of.

'I certainly will, Tessa,' I tell my new colleague before Leroy and I step out into the shadows of Kensington Palace into a frosty paradise.

The West End is so beautiful at this time of year, all lit up with blinking, twinkling lights at every turn. Shiny red buses trundle past through the faintest flurry of snow, carol singers gather on corners and in shop fronts, some just there for fun and others rattling buckets hoping for charity donations. A man dressed as Santa Claus asks an attractive passer-by for her phone number, but she replies something rude in German which leaves him wandering off, scratching his fake white beard.

Everywhere is packed to the rafters as shoppers take respite from bumper-to-bumper traffic. Corporates try to find a sandwich and a coffee to help them get through the latter part of the working day.

I have so much going through my head, most of it to do with Ollie, of course. I think of him when I wake up first thing in the morning, I write letters I'll never send in my journal when I stop on my walks with Nana in Kensington Gardens, and I toss and turn every night in bed wishing I was in his arms once more

'Distance is a bitch, but do you think Ollie was right? *Do* I run for the hills when reality kicks in?' I ask Leroy over dinner when we're warm and settled at our table in The Ivy. 'I mean, I hid my feelings from Sean here in London. And then I ran away from him too. Ollie sees right through me like no one else can.'

Leroy purses his lips and clasps his hands under his chin in thought.

'It wasn't real life with Sean. None of it was,' he tells me. 'And there lay the problem. A good dose of reality is needed to test a relationship, my dear. It tells you both how much you really want it, how much you want to fight for it. This distance, this time apart, is your reality with Ollie, but only if you both choose it to be. You've made your decision, so it must be the right one.'

I'm on a roll now. Having heard all about how Leroy fell for Anne from next door, I'm enjoying my analysis about why it all went wrong with Sean, and why I was so adamant that I couldn't go through all that once again with Ollie.

'Sean and I would only talk on the phone when he could fit me in around his working life,' I remind Leroy. 'Gosh, when I think about it, I don't know how we let it go on for so long that way. We saw each other maybe once a month if time and budgets allowed, and when he'd talk about the future I'd simply go along with it, because deep down I knew I was never going to be part of it.'

Leroy shakes his head slowly as I rant about Sean.

'You're going over old ground, digging up old bones, Miss Beatrice,' he tells me. 'Ollie isn't Sean.'

'He's building a new house, by the way,' I inform him, feeling my heart lift when I think of how Sean is much happier now, almost a year on. 'Shiny new girlfriend, shiny new Sean.'

'I'm delighted for him,' Leroy says. 'Everything for good reason, everything at the right time.'

343

'Do you really believe that, Leroy?'

'I do, because falling in love is the easy part, Miss Beatrice,' he tells me, swirling his golden whisky in his glass. 'You know, all the doe-eyed looks, the butterflies and the feeling like no one else in the world exists. But soon the claws of reality dig in and everyday life blurs the boundaries of the love bubble. Bills need paid, washing needs done, he leaves the toilet seat up, you leave the lid off the toothpaste, ex-girlfriends cross your path, ex-boyfriends appear like ghosts in the night to him too. That's reality. That's life. And if you can survive it all, then that's love. I always believed you and Ollie were the real deal.'

A lump in my throat makes me blink back tears when I picture how far Ollie and I had come in such a short time. Leroy is right. The past eleven months have been like some sort of love drug, running on the high of everything being so brand new.

Meeting Aunt Nora, seeing where he grew up, hearing all about his favourite things, trying out new places, making memories and sharing all those wonderful firsts together were amazing, but reality swooped in to remind us that we live and work miles apart.

And for me, that just doesn't work.

'This will be a very different Christmas for you, for sure,' Leroy reminds me. 'What does your mum say about it all? And Patsi?'

'Mum says it's my own decision, and that she's happy if I'm happy,' I tell him with a shrug. 'She's adopted that attitude since Peter died. I suppose when you experience that level of loss, it puts all of life's ups and downs into perspective.' I've chosen a succulent duck dish which goes impeccably with the Californian Pinot Noir, but my stomach is too nervous to appreciate it fully.

Leroy, on the other hand, is relishing his tomahawk steak, which he is rebelliously washing down with whisky rather than wine. He has put on a bit of weight lately and is looking so much healthier, thanks to the home-cooked meals and nurturing from Anne. The companionship she has shown him, with cinema dates, tennis matches and some light hiking around Brixton, is suiting him well.

'I still can't believe they offered me a pay rise and a promotion,' I tell him as we are sorting the bill.

'I can believe it,' Leroy nods. He puts his hand inside his jacket pocket and pulls out his wallet to pay the bill, but I won't hear of it. This is my treat on what is a very special evening for us both. 'Like I said, if I were the boss, I'd be putting your name in lights, or at least a gold plaque with your name on it outside the front door of The Carnation. And then I'd tell you to let us all get on with it while you go and make your own destiny in the world. I'd tell you to follow your heart.'

He winks at me knowingly as I link his arm. Then we step outside beneath the cold, dark sky and find our bearings towards the theatre where Sita will be waiting in the wings.

'And I may be biased, but if I had my way, Leroy, your name would be in lights somewhere too as a thank you for all your worldly advice over the years.'

'I had a feeling you'd say that, Miss Beatrice,' he chuckles as we walk towards the theatre. 'God broke the mould when he made you, that's for sure. I'm very blessed to have you in my life, young lady. Very blessed indeed.'

Sita knocked it out of the park, just as I knew she would. After an emotional reunion at the stage door followed by a few drinks, the three of us went our separate ways with our hearts full of joy, but now I'm home my flat feels empty and cold. It's been feeling more and more like this since I left the warmth of Oyster Cottage and nothing I do can fill the void that lives inside me without Ollie to turn to.

I yearn for him. I yearn for being back there with him so much it hurts.

For what feels like the millionth time today, I feel a huge wave of panic rush through me, tingling my skin and pricking my mind with anxiety.

'Please, Peter, send me a sign that I'm doing this whole life thing as I should be,' I say, leaning against my bed. I'm tipsy, tired and I wish I had my little brother to talk to in person instead of always wishing on a star to find him.

I feel around the carpet on the floor to find my phone.

I miss you, Bea.

His message is short and to the point. It's like every word stabs me in the heart.

Oh my God. It's Ollie, at last.

The phone bleeps again. I take a deep breath and open his second message.

I just remembered something I'd forgotten all about until now, he writes. In your brown suitcase, check the little pocket on the side. The one that doesn't zip properly. I hope it's still there. x

I stare at the case, wondering what it is inside that I could have missed last time when I unpacked my case after the wedding.

I haul the suitcase towards me and rummage in the first side pocket, but there's nothing. Then the second one, which I realise is the one with the dodgy zip. I dig my fingers down deeper until I'm met with what feels like a folded sheet of paper.

I pull it out on to my lap. I can't help but laugh out loud when I see his exaggerated, giant handwriting on one of the folds.

To Bea, it reads. *A Silly Christmas Poem for You with No Title (it probably sucks).*

I open it tentatively, my hands shaking in anticipation and my heart screaming for how much I've missed him since then.

And when I read the words on the page, I recall how I told him on that very first day last year to write stuff down when it seems too much for your mind to process. It looks like he has taken my advice and run with it, for he has penned me the most thoughtful, ridiculous, beautiful poem which is hands down the sweetest, most romantic thing anyone has done for me in my whole life.

I think of him lying in bed at home alone in Oyster Cottage, watching the clock tick by another moment apart, and perhaps waiting on me to give him my thoughts on what he has written.

But I don't want to text him. I want to hear his voice instead. There's something I need to ask him once and for all, and I don't want to skirt around the issue any longer. I hit his name on my phone, my hand shaking and my heart thumping in my chest. He answers the call with his camera on and the very sight of him makes my eyes well up instantly. He lies in bed with one arm draped casually above his head, the other holding the phone, and his bare chest looks delectable.

I've never wanted to be near someone so much in my entire life.

'What do you think?' he asks. His voice is a little hoarse, like he has just woken up. 'Pulitzer Prize-ready or do I need to work on it a bit more?'

I can't help but smile from ear to ear. I close my eyes.

'It's perfect,' I whisper. 'You're perfect. I've missed you.'

'I was wondering when you were going to realise that,' he says, shaking his head. 'You've no idea how hard it's been not to call or text you until now, but I didn't want to put you under any pressure. Then I couldn't wait any longer. I gave in.'

I take a deep breath.

'Can I ask you something?'

'Anything,' he replies. 'Actually, don't ask me to write any more poetry as that work of art was a one-off, never to be matched again.'

'What do you want, Ollie?' I ask him. 'What do you want from life? From me? For us? '

'Are you drunk?' he laughs. 'I'm joking. You don't have to answer that.'

'Tell me. I've just read what you've written and I'm in pieces here. What do you want?'

There's a brief silence.

'I want – some day when you're ready I want you to come here and live with me at Oyster Cottage,' he says. 'I don't want to force you. I want you to want it too. But that's my dream.'

I nod my head.

'I know now it's my dream too,' I whisper.

'I want you and I to make a life here. I want to make it ours,' he says. 'I want to make this place burst with our love like it used to when my parents had it, but I want us to do it our way, not theirs. You bring magic to this place that no one else could. You light up my whole world.'

I can barely breathe. My tears almost blind me.

'I want that too, Ollie,' I whisper. 'I want exactly the same as you do. We're going to make this happen. I promise you we'll make it happen.'

'After Christmas?' he suggests.

'After Christmas,' I say, as butterflies dance in my tummy. 'Let's make a start after Christmas.'

We talk as usual until our eyes are dropping shut, but I

sneak another read of his poem when he hangs up, and I read it over and over again until I fall asleep with the lights on.

> *You're the flames in the fire when I'm in from the cold,*
> *You're the bright crunchy carrot on the snowman's nose.*
> *You're the gold wrapping paper with a shiny bow,*
> *You're the first faint footprints on fresh white snow.*
> *You're the heavenly peace of a silent night,*
> *You're the rosy cheeks in a snowball fight.*
> *You're the fizz in the glass of the champagne on ice,*
> *You're the flickering glow of new fairy lights.*
> *You're a prayer in the morning, a hope that's forever,*
> *You're a black-and-white movie with crackers and Cheddar.*
> *You're the joy of a family all back together,*
> *Come live here with me, and forever will be*
> *Our best Christmas ever.*

Love Ollie, 3rd December, Oyster Cottage, written while you are sleeping. I love you x

Chapter Thirty

Ollie

Oyster Cottage, Teelin, County Donegal
Christmas Eve

I run.

I run through the village, past the pier and the boats that bob along the water.

I run past the shops and the houses and holiday homes that are scattered like someone has sprinkled the fields with little Lego-sized buildings in the distance. The wind feels like it's slicing my face, so I pull up my scarf, fighting with gravity when the long, slow gradient of the hills makes my calves tighten and my breath go short.

I stop.

I look across the water, I lean my hands on my thighs, bending over to get my breath back. It's Christmas Eve and I fear that if I don't keep moving, if I don't keep busy, then I'm going to crash, and I can't do that because I have to look after my aunt and the cottage like I promised my father I would.

I've no doubt he's out there somewhere.

It's where we left him, after all, but to me he is closer than the water's edge where I stand now, on the side of the road as the row of heather trains my eye to follow it down the sweeping slope and on to the sand.

My pockets are full of the shells he gave me that last day on the beach at Fintra. I can still hear his voice so clearly in my head. That's one of my biggest fears after losing him. I fear I'll forget his voice when I need to hear it.

I decide to walk the rest of the way home as my energy is slowly fading despite daily gym sessions mixed with saunas and swims. The ground is slushy under my feet, and I'm grateful to have made it this far without falling in a heap on the side of the road.

'If there's a tougher way of doing things, you'll find it,' I hear my father say. I plead with him to never stop leaving me messages, even if they're only in my head.

Aunt Nora has been at Oyster Cottage all morning, just like she has been every Christmas Eve since she moved in next to us. Every year without fail I'd look out the window to see her carrying all her baking equipment across the lane, from her house to ours, where the smell of cinnamon and freshly baked cookies, buns and puddings soon filled the air and seeped into the walls of Oyster Cottage so deeply, we often joked we could still smell it at Easter.

'Why are you cooking for a nation when there's just the two of us?' I asked her when we were grocery shopping a few days ago. 'I'm working until two on Christmas Day, don't forget, so we'll be having a late dinner, if you can wait for me to get home?'

She looked at the trolley which was full of biscuits, crisps, bottles of Shloer, tins of sweets, chutneys, cheeses, pâtés, crackers, goose fat, pickled onions, cranberry sauce – the works.

'Do you think I've got carried away?' she asks, pushing her glasses back on her nose.

'Just a bit! I thought we were having a quiet one this year?' I reminded her as I looked at the overflowing splurge in front of us. 'You know, just the two of us, a modest dinner, some board games and movies?'

'Maybe I *have* got a little carried away . . .' she said with a cheeky smile.

'That's overindulgence, commercialism and, dare I say, greed,' I replied, doing my best not to laugh at the shock on her face. 'The shops only close for one day, you know.'

'Which is fine if you live near a big town and not out in the middle of nowhere like we do, Ollie,' she said, shuffling behind me while I pushed the trolley towards the till. 'And we still have to get alcohol. Or is that overindulgence, commercialism and, dare you say, greed, too, eh?'

I took her to the off-licence in Carrick, and carried the basket while she filled it with beer, gin, Baileys and wine.

'Oh, I forgot to get vodka,' she said, trying to reach up to a higher shelf. 'I can't forget to get vodka. Pass that down to me, Ollie. No, not the cheap stuff, the other one, Scrooge.'

I shrugged and gave up commenting further, even when

she stared at me at the till to let me know we'd agreed to pay half on everything,

'I don't even know anyone around here that drinks vodka,' I told her. 'And you can't handle wine or gin. Are you inviting the neighbours round or are you planning a rave-up when I'm at work tomorrow?'

She rolled her eyes and drew her attention to the young man behind the counter.

'I always believe in being prepared rather than being caught short at Christmas,' she said to the boy, who looked like he was just about the legal age to be serving us and no more. 'There's nothing as bad as running out of something over the holidays, is there? Better to be safe than sorry.'

'I've no clue, my ma does everything in our house. I just eat and drink it,' he replied with a non-committal shrug.

I approach Oyster Lane after my run feeling like I've shed some of the emotional baggage I've been carrying since Bea and I finally made an agreement to make a fresh start in the New Year when she'll come and live with me here. She has already handed in her notice, but the days running up to Christmas seem to have taken forever and now all I want is to spend the holidays with her, even if it's just for one day.

But we can't make that happen. Not this year. Bea has to cover at the hotel, while I've committed to some shifts at the hospital.

I've thrown myself into work, making friends with my colleagues as well as keeping the banter going on the wards with my patients, and I'm delighted to have met some gems along the way.

'Get me the boy nurse,' I heard Bob, an elderly patient, say to the ward manager just a few days ago. 'You know, the nice-looking lad with the wavy hair. I want to say thank you for making me laugh when I was very scared after my surgery. He said if I was still here by Tuesday, he'd come back and see me again and now it's Tuesday, so get me the boy nurse.'

That made me smile for the rest of the day. My boss was impressed too.

I've had marriage proposals from female patients while coming round after anaesthetic, I've sung with worried men as I walk by their bed when they're wheeled into theatre and I've overheard a group of young student nurses comment in the staffroom that most of them have a crush on me, which was quite an ego boost if I do say so myself.

Sometimes, even when I'm really busy – be it doing routine ward rounds or day clinics like I used to in London for cardiac rehab patients – I find myself thinking of Scott and Jane, who have finally admitted they're much more than friends. I'm delighted for them. I think of returning patients like Leroy and Mary Doris. They were part of a very special chapter in my life, one which I'll always revisit in my memory with fondness. But that was then and this is now. I'm so excited for what our future holds that I could burst.

I open the front door of Oyster Cottage, lean down to pick up a bundle of mail in the hallway and make my way to the sitting room. I can hear Aunt Nora singing at the top of her voice in the kitchen as she bakes and cooks.

I don't know what I'd do without her here with me this year, and vice versa. She insisted we put up a tree in the hallway just like my parents did year after year, and we even played my dad's song, 'White Christmas', on repeat while we decorated the living room and kitchen with baubles, various Santa Claus figures in all shapes and sizes, a selection of angels and of course holly and mistletoe over each doorway.

Outside, I've made sure all of Dad's fairy lights are in full working order, and we even had a little ceremony in the garden where we counted down the switch-on in his memory.

Now, as I open Christmas cards from guests of yesteryear, all wishing me well and thinking of me on this first festive season without my father, I feel it all hit me again, and for the first time in a very long time I allow myself to cry.

I close my eyes and I see both my parents' happy, smiling faces, but no matter how much I imagine them together again, I can't help but feel sorry for myself that I'm left here in our home on my own, with only memories of Christmases past to cling on to.

In my mind I smell gingerbread men baking in the oven, I hear my mother's joyful laughter as she dances in the kitchen, warning me and Dad to stay out of her way while she cooks up a storm. I hear music from the past, the classic hits my mother loved like David Essex, Lionel Ritchie and Wham! She said they reminded her of 1982 when she had just turned twenty-one – the year she met Dad while she was working at a Christmas antique fair he'd stumbled upon in Bundoran.

I reach out my hands, wishing I could hold theirs once more, touch their faces, feel their skin on mine, but they move further and further away from me, their image fading in my mind like an old photograph.

And just like that, as soon as it has caught my breath and all of my attention, the loud whisper of grief passes like a tidal wave as quickly as it crept in.

It floats away like a ghost into the distance. I feel calm again, at peace.

I get up off the sofa, put a match to the fire and switch on the Christmas tree lights in the corner of the cosy room. There are presents under there, four in total.

I bought Aunt Nora the fancy patchwork quilt she's had her eye on in the craft shop in town, and I also wrapped up a Cliff Richard album just to wind her up. There are two gifts for me that sit side by side, wrapped in shiny silver paper with my name elegantly written on a matching tag. I know she'll have a card with some paper money inside tucked away somewhere as a 'surprise', just as she's always done.

Like all family traditions, Aunt Nora's carefully thought-out acts serve to seamlessly link each Christmas from year to year, filling in the gaps of loss by keeping memories of loved ones living long into the future.

But then I spot a new addition to our gift display, tucked behind my two packages from Aunt Nora. I shake my head at the cheek of her.

We'd agreed on no more than two gifts each this year – one

practical and one to raise a smile, hence my Cliff Richard vinyl. I hope she hasn't broken the two-present rule – but then again, she is known to break every rule in the book of life and get away with it.

'Aunt Nora, why have you bought me a third present?' I ask, calling to her up the hallway as I make my way to the kitchen. 'I hope you haven't been sneaky shopping?'

'It isn't for you,' she calls without turning to face me. 'It's for Murphy.'

Ah, that's OK then. Phew. I walk into the kitchen to find her.

'You've really pulled out all the stops. Are you a secret Instagrammer? This looks out of this world, but it's enough to feed a nation.'

The scene that awaits me is like something from a holiday movie, with hot cross buns, mince pies and a whopper of a pavlova, and the table is set like we are expecting royalty, with candles bouncing shadows on the walls, frosted branches decorated with fairy lights and a centrepiece of pine cones, greenery and berries.

'Who, me?' she asks, without stopping what she's doing, or even lifting her head. As always, she never ceases to amaze me with her energy and enthusiasm. 'I baked extra for you to take to work tomorrow for the staff and patients at the hospital.'

'You're the best, Aunt Nora.'

'And I also think we should make the most of today, don't you?' she continues, wiping her cheek with the back of her hand so that her delicate face is now covered in white flour.

'What's the point in having a quiet one? I'm going to be eighty next year if God spares me, and who knows what that will bring. So, treat every single Christmas with loved ones as precious. Who knows when it will be our last?'

'You speak words of wisdom as always.'

'I'm not finished,' she says, before I go any further. 'I also think each of us needs to find our Christmas love language and run with it.'

I am utterly speechless. Where on earth did she pull all that from?

'My Christmas love language is cooking and baking,' she tells me. 'What's yours?'

'I'm not sure what my Christmas love language is, but I think you might already know by the look on your face . . .' I reply.

'Yours is making sure the fire is stocked up and we don't go cold,' she answers swiftly. 'Now, the snow is coming down heavily outside already, so I don't think we'll get out of Oyster Lane for a few days according to the forecast. You won't be sneering then at my overindulgence, commercialism and what was the other thing?'

'Greed?'

'Yes, greed,' she says, nodding. 'Have you heard from Bea today? What a shame she has to work over Christmas. Imagine one year ago today you were seeing her for the very first time.'

I lift one of the mince pies from the table, expecting her to tap my hand and tell me off, but she doesn't. Murphy puts his paws up on the chair beside me, waiting for at least a crumb to fall, so I sneak him a bit of pastry when Aunt Nora isn't looking.

'Yes, it's a whole year already. And we're both gutted she has to work, but we'll make up for it in the New Year or at least that's what we're telling ourselves to ease the pain,' I reply. 'Right. I'll go and get some fuel for the fire before it's too cold to go out. Are you staying here tonight? You're very welcome to.'

She dips her head slightly and looks at me over the rim of her glasses.

'Are you expecting anyone?' she asks, cocking her ear to the side when we hear a car move up the lane. I've always said that despite her age, she could easily hear the grass grow. I glance out the window to see the bright beam of headlights moving along Oyster Lane.

'Unless Santa drives an Amazon van, no,' I tell her, as Murphy decides to bark at the top of his voice to warn off our uninvited guest. 'I'm sure I ordered some sports gear that hasn't arrived yet.'

'That will be it, then,' says Aunt Nora. 'All right, I'll finish up here and I'll leave you and Murphy to it. I'll just slip out the back door and head on home before it gets too dark or snowy. See you tomorrow, my love. And no peeking at your presents until I'm here to open them with you.'

I go quickly to the front door where I'm greeted by an exhausted-looking young delivery driver who hands me the parcel I'd been expecting.

'Happy Christmas,' I say to him, giving him a small tip in

return. 'Not much, but it will get you a drink over the festivities.'

He lights up like he has won the lottery.

'That's very kind of you, sir,' he tells me. 'You're my last delivery of the night, so I'm now officially off for Christmas. Have a good one with your family! *Nollaig Shona Duit!*'

'*Nollaig Shona Duit,*' I repeat, acknowledging his Irish language greeting.

I close the front door and check the time. This time last year I was already in love with Bea.

Now, a year on, I'm feeling it even more.

I check my phone to see if she has messaged at all, but there's nothing in the past hour or so. Maybe it's better she's busy at work tonight. Maybe it will take her mind off how we can't be together for Christmas, despite all our last-minute efforts to make it happen.

I stand in the hallway holding the parcel to my chest, doing my best to ignore the wave of grief and loneliness that sneaks up and clutches my insides. I breathe through it. I wait for it to pass. I always knew this would be a tough one to get through, and somewhere deep inside I'd hoped that having Bea here might make the first Christmas without Dad a tiny bit easier, but it wasn't meant to be.

'*One hundred and seventy-four steep steps,*' I hear my father's voice in my head from that day on Silver Strand beach. '*Not for the weak-hearted, but worth every single one if you're brave enough. A bit like life and love in general, Ollie. You'll know when you find the one who's worth the climb.*'

Now I know exactly what he meant that day.

'Come on, Murphy, let's go watch a movie,' I say to my four-legged friend. 'You want another tasty treat? Yeah, I do too. I won't tell if you don't. Let's go and stuff our faces in front of the telly. It's Christmas after all.'

There's another knock on the door, which sends Murphy bonkers. I do my best to calm him down, assuming the delivery guy has found another parcel, but when I open the door there's no one there.

'Hello?' I call into the still of the night as a sprinkle of snow falls on to the garden of Oyster Cottage.

'Hello?'

I call out again into nothing and take a good look around from the doorstep, unable to venture out too far with no shoes on. Murphy barks once more, drawing my attention to a large red box at my feet, tied with a huge matching bow.

'What's going on here, Murph?' I whisper, hunkering down to touch the box. 'This is just like when I was a boy . . . it's exactly like . . .'

The sight of it chokes me, transporting me back to Christmas Eve with my parents. I blink back tears as pictures and sounds of yesteryear fill my mind. I see the beaming pride on my father's face as I opened the box every year. I hear my mum, busy cooking in the kitchen, calling out to me to check the time.

I check the time now. It's 7 p.m. A shiver runs through my bones, and then I hear a voice from across the garden that almost takes my breath away.

'Some candy canes, some hot chocolate and marshmallows in a Christmas mug, new pyjamas, woolly bed socks, and you've no idea how much I had to search online to find them, but I managed to track down some 1998 favourites CDs,' she tells me. 'Oh, and as a little bonus, there's a photo album of memories of the three bears all together, but you can thank Aunt Nora for that one.'

I can't speak. I can't find the words. I wipe tears from my eyes when I see her standing under the ash tree where my mother once claimed all healing, magic and life begins.

It's Bea, her brown suitcase sitting next to her fresh footprints in the snow on the pathway.

'Happy Christmas, Ollie,' she calls.

'Bea?' I call back. 'This is . . . wow. You're here! But how?'

'I hope you don't mind, but I simply can't do this one without you,' she tells me. 'And I figured you might need me this Christmas too.'

Chapter Thirty-One

Bea

Oyster Cottage, Teelin, County Donegal
Christmas Day

It's Christmas Day, Ollie is due in from work any moment now. It's just gone three-thirty and my tummy is rumbling when I smell the feast of delights Aunt Nora and I have been working on all afternoon.

'Oh Bea, I can't tell you how many times I almost let our plan slip,' she tells me, for perhaps the fifth or sixth time, as we potter about the kitchen putting the finishing touches to our masterpiece. 'I said to your mother on the phone just yesterday, wait and see, I'll put my two big feet right into it at the very last minute. She said she didn't envy my task on keeping your surprise. She couldn't hold her own water either, or so she tells me.'

I still haven't quite got my head around how Aunt Nora is best friends with my mother, but it's so cute to hear of their conversations on the phone behind the scenes.

'Mum has been a great support in all my secret planning over the last couple of days to get here for Christmas Eve, as has Patsi,' I say, imagining what they're all doing now in Benburb. 'I can't wait to see them when we all go to Benburb tomorrow. We'll listen to some live music in the local pub, we'll dance and sing, and I'll show you and Ollie around the priory, the waterfall and the castle ruins where I spent the best days of my childhood.'

I see her face light up as she wipes down a worktop, then busies herself by drying off chopping boards and saucepans no longer in use.

'You know Ollie is only joking when he says I'll turn to jelly when I see Jacques,' she says firmly. 'If he dares say anything in front of your sister and her boyfriend tomorrow when we're in the same room as them, I'll be so cross with him.'

We both know he will say something. That's a given.

'Have I told you he snores "*comme un cochon*"?'

'*Je ne parle pas français,*' she replies, without changing her tone.

'Like a pig!' I tell her.

'Oh, I'm sure he snores like a symphony orchestra!' she crows. 'I mean it, if Jacques as much as utters an "ooh la la" in my direction, I might prove my darling nephew right by falling at his feet. Oh, show me that photograph again, Bea. You know, the one of him wearing the Santa hat.'

I find my phone on the kitchen table and scroll through until I get to the one she is after.

'I won't tell if you don't,' I say, showing her Jacques' smiling face on my screen.

Soon, with all our dinner preparation done, Aunt Nora and I retire to the sitting room where a blazing fire greets us in the hearth. It feels strange not to have had dinner at this time on Christmas Day, and the presents under the tree sit unopened, but we'll relax here with a drink until Ollie gets in from his shift.

Yesterday couldn't have gone any better, thank goodness. I've known about my surprise visit for days now, as has Aunt Nora, but it was a real challenge to keep it from Ollie who believed I had to work right through after handing in my notice at The Carnation. Next week after Christmas, I'll return to London to work the rest of my time there, I'll pack up my flat, and then I'll come back to Oyster Cottage. Ollie and I are already making plans for our future, and I've never felt more confident about a decision in my life.

'Here he is,' says Aunt Nora, as soon as she hears a car drive up Oyster Lane. 'At long last. My stomach was starting to talk to me, I'm so hungry.'

We both scurry out to the hall to greet him, smothering him in kisses as he takes off his coat and scarf. Even Murphy joins in to compete for his affection. And to my utter delight, when I look up behind him I see the faintest glow of a rainbow in the sky behind him.

'Ooh, a rainbow on Christmas Day!' gasps Aunt Nora. 'I don't think I've ever seen a Christmas rainbow in all my years!'

I think of Alice Charles with her words of wisdom and a warm glow fills my heart.

'Looks like I'm done chasing rainbows at last,' I reply, kissing Ollie on the cheek as he makes his way inside. 'You ready for dinner?'

'You bet, but can we do presents first?' he asks. 'I know I sound like I'm ten years old, but you started it all with the Christmas Eve box on the doorstep, Bea. I've been reliving that moment all day at work to anyone who will listen.'

'Your face was an image I'll hold on to forever,' I say, unable to hide my own delight when I picture it again. I don't know which was more of a surprise to him – the Christmas Eve box made exactly in the style his parents used to leave for him at seven o'clock, or the sight of me standing in the front garden beneath the ash tree.

'Isn't she the best, Aunt Nora?' he continues. 'And you are too for keeping it all hush. I've been telling everyone in work about that too. My colleagues Beth and Julie cried. I almost do myself every time I think of it.'

Before long we're seated at the table, which I've added my own little personal touches to, though Aunt Nora has played a blinder on my instruction of finding pine cones and greenery to line the centre.

'I should have known something was up,' says Ollie, tucking into his turkey and ham. The three of us are wearing coloured paper hats we found in crackers, we've toasted those no longer with us, especially Jack Brennan, of course, and we've said 'sláinte' to new beginnings. It couldn't be more perfect if we tried. 'I mean, the vodka should have been a giveaway as you're the only person I know who drinks vodka and tonic. The overflowing shopping trolley, the extra present under the tree Aunt Nora said was for Murphy, and all this stylish table decorating. I just don't know what to say, ladies. You've really made this a Christmas to remember.'

After a dinner that would win a prize, we spend the evening eating more and drinking lots, we flick through Ollie's new photo album and play board games by the fire.

'You're cheating,' Ollie teases Aunt Nora. 'You're not meant to look at the flip side of the card. That's where the answers are!'

I giggle as they argue it out, with Aunt Nora defiantly protesting her innocence.

And later on, with our bellies full and when we've laughed until our sides are sore, Ollie and I venture out in the snow to take Murphy for a Christmas walk.

'This place really is like something from a chocolate box, but it's people like you and Aunt Nora who make it so special,' I say to Ollie as we look back on Oyster Cottage with its twinkling lights in the snowfall and the faint glisten of the ocean in the distance. 'I feel your parents are very near this place, Ollie. And I know Peter is never far away from me either, no matter where I go.'

We look up to the sky as delicate snowflakes fall on to our heads and shoulders, dancing like little fireflies in the night sky.

'I like to think that too,' he whispers.

'You know I asked for a sign that night, just for reassurance

from Peter that this would all work out, and then you messaged me to look for the poem in my suitcase pocket,' I tell
him as he pulls me in closer.

I snuggle into him. He leans down and kisses the top of
my head.

'I never expected you to make such a huge move, but I
promise we'll make a wonderful team here at Oyster Cottage,' he says, his voice cracking with emotion. 'You remind
me of her a lot, you know.'

'Your mum?'

'Yeah.'

'That's a huge compliment, thank you,' I tell him. 'So, can
we talk about the wallpaper in the upstairs bathroom?'

'Too loud?'

'Verging on vulgar,' I reply.

'Aunt Nora told you to say that, didn't she?'

'I was never a good liar – yes, she did,' I confess, as I turn
around to face him, slinking my arms around his waist. We
are both wrapped up in hats, scarves, coats and gloves as
Murphy bounces around us in the snow.

'I knew you'd love it here,' he says. 'But we can make it
our own, in our own time. I want it to be yours, too.'

'That's the biggest honour you could ever bestow on me,
Ollie,' I tell him. 'Your parents are up there somewhere working their magic for sure. I can feel it. I only hope we can make
this place as vibrant and welcoming as they would have
wanted it to be.'

We walk hand in hand back towards what will be our new
home and my new place of work as we bring Oyster Cottage

back on to the market for tourists to enjoy, just as Eleanor Brennan always intended it.

Aunt Nora is thrilled to have me on board. She's already planning another long winter break to visit her sister in Málaga, now that she doesn't feel responsible for getting the B&B back on its feet again.

Leroy says he, Nana and Anne will be first to book in for a stay once we're up and running, and of course Patsi, Jacques, Mum and Dad will be here to visit as soon as we give them the go-ahead. Scott and Jane are planning a trip across too, now their romance is official.

'Come on, Murphy, let's get you home,' I call to the dog, who is having way too much fun in the fields that line the bumpy road known as Oyster Lane. With Aunt Nora tucked up in bed next door, her heart full of joy and her belly full of sherry, Ollie and I have a lot of catching up to do – which we'll start off on the sofa while watching a black and white movie.

'There's no place like home at Christmas,' says Ollie, pulling me closer to him. 'I'm so glad to hear you calling Oyster Cottage your home already.'

We stop under the moonlight, and he kisses me so tenderly I feel the earth has once again stopped on its axis.

'Did I hear you say you were going to run us a hot bubble bath to share?' he teases. 'I think we need some heat in our bones before our movie. Race you upstairs?'

I laugh and follow him indoors, into the warmth of the cottage, feeling fuzzy inside at the thought of whatever else is to come our way. I can't wait to spend my days taking care of the guests who come to sample the magic of Oyster Cottage, and when Ollie comes home tired from work after fixing broken hearts in hospital each day, I'll remind him how he will always be the keeper of mine.

And how I will always love him harder.

I watch him climb the stairs of this safe haven his parents created out of love. And with every step he takes, I know that no matter where we go from here, no matter where life takes us – be it London, Benburb, Donegal or anywhere across the world – I will always be at home when I'm in his arms.

I won't let one moment of life pass us by.

I won't take any day or season or celebration we share for granted. Because at last, I've found the rainbow I've been searching for. And as long as he and I are together, we will always have the best Christmas ever.

Acknowledgements

I'd truly believed 2024 was going to be a big year for me in so many ways.

I'd lots of plans, including writing this book and the production of a new musical I've been working on for ages, but at the beginning of March, my whole world was turned upside down with a shock diagnosis of an incurable blood cancer called multiple myeloma.

I'd never even heard of it.

I was right in the middle of some major rewrites of this book when I was diagnosed, and it took a huge effort to pull this story together throughout the grim, worrying early days. But during the following six months of chemotherapy and preparation for a stem cell transplant, I got there at last with *Maybe Next Christmas*, and for that I'd like to thank some very special people.

I always feel so confident, lucky and privileged having an agent like Sarah Hornsley at Peters, Fraser & Dunlop by my side. Thank you, Sarah, as always, for your words of wisdom, guidance and support which go much further than you could know. The patience, kindness and understanding you've shown to help me get this book over the line in such difficult times will never be forgotten. I adore working with you and always will.

I'm always so excited to see my books go out in different languages, and for managing all of that I'd like to say a huge thanks to the International Rights team at Peters, Fraser & Dunlop who have brought my festive stories to so many countries.

Thanks to my Katie Loughnane, my wonderful editor at Cornerstone, Penguin Random House, who has since moved on to pastures new. I miss you so much already, Katie! It was truly an honour to work with you on every level, and I look forward to the day when our paths cross again.

Staying at Penguin Random House, a huge thanks to Katya Browne (Assistant Managing Editor) and Jess Muscio (Assistant Editor); to Hope Butler (marketing) and M-L Patton (publicity); to Olivia Allen, Evie Kettlewell, Alice Gomer, Jade Unwin and Kirsten Greenwood (sales); to Anna Curvis and Linda Viberg (international sales); to Faye Collins (production) and Lizzy Moyes (inventory). And a huge thank you once more to Lucy Thorne (designer) and Jennifer Costello (illustrator) whose vision of Bea and Ollie, as well as Oyster Cottage, really brought them to life on the cover.

Thanks to Michael McLoughlin and everyone at Penguin Ireland, especially Leonor Araújo for all your publicity results and for treating me so well when I visit Dublin.

A book is just words on a page without readers, and I have the best, most loyal readers all over the world who I appreciate in every way. Thank you for your messages, reviews and enthusiasm that come with every release, and to those of you who are new to my writing, you're so welcome! I hope you stay around as I've got lots more stories to come.

I know a lot of you will be wondering if Oyster Cottage is a real place after reading this. Well, I can assure you that

Ireland is full of such delights, and I've based Ollie's home on some of the beautiful places I've drooled over in Donegal for a long time. Thank you to the gorgeous Eleanor Goan for her tips on Teelin and for sharing her memories of her Gaeltacht days on the pier drinking Coke and eating Twister ice lollies!

Benburb is a stunning place here in my native County Tyrone. Like Bea in the story, I have found great solace, peace and tranquility in the grounds of Benburb Castle by the River Blackwater. I am so appreciative to have been blessed by a relic of St Peregrine, patron saint of those suffering from cancer, on a recent visit to the chapel in Benburb Priory.

For those of you attracted by the brighter lights of London, the good news is that The Carnation Hotel where Bea works is based on The Milestone Hotel in Kensington, right down to Leroy's uniform, the red carnations and the most impeccable, individually styled rooms. I was lucky to spend the most glorious one-night stay there as early research for *Maybe Next Christmas* with my much-loved cousin, Maria Cussell, who was the best company. We had such fun and made memories for life. And yes, they do have a signature red velvet cake which was enjoyed immensely by the sales and publicity teams at the Penguin offices the next morning!

Thanks to Cindy Geslin and Lydia Cleere at Perowne International for arranging our stay at The Milestone, and to all the staff, including bar manager Angelo, chef Sam Saunders, duty manager Tom and doorman Tim, to name just a few.

The *Irish News* kindly printed a feature on our visit to The

Milestone, so for that I'd like to thank Features Editor Will Scholes and Jenny Lee. Thank you both for always helping spread the word on my writing.

On a similar note, a big thank you to Ciara and Lynette at *The Lynette Fay Show*, as well as Connor and Cameron at *The Connor Phillips Show* (BBC Radio Ulster), Pamela Ballentine and Petra Ellis at *UTV Life*, Niall McCracken at BBC Northern Ireland, Maureen Coleman, Niamh Campbell at the *Belfast Telegraph*, and all at *Local Women* magazine.

Thanks to all my writer friends, especially Claire Allan and Fionnuala Kearney who have been by my side on this journey from the very beginning. Our friendship goes so much beyond books by now. I'm so grateful to have you both in my life.

They say some friends become family, and that's very much the case when it comes to my 'sisters' at The Players Conservatory in Los Angeles. I've named a special character after our darling Deanna who we lost so suddenly in late 2023, and who we miss with all our hearts.

A huge thanks to Madeline and TP at Sheehy's Cookstown, and all the booksellers and librarians who recommend my novels. Thanks as well to the bloggers and influencers on social media who do lots of shouting and sharing when it comes to release time. I will never take your support for granted.

An extra special word of thanks to Sherry Frasier, a reader in the U.S., who with the help of her tiny grandson William, bought and delivered copies of my books to seven area libraries in her home county in Utah this year! Sherry also kindly bought copies for me to personally distribute here on my own home turf, to readers under the care of Causeway and Mid-Ulster Women's Aid, and to patients in the Mandeville Unit at Craigavon Hospital.

How ironic that on the very same week I delivered them on Sherry's behalf, along with my dad and daughter Jade, I'd be learning that I myself would soon be under their excellent care. Thank you to Dr Foy and all the medical team at Mandeville who look after me so well. I'd like to dedicate a short passage of this book, from Jack Brennan's letter, to each and every one of them, as well as to my almost-lifelong friend Katrina Loughran and her district nurses who call at my home once a week with loving care.

To help those suffering from ill health is a gift from God. I've always believed that nurses are walking angels who soothe frightened patients and ease worried loved ones.

Just a few moments with someone special can feel as good as a whole lifetime. Just a few words whispered when you need to hear them can sound like a whole symphony. And just a brief touch of a hand when you're frightened can reach right inside and hold your whole heart to keep it beating for a little while longer.

My biggest inspiration and source of strength in life and in my writing will always be my friends and family.

The amount of strength and solidarity I've been shown lately takes my breath away, from messages, phone calls, cards and prayers to visits and days out where possible, as well as lots of treats to distract me on those darker days. Some people I don't even know in person have been so kind and generous, leaving flowers and gifts at Jim's art gallery for me, or sending me stuff in the post to make me feel better from further afield.

I have the best siblings, aunties, cousins and friends, old and new, that anyone could ask for. You'll have noticed some references to rainbows in this story, which were written deliberately – every time I see a rainbow now, I feel closer to my cousin Ciara, who was taken from her family too soon in October 2023, just twelve months before this book was published. Ciara said she would send us rainbows. Her absence in this world is immense, but her vibrant colour, beautiful smile, stunning beauty and radiant glow will never be far away.

To my children, Jordyn, Jade, Adam, Dualta and Sonny (and our 'princess' toy poodle Lola). Each one of you has stepped up into different roles this year that no young person should ever have to in order to help us steer and sail this ship to the very best of our ability. You make me so proud in every single way. You always have and always will.

To Jim, my partner in life and love, there are simply no words to thank you for how you continue to prop me up and hold me together when the going gets tough. We've shared so many ups and downs, but I know that with the love of you and our children I can conquer anything that comes my way.

I've dedicated this very special book to a very special man who stands firmly at the top of our family. My daddy, Hugh McCrory, is truly one in a million, having raised six of us alone since the tragic day in May 1991 when he was widowed suddenly on the weekend of his forty-first birthday.

The pain of losing our mother as young children has taught me so much on the subject of grief, and while I pour it all out in my stories, I can never underestimate or express enough how my father has always helped us get through it quietly in the background with dignity and grace, oozing strength when we need him most.

Thank you, Daddy, for everything. You're simply the best.

To end on a truly magical note, I love it when a little bit of serendipity comes in to play when I'm writing a book, and this time round didn't disappoint.

The names of my main characters, Bea and Ollie, came to me one day out of the blue.

Bea and Ollie.

It was like they were real, but I don't know anyone, nor have I met anyone in real life called Bea or Beatrice. I've no idea where that name came from, but to me it was perfect.

Fast-forward to a few months later when, checking out after my stay at The Milestone Hotel, I paused as a book on display at the hotel reception caught my eye.

Its cover featured a fifties-style black and white image of a striking lady, so I went over for a closer look. When I picked it up, duty manager Tom explained it was written by the owner and founder of the hotel group.

She's in her eighties now, but still pops by to greet her guests at The Milestone Hotel, he told me.

I lifted the book and looked at her name which was printed below her photograph. My heart skipped a beat.

Her name is Bea.

Bea Tollman. A real-life Bea, who created the most beautiful place in London to base part of my story.

A shiver ran through me as I stared at her photo.

You see, little signs really are everywhere if we take the time to open our minds and eyes to see them.

And that's what I call catching rainbows.

I hope you catch yours too.

READERS LOVE
EMMA HEATHERINGTON

'Beautiful and tender… perfect all year round' ★★★★★

'I could not put it down' ★★★★★

'*This Christmas* is one of the standout stories of 2023' ★★★★★

'A delightful read' ★★★★★

'Full of charm, beauty, and romance – just what you want
at this time of the year' ★★★★★

'You actually feel you are living in the small village
and in Seaview Cottage with the characters' ★★★★★

'It was a real treat to read this book… festive,
poignant and lovely' ★★★★★

'Heartwarming' ★★★★★

'Just a gorgeous read, thoroughly enjoyed every page – warm,
endearing, wonderful and romantic. This may be
my new Christmas tradition!!!' ★★★★★

'Crying out to be made into a film.
Perfect Christmas escapism' ★★★★★

'The perfect read at any time of year' ★★★★★

'A magical story that made me both smile
and cry many times' ★★★★★

'Best Christmas book' ★★★★★

More from **EMMA HEATHERINGTON**